The Boys from Kalamazoo

A Novel

By

T. J. Johnston

T. J. Johnston

2003

Burd Street Press

Shippensburg, Pennsylvania

Maps drawn by author.

This Burd Street Press publication
was printed by
Beidel Printing House, Inc.
63 West Burd Street
Shippensburg, PA 17257-0152 USA

The acid-free paper used in this book meets the guidelines for permanence and durability of the Committee on Production Guidelines for Book Longevity of the Council on Library Resources.

For a complete list of available publications
please write
Burd Street Press
Division of White Mane Publishing Company, Inc.
P.O. Box 152
Shippensburg, PA 17257-0152 USA

Library of Congress Cataloging-in-Publication Data

Johnston, T. J., 1971-
The boys from Kalamazoo : a novel / by T.J. Johnston.
p. cm.
ISBN 1-57249-269-4 (alk. paper)
1. Michigan--History--Civil War, 1861-1865--Fiction. 2. Shiloh, Battle of, 1862--Fiction. 3. Kalamazoo (Mich.)--Fiction. 4. Sharpshooters--Fiction. I. Title.

PS3610.O39 B69 2002
813'.6--dc21

2002019459

PRINTED IN THE UNITED STATES OF AMERICA

Introduction

The Boys from Kalamazoo is a work of historical fiction, emphasis on historical, because as the saying goes, sometimes truth is stranger than fiction. While the central characters of James Lockett, Patrick McManus, Luke Bailey, and Matthew Bauer are fictional, the attitudes, events, and paths of the various regiments are based on historical facts.

At all times, I did try to maintain historical accuracy. At the end of this novel, brief historical facts are provided which I uncovered during my exploration of the boys from Kalamazoo. In the rare case where I did take literary license in the placement of a unit, etc., I have indicated it.

The Journey of the Boys from Kalamazoo

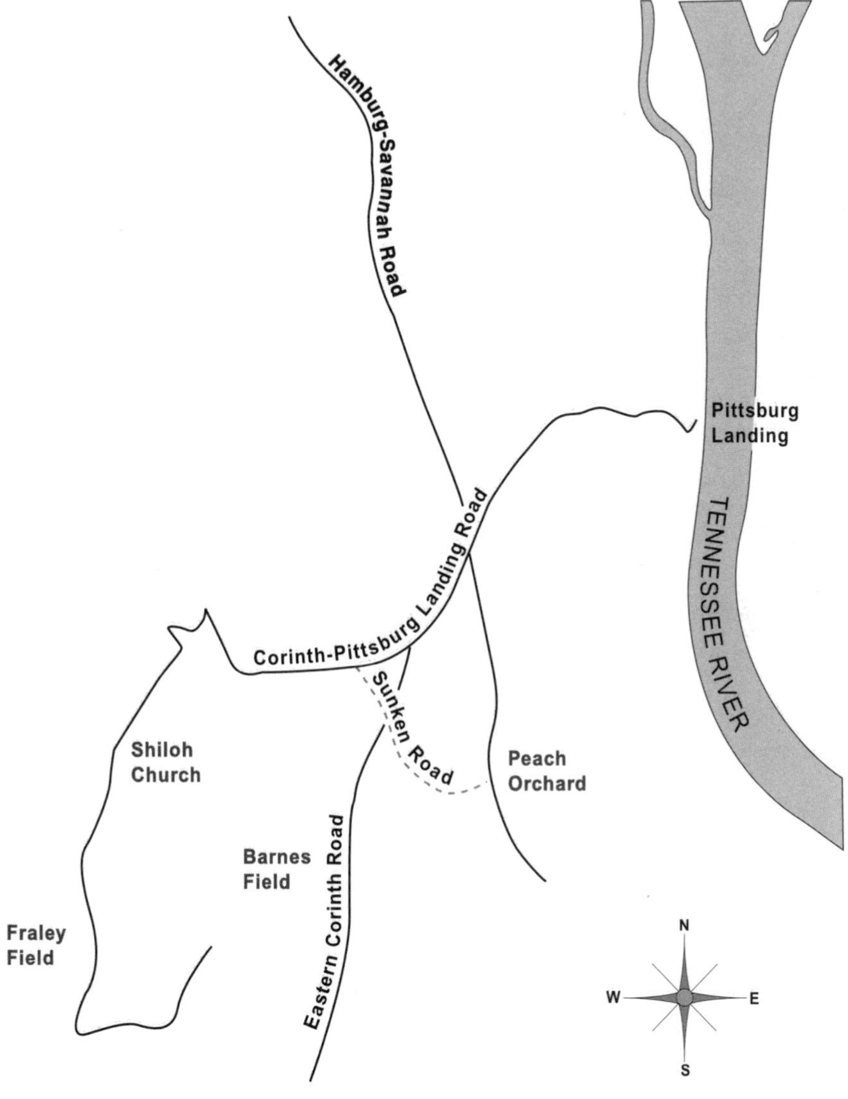

Battle of Shiloh (Pittsburg Landing)

I

The Boys from Kalamazoo

April 6, 1862

The morning mist had nearly lifted when Sergeant James Lockett saw the first few heads appear across the wooded rise. This time, it came as no surprise. They had all heard the sound of forty thousand pairs of feet crashing through the forest. The steady crunch of boots over sticks and underbrush seemed to echo throughout the hollow. It sounded like hundreds of men being trampled upon, bones being snapped in two, but the noise was less unnerving than the fact that the earth itself trembled beneath the approach of the Confederate army. James could swear that he felt the very ground quake, resonating up though the soles of boots into his feet, legs, and heart.

James stole a glance at his lifelong friend, Patrick McManus, standing shoulder to shoulder with him. It was a thin line of blue directly in front of the impending onslaught.

Patrick's steadfast blue eyes, sunk deep into a sun-blotched Irish face, flickered back at James. He was ready. McManus was no longer the bull-like young man he had been when they had started just six months ago. Illness in Missouri and his own personal tragedy had seen to that, but he was still as dependable as ever. James knew that for a fact.

Patrick turned his eyes back to the front, rifle already raised, poised at the enormous Confederate line that had reached the crest of the low hill. The Rebels hesitated at the top of the hill, leading one to think that they had second thoughts about descending into and then out of the shallow hollow, but the actual impression on the soldiers in blue, men from Colonel Everett Peabody's Brigade, was quite the opposite.

The soldiers thought that the Rebels were trying to intimidate them with their sheer size, and they were doing a good job of it. A few Federals gasped at the awesome sight of so many men lined shoulder to shoulder, while others muttered prayers. The unfamiliar soldier on James's other side took an uncertain step backward.

This was a sight that none of them had ever seen before, a sight never seen to date in the Western campaign of this War Between the States.

Stretched in front of James and his comrades were two tightly packed lines of battle, an army rumored to be forty thousand strong, and all of it appeared to be amassed here, directly in front of Peabody's insignificant brigade of less than three thousand.

There were more men than James could ever have imagined. When they had started out from Kalamazoo with one hundred men, that had seemed like a lot.

The Confederate line stretched far beyond the reach of James's eyes.

The unknown private next to James took another step back, causing James to turn and growl, "Steady!"

The private's eyes were as wide as saucers, but he did stop. In fact, he took a step forward so that he was nearly shoulder to shoulder with James again.

He looked at the unknown sergeant who had just addressed him with a menacing command that sounded strangely out of place with his physical appearance. Somewhat tall and lanky, the sergeant did possess some wiry strength. He had a grim, determined face and pale gray eyes, but the private never would have guessed that this sergeant possessed such a threatening voice.

Even though the soldier did not know who this sergeant was, he knew that he had been with the others who had first encountered this imposing Confederate army. Major James E. Powell's little patrol had slowed the Confederates for an hour before being forced back.

The private shook with fear, but he took solace in the knowledge that the lanky sergeant next to him had already experienced battle.

What the private did not know was that this would be the third encounter of an already exhausting morning for Lockett, McManus, and a few others from Major Powell's patrol. The soldiers had first laid eyes on the Confederates when their predawn reconnaissance had bumped into what they thought were just bushwhackers. After trading blows with skirmishers for a half hour, the patrol had been forced back by a tidal wave of Confederates.

Colonel Moore's reinforcements only delayed the Rebel advance for a matter of minutes, and now it was Peabody's turn to absorb the punishment.

Lockett already knew there were too many Rebels for such a piecemeal defense. This would be the third time that they would be pushed back, but they had to give the rest of General Ulysses S. Grant's army time to set up a defense behind them.

The entire army had been caught by surprise. It was only a fluke that Major Powell's patrol had bumped into the predawn attack. Were it not for that, the entire Union army would literally have woken to find Rebel muskets pointed in their faces.

James looked at the Confederate line readying itself for an assault, packing itself in tightly shoulder to shoulder. It was a futile effort, for such cohesion would be impossible to maintain once they began marching through the brush. Gaps would appear as men moved around trees and other obstacles. Still, it made for an imposing sight.

As James peered down the length of his Dimick deer rifle, he realized that for the first time today he was getting a good look at the men who would be trying to kill him. His earlier scrapes had involved only predawn silhouettes punctuated by blinding muzzle flashes and clouds of gunsmoke mixed with the damp morning mist. He had only been aiming at the muzzle flashes then and shooting randomly into the smoky fog. But now, James could see that he was actually aiming at men, at least until his own gunsmoke obstructed his view again.

Gently, he gripped the barrel of his Dimick rifle. It was still warm.

His shooting eye sighted along the length of the octagonal barrel, knowing that the wall of mismatched gray, butternut, and homespun was within range for himself and Patrick. After all, they had started out as sharpshooters, and still carried their own rifles. The grooves inside the octagonal barrel would put spin on the Minié ball, spiraling it so that it would cut through the air faster, straighter, and longer.

But the command to open fire had not yet come, and James knew why. As he and Patrick had retreated from their earlier defensive position with Moore's Brigade, James had realized right away that they were jumping in line with the new men from Wisconsin, and those boys all carried heavy Belgian muskets. The musket ball flying out of those smoothbore barrels would have no spin, at least no intentional spin. The range was much shorter than a Dimick, and the accuracy was similarly inferior. Who knew which way the musket ball would rattle out of the smoothbore, James sighed.

The tension was heavy in the air, and James swore he could actually smell the fear—a noxious, vinegary scent. It was the first battle for these Wisconsin boys, the first for many in Peabody's Brigade. Even James had to admit today was his first real battle. The run-in with Missouri bushwhackers was no comparison to the line of battle in front of him.

"Fah-wahrd!" the command of one of the Southern officers echoed across the hollow. The eerie quiet suddenly lurched into the sound of men moving again—broken underbrush, canteens and cartridge boxes rattling. Suddenly on the far left, the thunder and boom of cannon shattered the morning air. Even James flinched at the crack that was so much deeper and louder than the sound of rifles and musketry.

One by one, cannon were being lit off. It seemed unending.

James's ears rang from the abuse, and he realized that he could no longer hear the unnerving underbrush snapping beneath Confederate feet.

Still, he could feel the earth shake, not only from the cadence of 40,000 Rebels, some now whooping amidst the noise, but also from the Union cannon joining the fray.

It must be Hickenlooper's Ohio Battery, James thought blankly.

A few Rebels fired their weapons, more out fear and nerves than actual effect.

"Steady! Steady!" the order rang up and down the Union line.

Incongruously, James realized at that moment that his precious journal was back in camp, next to his bedroll and the rest of his belongings—a battered tin plate and fork. He felt a stinging sense of loss for a moment, but then pushed aside the thoughts with harsh, silent words for his mental wanderings. He turned his attention back to the Rebels.

Anxiously, men gripped their rifles and muskets, their impatience growing with each step that the Confederates took. To the left front of the Union line, a ghoulish yell rose up from the Rebels, echoing in the Federals' ears. A few Rebels even raised their weapons over their heads as they marched forward, full of defiance.

James's hand tightened around the barrel. Numbly, he aimed into the approaching wall of Confederates.

His mind wanted to open fire, but his will resisted.

At one hundred twenty yards, he finally heard the order reverberate down the length of their line, *"Fire!"*

The full Federal volley ripped through the air with one long, enormously brilliant flash. It blinded James for a second, and the puffs of smoke blurred his vision and stung his already reddened and irritated eyes. It was the first time that he had heard a brigade-sized volley that wasn't aimed at him, he realized.

The blast tore into the Confederate line. Many of the shots were wild, slashing through branches and leaves above the Rebels, but some of the shots smacked solidly into the advancing line, leaving men clutching chests, legs, arms, and necks as if in search of unseen protrusions. An entire section of the Confederate line broke and ran.

James could faintly hear voices with Tennesseean accents yelling, "Retreat! Retreat!" as they ran.

But most of the Confederates did not run. The volley had staggered them, but the Rebels did not run, rather they slowly inched back. The cannon continued its thunder, and the Rebels fell back behind the low rise.

A few Union soldiers cheered, including the private next to James, but James shot him a nasty look and the man stopped.

The Rebels had been stunned, but they were only gathering themselves for another push. How many times have I seen this already today, James wondered as he began to reload, and it's not even midmorning yet!

The cannon to their left roared again and then slowly began to lessen its pace.

"Who's to our left?" James asked the private. The man was still shaking from his first taste of battle, however brief and abbreviated it was.

"Miller's Brigade and Hickenlooper's Battery, I imagine," the man, who James now noticed was really just a boy, replied in a tight voice.

"How about to our right?" Patrick asked, as he finished ramming another Minié ball home.

"Our right?" the boy said with a puzzled look. "No one, I guess."

Patrick looked at James with little more than a shrug, already knowing their piecemeal defense would be no match for the long Confederate line of battle. It was only a matter of time before both flanks were overlapped. Where were General Sherman and his men?

"Best reload, friend," Patrick said to the private as he slid his ramrod back down into place beneath the barrel of his Dimick. "They'll be back in a few minutes."

Patrick was right. A few minutes later, the Confederates appeared at the crest of the low hollow again, and this time they meant business. There was no pausing at the crest to realign. The Rebels simply came over the rise and continued advancing.

The Union fire was less directed. Rifles and muskets spat at the Rebels well before one hundred twenty yards this time, but it did not slow them. The massive front moved toward them...one hundred seventy-five yards out...one hundred fifty...

James had already fired when the Rebels were two hundred yards out, which he knew was a mistake afterward. Although, he was confident that his aim was true, his action encouraged the Wisconsin boys around him to also open fire with their Belgian muskets, and from that range, they did little damage.

James rushed to reload, working through the familiar process. Taking another paper cartridge from his cartridge box, he used his teeth to help tear the end off, and then dumped the grainy black powder down the barrel, stuffing the remaining Minié ball in after it, paper and all. Using the ramrod, he quickly rammed it all down and replaced the ramrod on the underside of the barrel in one smooth motion. Reaching into the cartridge box again, he took out a percussion cap and placed it on the nub of the rifle, where the hammer would fall on it.

Looking up into the gray gunsmoke, James saw a Confederate officer among his men, yelling something that could not be heard above the deafening din. With his gray uniform trimmed in golden braid, a broad-rimmed officer's hat, and gleaming saber, the Rebel officer cut quite a contrast to his ragtag men. Suddenly, the Confederate officer slashed his sword downward, and James knew what the order had been.

He saw the flash of the thousands of Rebel rifles and muskets.

In the split second after the flash, his mind spun faster than he ever could have imagined possible. The last six months exploded into his head in detail. He remembered the fateful day that he had volunteered with the others to join the Kalamazoo Sharpshooters. He remembered the life-changing experiences in Missouri, fighting his own officers as much as the bushwhackers. He remembered his own odd path to a place as sergeant in the 12th Michigan.

Six months that seemed like an entire lifetime, all leading him here.

Chapter 2

I have done it. Against my own good sense, I have done it. Hours have passed since I signed the sheet, but I still feel this unexplainable flush of energy. I am a volunteer now.

War fever has hit Michigan.

—The Diary of James Lockett

November 1861

Kalamazoo, Michigan

"...our esteemed congressman, Charles Vincent!"

The applause erupted in the cool November afternoon air, and it struck at least one person in the crowd that the ovation for Charles Vincent was greater than the reception Kalamazoo had given the unknown Abraham Lincoln two short years ago.

Two years prior, Kalamazoo had listened attentively to Lincoln with polite nodding heads.

But now, the talk of *action*, embodied in the refined figure of Congressman Vincent, stirred the crowd's enthusiasm. They were unleashed, unabashed! They were ready for this message!

As young James watched the goings-on with a curious detachment, he wondered whether Lincoln himself would have received such a reception today as Charles Vincent had.

Was it the man, the message, or the mood?

Of course, Abraham Lincoln was president of the entire country now, but Lockett still wondered. The country was now at war with itself, and while a wildly contagious fervor had swept through Michigan, stories of defeat out East in far-off Virginia bridled many in this small Midwestern farming and logging community. The citizens were anxious for action, for battle!

Certainly President Lincoln would be received warmly again in this antislavery hotbed, James thought to himself. Yet, if the president shared the stage with Congressman Vincent, the tall, gaunt president would without a doubt pale in comparison to the confident and handsome congressman. To James, Abraham Lincoln and Charles Vincent had nothing in common other than their loyalty to the Union.

James remembered Lincoln to be so unusually tall, almost all limbs, although he did not move with the awkwardness that one would assume from someone so lanky and angular. In contrast, Vincent was of average height with an unusually long torso and when combined with his habitually puffed-out chest and short legs, he gave the impression of being much shorter than he was.

The congressman surveyed the large crowd that had gathered in front of the courthouse. Vincent knew there were scarcely twenty-five thousand people in all of Kalamazoo County, and as he smiled into the sea of expectant faces, he knew that at least half of the county now waited for him to speak.

They crowded the broad dirt strip that was Main Street, spilling out onto the wood planking sidewalk on both sides of the thoroughfare from Gibson & Brothers Dry Goods to the Burdick Hotel. A few even leaned anxiously out on the second-floor balconies above the shops, saloon, and hotel.

Vincent smiled, nodding at a familiar face in the crowd before turning to the powerful ring of businessmen and town founders who stood with him on the raised platform. They too applauded him gustily.

The state congressman paused to enjoy the moment. Perhaps only U.S. Senator Charles Stuart was more popular in Kalamazoo County.

As a fit-looking man of forty with thick black hair, oiled back on the sides, Vincent knew that he cut a sharp contrast to the plump mayor who had just introduced him. Square-jawed, clean-shaven, and sharply dressed in his new brown suit, Vincent knew that every pair of female eyes was on him, and that was the way he liked it.

"Thank you for that nice ovation," Vincent began. "And thank you for coming today to hear this important message..."

His booming voice allowed those in the rear to hear him with ease. Even a skeptic, like young James, had to admit that the congressman knew how to address a crowd. But as James shifted his feet, he grew impatient with the congressman's style, impatient with waiting for the message that he knew would be delivered. But first, the congressman waxed on the topics of unity, slavery, the Founding Fathers, and business…but, eventually, the message they were waiting for came.

"...as many of you know, fellow Michiganders in Van Buren and Berrien Counties have already taken up arms." There was a small cheer from one corner of the crowd, and Vincent paused to let it play out. "And that is why I am here before you today. This Secessionist rebellion needs to be extinguished quickly! And there is no quicker way to squash these traitorous vermin than to bring the rifles of Kalamazoo County..."

A throaty cheer sounded from a separate corner of the audience.

"And so I come today looking for other courageous heroes to join me in forming a company of Kalamazoo Sharpshooters!"

This time, the entire crowd broke into applause. James looked around, and every man, woman, and child clapped with a devotion that must have made Reverend Joseph Bailey envious.

Five months earlier, the South had fired on Fort Sumter and President Lincoln had called for the mobilization of state militias. The initial confidence of immediate victory had been dampened by the defeat at Bull Run in July, but as James scanned those around him, all he saw were confident faces.

From the back of the crowd, James had a clear view of the many nodding heads in front of him. Vincent's message had obviously been well received, but James turned around and looked down the other end of Main Street. Empty, it looked rather like a ghost town, and with the mighty cheering going on directly behind him, it all seemed strangely unreal. His mind wandered as his eyes followed the dirt strip out of town and across a low, rising, grassy hill. Behind that hill, a few miles down the road, through a strand of birch trees was the Lockett farm.

James bit his lip, already feeling guilty about being here. His place was back on the farm, toiling in the earth, which he did every day, trying to scrape together a living for the family—just as he had for so many years now. If it weren't for him, he wondered how they would have survived.

James had assumed the family mantle after his father had died five years ago. He could still hear his father's terrible hacking cough; the gut-twisting, deathly smell of the room was still in his nostrils. James was sure that the terrible odor would never go away.

How many times had he awoken in the middle of the night, sitting up straight in bed, that smell burning like an acid in his nostrils? How many times had he pounded his chest, wondering whether he too would start a mysterious hacking cough that came from nowhere, a cough that wouldn't stop, an incessant cough that he thought his lungs would explode from his body.

But the cough was never there, and neither was Pa anymore. Since then, it had been up to James to take care of Mother and his three younger brothers. He loved them all, but did they really understand how much he did for them? Daniel was the closest in age, but he had nothing in common with his older brother. Daniel was always sneaking off, laughing, trying to get out of work, forever talking. Nothing ever fazed Daniel; nothing was ever serious for the curly-haired younger brother.

Often, James spoke to himself in the dying shadows of daylight while he struggled in the field. How could it be that Daniel and he came from the same seed? When would Daniel ever understand how serious work must be?

James knew that he was quiet and somber, even his reflection in the pond behind the farm was always serious-eyed and determined. But I have to be, to get them by, James thought bitterly.

And that was what pained him as he stared into the distance at the unseen farm. He knew he shouldn't be here in town today. There was only one reason to be here today. Everyone knew that Vincent intended to raise a volunteer company.

And James knew that he wanted to join. It didn't make sense, but he knew he wanted to.

"What do you think, James?" Patrick said, tugging on his friend's sleeve.

"He's a good speaker," James replied, knowing that he was avoiding the question.

The red-haired Patrick gave no reaction to his friend's reply. He had known James all his life and was accustomed to his coy answers.

"You mean you're not going to volunteer?" Daniel spouted incredulously. James's younger brother was even more bright-eyed than normal today. He was obviously excited, and James knew this was the other reason he was here today—to stop Daniel from signing up.

"He didn't say that," Patrick answered for James, comparing the two brothers as they stood side by side.

James and Daniel had always looked like different sides of the same oak leaf, one so shiny and vibrant, the other so dull and grayed. It seemed that one had inherited all the seriousness, and the other all the humor, but Patrick knew that this was misleading. Despite all his grayness, James was actually a good-natured, wryly humorous person, as long as he wasn't thinking about the farm. James probably couldn't recall, but Patrick remembered what the elder Lockett brother had been like before his father's death. James wasn't really the limp-haired, weather-etched young face that he appeared to be. Behind those gray eyes, there was a mind that worked like the large clock above the Gibson and Brothers' sign, never out of step and constantly whirling. That was James's problem, Patrick thought, James was too smart for his own good.

Daniel on the other hand...

"Well, I'm going to volunteer," Daniel said, starting to pick his way through the crowd only to be jerked back by his shirt collar.

"You're way too young, Daniel," James said, holding firmly to the collar.

"But—"

James's eyes narrowed, cutting his brother off with, "Besides, someone is needed to watch over Ma and the farm while I'm gone, Daniel."

"But—"

"There are no buts, Daniel," James said sternly.

The soft brown eyes of the carefree Lockett brother flickered. "Yes, James," Daniel said finally, unsure that he had heard his older brother correctly. Was James really going to sign up?

James relaxed his grip on Daniel's shirt and wondered whether this was such a wise decision. For the last five years, he alone had taken on the role of head of the house. Too many times, it had been he alone who carried the burden, but his brothers were maturing. They should be able to carry the load if necessary. Or at least, so James hoped.

He knew that at times he had been severe, sometimes even cruel, with all three brothers, especially impulsive Daniel. It bothered him that a natural distance and barrier had developed between them, but he knew no other way at the time, and it was too late to change that now.

"You're really going to volunteer?" Daniel said in a stunned voice.

James nodded. Despite the difficulties of the Locketts' lot in life, James knew that this country had given them so much. His father had impressed that upon him well before his death, and James thought that the country needed him now. He knew his father would understand; he just hoped that his mother would, and that his brothers could carry on in his absence.

"I tol't ya. There was never a question, Daniel," Patrick said.

The red-haired, sun-blotched Patrick grabbed Daniel by the shoulders. Growing up on the farm next to the Locketts with four sisters, Daniel was as close to a younger brother as Patrick would ever have. His thick, sun-dried knuckles playfully rubbed Daniel's head.

"Aw, leave me alone," Daniel fussed, breaking free of Patrick's grasp.

Patrick smiled broadly. Broad-shouldered and built like a bull, he slapped James on the back. His blue eyes, set deep into his sun-battered Irish face, sparkled at some unseen joke.

"Now, let's go sign up, James," he said.

"What?" James said. "You can't sign up!"

"And why not, my good friend?" Patrick said with a cheery obstinance.

"Now, I know you're as impulsive as Daniel here, but you just can't sign up, Patrick."

"Bless your caring heart, James Lockett. Again, why not?"

"Because you have a wife!" James said. "What about Martha? What will she do? What about the West Field?"

Patrick smiled and placed his hands on his hips, making his wide frame even broader. Married just over a year, Patrick had labored all summer to finish the little house on the edge of the West Field of the McManus family land, land given as a wedding present.

"She'll be fine. I finished the house, you know. Besides, it won't take long. We'll whip them Secessionists once and be back before spring planting."

"Now you sound like one of these fools," James said, motioning to the crowd without looking. Congressman Vincent had long ago resumed his oration, but that hadn't stopped numerous murmuring pockets to break out in the crowd. "This will not be over in one little fight as they say, Patrick," James added.

"And why not? They're just a bunch of Secesh..."

"It won't be over so quick, Patrick."

"And what makes you so God blessed smart, James. What do you know that the rest of the Michigan doesn't know?"

"Patrick," James answered with frustration, "think about it. We're talking about invading someone's home. They'll fight—"

"But, James," Daniel interrupted.

"This has been brewing our entire lifetime," James continued. "I can't see it ending just like that. No, sir, it can't end so quickly."

"Maybe you're right," Patrick relented with an ease that put James on edge. "But that doesn't change my mind. If anything, I have more reason to go now. Someone has to watch out for you, James."

James stopped arguing and looked at his old friend with resignation and then a chuckle.

"I suppose I should probably be thankful for that."

"'Course you should," Patrick said with another heavy clap on the back.

"...who will be the first to join me?" Vincent finished. His oratory admonishing the sins of slavery and the disgrace of Secession was finally complete. "You, there. Aren't you, Matthew Bauer?" He pointed to a young man in the front row. "Didn't you win the contest this summer? Why, you're the best shot this county has ever seen!"

The young man, with brown hair and boyish features, blushed slightly at the recognition, but gave his characteristic eager smile nonetheless. With his smooth, whiskerless cheeks, Matthew looked far younger than his eighteen years. Thin-boned, with large hands and long limbs, he clearly had not grown into his body yet. But that had not stopped him from winning the shooting contest at last summer's county picnic.

That day, boyish Matthew had made a name for himself, and he found that he liked the attention. He liked the adventure. There was no adventure in his father's small lumber mill, hoisting birch trees up onto the platform to be cut into planks, most of which would be sent away to Chicago by train.

Matthew had been one of the first in the crowd to gather today. He wanted to be right at the front to listen to Charles Vincent's call to arms.

"That is me, Congressman," Matthew replied loudly to Vincent's query, not at all surprised that the congressman recognized him, "and allow me to be the first to join your company of volunteers."

The crowd erupted in loud applause again, and there was a clamoring of men to get in line behind Bauer.

"We're right behind you, Matthew," Patrick said, grabbing Matthew's thin shoulder with a meaty, calloused hand.

"Patrick, James," Matthew acknowledged his two friends, "you ready to teach them Rebs something?"

"Something like that," James said without the gleeful enthusiasm that had consumed the entire Main Street.

"C'mon, Patrick," James said, "we best be getting back before Martha starts to worry." James also wanted to get back so that he could talk to Daniel, who had left in a huff when it became clear to him that James would not let him volunteer.

"She'll wait," Patrick said, turning back to the game of cards that he had started with Matthew and two other volunteers.

The sun was slowly sinking, but there was still plenty of activity around Main Street. Most of the volunteers still lingered. Their cocky voices carried easily across the crisp air. Some were familiar faces to James, but most were not. He hadn't thought that the county was that big, but now he knew he had been mistaken.

"You're a worrier, James," Matthew said with a smile. He looked particularly young sitting next to burly Patrick and the two other volunteers whose full beards made Matthew's cheeks look cherubic. Still, despite the obvious age difference, it didn't diffuse Matthew's confidence at all. With a pleased look, he laid a pair of aces on the crate that they used as a table.

"Again?" one of the men said disgustedly, getting up from his spot on the raised planking sidewalk.

Though his eyes were watching the other losing hands being laid on the crate, it was James whom Matthew addressed. "You worry too much. You worry about your brothers, about Patrick's wife, and probably a dozen things about me alone."

"Aye, there's plenty to worry about with you," Patrick joked.

"Yes, but..."

"And James has to do all your worrying for you," Patrick continued, "because you were born without a worrisome bone in your body."

Matthew looked up at James's frowning face, knowing that James disapproved of card games, even the stakeless version that they had just been engaged in. James was about to speak when the sound of rapidly approaching hooves interrupted them. They turned to look down the dusty street.

"That looks like—" Matthew began.

"Luke?" James finished with a puzzled voice.

The rider continued to urge his mount on with haste, tufts of blond hair flapping in the wind beneath his hat. Spotting the three of them, the rider steered his horse in their direction, pulling on the reins at the last second.

"Luke Bailey!" Patrick bellowed happily, "you're back!"

"What are you doing here?" James questioned in a confused voice.

The tall, athletic Bailey dismounted and smiled broadly. Rawboned, he was taller than both the bullish McManus and the lanky Lockett, and though the white blond hair and blue eyes looked fittingly choirish for a preacher's son, he was surprisingly muscular and walked with an erect posture and confident gait. James often thought that Luke would cut an impressive figure behind the pulpit when he was done with his studies.

"You didn't think I'd let you boys go off to fight God's war without me?" Luke said happily, shaking Matthew's hand.

"Welcome back, my friend," Patrick laughed with a bear hug of Bailey.

"But what about your studies?" James said.

"There will be time for that later, James. What? Not glad to see me?"

"Don't be absurd," James said, snapping out of his confusion and shaking Luke's hand.

They all laughed, feeling more like little boys than like men on their way to war. James looked at the other excited faces in the background. It was a full-blown epidemic. War fever had struck Kalamazoo County. So many eleven and twelve year olds had clamored to be the drummer boy that Congressman Vincent had allowed a little contest to aid in the selection.

James supposed it shouldn't surprise him. The rhetoric of Reverend Bailey and others had long since stirred up this county. He also decided that it shouldn't surprise him that Luke had left school to join the fight. Of all of his friends, Luke was the most likely to join this battle. It sounded strange that the preacher's son would be the most likely to go off to war, but you only had to hear one of the Reverend Bailey's sermons on the evils of slavery to know that there was nothing more central to Luke's life than fighting slavery. Luke and his father even aided fugitive slaves on their way to Canada, but that was a well-kept secret, lest the slave catchers catch wind of it.

No, it was no surprise to James that Luke was here to volunteer.

"Am I too late?" Luke asked. "I was already on my way back when I heard that Vincent was forming a company of volunteer riflemen. I hurried back as fast as old Burt would bring me."

"But you? A rifleman?" Matthew laughed. "That's a good one!"

"A good one indeed," Patrick chimed in. "Have you ever picked up a gun, preacher's son?"

"Never needed to until now," Luke said, still composed.

"I suppose Matthew can teach you a thing or two in a hurry," Patrick chuckled. "After all those times we tried to get you to go hunting with us...never thought I'd see the day."

"Never thought I'd see the day when we would rise up to stop these slaveholding devils," Luke said with cold seriousness. "We will be God's sword."

Luke's words chilled James slightly, but he brushed it off, knowing that Luke was saying what he believed.

James's mother had often said that the issue of slavery was a black and white issue in the Bailey house, and she was not referring to skin color. There was a right and a wrong in the world and Reverend Bailey left no confusion about which was which.

But *"God's sword?"* James thought to himself. As he looked at the other volunteers, he guessed that many of the faces would have agreed with Luke. After all, many of them had heard the same sermons.

November 16, 1861

I fear Patrick is making a terrible choice. On my way to gather him for drill, I overheard them arguing. A more shrill cry I have never heard. Martha is not at all well with her husband's choice. But it is too late to change now. Patrick has already signed the papers just like the rest of us volunteers.

The sound of the weeping makes me uneasy. Even when Father died, Mother never cried. I suppose she remained so stable for our benefit. She has said before how guilty she feels that we must carry such a burden without a Father. Despite my responses that it is not so and she is not to blame, Mother takes no solace.

She urges me to court. I suspect she would like another woman in the house, but there is no time with the farm. But I had promised her that I will take care of the farm so that Daniel will be able to court. He is nearly of age. Naturally, he will need no urging to avoid the work of the farm!

But am I liar? How can he court if I am not here to run the farm?

But it was the only way I could think of to stop Daniel from volunteering. With me gone, he has to stay to take care of the others, and he knows it.

—The Diary of James Lockett

November 18, 1861

James shoveled the manure out of the barn. He turned around for another shovelful and saw Daniel standing in the entrance, the reddish orange hue of the dawn framed behind him. Daniel's usually affable face was stonelike, save for the red cheeks that were caused by the morning chill. James could tell what was eating away at Daniel.

"You won't make a good soldier," Daniel blurted out.

"What?"

"I said, you won't make a good soldier. What do you know about fighting?"

"Fighting?"

"James, you know about shoveling manure and plowing the fields. What do you know about excitement and adventure? What do you know about fighting?"

"About as much as you, Daniel—"

"But," Daniel interrupted, "your place is here."

"On the farm?" James finished for him, feeling his own anger rising.

"Yes, on..."

"On the farm, where I can keep this family together? Where I can do the work of two men, because my lazy brother would rather fish down at the creek, or tease Mary Elizabeth Collins, or do anything other than work?" The words were spilling out of James faster than he could have imagined. "Is that what you're saying, Daniel? My place is here?"

The intensity in his normally placid older brother took Daniel by surprise. While they had often argued, he had never seen his brother so charged with emotion; he had never heard his brother's true feelings come out in so naked a form.

"Is that what you're saying?" James fired on.

Daniel gave no answer. Instead, he stood open-mouthed at his glaring brother for a moment. Then, he turned and ran.

Alone in the barn, James answered his own question, "Because maybe you're right, Daniel."

"No, no, no," Matthew repeated to Luke. "Don't jerk back on the trigger so hard."

"Don't close your eyes beforehand either," Patrick added with a laugh.

"I'm not trying to do that," Luke said with exasperation.

"Try it again. Squeeze it gently. When you jerk back, it goes high. It kicks high in any case and..."

"In your case, very high," Patrick needled.

"Quiet, you big Irish ox," Luke said, concentrating on the target. The large hay-filled target swung lazily in the breeze as it dangled from a tree limb. "Look at it, it's moving," Luke complained.

Patrick rolled backward in laughter. "I'll tell...them Southerners...to sit still...for you...when we see 'em," he said, struggling to get the words out between laughing gasps.

Luke looked down again through the long barrel of Matthew's Dimick rifle, slowly going through the checklist that the others followed so automatically. He pulled the trigger, and the rifle kicked back fiercely into his shoulder. He knew he had long since bruised it, but he didn't care at this point. Though his friends were trying to teach him how to shoot without the other volunteers knowing, Luke knew that he was the laughingstock of the company.

And Luke had never failed at anything before. He wished he had learned to shoot a gun earlier, but it was the lack of improvement that irked him most. Still, he was determined not to fail.

With eyes beginning to water from the rifle smoke, he looked down at the target, still swaying unharmed in the breeze.

"That was a better shot," Matthew said positively.

"What?" Luke asked.

"You were on line that time. At least I can see where this one hit. That's a start."

"What? Where?" Luke said excitedly. The most frustrating part about all of this was that his aim was so bad, he hadn't even left a mark anywhere to give him a clue as to how close he was to the target. Actually having hit something, anything, was an improvement.

"The tree limb," Matthew answered, "look at the tree limb above the target."

"Aye," Patrick said encouragingly, "that's a big improvement. You're just too high and a little to the right."

"I can fix that," Luke said, quickly reloading.

"There you are," a soft, timid, feminine voice said from behind them.

"Martha," Patrick said in surprise, "what are you doing here?"

Matthew eyed the large picnic basket that she lugged with two hands.

"I thought everyone could use a good meal," she said, rising on her tiptoes to kiss her husband as he took the heavy basket from her.

"Some army this will turn out to be," Matthew said, but smiling he added. "But as long as you're here, what do you have?"

"Plenty for all four of you," Martha said. "Where's James?"

"Off to find the latest rumors for us," Matthew said.

Crack!

Martha jumped at the sound, her already pale features turning even more white.

Luke lowered his rifle and peered through the smoke. "Nothing!" he cried dejectedly.

"Time for a rest, Luke," Patrick said, gently taking his wife's visibly trembling hand.

"Sorry," Luke said, turning around and looking at Martha.

"It's alright," Martha said in calm voice, the color returning to her face. "It just startled me that's all."

Chapter 4

Luke and Matthew walked back to the drill field. The one-time horse pasture on the Brandt family's land still looked relatively undisturbed. James had said earlier that he wished that the yellowing of the grass had been more worn from marching, but for the most part it still stood stiffly in the wind. That was just fine with Matthew. He couldn't see how parading around like a team of trained horses did much of anything.

A bubble of laughter floated by, and Matthew looked at three other volunteers laughing around a small cookfire. The smell of burning birch wood drifted by. A few small cookfires were being started.

"Hallooo, Matthew," a friendly voice said from a nearby cookfire, and Matthew looked to see old Wil Fulgham waving him to come over. The balding, rotund shopkeeper looked oddly out of place in his new jacket, sitting next to one man in a buckskin coat, and two younger men with cheap sackcloth tucked inside their trousers. Now that he thought about it, Matthew noticed that there weren't two men in the whole camp who wore the same clothing. A few wore handsome-looking winter coats, but most wore mismatched, homespun ensembles.

One of the younger men in sackcloth offered a canteen. "Have a seat, friend! Wan' some mule kick?"

Noticing that Matthew was examining his clothing, the man slurred, "Beeeen es-pecting winter." He coughed, cleared his throat, and spat before tilting the broad-rimmed hat on his head to a jaunty angle. "Do I look ready to go fight 'em Rebels?" he gurgled.

"Don't mind Sam," the other young one chirped. "He's had too much of his Uncle Seth's mule kick. He's normally not like this. I'm John Quinlan, and this lump here is Sam Barker."

Matthew shook hands with John. He looked about the same age as James, maybe slightly older. Long-faced, with a wide mustache that drooped around the corners of his mouth, John could look both saddened and morose, but his inquisitive eyes were a truer guide. He wore similar clothing to Sam, although his buttons did not have quite the struggle that Barker's were engaged in. Unlike his friend, John did not wear his wide-brimmed hat to the side. Rather, he wore it straight across, tilted back ever so slightly as to give the appearance that he was relaxing.

"I'm Matthew Bauer." He shook hands with both men, wincing in Sam's thick hand. The man had a grasp like a bear.

"What do you say, Matthew?" old Wil said from across the cookfire. "Ready to go chase these Secessionists all the way back to Fort Sumter?"

Luke observed one of the volunteers reading a Bible. The volunteer was older than most of them, short and stocky with a gnarled, thick, black beard. The man sat on the log, smoking a battered clay pipe and ignored Luke at first when a younger man sat next to him. Eventually, Luke lured George VanderJagt into a conversation and was surprised to learn that VanderJagt had never heard of his father, Reverend Bailey. Luke had always thought that everyone in the county knew of Reverend Bailey.

"You're not from around here, are you, George?" Luke asked with a smile.

"No," George answered in his gravelly voice, twinged with an odd accent that Luke could not place. "Moved 'round most of my life, spent a good while in Texas. Came here eight months ago to go into business with my brother-in-law, but it didn't work out. Don't got no head for business, unlike my poor brother-in-law. I was a terrible burden to him. Then, all this happen'd. Figured it was time to go back to what I know, the only thang I know."

"What's that?"

"The army life, of course, boy. Ol' army blue."

"You were fighting the Mexicans in Texas?" Luke asked, guessing the man looked old enough.

"Smart lad, very smart. Yup, fought 'em when I was even younger 'n you. Stayed in another eight years before I wen' back to Texas to try farmin'. Worse at farmin' than I am at business!" George cackled loudly.

"Did I miss something?" Matthew asked, walking toward them with his rifle across his shoulders.

"George here was telling me his life story," Luke said, introducing the two of them.

"So what do you think?" Matthew said. "Are we ready to send those Rebels scurrying?"

George's yellow smile disappeared instantly, and he became coldly serious. "We're 'bout ready to get a whole lot of you boys sent home in pine boxes."

The look of certainty took Luke aback, but it didn't seem to bother Matthew. "Oh, yeah? You ain't seen me shoot yet, old man. I'll take out a squirrel's eye from two hundred yards."

"T'at a fact, boy?" VanderJagt said, a scowl on his face.

"It is," Matthew answered confidently.

"A lil' contest then?"

"Contest?" Matthew answered with a sly smile. "I'm always ready for that."

"Gus!" VanderJagt called over to a large man with tiny wire-rimmed glasses and a shock of hair nearly as blond as Luke's.

"My nephew, Gus Jeltema," VanderJagt said. "Promised my sister I'd look after 'im."

"I'm Matthew Bauer," Matthew responded, pleasantly shaking Gus's hand.

Luke looked up at Gus, bookish and timid looking from the neck up, a pleasant Dutch boy face. But the rest of him could not be confused as boyish. He was a giant with thick shoulders and long legs as wide as tree trunks.

"We're goin' to have a lil' contest with Bauer here," VanderJagt said to Gus. Taking his nephew aside, VanderJagt pulled on the man's shoulder until he was down to his uncle's height. The old man gave Matthew one last look and then whispered into his nephew's ear.

Gus straightened up and looked at his uncle with an uncomprehending stare and then stole a glance at Matthew. A second look at his uncle's scowling face seemed to erase the indecision, and he marched off until he was about sixty yards from Matthew.

"Where's he going?" Matthew asked.

VanderJagt ignored the question. "The tar-gits are those two stumps out thar'."

Matthew looked at the two hacked-off tree trunks with a puzzled face. "That's easy," he said, completely mystified. "Anyone can hit those, especially from this range."

"Y'all git to prove it," VanderJagt said.

Matthew unslung his rifle and loaded it, pinching a percussion cap onto the nub after he finished. He raised it to his shoulder and said, "And what are your nephew's targets?"

"His tar-git is different," VanderJagt replied as Matthew took aim on the first tree stump.

Matthew fired.

"It's a race of sorts, boy!"

Matthew leisurely turned his attention from the first tree trunk to look over his shoulder at the now madly rushing Gus, carrying his musket by the muzzle like a club.

"You best hit that second trunk before he gits here," VanderJagt said calmly.

Matthew blinked in surprise at the sight of Gus's huffing, red face bearing down on him.

"Hurry, boy, hurry!"

Matthew rushed to grab his powder flask, dropping it in his haste. He quickly picked it up and poured the powder down the muzzle. Next was the bullet. He looked up as he withdrew the ramrod, stuffing it all down. Gus was nearly upon him. Matthew tried to raise his rifle, but he was too late. Gus swung.

The panting of the large Dutchman blended with the swooshing sound of Gus's weapon swinging through the air. Suddenly there was a loud crack as the blow was blocked by another rifle just before it could complete its arc into Matthew's ribs. So great was the force of the blow, that the wood of Gus's gun snapped in half, flinging its remains to either side of Matthew's quivering body. Matthew blinked and looked up to see that VanderJagt had parried the blow with his own rifle.

Though Gus was panting loudly from his sprint, Matthew's own gasping breath was louder. "That was unfair," he managed.

"Hit the target now, boy!" VanderJagt bellowed with such ferocity that Matthew was more frightened of the voice than he had been of the onrushing Gus. With shaking hands, he managed to raise the rifle and to squeeze the trigger, knowing that he was breathing too hard to be perfectly accurate, but it was only a tree trunk. He knew he could hit it. Squeezing the trigger, the hammer fell with a soft metallic click.

Matthew blinked in surprise, completely befuddled.

"You forgot the percussion cap, boy," VanderJagt said in a surprisingly gentle voice.

Matthew looked at the nub of the firing mechanism, at the bare spot that should have held a pinched percussion cap, which would trigger the explosion needed to fire the projectile. In his haste and worry, he had forgotten to place one on the nub.

"Let that be a lesson, son," VanderJagt said. "Fightin' is more like a race than target shooting."

With that, VanderJagt pulled his nephew away, saying as they left, "Sorry about that Brown Bess, Gussie, but I told you that you would wan' a rifle, not a musket, once this starts anyway."

I believe there are two types of men in camp. There are adventurers and moralists, like Matthew and Luke, ready to fight for the Union of this great country. But there is another type of man here. These are generally loathsome types with no better prospects than to sign up. They drink and look for fights. I have no doubt that some would stick a knife in a man's back.

Our little group has already had a run-in with one of these characters, a particularly large and foul-smelling drunk by the name of Hiram Walker. For some reason, he picked a fight with Matthew and then with Luke when he tried to play peacemaker. Fortunately for the two of them, Patrick was nearby, and Hiram Walker will not soon forget that famous Irish uppercut.

—The Diary of James Lockett

November 19, 1861

The trunk gave a satisfying thud as James and Matthew set it on the table in Captain Vincent's room at the Burdick Hotel. There was the faint smell of perfume, and a bulbous oil lamp burned dully despite the fact that there was plenty of light showing through the half-shaded window. With a self-conscious awareness, James tried to tread lightly over the thick red rug, worried about the mud from his boots.

"That will be all, men," Captain Vincent said, waiting for them to salute.

James and Matthew stood there for a moment before realizing with a start what the captain was waiting for. "Yes, sir," they said with flaccid salutes that would make no officer proud, although Captain Vincent did not seem to notice.

It would be a short walk back to camp for them now. The errand that they had been randomly selected for was complete. The small, but heavy, trunk was now off the wagon and in the captain's room. They emerged on Main Street, and James looked over at the large white clock that hung above the dry goods store.

"Got somewhere you need to be?" Matthew asked with a teasing smile.

"No," James said with a shake of the head, not quite catching the humor. "Where would I need to be?"

"I didn't mean...oh, never mind."

"I was just looking at that clock. You ever wonder how it keeps working. Honestly, how does it keep such exactness? Always keeping time, always."

"I don't wonder about those sorts of things, James," Matthew said with a tone of slight condescension. He straightened his wide-brimmed slouch hat against the glare of the sun and added, "You ready to go?"

James nodded, his eyes still on the clock, not paying any attention to the rider reining in his horse in front of them. "You there!" the rider said as they began to walk away from the hotel. "Is this where Congress...I mean Captain Vincent is staying?"

Matthew turned and answered the well-dressed rider. "For now. But we should be leaving in a few days."

"We?" the rider said, sliding off his horse. "You're one of the volunteers, boy?"

"Yes," Matthew said, reddening at being called a boy.

The rider was of average height, slightly taller than Matthew, slightly shorter than James. He looked at Matthew with a pair of disdainful eyes over a patrician nose and trim brown mustache. There was an arrogance on his face and in his eyes. With a lordly look, the stranger added, "Take care of my horse, boy, while I go see the captain."

Matthew bristled. Didn't this man know who he was? He was Matthew Bauer, best shot in the county, and now a soldier! "And who are you?" Matthew asked sharply.

"Orrin Long," the man answered firmly. Clearly displeased, he stopped in his tracks for a moment before slowly turning around to glare at Matthew with malevolent eyes. "Your new lieutenant."

Matthew said nothing beneath the disdainful, withering glare.

"And he needs some water too," Lieutenant Long added, pointing to the horse.

James watched the officer disappear inside the hotel and commented sarcastically, "It just gets better and better."

"Oh, be quiet," Matthew said with some embarrassment. "How was I to know that he would be one of our officers?"

"He certainly seems comfortable giving orders."

Lieutenant Long took his flawlessly polished boots back with one hand and flipped a coin into the air with the other. The small boy spun around, and his hand flashed high to catch the coin. With a hoarse laugh, the officer gave the boy a gentle kick in the rear and sent him sprawling down the hall of the hotel. Still laughing, he closed the door to his room and focused his attention back on the lieutenant's blue uniform that hung on the crosslike rack across the room. Brushed blue wool with shiny brass buttons, it looked perfect in its newness.

Long smoothed his thin mustache with the back of one finger and licked his lips like a hungry wolf. He really had never thought much about becoming a soldier. When his Uncle Charles had raised the possibility of leaving the state congress to form a company to fight in this "grand cause," Long had little choice but to eagerly nod that it was a brilliant idea.

As his uncle's congressional assistant, Long had little means of his own. His only direction was to assist his uncle and take advantage of the opportunities that presented themselves. Of course, in the state capitol, there were always plenty of opportunities.

Graft is what some called it, but Orrin saw it only as business opportunities. In many cases, he was convinced that by taking the money to encourage his uncle to vote a certain way, he was actually helping the state. After all, business enterprise was the true goal of the state, the only reason for doing anything.

Yet despite his last three years in Lansing, Orrin still had little to his name, certainly not enough money for his ambitions and aspirations. But that would soon change. Upon his return from this odyssey, he planned on marrying Big John Moffat's daughter. As the son-in-law of Big John Moffat, Orrin knew that he would never want for anything again and would have all the power that most men could ever want.

Except Orrin was not like most men. Simply marrying into power would not be enough to sustain him. In the heady air of the elite, he would need something else to aid him. And with that thought, he took the uniform from the rack. He was starting out as a lieutenant, and with any luck, he would be much higher in rank by the time he finished. "A major?" he wondered aloud. Yes, that would be enough—Big John's son-in-law and a respected major, a war hero. "Yes," he murmured in a self-assuring voice. With those credentials, the sky was the limit. He had already learned much about elections from helping his uncle. Governor, perhaps? Yes, he smiled wolfishly.

Of course, it would be discomfiting work to lead this rabble. He had ridden past the sharpshooters' camp on his way into town. A dirty mob of ignorant farmers and loggers is what they were. He frowned, good for nothing but menial labor, probably not one brain among the hundred of them, but he had expected as much. With troops like that, they would definitely need officers like me, Orrin thought. They would need someone to make the decisions for them.

But the thought of the Kalamazoo farmers and loggers-turned soldiers quickly passed from Orrin's head. "Governor Orrin Long," he practiced aloud. "Yes, that has a nice ring. Someday."

Captain Charles Vincent and his officers looked the part. Their bright blue uniforms were crisp and new. The golden trimmings on the

shoulders sparkled in the bright November sun. It made our pitiful appearance look even more bland and unworthy.

Lieutenant Orrin Long and Lieutenant Walter Simon were introduced as our new officers. It took me all morning, but I finally remembered where I had seen Orrin Long. It wasn't until he walked behind the captain that it hit. He is Captain Vincent's nephew. I remember him from the last election.

George VanderJagt is the sergeant now. Captain Vincent must have been compelled to make him so after it became clear that George was the only one among us with any experience in the army.

Lieutenant Simon is organizing a vote later today to elect a corporal. Our 2nd lieutenant seems attentive enough to his duties, but he is young and nervous about it.

But there is only thing that the camp is talking about. We leave tomorrow for Chicago and eventually Benton Barracks in St. Louis to join Birge's Western Sharpshooters.

It has begun.

—The Diary of James Lockett

November 20, 1861

"I don't understand it," Captain Vincent declared, pacing his hotel room with quick little steps.

Lieutenant Walter Simon looked over at the senior lieutenant, Orrin Long. There was the reaction of a sycophant's nodding sympathy on Long's face.

"I can't believe that I was robbed, right out of my own hotel room," Captain Vincent repeated for at least the fifth time. He looked at the small trunk that the two privates had carried in the room for him yesterday. The papers were still there in their half of the trunk, but the square strong box that contained the silver coins was gone.

"I intended to give every man a small advance for their service—a reward for their prompt devotion to their country. It was to be a morale lifter before we left our warm homes."

"Morale," Lieutenant Long scoffed. "We don't need any more morale to scotch these Secesh bastards."

Lieutenant Simon looked at him with undecided eyes. Lieutenant Long certainly had the attitude and gave the impression that he knew what he was doing, but his actual words sometimes betrayed the impression that his physical presence emitted.

"Morale," Long continued and then stopped short. Realizing that his words could be taken as a reproach of his uncle, he quickly added, "It would have been a beautiful gesture, sir, of your generosity."

"Shall I inform the sheriff?" Simon finally spoke. He had been silent all throughout the captain's ramblings.

"No," the captain grumbled, smacking a fist into his other hand. "That is the last thing we would want now. Such disappointment would damage the men's morale once the word spread. I don't want to begin my Kalamazoo Sharpshooters on such a note! By God, no, Lieutenant Simon, that is not at all a good idea. I don't want word of this to leave this room."

"And we leave tomorrow," Lieutenant Long added with a mischievous look in his eyes. "There isn't even time for us to look for the thieves."

Captain Vincent shook his head sorrowfully. "You are too right, nephew. Those thieves could not have timed it any more fortuitously. I shall have to put it out of my mind, but by God, that burns me!"

"So when do you think we get our uniforms?" Matthew asked James as they milled about at the end of Main Street, waiting for Captain Vincent.

James looked around at the motley collection of clothing. None of the men had uniforms, and no two men were dressed alike, although a number of them were sporting squirrel tails on their wide-brimmed slouch hats. "Don't know, Matthew. We don't look much like an army, do we?"

"We're a citizen's army," Luke said brightly. "Don't worry, I'm sure we'll get uniforms in Chicago."

"Hope so," James said, looking at a couple of their comrades dressed with sack coats inside their trousers.

"So we're going to be in Birge's Western Sharpshooters too," Matthew mused. "Right with those boys from Van Buren and Berrien Counties."

"Is that where they ended up?" Patrick said. "I thought they went out East."

"No," Matthew answered. "They're with Birge, and I guess he's in St. Louis."

"Wish we could get going. At this rate, the war could be over before we even get to St. Louis," Luke sighed. "Where is our captain? I thought the army was supposed to be a punctual place."

"Maybe," James shrugged with a small smile. "But none of us would know much about that. Would be nice if we could leave in some reasonable order. The longer we mill about here, the more likely..." James stopped in mid-sentence and leaned an ear into the breeze.

"Horses," Matthew said accurately.

Finally, Captain Vincent and Lieutenant Long galloped up with the lieutenant carrying a large bag. It took a couple of minutes until the contents were distributed to the men of the Kalamazoo Sharpshooters.

"Here ya go," Sergeant VanderJagt said eventually, handing James a bright red scarf.

"What am I supposed to do with this?" James said.

"Look! I'm a bandit," Matthew said, tying his around his face.

"Don't ask me what we're s'posed to do with this frill," VanderJagt said gruffly. "God knows why we wan' to wear these."

"The women of the town took up a collection to buy them," Patrick said softly from nearby.

"What?" James said in surprise. "How do you know that?"

"Wives," Patrick said. "It was supposed to be a surprise, but Martha told me. She can't keep a secret for anything."

"Women!" VanderJagt snorted. "'Splains everything." He left them to distribute the remaining scarves to the other men.

The Kalamazoo Sharpshooters departed via an impromptu parade. Each man was surprised at the number of people who lined the dusty street to watch them—one hundred and two strong—march by in ragged rows of four.

More pack mule than soldier, they beat down the road west towards Chicago. Many men carried an odd array of heavy clothing and accoutrements. Some carried revolvers given to them by loved ones in addition to their precious rifles. Almost every man carried a heavy hunting knife, skillets, a pot, and tinware. They were a walking, jangling caravan. The only exceptions were Sergeant VanderJagt and his nephew. They were traveling light.

November 24, 1861

Dearest Martha,

I write you only because I promise. You know I ain't good with ABCs like James.

We ain't gone far yet. But many feet already hurt. At this speed I wonder whether we will git to Chicago. Sergeant VanderJack tries to push us to cover more ground each day, but it is no good. By the time Captain Vincent readys hisself in the morning, half the day is gone. One of the wagons is his alone with a tent so elaborate he should be the king of Egypt, not a congressman. I reckn that a early storm will swing down and catch us, but so far the wether has ben nice. That must be a first for Michigan.

There is a pair of twins from Galesburg who know your cousins here. Their name is Dobbins.

You know that I ain't much for correspondence, but I wanted to let you know that I'm fine.

Your Husband,
Patrick

December 4, 1861

"Chicago," Luke thought aloud.

He was standing in the crowded church on Michigan Avenue. It was a small, stone building, the only nonwooden structure that he had seen for blocks. Standing near the pulpit listening to Reverend Wallace Armbaugh, Luke's mind wandered back to his father's own small congregation in Kalamazoo. He wondered whether his father had come to grips with it yet. The "it" in question was the fact that his son had volunteered to take up arms.

Though vehement in his denunciation of slavery, Reverend Joseph Bailey had surprised his son by trying to dissuade him from leaving with the Kalamazoo Sharpshooters. Luke still did not understand his father's logic. A cause such as this needed him, he thought. Luke and the others were to be God's sword, freeing his captives in the South and destroying the rotten fruit.

The idea of killing did trouble Luke when he allowed it to slip into his thoughts, but so far, he had been successful in pushing it out of his mind. Sometimes painful things needed to be done, Luke told himself sorrowfully, reflecting on the Old Testament story of Abraham and Isaac. God had tested Abraham's faith, and now he was testing Luke's and many others.

Luke's eyes locked on another pair in the crowd who bore right through him with their intense curiosity. The dark orbs belonged to a young black woman with a slight build. She appeared to be listening to the reverend as inattentively as Luke was. Her attention was clearly on the tall, blond man who looked back at her.

Reverend Armbaugh had told Luke before the service that there were a number of freedmen in the congregation, and Luke wondered whether this particular woman had at one time been a slave. More than once, he and his father had housed runaway slaves on their way to Canada in their secret room attached to the small library. A closet was probably more appropriate than calling it a room, but no one ever complained. It hid the refugees from the callous slave hunters.

Though his father had been willing to put them all in danger to protect slaves on this underground railroad, he was incapable of giving Luke his blessing on this decision. Is it because I am all he has? Luke wondered. His mother had died ten years ago, and there were no other siblings. Even Luke's Uncle William had died two years ago. Truthfully, he was the only kin left for his father. That must surely be it, Luke reasoned. But sometimes one had to place his faith in God and prayer. His father would come to see that eventually, Luke prayed.

Reverend Armbaugh pounded the pulpit to emphasize his plea on pushing President Lincoln to officially emancipate the slaves. The sharp thud snapped Luke's attention back to the present. It was strange to Luke that no announcement had been made yet. He knew that was what they were fighting for, although he had learned the hard way that freeing the slaves was not the only reason that the men from Kalamazoo County were heading off to fight.

Still, Lincoln's delay disturbed him. Little hope of reconciliation existed after Bull Run, even if either side desired it, and Luke, for one, did not pray for reconciliation if it meant a continuation of slavery for some of God's children.

"...one of our brave citizen-soldiers, a man in God's army," Reverend Armbaugh finished saying, gesturing towards Luke.

Luke felt his face flush, more from being caught daydreaming than from the public attention, but he quickly recovered and seventy expectant eyes followed him to the pulpit. Out of habit, Luke rested a hand on the corner of the Bible opened on the pulpit. "Not everything can be wrought by words," Luke said, not knowing where the words came from or how they went into his mouth so quickly. "Sometimes, God's will must be served by the action of his humble servants."

December 6, 1861

Dear Father,

We have arrived and departed Chicago. We are now in St. Louis at Benton Barracks. Have seen nothing of St. Louis, being night when we arrived. The train ride from Chicago was a blur of scenery. How flat Illinois is! Despite my excitement, I quickly fell asleep. The clickety-clack of the rails could put anyone to sleep.

We are now called Company J. I liked the Kalamazoo Sharpshooters much better. How many stories of heroism can there be about Company J? It lacks the vim of the Kalamazoo Sharpshooters! Next, they may take away our red scarves. I pray not!

Now that we have reached camp, I've no need for my powderhorn. The army will provide paper cartridges for my Dimick.

Our spirits are high, and we are ready to teach the traitors a lesson. Luke's improvement with your rifle has been steady. It won't be long until he is a tolerable shot, but he is still learning. He wishes me to thank you again for loaning him your Dimick. I thank you too, because I hesitate to say what he would hit with an old smoothbore! My only fear is for James. His mood is dark and comments dim. He was always the cautious sort and doesn't seem to be filled with the fire of the other boys. I don't think he has what it takes to be a soldier.

Matthew

December 8, 1861

Sergeant VanderJagt drilled us into darkness today. Most of the men hate him right now, but I think most of them know now that Vincent made the right choice in making him sergeant. We are becoming very familiar with the commands and how to march. Some still don't understand though, and I wonder whether some of them even know which is their left, and which their right. It is obvious to me that we are not performing as well as the other companies, but VanderJagt is determined to correct that. I only hope that Captain Vincent and Lieutenant Long will be as well prepared. I didn't see hide nor hair of them today. The drilling was handled by VanderJagt and Lieutenant Simon. Simon seems to know what he is doing. I was told that he was in the militia before leaving for the university, and that he is why he is so familiar with the commands. He is a bit distant, and some of the men have taken to ridiculing him. He doesn't look nearly as impressive as Vincent or Long, I agree, but I like him in any case.

As I write this, the draft in the barracks makes my candle flicker, or perhaps it is the snoring of a hundred men. Regardless, I am too tired to write more, but I still look forward to tomorrow.

—The Diary of James Lockett

December 9, 1861

"You know what one of the Ohioans in Company G told me?" Luke said to Matthew as Matthew worked on molding his bullets and cutting his own patches. VanderJagt's pronouncement that the army would provide paper cartridges proved to be an overstatement. Though promised, most of the cartridges had not arrived yet, and for now, it was up to each man to mold his own bullets and cut his own patches for his Dimick rifle. Working the pliers-like device, Matthew molded the soft lead of the bullet.

He stopped for a moment and looked into the barrel of the gun studying the long grooves that ran from the bore. Such a simple thing, Matthew thought, the grooves would put a spin on the bullet, allowing it to cut cleaner through the air, giving it better accuracy and more distance. So simple, yet so important. He knew full well the difference in accuracy of a rifled shot versus the ball of a smoothbore.

Luke watched Matthew examining the gun in religious silence, knowing that Matthew put more stock in his rifle than in his soul. That was something that Luke intended to change.

"Now, what was it you wanted to tell me?" Matthew asked as he looked up.

"Tell you? Oh, yes, I was talking to one of the Ohioan boys in Company G. Did you know the Western Skirmishers were General John C. Frémont's idea?"

"Frémont? Who's he? I thought our generals were Halleck and Practice."

"Prentiss," Luke corrected, "General Benjamin M. Prentiss. And you're right, Frémont's not our general anymore. He's out East somewhere, but he ran for president, remember?"

Matthew shrugged. "No. Never heard of him. What's your point?"

"Point? Well, I suppose, I don't really have a point, I just didn't know about that."

"Did this Ohioan tell ya that we're supposed to be used as skirmishers too?" Matthew looked back down at his rifle, gently fingering the trigger. Perhaps, if he filed it down to make it even more sensitive that would further improve his accuracy.

"Skirmishers?" Luke responded, "No...what's a—"

"The advance guard, sort of. We go out in front of the main body. Scout where the enemy is so the main body doesn't blunder into a trap."

"What main body?"

"That's my point, we don't have a main body, just skirmishers."

"That doesn't make any sense."

"Either does having no uniforms or ammunition."

"You're starting to sound like James now," Luke laughed.

"Bah," Matthew said. "We'll still whup them bushwhackers out there. Jus' seems a mite disorganized, you know?"

"I know. I overheard some of Wisconsin fellas in Company A talking about how it's been a mess since they got here. They just want to get out of camp and get after the Rebels."

"Me too," Matthew agreed.

James and Patrick followed Sergeant VanderJagt to the front of the barracks where Matthew sat and Luke stood.

"Where are the uniforms?" Luke said, noticing that they were empty-handed.

"No uniforms," Patrick snorted.

"The quartermaster has enough for one company, but seeing as how there's us and Company I, not to mention that G doesn't have 'em yet either, he's not going to give them out to anyone."

"What?" Luke said, puzzled.

"Welcome to the U.S. Army, boys," VanderJagt said.

"Who's he going to give the uniforms to?" Matthew asked.

"That's just it," Patrick said. "He ain't givin' them to no one yet, not until somebody higher up decides who should get them first."

"Crazy," James muttered.

"Where are the rest of the uniforms? Aren't there more coming?" Luke asked.

"Should be, but only God knows where they are at."

Dearest Martha,

We made it to camp in St. Louis and ben training hard each day. The barracks ain't bad, tho Luke keeps complaining about sleeping on hard boards. The bunks are in three tiers and each barrack holds a hundred men with the officers at the end. Captain Vincent keeps other arrangements, but none of us miss him. For all his fancy talk, he ain't much in person.

We still ain't got no uniforms, and it is a good thing that we brought our own rifles or we would be walking 'round with sticks like some of the Ohioans.

I long for home. There is talk among some men about reenlisting at the end of our three months, but I am not so sure.

Your loving husband,
Patrick

December 11, 1861

Luke could hear the cries of anguish as plain as day. They were cries he could never fully understand, cries that he could never imitate, cries that he had never actually heard. Yet somehow, as he stared at and read the sign "Jack Cobb – Slave Trader," he could hear the shrieks and sobs.

The door to the narrow store front was boarded shut, and the sign out front dangled perilously from one hook. But it wouldn't fall. Like some sort of harbinger, "Jack Cobb – Slave Trader" dangled stubbornly despite another stiff wind that was blowing this evening. The wind pushed the sign back and forth, twisting all the while.

Luke's eye caught sight of the small stump out front of the door. Was that where the auctioneer stood, he wondered. Or was that how the slave was presented to the crowd? Did they have to stand upon the stump so that slaveholders could gawk, judge his value? Bid on him? On her?

He could feel the fear now...again.

But his fear as a timid little boy had been nothing compared to what his African brothers must have felt on the slave trader's stump, and he suddenly felt ashamed.

Luke could remember his father's voice telling him that he did not have to go. But every time, little Luke would pretend to swallow his fear and hop into the wagon beside his fugitive-assisting father. They would conceal their human cargo beneath a simple blanket in the back of the wagon and bounce along the rutted dirt roads for fifteen miles to the next stop on the Underground Railroad. Luke had accompanied his father every time, and in later years, Reverend Bailey had told his surprised son that the presence of his little boy had calmed his fears. Whether it was Luke's mere presence or being less conspicuous by having the little boy with him, Luke was not sure.

What Luke did know for certain was that he had been terrified on every trip! He had lived in paralyzing fear that a fugitive slave hunter would stumble across them. Little Luke had clutched the sides of the jolting wagon seat until he thought his hands would bleed. Every time it was the same. The fear disabled him. All he could do was grip the wagon, frozen in place.

Now standing in front of Jack Cobb's sign, here in St. Louis, Luke rebuked himself for such fear. It was nothing compared to the fear of those the Baileys were helping. His fear had been irrational, irrelevant.

There had been so many terrified and anxious faces that they had saved. The ebony faces had peered at him with such anxiety, yet those courageous souls always put themselves into such blind trust. Were they able to peer into the Baileys' souls? How did they know that the Baileys were friends and would not turn them over to the fugitive slaver hunters? Those lucky enough to make it to the Baileys in Kalamazoo or the Hendersons in nearby Schoolcraft were the lucky ones. They had already cleared the largest hurdles barring their way to freedom in Canada.

Had any of those who made it to Kalamazoo started here in St. Louis? Had they been forced upon the stump in front of Jack Cobb's? Luke stared with festering rage at the narrow store front. Why? Why did God allow such evil? How could the building still be standing? Why had President Lincoln not emancipated all of God's children yet?

So possessed by his thoughts, Luke did not notice that he was no longer alone. It was only after the man cleared his throat politely a minute later that Luke turned to see a short, squat man with a flat face looking at him. His wide-brimmed hat was battered and pulled low over his eyes, but he smiled and tipped the hat up slightly. The eyes hinted at mischief, but the voice was pleasant enough as he said, "Didn't wan' to interrupt you. Looked like you were in some deep thinkin', friend."

Luke nodded and looked once more at the dangling sign. Why wouldn't it just fall?

"Ol' Jack Cobb is long gone," the man continued when it was obvious that Luke was to make no reply. "They chased him out of town a long time ago."

"Not long enough," Luke responded with a thin-lipped gaze.

"Terrible thing, terrible," the man mumbled with a shake of his head.

"The enslavement of God's children is more than terrible. It is an affront to God himself," Luke declared, carefully eyeing the man for his reaction. After all, this had once been a slave state, and he had been told more than once since they had arrived that this sentiment was largely unchanged even though St. Louis was in Federal control.

But, the man across from Luke did not flinch; in fact, he gave no reaction at all to Luke's words. The man's reddened eyes still looked at Luke with that same hint of mischief, as if he knew a joke that Luke did not. Luke searched for malice in those eyes but found none. The man's next statement cleared any doubt in Luke's mind as to which side he was on.

"Always good to find another wise in God's ways," he said. "Jack Cobb! Hah! I spit on him!" With an audible splatter, the man sent a wad of tobacco juice onto the front stoop of the building. "You're not from around here, friend."

"Michigan," Luke answered.

The man nodded appreciatively. "You've come a long way to look at a boarded-up slaver's hole."

Luke was about to reply, but the man gave him no chance.

"Was on my way to see some other Wide Awakes."

"Wide Awakes?"

"Wide Awakes," the man said in an almost annoyed voice. "Men like Lyon and Blair—men who kept the armory from Secesh hands. By God, they made some hard enemies! But the Wide Awakes kept St. Louis from falling into Rebel hands."

"Oh, I see," Luke replied feebly.

"Yep," the man continued, grabbing Luke by the elbow and leading him down the street. "The Wide Awakes and Minutemen nearly turned the whole city into a funeral pyre. Price's Minutemen setting up camp across from the armory."

"Sterling Price?"

"The one and the same. Yep, those Minutemen could stir up trouble with the best of them. Running a state flag up the Federal courthouse. By God, that got the dander of the Wide Awakes!"

"State flag?"

"Back in March. Didn't stay up long, but the crazy flag they put up over the Bethold mansion, now that caused problems."

"What kind of problems?"

"The worst kind. Some of Dickey's Wide Awakes wanted to storm the place, 'course that is exactly what the Minutemen wanted. They had a hundred muskets and a swivel gun ready to stop them."

"A hundred men?"

The man gave Luke a sidewise glance but continued on. "Next thing I knew, Dickey had a knife to his throat."

"You were there?"

"'Course, most of the St. Louis wanted to see the outcome. But that was just one of many encounters."

Luke could hear the sounds of raucous laughter growing louder in the darkening night and knew that his new friend was leading him towards the saloons of St. Louis. That would be where most of the Kalamazoo Sharpshooters were, enjoying their brief night of freedom before they left for the bushwhacking country of middle Missouri the next afternoon.

No doubt most of the other Kalamazoo Sharpshooters were enjoying this brief and unexpected privilege that Captain Vincent had granted them. Sergeant VanderJagt had groused incessantly that it was a terrible idea the day before they were to leave. The gruff, old sergeant had made it a point to remind each of them the punishment for desertion was the firing squad, and VanderJagt announced that if any of them deserted, he would personally handle the duty.

Luke had shrugged off the warning like most of the others. There was no need to desert now. They finally were getting what they wanted, out of the barracks and into the action.

More likely, there would be problems with VanderJagt's second warning. The policing provost guard would not treat brawling or thievery lightly.

That warning fell on similarly deaf ears, Luke knew.

Luke's companion was still talking, completely unaware that Luke had stopped listening for the last two minutes. "...'course, ain't be a prob'm if the armory wasn't here in Sain' Louie. Sixty thousand stands of arms and twenty-five cannon would have been a nice prize for those wan'ing Secession."

Luke gave a low whistle. "Sixty thousand muskets!"

"Damn right," his companion agreed with gusto and a slap on the back. "Now, you can see why the Wide Awakes and Minutemen had their blood up so!" He tugged on Luke's arm and steered him through an alleyway that cut through to the street behind. "Shortcut," he said.

The alley was pitch-dark and stank of urine and excretions, but Luke followed nonetheless. "Where did you say we were going again?" Luke asked.

"Right here," the man said, grunting with effort on the last word.

Something heavy hit Luke in the back of the head, and he dropped to his knees. His ears were ringing with a strange sound and pain shot down the base of neck while purple and yellow bolts appeared before him even though his eyes were closed. He knew he was on all fours, and he could hear the surprise in the man's voice. "You got a hard head, Michigan."

A series of boots to the midsection toppled Luke flat to the ground. "Negro-loving bastards in Sain' Louie!" The toe of the boot crashed into Luke's temple; and then Luke did not feel the next dozen blows to his body or face.

Dear Daniel,

As I have 10 minutes, I will spend them in consideration of your interest in our activities. Camp life is a bit boring, and most are ready for some action. Drills have been improving, even Captain Vincent seems to have taken an interest in it now and his presence has probably helped. I have trouble judging the man. Often, I find myself detesting him, but the next, I find that he has some redeeming qualities.

The weather has improved just as Matthew said it would. He is ever chipper, almost gay, and I find that rankling me, although I dare not let it show. Perhaps, I am just ready for action like the others. I have found myself wide awake before reveille for the second straight morn.

We still have no uniforms, and no one expects them soon. We look quite the hodgepodge with our country dress, bright red scarves, and floppy hats. More of the men are taken by the squirrel tail in the hat, and the tails have begun to actually fetch a decent price since there are no squirrels around camp. I'm sure that you find it hard to imagine that a squirrel tail would have any value, but that is camp life.

I hope this obliges your curiosity for the moment. Please give my affections to all and keep us in your prayers. We leave for central Missouri to chase bushwhackers.

Your brother, James

"Ninety-nine, one hundred," Lieutenant Long mouthed silently. He looked up at the troll-like little sutler with the greasy side whiskers.

"It's all there," the sutler said with a raspy voice. He held out a battered flask that was more discolored than silver. "Drink to the deal?"

Long frowned at the grotesque little man and wrinkled his nose. The man's strong odor was becoming a more repulsive stench the longer he stood there.

"Suit yourself," the whiskered sutler cackled and took a long pull on the flask.

Long pulled fifteen dollars from the one hundred that he had just received. The fifteen was for the labor of Walker and his friends, loading the army supplies into the wagon, as well as providing Long with protection. He doubted he had much to fear from the little sutler, but there was no trust in the selling of contraband. It was far better to project a sense of force, and that was what Hiram Walker and his four brutes did.

Of course, Walker and his dull-witted cohorts had no idea how little their cut was, and Long had to smile at that. The selling of the army's property to greasy little sutlers like this man was a profitable business—all profit in fact.

"Same time next week?" the sutler asked, scratching furiously at his side whiskers for the louse that had somehow crawled in there.

"No, we leave for Centralia tomorrow afternoon," Long said.

"Too bad. This could have been quite profitable for both of us."

Long grunted, turned around, and walked away. He stepped into the dark alley where Walker and the others were waiting. They would have to hurry. It would be dawn in a few hours. The haggling had taken longer than he expected.

"Ready?" Walker asked him.

"Yes," Long said, but Walker did not budge, and Long looked at him with momentary confusion. With a flash of realization, he put fifteen dollars in Walker's hand.

Walker gave a yellow-toothed smile and said, "Ready now."

There was a low moan from the depths of the alleyway, and Long turned quickly on his heel to see a figure stagger to his feet in the darkness of the alleyway. "I thought you checked the alley," Long said fiercely to Walker. The figure moaned again and staggered forward a step. It was clear that the man was in bad shape.

"I'll take care of it," Walker grunted, pushing Long gently into the shadows. Walking towards the figure, who was stumbling slowly towards them, Walker said, "You all right, friend?"

Though no face could be distinguished in the darkness of the alley, there seemed to be something familiar about the man struggling closer. Gripping the revolver, Walker stopped and let the man come to him.

The man moaned pitifully again and clutched Walker's sleeve with a desperate claw, as if he was trying to pull himself erect. In the dull grayness of the early morning, there was a flash of astonishment and recognition in each man's eyes.

"Preacher boy," Walker said, looking at the battered face of Luke. "Hope you didn't see anything tonight." The butt of Walker's pistol sent Luke crashing back down to the horse manure. "'Cuz if you did see somethin', that will be the least I'll do."

Walker returned to Long and the others. "There's no problem. Let's go."

December 12, 1861

The sharpshooters were finally moving toward battle, James thought to himself. The dust of Benton Barracks was behind them, and despite their continual supply problems, Birge's Western Sharpshooters were headed for war.

The flatcar bounced along the track at thirty miles per hour. The regiment had departed from St. Louis a half hour ago for points west. Their objective was to quell Rebel bushwhackers and to intimidate Rebel sympathizers in central Missouri. Every man was perfectly confident that they could accomplish that, and their spirits were high.

Ahead of the flatcar, the locomotive belched thick black smoke. The train rattled and bounced across the tracks, but what most of the men on the flatcar noticed was the cutting wind that knifed through their thick clothing.

Most of Birge's Western Sharpshooters were crammed into the passenger coaches, but the capacity was much less than the one thousand men of the new regiment. Though the wind turned bitter cold at these speeds and exposed positions, a few men chose the elbow room of the flatbeds over the sardinelike passenger cars. There were twenty hardy souls aboard this particular flatbed.

James looked at the bruises on Luke's swollen face. Luke looked even more miserable now than when Sergeant VanderJagt had dragged his semiconscious body back to the barracks just before morning reveille. Luke was lucky. VanderJagt had taken a small party to find any stragglers from their night of revelry. They had found two Kalamazoo Sharpshooters passed out from drink in one of the saloons, pockets picked clean. On their way back to camp, they had cut through an alley and had been shocked to find Luke bleeding and unconscious in the foul alleyway.

Luke had said little about it through his swollen lips. His peaceful features were obscured by the purple swollen eye, twisted nose, and knot on his forehead. Everyone knew that Luke was plainly embarrassed about being suckered, but what bothered Luke was the bizarre dream that he had dreamt. For some reason, he had dreamt that Hiram Walker had found him first in the alley. How strange that one could dream while unconscious, Luke mused.

Maybe later when he didn't feel so miserable, he would tell them. But right now, he sat sphinxlike on the flatbed with James, Patrick, Matthew, and a few other Kalamazooers of Company J, plus a dozen Wisconsin natives from Company A.

"It's a bit colder than I suspected out here," John Quinlan said, his cheeks flushed bright red.

"But the fresh air and view," Matthew said, his boyish face hidden behind his red scarf to protect it from the cold, "you couldn't pay me to go back there."

"The smell of all those Ohioans packed together is reason enough," joked one of the Wisconsinites.

"This is like summer back home," joked another private from Company A.

"Never been to Wisconsin," Matthew began.

"You ain't never been anywhere," Patrick interrupted, drawing out full laughs from all those huddled around.

"For the sake of company unity, I'll pretend I didn't hear that," Matthew sniffed dramatically.

"Anybody got some tobacco?" another Wisconsin man asked. "I haven't had a decent smoke in two days." He removed a long, drooping pipe that dipped so low it looked as if it balanced on his chest.

"Would warm ya up," another added.

"What you need is a beard," Patrick said, rubbing the reddish-brown scruff that he had started to grow five days ago. "Too bad we didn't leave a week from now. It'd be filled in by then."

"How far away we goin', Sergeant?" the first Wisconsinite asked the tobacco smoker.

"I heard the colonel tell Captain Wallace it was a hundred fifty miles."

"One hundred fifty miles of this?" Matthew said, sweeping his hand out across the flat prairie, interrupted only by a few low hills and bluffs.

"Why, we should be able to see it already," laughed one of the Wisconsin men, standing up on his tiptoes and peering out with a hand blocking the sun from his eyes. The train took another bounce along the track, and he lost his balance, falling squarely on his buttocks, leading to another chorus of laughter.

"This place is awful flat," Matthew agreed after they regained their breath from laughing so hard. "You think there will be any Rebs left when we get there? They should see us coming for miles and take off."

"I dunno," James argued. "It's not that flat. Some of these bluffs are decent sized. I'd say Kalamazoo is flatter than this."

"Not even close," Matthew disagreed.

"In any case," Patrick said, "we have bigger trees."

The conversation gradually turned to the divided nature of the state of Missouri. Many in the state were pro-Secession, like the governor, but many others were Unionists. The state had a long and fractious history, never more so than now. Regiments of volunteers had been drawn from the state already, some fighting for the Union, some for the Confederacy.

"There will still be Rebels. Don't you worry, Michigan," one man finally answered Matthew's question.

"The whole damned state is proslavery," another Wisconsinite chimed in. "It's just a good thing that somebody thought ahead about capturing the armory in St. Louis, or they might have outgunned us."

"They say Sterling Price has an army here and is recruiting more everyday."

"People say a lot of things, Merkeson," the sergeant replied with some disgust. "Ain't nothing but some bushwhackers out here. Nothing more than glorified bandits."

James and the other Kalamazoo boys curiously watched the exchange. Having arrived so late, they knew little of what was out there, and even less of what was expected of them.

"So vhat are ve going to do out in the middle of here any-vay?" a second Wisconsin man added. "E'f they are bandits, get the sheriff."

"What? Did they just pluck some of you Danes right off the boat?" the sergeant said. "They're all traitors here. There is no law. We're the law. If we don't get in there and wipe out these traitors, they might recruit the whole state."

"Missurah," Merkeson said, "they can have it."

"Ain't much of a state," the sergeant agreed, "but we got to start somewhere."

"Would be nice if they gave some of you boys uniforms first though," Merkeson said, nudging James.

"Can't tell you from bushvackers," the Dane added with a toothy smile.

"Ain't gonna impress the locals looking like that," the sergeant agreed. "I thought some uniforms came in. What happened?"

"Only enough uniforms for one company," James explained. "And they're still trying to figure out who's the lucky one."

"Humphh," the sergeant said. "Sure looked like more uniforms than that, but I'm just an old lumberjack, so what do I know."

December 16, 1861

Dear Father,

We have finally begun this holy fight to rid our land of that plague, slavery. We are camped on the prairies of Missouri, near Centralia. Half of the regiment is here, the other half being in Renick. All around us are Rebel sympathizers and bushwhackers. There have already been some skirmishes, although none have involved us. Rumors say that there is some cavalry out there too, but no one has seen them yet.

We still have no uniforms, and therefore, have been assigned to guard duty and other less important roles. Part of why we are here is to impress the Missourians with our strength, and we do not look much better than the Secesh without uniforms. I cannot understand why they don't get the rest of the uniforms, much less release the ones that they have here.

The army is a strange place, Father. Many of the men need spiritual ministry, though they don't realize it. I have tried to hold a number of prayer meetings, but they have been more poorly attended than I expected. But I will continue to have them.

Keep us in your prayers.

Your son,

Luke

December 18, 1861

James, Patrick, Luke, and Matthew sat around their cookfire eating a dinner of salt pork and hard biscuits. From the first days of its formation, the company had settled into groups of four messmates. In most of these groups, cooking duties rotated. Tonight, it was Luke's turn.

"Not bad," Patrick mumbled with a mouthful. "Not like Martha," he added after swallowing, "but a good sight better than old James here."

"What?" James replied in mock surprise. "You don't like my cooking?"

"Little Mary cooks better than you," Matthew agreed, speaking of his niece, "And she's only four."

"You certainly can't blame it on your blood," Patrick said. "'Cuz your mother is one the best cooks I know."

"And to think I went out of the way for you, my good friends. Why, next time it will just be hardtack all the way around."

"I imagine we'll be having plenty of that over the next month," Patrick sighed.

"Hallo, boys!" Gus called as he approached their campfire with a wide smile set across his face.

"What are you so happy about, Gus?" Luke said.

"Uniforms," Gus said proudly. "They've arrived. I just saw them."

"Uniforms?" James said skeptically. "Are you sure?"

"Or is there just enough for one more company?" Patrick added.

"No, enough for all of us. I asked one of the teamsters what he was hauling, and he said uniforms, so there has to be enough for all of us."

"Uniforms," Matthew said, pondering. "Maybe that means we can get off guard duty and actually get out of this camp."

"I'll be," James said, watching Lieutenant Simon, leaving the quartermaster. "Judging by the look on the lieutenant's face, I'd say you're right, Gus. We're finally going to get our uniforms."

December 19, 1861

"Finally," Matthew said, "we get to do something."

The boys of Kalamazoo County stood proudly in two rows, their new blue uniforms topped by their bright red scarves. Some of the men fiddled with their belts and cartridge box straps. Many did it more out of newness and wanting to touch the uniforms than out of actual need to adjust anything. Some of them just wanted to touch it to make sure they weren't dreaming.

"Uniforms, hallelujah," Luke said, leaning around James to address Matthew.

"Stop the yapping down there," Sergeant VanderJagt said from the end of the line, immediately curtailing that conversation and a few others.

Captain Vincent walked from his large tent with deliberate slowness. His chest puffed out and face colored from the brisk morning wind, he came to a halt in front of his men, pausing to reflect upon their first "real" orders.

"It is my great pleasure to inform you men that today will be our first patrol into the Missouri countryside. As with the other companies of our regiment, our mission is to seek out Rebel bushwhackers, who may be roaming the countryside, or to seek information on their whereabouts. Further, we are to bring to justice those who willingly aid the Rebels and to be a show of force to dissuade others from doing so." The words were loud and clear, spoken with a sense of righteousness. "There is no neutrality, men. The citizens of Missouri are either loyal Americans or traitors. Obviously, those who openly work against us are our enemy. But understand this, those who provide information or aid to these bushwhackers and bridge burners are also the enemy and must be arrested."

These were General Prentiss's orders. Those who provided the traitors with aid were to be arrested, woman and child alike.

Captain Vincent continued, "Due to the amount of ground we have been assigned to cover, we will split the company into three detachments." Vincent stepped forward closer to the ranks, directly towards James. "You men from here," he said, placing his arm between where Luke and James stood, "will go with Lieutenant Long." He moved farther down the line. "You men will go with Lieutenant Simon. Those in the middle section will go with me."

James's face betrayed no second thoughts, but he knew this went against the practice of the other companies. They always left in force and never divided up. To date, there had been no serious engagements, just skirmishes with bushwhackers hiding in the woods. Still, the idea of marching around the slave state of Missouri in groups of thirty or so did not seem wise to him.

They marched two abreast down the dusty road. Their feet kicked up a cloud of dust that was caught in the cool breeze and sent whirling into the blue sky. In the horizon, they saw nothing but more grassy prairie.

They were finally going to play their role in this conflict between the states, James thought. Even the knowledge that Missouri had been a battlefield long before 1861 couldn't slow the surge in his veins.

Missouri had been at war with itself in one way or another for nearly twenty years. From John Brown and antislavery Kansas jayhawkers to the proslavery vigilantes, Missourian soil already had absorbed much blood.

"Think Luke and Patrick will find more action than us?" Matthew asked James in an excited voice.

As they marched, James looked behind their detachment. Patrick and Luke were with Captain Vincent's party, and they had since departed from view, searching for bushwhackers west of where James and Matthew marched.

"It's just good to be out of that camp," James said, looking around at the open spaces. "So flat. I wonder how much snow they get here?"

"As flat as it is, the drifting of the snow must be awful."

"You think they get much snow then?"

"Dunno, but I'd say it was cold enough, in the morning at least. Though I was talking to one of those boys in Company E from Edgar County, he said they don't get much snow down here, not like we're used to at least."

"That's good because we'd need to start building some shelters soon." No one in the detachment was paying attention to anything in particular. Everyone engaged in their own animated conversations, even Lieutenant Long spoke with Hiram Walker at the front. By now, James knew all the men in the company, knew their family histories—wives, sisters, fathers, everything. He already had known some of them before starting this journey.

The one group that James did not know much about, nor care to know much about, was Walker and his friends. As James had said once around the fire, Walker and his friends were half-witted brutes with no prospects at best, criminals on the lam at worst.

Luke, of course, had tried to start a debate about the redemption of every soul, but for once, no one else was having it.

But as luck would have it, where Captain Vincent had split the company, all of Walker's eight or so friends, James, Matthew, and a few others advanced with Lieutenant Long.

The men had marched past noon, and James was beginning to wonder whether they were ever going to see even a little shack to break the monotony. Finally on the horizon they saw two farmhouses and a rare patch of trees.

There was a farmhouse on each side of the dusty road, and the one on the right was located well off the road, back near the small copse of trees. As they neared the houses, James could see that the house on the right even had a small barn.

"Finally," Lieutenant Long said with a touch of impatience. "All right, let's see what Rebel scum these two farmsteads have. Corporal Holleck?"

"Yes, sir."

"Take fifteen men and investigate the house on the left. The rest of us will go to the right."

As ordered, James and Matthew followed Walker and his friends behind Lieutenant Long. The men made their way down the dusty drive to the small, but well-kept, white farmhouse. James looked at the long ago-harvested fields and judged the landowners to be rather successful corn farmers. He studied the house for any movement, but saw none, nor did he see any signs of "Rebel scum" in Lieutenant Long's words.

"The problem with this," Matthew said accurately, as if reading James's mind, "is that in Missouri, they may be Confederate, or they may be Union, but you never know."

"They're Rebel," Walker said in front of them, surprising James and Matthew.

"How do you know that?"

"He can smell 'em," laughed Isaac Washburn, one of Walker's messmates.

"Don't matter," Walker said. "They're all Rebel 'til they prove otherwise."

Matthew and James looked at each other but said nothing.

At the top of the drive, Lieutenant Long stopped and looked at the house. The drive forked with one path leading to the house, the other to the small barn.

Walking towards James, Long said, "You men from here, back, check the barn. Private Walker, you and the rest come with me."

"Yes, sir," James said with an amateurish salute, turning toward the barn, keeping an eye on the small woods behind the barn. Too small and too sparse to hold much of an ambush, he still kept his eyes on it, even as he unshouldered his rifle and held it in a ready position. Without a word, Matthew and the others did the same.

"Anybody see anything?" James said, as they paused at the front of the barn.

"Nothing," Barker replied, as Matthew wondered how James had become the leader of their small expedition, and why they were all so timid at the moment.

"This is silly," Matthew said. "What are you afraid of, a bunch of horses?" He jogged forward and quickly opened the broad barn door.

"No horses," Barker said.

"Nothin'," Quinlan added.

The barn was empty except for a small amount of hay in the corner.

"That's funny," Quinlan, who was also a farmer, added. "Where's the plow?" He swung around, as if to make sure that there were fields outside.

"I don't...," Matthew began, only to be interrupted by the sound of a single gunshot from inside the house.

James was the first to react, taking off in a full sprint to the house. His long legs immediately increased the distance from the others as he leapt up the steps and into the back door of the house.

He brashly opened the door and found that he was in a kitchen. In the corner, a soldier pinned a small, crying five-year-old boy to the floor with his foot. He whimpered in an odd, subdued way, and James noticed a small amount of blood dripping from the side of the little boy's head, turning the child's red hair darker.

James looked in bewilderment at the dazed child and then at the soldier who held his rifle in one hand and an ancient-looking musket that still trickled smoke in his other hand.

"What's going on?" James said, finally turning his eyes on the remainder of the room.

"That boy nearly shot my foot off," Walker said, tapping a hole in the wooden floor for emphasis.

"He probably can't even lift that musket off..." James stopped in midsentence.

No longer obscured by Walker's massive body, a woman rose shakily from the floor.

"Where do you think you're goin'?" Walker snarled, grabbing her by the throat with one hand.

"What are you doing, Hiram?" James said. His voice sounded tinny and weak; yet, his mind told him that he knew exactly what Hiram was attempting to do. The woman looked pleadingly at James with her blue eyes.

The boy's red hair matched the woman's, James realized, and the woman's face began to turn blue from Walker's grip. The front of her plain dress was already torn on the right side, and though she was in the midst of choking to death, she struggled to lift up the torn flap to cover herself.

"Let her go, Hiram," James growled, feeling a slow fury building inside him.

"Get out of here, Lockett," Walker said without concern, not bothering to turn his attention away from the woman's face. He was clearly enjoying the bulging of her eyes and her useless attempts for air.

"I said, '*Let her go*'," James said in an emphatic voice. The tinniness of his voice disappeared as the wellspring of fury began to fuel his veins.

"What?" Walker said with more annoyance than fear as he turned to find James leveling his rifle at him. Walker did not seem fazed at all. "I think you should rethink that, Lockett," Walker said smugly, enjoying himself even more now.

From the corner of his eye, James saw Isaac Washburn and Bart Randle, two of Walker's cronies, aiming their rifles at his midsection.

"Now, why don't you be a good boy, and step outside so as I can get down to bisness."

Swallowing hard, James tried to think, but all that raced through him was rage. It was a feeling of intensity that he had never felt before, and it swelled his muscles and subdued any commands that his brain might initiate. His eyes were charged with lightning and his jaw clenched reflexively in determination.

"Let her go now," James commanded in a determined voice, thumbing back the hammer on the rifle. He gripped the Dimick tightly and pressed the muzzle to Walker's temple.

Stunned, Walker said nothing. Completely caught off-guard that James had not been bullied into submission, Walker was not at all sure what to do.

"Private!" James heard an authoritative voice say. "Drop that gun now. Private Walker is following orders."

His jaw slackening, James turned slightly to see Lieutenant Long standing in the corner with his own revolver aimed at James. James's aim wavered more out of surprise than obedience. Then, they all heard a great commotion outside the house.

"Lieut'ant! Lieut'ant!" Barker yelled, as he came bursting in the front door. "The Rebs! They're here!" Barker yelled again as he looked for them.

"I'll be back," Walker told the woman with a backhanded slap that knocked her cold to the floor.

They found Barker halfway up the steps to the second floor, oblivious to anything else that had been occurring in back of the house.

"There you are! They're here, sir!"

"Who? Where?" Lieutenant Long asked them.

"Up the road. Cavalry, maybe ten to fifteen of 'em!"

"All right, everyone outside!" Long ordered, "Into line of battle!"

James, dumbly, followed the lieutenant outside, not at all comfortable that he had his back to Walker. Everyone formed a line of battle outside the house as if nothing had happened.

"Some line of battle," Matthew said, as James fell into place beside his friend, "Only fifteen men."

"Hope Perry has seen 'em too," Barker said excitedly from the other side of Matthew. "There they are!" he added as Corporal Perry Holleck's fifteen men left their farmhouse from across the road.

"What's wrong?" Matthew said, looking at James for the first time and seeing the fiery eyes, red face, and still clenched jaw. Thinking that it was nervousness at the prospect of their first fight, Matthew added, "We got 'em outnumbered two to one, James. We'll send 'em running after one volley."

"Later," James whispered, noticing Lieutenant Long coming around the side of the line taking them to join up with Corporal Holleck.

In the distance on the road, thirteen riders shifted in their saddles, as they watched the Yankees form a thin line of thirty-three rifles. With some amusement, Long and his men watched the Confederate soldiers slowly ride down the road.

"This is no way to fight cavalry," Matthew said as they moved closer. "By the time we get within range, they'll just ride off."

Exactly as Matthew predicted, as soon as the thirty-three Kalamazoo Sharpshooters came close to being within range, the horsemen turned and rode away from them.

Lieutenant Long stopped and watched them ride away, momentarily unsure what to do. "Very well," he said finally. "Corporal, did you find anything or anybody in your house?"

"Not a thing," Corporal Holleck said, casually taking off his cap and scratching his head. "What do you want us to do now?"

Long said nothing while he adjusted his scarf, which had become loose in the commotion. Satisfied that he had returned it to a properly jaunty position, Long turned to face the corporal. "Wait for us on the road and keep an eye out for those bushwhackers. We're almost done in the house."

The men turned and walked back to the farmhouse. A sense of disappointment hung in the air for most of them. Lieutenant Long, Walker, and two others returned to the house through the front door. James walked with trepidation towards the back door. With each step, he became more and more uncertain about what he was going to do. Now that the moment had passed, his brain was able to function above his anger again, and he wondered what he could do now to stop Lieutenant Long and Walker.

He had hoped originally that cooler heads would prevail now that there had been an interruption, but judging by Walker's eagerness, there was little chance that the situation would defuse itself.

"Obviously, I can't stop it all on my own," James mumbled quietly. Could he rally the men against their lieutenant and Walker at the injustice that was about to take place? Judging the chances of that, James looked into the flat horizon across the fields, blinked twice, and squinted into the distance. Riding away at a fast gallop with dress streaming behind her and with her child holding tight, James saw the shape of the woman grow smaller and smaller.

From inside the house James could hear cursing and yelling now, when Randle stuck his head out the back door and yelled angrily, "There she goes! She must have hid a horse in the woods!" He turned to see who was watching him. Upon seeing James, he spat ferociously and glared at him before retreating back inside the house.

"Thank God," James muttered softly, "thank God."

"What was all that about?" Matthew said, coming up from behind. "Why'd Randle give you that look?"

"I'll explain later," James said softly, turning slowly and walking away.

"What happened in there?" Matthew said, "And..." He stopped and a look of puzzlement crossed his face. James turned to see that Matthew was looking through the window into the kitchen. Together, they watched Walker and Randle stuff silverware into their haversacks.

"What," Matthew said in utter confusion. When James said nothing, he continued, "They're stealing their silver!" At most any other time, the bewilderment in Matthew's voice would have been humorous, but what they were witnessing was too disturbing for anything like that. "I can't believe it. We have to..." James put a firm hand on Matthew's shoulder as Matthew took a step towards the back door. "Why are you—"

"Leave it, Matthew."

"But," Matthew stopped. His eyes amazed now as he saw Lieutenant Long participate in the thievery.

"We can't stop them," James said in sad, knowing voice.

"But that's probably the most valuable thing these people have. Probably heirlooms, from the looks of it, they can't have much else."

"They have one thing more valuable, Matthew," James said heavily, "and they only barely got away with that."

Luke stared up at the sky as the soldiers marched. The thick, white clouds looked like inviting islands on the heavenly blue sea. Today, the beauty of God's creation tugged more powerfully than normal. Everything appeared so alive and so right to him at this moment. He pondered the fact that he was serving God's country, confronting its most immoral sin.

But the fear still would not dissipate. There was the fear that he would fail himself and God; the fear that he was a coward; the fear that he was incapable of fighting.

The other men had started whistling a tune long ago on this march, and now, without realizing it, Luke found himself whistling along with them. He could not imagine the spirits of the boys from Kalamazoo being any higher.

"If you're going to whistle," Patrick said to Luke, nudging him to make certain that his dreamy friend heard him, "at least whistle with some sense of tune."

"Sorry," Luke said. "I suppose God didn't bless me with much musical talent. Even in church, I try to sing the hymns as quietly as possible."

"I always thought God wouldn't care about the quality of the voice," Patrick commented.

"Oh, you're right," Luke answered immediately. "I do it more out of consideration for others. There are some beautiful voices in the congregation, and I would hate to think that mine would ruin that sound."

"Don't like to sing much myself," Abraham Dobbins added from behind. "Never have."

The short, muscular young man was the more talkative of the Dobbins twins.

"I never have either," Luke said, "although that was more because of my mother." He paused with a nostalgic look on his face. "She had a voice like an angel, and I could never wait for each Sunday so that I could stand next to her in church and hear her sing."

"She passed on?" Abraham asked.

"Ten years ago," Luke said with a more unemotional voice than he could ever have imagined ten or even five years ago.

"Ours too," Jimmy Dobbins added, surprising them by speaking up before his more exuberant brother.

"In childbirth," Abraham added.

"Well, I'm sure they're up there together now, looking down on us as we undertake God's work," Luke said.

No devout Christians, neither of the twins said much, although the comment didn't surprise either, as they had seen Luke try to rally the company for prayer meetings more than once.

"Do I see civilization ahead?" Patrick said with feigned astonishment.

Luke craned his head above the small column of men, examining what was little more than a crossroads with a sturdy-looking wooden house on one corner.

"Ya think thar're Secesh in that house?" Abe said excitedly.

"If thar're," his brother said, looking at the size of the home, "I'd say we got them heavily outnumbered."

"I didn't mean troops," his brother said elbowing him roughly. "I meant more like...more like..."

"Sympathizers?" Luke offered.

"Yeah, that's it."

As they neared the house, the front door opened slowly and a woman, followed by six children of various ages, spilled out onto the cramped porch. Smiling and cheering, the woman waved a small Stars and Stripes flag while her children stared in various degrees of fascination at the soldiers. Luke noticed the oldest, a girl, of probably fourteen, staring at all of them with extra scrutiny.

"Ma'am," Captain Vincent said, riding up on his impressive bay horse, "I'm Captain Charles Vincent of Birge's Western Sharpshooters."

"Birge's Western Sharpshooters!" shouted the eight year old, as he marveled at the shiny buttons and sword of the Union captain.

"Hush," the woman said, embarrassed at his intrusion. "Yes, Captain. I'm Elizabeth Landon. It's a pleasure. We haven't seen Union troops since my husband left with the 1st Missouri Cavalry three weeks ago."

After receiving permission, Luke and the rest of the detachment rested around the Landon house while Captain Vincent spoke with Mrs. Landon about recent Rebel activity she had seen or heard.

"Where are y'all from?" a pleasantly inquisitive female voice asked Luke as he leaned back against a tree.

He turned to face the oldest daughter, who stared at him with vibrant, dark eyes. Her dark brown hair was pulled up in a bun to make her look older. However, it actually had the opposite effect by revealing the complete smoothness of her unblemished young face.

"Kalamazoo County," Luke answered, watching her look him over with a careful eye.

"Where?"

"Michigan," Luke said. "Sorry, I forget that I'm a long way from there now."

"That is a long way."

"I'm Luke Bailey," he responded, offering a hand.

She smiled broadly, her small hand disappearing in his grasp.

"Rebecca Landon," she replied, trying to sound as old as possible.

"Rebecca?" said one of her younger brothers, idling up. "You were always Becky before."

"Hush you," she said angrily, chasing him off with a swooshing of her hand.

"Nice to meet you, Rebecca," Luke said, with a small grin on his face.

"Have y'all done much fighting?" Rebecca asked trying to be shy but losing out to curiosity.

"No, no, not yet," Luke said.

Rebecca waited for him to continue, for some of the boastful talk that the soldiers in the cavalry had offered, but none came from the tall man from Michigan whose face still carried some fading bruises around his eyes and nose. He certainly looked like he had seen some fighting.

"Seen any Rebels around here?" Luke finally asked, more out of jest than actual seriousness.

"Most every day," she replied.

"What?" Luke said, the surprise showing on his face.

"Maybe not every day," she hedged. "But every day has some rumors. And we do see some bushwhackers once in a while. They scare Mother so, especially now that Father is gone."

"It's good to see that not everyone is a sympathizer in Missouri. The way some people talk—"

"Everyone!" Rebecca said aghast. "Gracious, goodness, no. Why everyone around here are loyal Unionists!"

"Everyone?"

"Maybe not everyone, but we're not the only ones. The Robinson farm," she said, pointing down the road, "they're all Unionists...hmm, almost all. The oldest son, Billy, he ran off with Sterling Price in September, but the rest of them, all Unionists!" She paused and looked at the ground. "I still can't believe Billy ran off with those scoundrels." Then she looked up at Luke with a fierce look on her face. "'Course, Billy will get what's comin' to him!"

Deciding that there was more to this story, and not wanting to rile her even more, Luke tried to change the subject. "How about bushwhackers, Rebecca? Seen any bushwhackers roaming around here?"

"Not lately," she said. "Some passed through a few weeks ago, for good probably. I heard that there was a whole Union army in Centralia, and we haven't seen the bushwhackers since. 'Course, I heard the lot of them ended up in Hallsville for now. Are you going to go down there next?"

"Maybe," Luke chuckled. "But the problem with being a private is that they don't tell you anything in advance."

"Hope you have more men somewhere else though," Rebecca said, tapping the side of her cheek in thought. "'Cuz there's less of y'all than there are of those vermin. I thought you were supposed to be a whole army?"

"Don't worry, there's more of us," Luke reassured her, although he knew they were just one regiment, nowhere near an entire army. "Hallsville, you say."

Our first day of real soldiering is over. My feet are sore and heavy, but not as heavy as my heart. Even Matthew seemed burdened by the thievery we witnessed. He said little the rest of the day, and I too felt no need for conversation. If this is the army I serve, would the South be better off without us? I shudder to think what Hiram would do had there actually been real wealth displayed in front of him. Will these men have the discipline and morals to resist the plunder that could be laid before us, the conquering army?

Luke and Patrick fared better than us, although I was surprised that Luke confided in me about his fear of cowardice tonight. It weighs on him. I would not have thought him a coward before, and still don't. Yet his apprehension was genuine. If it does turn to be true, why did God create a world where Luke does not fight bravely, yet men like Hiram do? I pray that those predictions are wrong. They are too depressing to consider.

—The Diary of James Lockett

December 26, 1861

My dearest Martha,

Merry Christmas! Sorry I ain't got to hunt that terkey for everyone this year. Next year, I promise, I will be back and bring you the bigest bird in the county.

Our Christmas supper was bacon and hardtack. We march again. We left Centralia yesterday, and today captured Columbia at daylight with little effort. We were in reserve and did not see action yet again.

The bluffs around the Missouri River at Columbia was mountains after spending so much time on the prayeree. Now, we are on the way to Sturgeon to meets up with the General and his cavalry. It is silly to march around like we do and fight no battles. So far, none of the Kalamazoo Sharpshooters has fired a shot in anger. You must be pleased to hear that, but the boys are anxious. I must agree with them. We need a battle so this whole thing can be over, and I can return to you. I hope you enjoy this long letter. It is my Christmas present to you.

Your Husband, Patrick

Dear Daniel,

I appreciate your enthusiasm, but you already know the answer. You cannot leave the farm. Mother and our brothers need you too much right now. I realize that you feel like you are missing out, but that is the way it must be right now. Besides, you are not missing anything. Somehow, the Kalamazoo Sharpshooters always seem to miss out on the skirmishes.

I have seen enough torn-up track and burned bridges to know that there are bushwhackers out here, but there is little we can do as infantry. If only half of us were mounted, we would fare much better. The bushwhackers lurk about but do not stand and fight when confronted. It is very strange, little brother, but often, we even know the names of our foes and where they live. Their neighbors have told us the names. Can you imagine a fight in Kalamazoo with neighbor against neighbor? Thank the Lord no such rift has occurred between us and our neighbors like the McManuses. But without horses, there is little we can do to clear these bushwhackers out of central Missouri.

We are on the march again to join up with General Prentiss and his cavalry, perhaps then we will see action.

Take care of mother and our brothers. I will write again soon.

Your brother, James

December 27, 1861

The dust swirled behind them, seemingly in tune with whistling of the Kalamazoo Sharpshooters as they marched. Spirits could not have been higher, and the voices of the soldiers were filled with pride and the excitement of expectation. Battle! That is what they wanted, and for once it seemed likely! They had already given three hurrahs for their captain.

"See what having a man like Captain Vincent can do," Abe cheered. "Only he could have convinced General Prentiss to give us the honor!"

James didn't dispute the fact that the task at hand was due to the captain's work. What he would have disputed was how much of an honor it really was and whether the captain was the man to accomplish the given task.

The day before, General Prentiss had learned of the presence of a band of bushwhackers in nearby Hallsville. According to his information, it was only a small force, but still of considerable size to deem worthy of a company of Birge's Sharpshooters. The hope was that for once the Rebels would feel like engaging them in battle.

The sharpshooters had tired of chasing shadows that evaporated whenever they appeared. The burned bridges and torn-up railroad track were clear evidence that there were bushwhackers around, but to the sharpshooters' dismay, the bushwhackers would run at the slightest chance of a direct conflict. It was a type of warfare that none of them had expected or understood. Matthew, like most in the company, was convinced that the tactics demonstrated a distinct lack of courage on the Rebels' part.

Luke thought he had read in a history book about similar tactics in Spain during the Napoleonic Wars, guerillas he called them.

Patrick wasn't at all sure what gorillas had to do with this, but he was frustrated also. They were getting nowhere like this. At this rate, he would never get back to Martha whom he found himself missing more and more with each passing day.

James could only shrug his shoulders. He had not expected to futilely chase men around the prairies either. Not only did the bushwhackers' horses give them a distinct advantage, but they also knew the land and the people. Often, they would strike at night, knowing that the Union troops were usually in their camps then.

But this march on Hallsville seemed like the opportunity that every Union soldier wanted—a stand-up fight. If Rebel bushwhackers controlled the town, maybe they would be more prone to fight for the town rather than run.

However, James was still troubled, because for once, General Prentiss was breaking his rule about moving in force. "Why is the general only sending one company?" he mumbled out loud, not really meaning to bring up the subject.

Not surprised by the comment, Matthew looked at James's troubled face. "It's only a small band of scum, James," he said with some irritation. "We can handle them." Matthew frowned in annoyance at James's constantly cautious and pessimistic nature.

James's voice was quiet. "Still, why only one company when the general has passed orders for everything else to be done in force?" He really didn't expect much of an answer and really didn't want one. The subject was a moot point; the decision had already been made.

"Maybe," Luke said thoughtfully, "maybe the general thought a larger force would scare them off. This time he wants an actual engagement."

Patrick pursed his lips and nodded agreement. "That would make sense to me. How about it, James?"

James looked at Luke with equal consideration. "That does make some sense." Nodding again, he added, "Perhaps, you have it, Luke. If it is a reasonably equal fight, they would be more inclined to make a stand."

"It's supposed to be a smaller group of Secesh, though," Matthew interjected. "Only about fifty men."

James shrugged, but it was Patrick who spoke. "We haven't been here that long, Matthew, but I think by now we all know that there's a lot of cross-eyed folks in Missouri. When they see ten Rebels, it usually means that only two were there. But then sometimes, it works in reverse."

"Doesn't matter," Matthew said stubbornly. "We're all ready for a fight."

"I wouldn't worry, Matthew," James said. "I have a strange feeling that for once, you will have your fight."

Despite the few miles that separated Hallsville from Sturgeon, the march took forever. James imagined that they should be more serious and concerned about an ambush, but the conversational pockets did not die down even with the knowledge that they were getting very close to Hallsville.

"They're goin' run away again," Abe said with frustration. His hawklike face wrapped itself into a fierce scowl so that the veins in his forehead popped out like a curved web from his hairline to thick brow. The nostrils in his curved, beaklike nose flared slightly. "They ran away before we even caught wind of them this time."

"Too early to tell," his more mild-mannered twin countered. "Why, they could be in those woods over there." He motioned toward the barren woods a quarter mile away.

"Those woods are so sparse," Abe argued. "They couldn't hide an elephant, much less some Secesh."

A few men chuckled, when a cry from the front ranks of their column. "Over there!" They all looked forward, searching for the cause of the cry and warning. For the briefest second, they saw a man on horseback rushing away from them. He disappeared almost instantly, below a low bluff that their road would eventually wrap around.

"It won't be a surprise now," Patrick said, itching his now thick reddish-brown beard.

"I guess we'll see whether Luke's right," James said, "If they're still in Hallsville, it will be because they want to fight us there, not because we caught them there."

Matthew stood with his rifle ready, in one long, thin line of battle with the rest of the Kalamazoo Sharpshooters. They faced a meadow that looked into a small woods. Matthew could detect a few figures in the trees, although it was impossible to accurately judge how many. His heart was pounding, and Matthew knew his boyish face must be flushed to a deep red. To his left ran the road to Hallsville, cutting through the trees. The narrow dirt strip was barricaded at the woods line by a felled tree and wagon behind which he could see at least five heads watching the thin blue line as it stood at the ready.

Battle, Matthew thought, finally! He wiped a sweating hand on his trousers, thinking it must be the excitement.

Patrick gripped his rifle with unthinking white-knuckled strength. It was like they were playing a game, he thought, standing here, facing the enemy, neither side moving, just staring across the empty space.

Ominously, there was no sound. No fallen leaves blowing in the absent wind; no man moving yet in the dead winter grass of the field; no commands being given since Captain Vincent had ordered them into line of battle. One good volley, the former congressman had said, and the Rebels would scatter like frightened chipmunks. Patrick continued to wait, wondering how it could be so impossibly quiet at a moment like this.

Luke toyed with his own thoughts. He couldn't see the faces across from him, and he wondered whether the Rebels were as scared as he was. Anxiously, he looked down at the Dimick rifle that looked so foreign in his hands. For a panicky second, he couldn't remember how to reload it, and he closed his eyes and swallowed the lump in his throat. "The Lord is my Shepherd...," he began silently. Before he was halfway through the Twenty-third Psalm, the anxiety had passed, and he could remember how to load again.

James looked up and down the line of blue-coated, red-scarfed soldiers from Kalamazoo. He himself was standing to the right of the middle. At the left end, just across the road, stood Lieutenant Simon and Corporal Holleck. James's eyes moved further along the line to the left middle where Sergeant VanderJagt stood just behind the line. James wondered for a passing moment why the sergeant was just behind the line instead of on it.

Captain Vincent had been riding up and down the line on his magnificent horse, and at this moment, he was stopped and in conversation with VanderJagt.

To his right, James watched Lieutenant Long's sword flash in the weak sunlight of the overcast day. Next to him, Walker, Randle, and Washburn waited.

Overall, James judged few of the faces in the Kalamazoo Sharpshooters to be showing concern. Most wore masks of uncertainty. Some were shaped into expectant stares. A few scowled already at the Rebels. James's own face was set in a calm look, devoid of clues about his thoughts. One might have said it was a blank look, except that there was something that hinted at concentration and determination in his gray eyes.

"Sir," VanderJagt said again to Captain Vincent, "please come down off the horse. You are too much of a target up there."

"Nonsense, Sergeant. I can lead the men much better from old Victory here. Now back in line."

VanderJagt saluted appropriately, but inside he shook his head in dismay. Not only because of the captain's stubbornness, but also because there was a reason that he was behind the battle line in the first place. From there, he could have kept an eye on the men. In their first battle, the cowards would come out and try to break ranks. From behind, he could give them a not-so-gentle shove back into position, but VanderJagt knew it was useless to explain that to Captain Vincent now.

Squeezing in next to his nephew, VanderJagt took one last look down to their left flank. He could see Lieutenant Simon and Corporal Holleck across the road, but beyond them, further to the left, some trees followed the Union flank along the approach to the blocked road. VanderJagt could see no movement in the dead woods; however, if he were the Confederates, the woods would be the place to put men along the Union flank.

VanderJagt had already asked Vincent whether he wanted skirmishers to approach that flank, only to be told that they would form in line of battle and approach the Rebel positions. While VanderJagt was a believer in massive volleys too, he knew that this was no parade ground, even if the flat field with the small knoll in the middle did resemble one. But being only a sergeant, he was in no position to debate tactics with his captain, even if he felt that confident about them.

"Forward!" Vincent ordered, stiffly pointing his saber toward the Rebels.

Spastically, the line moved forward, some sectors moving before others, only to slow down and allow their comrades to move up to their shoulders again. With rifles tilted ready in a ten o'clock position, they moved forward like a lumbering beast.

James tried to measure their speed as they moved, deciding that it had to be half as fast as their normal marching pace. Lurching forward so painfully slow in the face of the enemy made absolutely no sense to James, but hurrying onward without the rest of the line would do him no good either.

Patrick noticed that there was still virtually no sound, just the crunch of dead grass being trampled, mixed with the jangle of men's canteens and cartridge boxes.

Earlier, while Captain Vincent had ridden behind the men, he had ordered a stop at sixty yards for a massed volley. He had given no orders beyond that, and James wondered whether they were supposed to charge after that or reload and fire again.

They continued to close on the bushwhackers, but there was still no reply to their advance. James looked down to make sure that his percussion cap was still secured to the nub. He had already double-checked that while standing in line. He hoped all of them did. Satisfied, he lifted his eyes forward again and wondered whether he should lock his eyes onto a particular target. But he found that impossible at the moment, and his anxious eyes scanned the entire forest before him.

He looked at Matthew next to him and observed Matthew nervously tapping the trigger guard of his Dimick. They were within one hundred yards now, well within the range of the riflemen, especially those like Matthew, and James could see the impatience eating at Matthew as they neared the small knoll in the field, which was capped by a large tree stump.

Yes, James reasoned, a massed volley did have a powerful impact, but getting this close to their adversary would take away some of the natural advantage that the riflemen possessed, their long-range Dimicks.

Further to James's left, Captain Vincent calmly rode behind the line, completely oblivious to the incredible target he was offering. The line was now within eighty yards, and Vincent prepared himself to give the order to fire, but before he could, a smattering of loud cracks broke the air, followed by a number of white smoke puffs in the tree line.

Rather than one well-timed volley, the Confederate fire seemed to spread sporadically from the middle of the forest. Almost immediately there was an odd thumping sound and an abbreviated whinny from Vincent's horse. Four musket balls smacked into the front of the proud animal. A fifth shot slammed into the animal's skull, a sixth tore off one of the shoulder boards from Vincent's uniform. Before he could react, Vincent's horse awkwardly hit the ground, pinning the stunned captain. The men in front of Vincent looked down at two of their comrades in a state of puzzlement, perplexed at the strange thumping sound they had just heard.

Only when they saw two of their own on the ground, did they realize it was the sound of ball hitting against flesh. With the loud crash of their captain's horse finally registering in their shocked brains, a few sharpshooters stopped and turned around in confusion.

"Don't stop you bastards!" Sergeant VanderJagt yelled at them immediately, raising his rifle for effect. "Advance!"

Satisfied with being given a command, any command, the men faced forward and continued. VanderJagt lingered behind them for a moment, pulling their dazed commander out from under the large horse. It was difficult work given the size of the animal and Vincent's complete lack of help.

Though Captain Vincent appeared unharmed physically, VanderJagt could see that the former congressman was stunned beyond immediate recovery. In fact, given the look on the man's face, VanderJagt wondered whether the captain even knew where or who he was.

The initial sound of the enemy's rifles put the Kalamazoo line into immediate disarray. Many stopped in surprise at being fired upon while a few, like James, Patrick, Matthew, and Luke, continued on, if only because that was what they had already programmed their minds to do.

James, Patrick, Matthew, and Luke reached the tree stump on the knoll and realized that they were alone. All of their comrades on their left and right had stopped marching at the sound of the gunfire. Worse yet, no command to fire had been given yet. "Find some cover and fire!" James reacted before he could stop himself.

Matthew happily obeyed and took a bead on a figure behind a tree that seemed to be aiming at him. The kick of the rifle against Matthew's shoulder calmed him, and he found that he had been holding his breath since the first sounds of battle. Hungrily, his lungs sucked in air, and he busied himself with reloading the rifle. He was down on one knee now, and that slowed the reloading process, but Matthew found himself quite happy to fight "Injun" style.

Patrick flopped down next to James behind the tree stump after he fired and reloaded himself.

Only Luke hadn't fired yet, and as he stood there, he looked around with unbelieving eyes. To their right, Lieutenant Long and those men had disappeared. Only when he looked behind their position did he see them, fleeing as fast as they could.

To their left, some sharpshooters stood and fired in haphazard fashion, but Luke could already see three blue-coated forms facedown in the field. Most disturbing of all, Luke saw a dozen spouts of flame come from the forest to their far left, pouring fire into the company's left flank. Corporal Holleck turned to face the new threat but too late. He fell to his knees, both hands grasping his stomach.

"Over there," Luke finally uttered, as James pulled him down.

James looked left to see what Luke was talking about.

Crack! Crack! Crack! Crack!

It was chaos all the way around. The air was full of rifle and musket pops and the zings of whizzing balls. A cheer erupted from the left, and James saw a number of men—dressed much like the Kalamazoo Sharpshooters had appeared just days ago—swarming down on his comrades. Splinters flew over James's head as a ball clipped the top of the tree stump that he crouched behind.

"We can't stay here," Patrick said, as he looked over the stump and fired. "The whole company's given way."

More Confederates came streaming out of the woods now, chasing those who were fleeing and those who still stood in the middle of the field. Luke imagined that some of the sharpshooters still stood rooted like trees in the pasture because their legs were paralyzed by fear like his.

"He's right," Matthew agreed, taking aim on a particular Confederate leaving the safety of the trees. Without bothering to see if he hit the target, Matthew slid back down on his knee. He struggled to reload from this position, but he didn't dare change it. Using his teeth to tear open the paper cartridge, he poured the black grains down the barrel, then pushed the Minié ball, paper and all, into the barrel. Removing the ramrod from beneath the barrel, he jammed it all down and replaced the ramrod. Finally, he pinched another percussion cap onto the nub.

"No retreat!" James said angrily, firing his own Dimick. The others looked at his smoke-irritated eyes to see an intensity and anger they were unaccustomed to seeing in their lifelong friend.

"There's too many, James," Patrick cried, grabbing him by the shirt collar and pulling him back.

"No one's shooting me in the back," James growled, turning around to face the Rebels again. Slowly, he backpedaled, reloading and firing as he went. Unsure why, but noticing it nonetheless, James noticed his three friends did the same.

It seemed an eternity as they backed way, firing as fast as they could reload. But none of the bushwhackers noticed or cared about the four Union soldiers slowly backing away. They were too busy rounding up prisoners from the decimated left flank. Luke watched with frustration as he saw Abe clubbed by two Confederates. The twin tried to defend his wounded brother, who struggled to lift his bloody body off the ground only to be stopped by a rifle butt to the top of his head.

Finally, they reached the tree line behind them, and James heard VanderJagt's guttural voice call out to them from nearby. "'bout time you boys made it back. That was an excellent fighting retreat, but those don't matter a damn when there's only four of you. Now, c'mon, we best catch up with the rest of this sorry bunch before the Secesh round up us too."

James spat some of black gunpowder out of his mouth and followed VanderJagt back to the main body which was hurriedly making its way down the road, back to Sturgeon.

The march back was as solemn as a funeral. For all their chatter and boasting on the way to Hallsville, they had been whipped, and it muted the company. Not a man spoke a single word. Occasionally, a man would look behind them, but the Rebels were not chasing them.

With their failure so complete and shocking, there was nothing to be said, only to trudge back to camp. Luke and another soldier acted as crutches for Andy Baker, who had been shot in the thigh. Despite pulling the tourniquet as tight as physically possible, James watched the trail of blood behind Andy. He wasn't going to last much longer.

In the front of the line, Captain Vincent shuffled along. There was no fiery oratory from him today, no lifting of his men's spirits. The captain's dampened spirit dragged the boys of the Kalamazoo Sharpshooters even lower into the morass of their own depression. Vincent still in a daze certainly looked out of place walking alongside of them instead of riding on his towering horse.

James himself was also out of sorts. He could still taste some of the grains of gunpowder in his mouth. No amount of spitting removed the bitter taste. Similarly, no amount of fresh air cleaned the acrid smell of the white smoke from his nostrils either. He knew his face was set in a nasty scowl, but he couldn't change it despite his best efforts. The knowledge that the sharpshooters had all crumbled so easily burned him. For all their boasting, he had expected more from them and from himself. Though he had performed more admirably than most of the others, there was more he could have done. He had known many of these men for a long time, most of whom were not cowards. They just needed a leader.

He hoped that they now knew what to expect and would bounce back, but it would be difficult if Captain Vincent did not step forward and rally them. The only soldiers who appeared to be unaffected by the catastrophe were VanderJagt and Gus. VanderJagt still wore his customary grimace, and Gus, as usual, marched alongside his uncle, ever obedient and serious-eyed.

Each section of messmates had settled in around their fires for the night. The men of Company J were keeping to themselves tonight, and the other companies were happy to leave the mauled company alone. Already the rumors of their cowardice had run through the camp. Their shame was now complete, James thought.

The chill of the cloudless night air made James shiver, and he reflected on how terribly quiet the fires were tonight. There was no fiddle playing or singing or boasting, hardly even a conversation and those were abnormally hushed and restrained.

"Mind if I join you, boys?" VanderJagt asked, sitting down next to Luke, close to the fire.

There was a very long pause before the next words were spoken. All five of them were silent as they watched the small yellow flames of the fire dance in the night air.

"A lot of boys saw the elephant today," VanderJagt said slowly. "And they didn't like it."

Luke's confused look turned from VanderJagt to Matthew, wondering whether VanderJagt had been mysteriously wounded in the head today.

"He means we all saw our first battle today," James clarified.

"Oh," Luke answered.

"I don't know that I'd call it much of a battle, James, but the men got their first taste of fire today."

"We weren't ready yet," James said, sounding like he thought VanderJagt was criticizing them.

"You boys were plenty ready," VanderJagt pointed out, looking up suddenly from the fire. "I saw you boys standing there today, giving it right back to the Rebs. Some of the other men saw it too, if they weren't already running for their lives. And if y'all are ready, then...well..."

"Everyone panicked when Captain Vincent went down," Patrick said in a hushed voice.

"He should have rallied us," James criticized.

"He was too dazed," Matthew argued.

"You're both right," VanderJagt said, ending the debate. "But it wouldn't have mattered anyway with both flanks gone."

"Aye," Patrick said. "Lieutenant Long was running so fast, the Secesh couldn't have got a second shot on him even if they wanted to."

"Poor Lieutenant Simon," Luke interjected.

"He'll live," VanderJagt said. "But the boy won't ever look the same again."

Though quiet, and the type to keep to himself, most of the men liked their young second lieutenant. When his flank had been ambushed, Lieutenant Simon had been among the first to go down, but he was fortunate. The musket ball that had torn through his cheek had somehow missed bone and teeth. While his face was a bloody, ragged mess, he'd live.

"What was the total count, George," James asked, although he had already done a mental calculation in his head.

"Four killed, twelve wounded, half of 'em captured, another ten missin' presumed captured."

"Twenty-six," Luke said quickly, "out of one hundred two?"

"A poor start for the famous Kalamazoo Sharpshooters," James said derisively.

"We were outnumbered," Matthew countered, but he didn't sound believable.

"Don't think so, boy," VanderJagt answered. "If we were, why didn't they pursue us and capture the whole lot of us? We were a sorry bunch by then. The reason is because they were even smaller than we were."

"Just more prepared, waiting for us," Luke said.

"Exactly," VanderJagt agreed with a sour face. "'Course, you could be right, Matthew," VanderJagt continued acidly. "Captain Vincent told Colonel Birge that there were three Secesh companies there, but I sure didn't see that many."

"I think it was only a dozen or so men that hit the flank," Patrick added.

"There you have it then."

"We were licked by a force half our size," James said disparagingly.

Suddenly, Matthew leapt to his feet and charged James, angrily shoving him off the log that he sat on.

James sprung back to his feet, but Patrick was already in the middle, an iron arm in each man's chest, separating them.

"Get your hand off me!" Matthew cried angrily, trying to brush Patrick away.

"Save it, you damn fool!" VanderJagt ordered.

"Relax, Matthew," Luke said more gently.

Matthew clenched his fists angrily at his side, glaring at James. With a sharp turn, Matthew pivoted on his heel and headed off into a different portion of the darkened camp.

December 28, 1861

The damage from yesterday seems irreversible. Even the close of today and the good news that it bore has done nothing to lift our spirits. We endured the jeers of the other companies all day, especially Companies A and H after they returned. At first light today, General Prentiss left with two of our companies and all five mounted companies of the 3rd Missouri Cavalry. After routing one company of Secesh in Hallsville, presumably the same one we encountered yesterday, they proceeded to Mount Zion church, having been given information that this is where the rest of the bushwhackers were. One of the mounted companies and both of our sharpshooters engaged the enemy in heated fighting, eventually driving them from the woods. I am told the fighting in the Rebel camp was hand to hand, but eventually the enemy gave way and left us on the field. General Prentiss complimented Colonel Birge and his sharpshooters on their "gallant behavior." Though this redeemed the regiment on a whole, it has only increased the disgrace of our little company. Some are calling us the "yellow company." I pray the name does not stick.

Sadly, we also had elections to replace Perry Holleck as corporal, God rest his soul. More proof that this is a sick world, Hiram Walker and his friends bribed enough votes with liquor so that somehow, he is our new corporal!

—The Diary of James Lockett

James looked up at the night sky. Overwhelmed by the number of stars in the clear prairie sky, his wonderment grew as he began counting God's pinpricks in the black cloth. The stars shone even brighter without a moon tonight, and James decided that drawing picket duty for the night wasn't so bad.

Next to him, Luke looked across the flat spaces of the prairie. The moonless starlight provided barely enough light to make out the difference between land and sky, but Luke maintained his vigil with utmost determination.

More quiet than usual, James watched his old friend perform this duty with unnecessary extra effort. To James, it looked as if Luke was trying to train his eyes to see through the darkness, overcoming the human impossibility.

"James?" Luke said abruptly with a soft voice, as if he feared waking someone up.

"I think you can speak a little louder than a whisper, Luke. We are a good ways from camp, remember?"

"I know," Luke replied, but his voice was still soft. James said nothing, and Luke continued on. "I think," he began and then stopped.

"What?" There was no answer. "What? What, Luke?"

"I'm just...thinking..."

"About the battle?"

Luke nodded, and although James couldn't see that, he judged by the silence that his guess was correct.

"What's on your mind?"

"I think...I think I made a mistake, James."

"Mistake?"

"Yes."

"What are you...talking about?" James said, stifling a yawn in midsentence.

"I shouldn't be here. I'm a...," Luke struggled, finally bursting out with the word, "coward!"

"What?" James said, feeling the distress in Luke's voice, knowing that he must have been struggling mightily with this since the battle.

Luke gave no answer, and James was too impatient to wait long.

"What are you talking about? You stood right next to me and fired on them. We didn't run. We were the only ones who didn't run!"

"But I didn't shoot at first."

"Huh?"

"When we were on the ground, on that little hill. I froze. I couldn't move, James. I was terrified."

"I was scared too."

"But not like me, James. I was worthless. I couldn't fire my rifle. I don't think I could have even run."

"You fired as we backed our way out, didn't you?"

"Yes, but..."

"And you stood right next to me, shoulder to shoulder, as we backed away."

"Yes, but..."

"A coward would have took off running then, like Lieutenant Long, but you slowly backed away, firing as you went."

"But..."

"But what?" James demanded more harshly than he wished.

"But I couldn't have done it if you hadn't given the order. My mind didn't work..."

"Rubbish," James said angrily. "So you did it after I spoke. So what!"

"I can't always depend on you to pull me out of it."

"You don't need me to do that anyway. You would have done the same if I hadn't been there..."

"No, I wouldn't!" Luke snapped back, knowing that James wasn't getting it.

"It was your first battle," James said without hesitating. "I know you, Luke Bailey. I've known you all my life, and you're not a coward."

"But..."

"Luke, remember fishing down at the Kalamazoo River? Remember when we would hang off that old tree limb over the water?"

"That was a long time ago," Luke said wistfully, "Before your er..."

"Yes, before my father died."

"I remember," Luke said, his mind immediately flashing back to the days of his boyhood, playing with James back when James had hair nearly as blond as his.

"You, me, and little Thomas," James added.

"Yes, Thomas was always such a tag-along then."

"Remember when that old tree limb snapped and Thomas fell in the water? He was only four years old."

"I remember," Luke said in a reflective voice.

"You were the one who dived in immediately, Luke, not me. And you weren't even the best swimmer then."

"I remember," Luke repeated. "Mother was deathly afraid of the water. She never wanted me to go near it. When she found out we had been fishing, she gave me such a scolding."

"You're no coward, Luke. I stake my life on it. A coward would not have done that."

"But that was different."

"It is not different!" James insisted.

"But I froze!"

"This time, maybe. But maybe, Luke, just maybe you were caught up in looking at it. Regardless, next time will be different."

"I don't know..."

"It all happened so fast today, Luke. Next time, you'll know how to react."

"But James, how did *you* know how to react?"

James shrugged. He had wondered that also. His mind had moved with such speed and precision when it all happened. He couldn't understand that either. "Don't know, Luke. Just instinct I guess."

"James," Luke began only to be interrupted again.

"Remember why you signed up in the first place, Luke? Nothing has changed, right?"

"I volunteered to stop slavery."

"Nothing has changed?"

"My reason hasn't, but...," Luke said slowly.

"God is in control," James broke in."You believe that, don't you? God is in control."

"Yes, of course He is."

"Then, trust him Luke. He will see you through."

James let the words hang in the air. He knew this would get through to Luke.

"I know," Luke said slowly, James's words ringing clear in his head, "God is in control."

"He surely is, Luke, and He will give you the courage when you need it most."

Luke was silent for a moment before laughing softly. "What is this, James? Have you been listening outside of my prayer meetings?"

"Is that what you and Johnny Quinlan have been doing?" James joked. "I thought maybe you were playing cards."

"They haven't been very well attended," Luke chuckled with a nod.

"Maybe it's time to have another."

"Maybe it is," Luke said, nodding, "maybe it is."

December 30, 1861

Hallsville seems to have affected us in ways that I never would have imagined. First, Luke tells me that he thinks he is a coward. Now, this morning, Patrick tells me that he is worried about freezing to death out here in the Missouri winter. The look on Patrick's face was like nothing I'd ever seen before. Three years ago when the crops failed, I could always count on Patrick to have a smile and try to lift my spirits. But not anymore.

Maybe we will split up into three groups and find winter quarters. That is the latest rumor. But even that reminder did not ease Patrick's anxiety. It is unnatural for him and unnerving to me.

It took ten minutes, but I finally got what was troubling him. He misses Martha and thinks he might have made a mistake in enlisting so quickly. Patrick's parting words still linger in my head, "I can't leave her a widow..."

—The Diary of James Lockett

December 31, 1861

Luke looked around the fire in surprise. He had expected more souls to show up for this prayer meeting than in the past, maybe fifteen men, but around his fire tonight there were close to one hundred, half of whom were Kalamazoo Sharpshooters. He hardly knew what to do.

"Nothing like fear to stir men's souls," Lieutenant Simon mumbled through his bandaged cheek.

He stood next to Luke holding his own small Bible. Over the past few days, Luke had spent more time with his wounded Lieutenant, offering to help him out with his daily chores while he recuperated.

Luke found a great deal that was likable in the company's young lieutenant. His commission had been arranged by his father, Judge Simon, and although Walter Simon had little desire to lead men, he did his best.

Even though wounded, Lieutenant Simon impressed Luke with a cheerful nature, and Luke decided that the man must feel lucky to have escaped death.

Simon hadn't been a particularly handsome young man to begin with. With a narrow face, large nose, and a sunken jaw two sizes too small for the rest of his head, he could never have been considered dashing. Luke thought that he embodied Washington Irving's Ichabod Crane.

He was unperturbed and even-keeled, so much so that one half-wondered whether he was dull-witted, but according to what Luke had heard from the survivors on the left flank, the lieutenant had acted with surprising aplomb as he issued his calm commands, seconds before being shot through the cheek.

Now, they stood in front of a crackling orange fire and faced nearly a hundred of their comrades. The Kalamazoo Sharpshooters now had a two common bonds: their shame and a renewed desire to talk to God.

Luke opened his small Bible to the passage he had preselected. He cleared his throat softly and began reading the passage aloud. Many of the men thought that he sounded remarkably like his father, Reverend Bailey, just a younger, larger, more vigorous version. As if mesmerized, they listened to the strong voice, instantly feeling a sheltered comfort that was due as much to the reassuring voice as to the scripture passage.

When Luke finished, he looked up to find a silent crowd with heads reverently bowed. The crackle of the fire was the only sound for a very long time. Then one voice from the middle began, "Our Father, who art in Heaven..." Immediately, the rest of the men joined in, and Luke looked out across to the campfire, astonished at the oneness of the response.

Feeling the swell of duty and conviction rise in him like a morning sun, Luke realized that James had been right. He was where God wanted him to be. Why this had all reached this point, Luke knew he would never understand. What he did understand, is that God wanted this scourge cleansed, and he wanted it done by ordinary men like Luke, Patrick, Matthew, and James.

"I will not be afraid," Luke whispered silently, an instant before a hushed, "Amen."

Chapter 9

January 3, 1862

We have left our camp for the town of Sturgeon. I have never thought I would look forward to sleeping in a stable so much. The temperatures have dropped drastically, and we saw our first snow. With two other companies of Western Sharpshooters, we have overwhelmed this tiny town. The boarding house above the saloon is even more full than the livery. The captain and Lieutenant Long have occupied the house of a Secesh who joined up with Sterling Price's men.

There have been a few small skirmishes with no casualties. Since Mount Zion, there hasn't been any major sightings, but there is still the occasional torn-up track and burned bridge. I imagine this will be normal for the winter. Maybe after the thaw there will be more to do.

—The Diary of James Lockett

January 7, 1862

"What are you always writin'?" Sam asked James as he sat in the corner of what had once been a horse stall.

"This?" James asked, holding up his small, black book. At one point, it had looked brand new, but after two months of marching and army life, it had taken on a more battered, well-used appearance.

"Yup, what is that?" Sam said. "You're always writin' in it. I thought Luke was the student. Or are you one too?"

"No," James laughed softly, "I'm just a farmer."

"But he does have a way with words," Patrick broke in from the other side of the stall, his hat pulled over his face as he dozed in the corner.

"I do like my readin' and writin'," James agreed. "It was always the numbers that gave me problems."

"Could never do my figures," Sam said with some embarrassment.

"Didn't even know that you ever tried," John quipped from across the livery.

"Shut your trap, Johnny. You know I tried."

If there was one thing that James had noticed about Sam Barker, it was that at times he could be surprisingly sensitive about his intelligence. "This is my journal, Sam," James said, diverting his attention.

"Journal?"

"He's recording our history," Patrick said.

"Really?" Sam said incredulously. "Am I in it?"

"I wouldn't really say it is a history as Patrick said. It's more of a diary, Sam. Just some of my thoughts. Though, I guess, I do write down some of the events that have happened."

"Like Hallsville," Sam said tightly. Though the jeering from the other companies had subsided somewhat, the memory of their failure still clung tightly to the Kalamazoo Sharpshooters. The inactivity brought on by winter only made it worse. Many, like Sam, were anxious to redeem themselves.

"And other events," James nodded.

"Why you goin' through all that effort?" Peter O'Shea asked. "Seems like a waste of time to me. Who's ever goin' want to hear about us?"

"I like it," Sam disagreed. "You're a smart feller, James. Don't let Pete tell you nothin' else. Even if no one ever reads it, it's still a good idea."

"I don't expect anyone to ever read it," James said honestly. "That's not why I'm doing it."

"Does pass the time," Pete admitted.

"Especially on a day like today," John said in a lonely, bored voice.

Luke opened the livery door and reentered his new home, snow swirled in from outside and the wind howled with such ferocity that Luke had to lean a shoulder back into it to close it.

"Any let up out there?" Patrick asked, still not looking up from his dozing position.

"Not yet," Luke said, shaking some of the snow off his new, thick, blue topcoat. "Must be almost a foot out there now."

"Must be some good drifting with that wind too," Quinlan said.

"Only thing good about a day like today," Luke said, "is that the Rebels are as inactive as us."

January 15, 1862

Warm weather melted the snow that had swept across Missouri, and at least for the moment, there was a slight reprieve from the low temperatures. With a growing sense of curiosity, Luke and Matthew waited outside of the small house that served as the officers' headquarters in Sturgeon.

They waited for Lieutenant Simon to give some orders. The door opened and Lieutenant Simon came out, followed by two civilians. "How are you today, Luke?" Simon asked. The wound in his cheek had healed about as well as could be expected. The pinkish, new skin folded in on itself in haphazard fashion, leaving an ugly, puckering pocketlike scar that stretched from his cheekbone to his lower jaw. Matthew found it impossible not to stare at it, although Luke seemed not to notice.

"Fine, sir," Luke replied, pulling himself to complete attention.

"This is Mr. Branson and his assistant, Mr. Kotler."

Luke's eyes flashed first from the fleshy, white-haired man to his younger, mustached assistant. The older man returned Luke's scrutiny with accusing eyes set behind a hooked, hawk nose and a wrinkled, heavy brow. The younger man, named Kotler, with friendly brown eyes, smiled in acknowledgment.

"...they're from the railroad company and are here to examine the track west of town. The captain decided that since there has been no activity since Mount Zion, it would be quickest and easiest if these gentlemen were taken out by handcar. You and Bauer are to help them in whatever fashion they require."

"Yes, sir," Luke answered.

They waited outside of the saloon with Kotler. Luke guessed he was about ten years older than him and about twenty years younger than Branson. The pleasant-faced Kotler had an overall well-kept appearance that the soldiers of Birge's Western Sharpshooters had lacked for some time. Though Luke still went clean-shaven, and Matthew appeared not to shave yet, their uniforms were rumpled, soiled, and possessed a noticeable odor if they stood in a closed room for too long. The only thing clean and polished about them was their rifles, which Matthew made sure the soldiers cleaned fastidiously.

Looking down at his ruined boots and trouser cuffs, Kotler grimaced. The warmer weather had temporarily turned the roads into a shallow mud that now caked their boots. "Nice weather you boys are having. Be glad to get back up on the track and out of this stuff," Kotler commented with a friendly voice. "Call me Thomas by the way."

"Nice to meet ya, Thomas," Matthew said, taking Thomas's extended hand. "Matthew Bauer."

"Luke Bailey," Luke added.

"You boys don't sound like you're from around these parts," Kotler said, his own accent sounding similar to theirs.

"Michigan," Luke answered.

"The Kalamazoo Sharpshooters," Matthew added. A few weeks ago, he would have said it with a chest full of pride that bordered on arrogance, but now, he spoke in a matter-of-fact tone.

"Ah," Kotler said with a smile. "Ohio myself."

"Mr. Branson from there too?" Matthew asked.

"No, St. Louis actually. By the way, don't mind him too much. I mean, he, ah, rubs people the wrong way sometimes. He doesn't mean anything personal by it, treats everyone like that."

Luke gave an unconcerned shrug. "Think we can live with that for a day?" he asked Matthew.

"S'pose we'll have to," Matthew replied good-naturedly.

"Just thought I'd warn you. It could be worse though. You could be me and travel with the old coot full-time."

Luke and Matthew started to chuckle as the balding, white-haired Branson emerged from the saloon/boarding house.

"Let's go," he said gruffly, walking past them towards the train station with a heavy-footed gait. "Hope you boys are stronger than you look," he added as they trailed him. "These handcars can be hard work."

"Don't worry, they're pretty easy on the flat of the prairies," Thomas said softly.

"Huh? What's that? Kotler, you say something behind my back again?"

"No, sir."

"'Course not, never do, do you, Kotler? Always the wind playing tricks with my ears, eh?"

"Just telling our escort that the handcars aren't complicated."

"Complicated? 'Course not. A monkey could do it. You just pump the bar up and down. Complicated, that's the dumbest thing I ever heard. Don't you boys know anything? No, 'course not, right off the farm. I still can smell the manure on you."

"Actually, neither of us are farmers," Matthew said, causing Branson to frown, but he ignored the interruption nonetheless.

"Just hope you boys are strong enough, because I don't do the manual labor. Do you understand me?" He stopped to look Matthew straight in the eye. "Kotler here may offer to spell you once in a while, but I never do. Got it?"

"Yes, sir," Matthew said.

"'Course, you do. And Kotler, they're not an escort, they're the muscle to move the handcar. Understand? The army has assured me that there is no more Secesh trash wandering around this part of Missouri since these boys chased off that Colonel Dorsey and the rest of his band of thieves and murderers."

Matthew was about to say that there were still occasional skirmishes with bushwhackers, but Luke elbowed him gently in the ribs before he could. Matthew looked up in surprise, and Luke shook his head.

They reached the small square hut that was the Sturgeon train station and looked at the handcar that waited for them at the switch.

"Kotler, I have one thing left to take care of before we go verify the condition of this track. I'll be right back," he added gruffly and waddled inside.

"Ever done this before?" Kotler asked the soldiers as they walked over to the small contraption.

"Looks easy enough," Matthew said, examining it.

"It's a simple device," Thomas said, pulling himself up onto the wooden platform. "You just grab this handle and pump it up and down."

"One of us on each side?" Luke asked.

"I think that works best."

"How does it know which way to go?" Matthew asked, as Luke climbed up.

"See that big lever down there?"

Matthew looked underneath the wooden platform, between two of the shining metal wheels. "Yep."

"Just pull it, and it reverses the direction of the pumping motion."

Matthew made an appreciative face and jumped up onto the platform with Luke and Thomas. "How far we going?"

"Good question," Thomas said. "I'm not real sure. It's up to Mr. Branson."

"No difference," Luke said, looking at his rifle. "It's better than sitting around here cleaning this again."

Matthew's eyes wandered across the flat plains as he and Luke propelled the cart with a steady up-and-down pumping motion. Thomas had been right. It wasn't that difficult once they got the speed up.

They sliced through the cool wind, but the temperature did not bother Matthew. In fact, it was very refreshing, and he hoped the fresh air would clean some of the stink off him. This way is much preferred over a dip in freezing water, he thought to himself.

"So you say neither of you are farmers?" Thomas called from the back. While Luke and Matthew pumped the lever in the center of the car, and old Branson situated himself in the front of the cart looking for damaged track, Thomas lounged near the brake lever in the rear.

"What?" Luke asked, facing the rear.

"I think Matthew said neither of you are farmers."

"That's right," Matthew said, looking over his shoulder. "Luke is Reverend Bailey's son. He's about the most famous person in the whole county."

"Sorry. Never heard of him," Thomas said after noticing that Matthew had paused, waiting for a reply.

"He's not that famous," Luke countered. "Matthew's exaggerating. He's just a small country preacher."

"But he goes to Chicago to speak at the abolitionist meetings."

"Prayer meetings," Luke corrected. "And that doesn't mean that he's famous."

"So your father is one of *those* people," Branson broke in with a condescending tone. "It's because of people like that and their Mr. Lincoln that we're in this mess."

"It's not the God-fearing abolitionists who have caused this," Luke replied calmly. "It's those who enslave God's children."

"God's children?" Branson laughed. "How many of these children have you met in your life? How many Negroes, boy?"

"Many," Luke snapped. "There have been dozens who have stayed with us on their way to freedom."

"Freedom? Are you trying to tell me you hid slaves?"

Luke said nothing, but the look on his face was answer enough.

"You're a lawbreaker. You realize that? You, who claim that the South has no right to secede, and you're a lawbreaker yourself."

"I'm obeying a higher law," Luke said without hesitation.

With annoyance, Branson turned back around to face the track. Kotler broke the uncomfortable pause. "What about you, Matthew? You're not a farmer either?"

"My father owns a small sawmill. Kalamazoo is big lumber area."

"Interesting," Thomas said for lack of a better reply.

Without thinking, Matthew wondered how his father was doing. He could see the old man hoisting lumber up onto the platform for cutting. He was surely missing Matthew's back in that task. And though Matthew did not miss that particular aspect, he did miss hearing the reassuring swirl of the creekwater which provided the power for his father's sawmill.

The monotony of the pumping motion and the steady click-clack as they rolled from one rail to the next only served to add to Matthew's daydreaming. Eventually the soldiers' backs and shoulders began to tire. Luke and Matthew began to alternate to give the other a brief rest, and Thomas also obliged them by lending a hand. Overall, their speed was dropping, but there was no rush. The track was fully intact, and they had seen no evidence of damage.

Bored of the silence, and not caring that it might further rile his boss, Thomas asked Matthew whether fighting slavery was why he had volunteered.

"Slavery?" Matthew said. "Not really. Not that I think any man should be put in chains, but I never thought about it much and still don't. No, I volunteered because it seemed like more fun than loading trees into a sawmill from dawn till past dusk."

"This does sound more exciting," Thomas agreed.

"Maybe you should get it over with and volunteer yourself, Kotler," Branson interjected from the front.

"I could never be a sharpshooter," Kotler said with a shake of the head. "I'm a terrible shot."

The comment struck Matthew as funny, and he laughed aloud.

"Don't worry," Luke said, noticing Kotler's quizzical stare. "He's laughing at me, not you."

"Oh?"

"Matthew, well, he's the best shot in all of Kalamazoo County, but me...well, I'm not so good."

"Not so good?" Matthew teased. "You couldn't hit the broad side of a barn when we started."

"And you're a sharpshooter?" Thomas asked with some confusion.

"I had to volunteer somewhere," Luke said lamely.

"But he's getting better," Matthew added, stopping his laughter momentarily. "He's hitting the barn door now." Matthew started laughing again.

Ignoring him, Thomas continued, "So how has it been? It sounds like you boys had some excitement at Mount Zion Church."

Matthew stopped laughing and bit his lip. Luke also said nothing, but they were saved from answering by Branson's yell.

"Whoa! Brakes, Kotler, damn you!"

Immediately, Luke and Matthew stopped pumping, and Kotler slowly applied the brake with increasing pressure.

"Good, good," Branson said. "We have some torn-up track ahead."

It wasn't clear to Luke or Matthew if the first comment was in regard to the brake job or the track, and they peered over the old man's shoulder as they came to a complete stop. Twenty yards ahead, the rails had been ripped from the ties. They could see some of the rails lying next to the track, a few others were pulled even further away.

"I guess there are still some bushwhackers out here after all," Kotler remarked.

"Nonsense," Branson replied. "This track hasn't seen a soul in three weeks. It's probably been like this since then. I'm sure the army is quite correct in their assessment that any bushwhackers have headed to safety in southern Missouri."

Luke looked at Matthew and gave a silent chuckle at the grimace that his friend gave.

"Now what?" Luke asked after another moment. "Do we fix it?"

"No spikes," Kotler answered before Branson could. "Besides, that would be a big job for just two of you."

"Let me examine the track a little more," Branson said, lowering himself down to the ground.

"What about that farmhouse?" Matthew asked. "Should we see whether they've seen anything?"

They all looked to their left where Matthew was pointing at a small farmhouse about three hundred yards away that no one had noticed earlier.

"Looks more like a shack than a house to me," Branson said contemptuously, and Luke had to agree with him. Even from here, the small wooden structure looked to be defeated by the weather. Luke wondered whether there was anyone still living there, or whether it was abandoned like many farms owned by Confederate sympathizers in North Central Missouri.

"Might as well see what they know," Branson declared, taking one last look at the small stretch of torn-up track. Stumping toward the house with the others in tow, Branson added, "Let me do the talking."

"Yes, sir," Luke answered, trying not to laugh.

The house was situated in the dead middle of the flat farm. Luke imagined that the house must be incredibly drafty in the winter. A quarter mile behind the house, there was a small forest, and Luke decided that the trees provided some protection from the wind.

"Luke," Matthew whispered, "while Branson does all the talking, I'm going to take a quick run into the woods. Call of nature."

While the others went straight to the front door, Matthew headed around the side of the house. Looking at the edge of the woods, he wondered whether there were any squirrels or game in the woods. Some fresh meat for dinner tonight would be a real bonus to the trip.

Old Branson knocked on the door, half wondering whether the decayed wood would give him a splinter. Surprised, the men heard a coarse voice yell from inside, "What are y'all knockin'?" The door opened slowly, and a dirty-looking man with a short, greasy beard stopped in midsentence, his mouth agape, his eyes flashed immediately to Luke's blue uniform and shoulder-slung rifle.

"Sir?" Luke said before remembering that he wasn't supposed to speak. It wouldn't have mattered since Branson appeared to be stunned by the man's appearance.

"What do you want?" the man said suspiciously. His tongue curled over yellowish teeth, and he took a step back, quickly glancing to his right.

Suspicious himself now, Luke was about to speak when Branson recovered. "May we come in?"

"In?" the man said slowly.

"We want to ask you some questions about the track."

"Track?"

"The railroad track in front of your farm has been torn up."

"It has," the man said with a slow deliberateness. Luke wasn't certain that the man's reply was either a statement or a question.

"Do you know when that happened?"

"The track?" the man said.

"Yes," Branson said, his annoyance with the man's behavior now growing.

Matthew began to purse his lips and whistle when his eyes skirted to another section of the forest. Stopping short, he looked at the section of the woods that had previously been obstructed from view by the farmhouse. It took a few seconds for it to register what he was looking at.

At the edge of the woods, there were a number of tents and a small cookfire. Matthew looked uncomprehendingly at the men in simple, winter clothing gathered around the fire, talking, unaware of the intruder.

He could hear the booming laughter of one of the men echo across the field, and slowly, Matthew began to back up. Looking a little further to the right, Matthew could see a dozen horses tied to trees.

"Bushwhackers," he whispered, as he turned and ran back to the front of the house.

"May we come all the way in?" Branson asked again with some annoyance.

Stepping to the side, the man answered with a crooked smile, "Of course."

Luke looked at Kotler who shrugged in reply.

"Again, Mister..."

"Cole."

"Mister Cole, did you see who ripped up my track?"

"I did. I did indeed, suh."

"Well?" Branson said impatiently.

Lunging with surprising speed toward the crude fireplace, the man yanked an old smoothbore musket off its pegs above the hearth. Before anyone could react, he had the musket pointed at Luke's chest.

"Don't get any ideas, Yankee!" Cole snarled, causing Luke to drop his hand from the sling of his still-shouldered rifle. "I saw exactly who tore up your track. It was me and the rest of Colonel Webb's Marauders!"

Just then, Matthew violently opened the front door, causing the Rebel to spin to his right and fire. The crack of the musket was deafening inside of the small room. Frozen in place, Matthew stood with his mouth open and looked at the door. Just below his hand, there was a new hole in the rickety wooden door.

Realizing that he had missed in his haste, the man stood stock-still for a moment, unsure what to do. Finally, he took a step toward the new intruder blocking the doorway, but Luke was ready this time. The crack of the man's gun had brought Luke into action, and he jabbed his now unslung rifle into the side of the man's head.

The man had scarcely hit ground before Matthew could mumble, "Bushwhackers." But like a magic spell, the word broke the look of dazed wonderment on everyone's faces, and he repeated it again, this time full of energy, "C'mon, there's a whole mess of 'em in the woods back there!"

They scrambled out of the small, one-room shack and raced for the handcar. The small contraption seemed miles away from them at this moment and particularly distant to old Branson as the three younger men began to quickly outdistance him.

Craning his head around, Matthew could see a few bushwhackers coming in an unconcerned jog to see the cause of the commotion. They suspected old Cole was drunk again and had accidentally discharged his rusty musket again, until they saw the four Yankees running.

Matthew could not hear what the bushwhackers were yelling to their comrades, but he could tell by their motions that the others were being directed to their horses.

"Hurry!" Matthew hollered at Branson.

The old man's face was bright red and contorted in pain as his tight-legged gait struggled hopelessly to keep pace with the younger men. Matthew unslung his rifle, placed a percussion cap on the firing cone, and aimed at one of the bushwhackers running after them. Ignoring Branson as he struggled past him, Matthew relaxed his body and focused on the running figure carrying his own weapon in his right hand. The man did not bother to shoot at the fleeing Yankees, figuring they were too far away for an accurate shot, but the distance did not stop Matthew as he squeezed the trigger.

The rifle gave its customary kickback into Matthew's shoulder. Pausing for a second, Matthew lowered the rifle and watched the man snap backwards like a puppet whose puppeteer had suddenly snapped taut the strings. The rifle flew from the man's hand, and he landed flat on his back. By this time, Matthew had already turned to run. He was too scared for it to occur to him that he had just killed his first man.

He quickly caught and passed Branson again, and he took a moment to stop and load his rifle while the old man repassed him. Matthew followed in a jog, jabbing the ramrod back into place underneath the barrel and pinching another percussion cap onto the firing nub.

"C'mon!" Luke yelled from the handcar. Below him, Kotler swung the lever on the handcar to change the direction of the pumping.

"Hurry!" Matthew yelled to Branson again. "Only fifty more yards." Turning to look at their pursuers again, Matthew saw a group of riders breaking out of the woods.

Finally, Matthew and Branson reached the handcar. Luke yanked Branson onto the car. "Go! Go! Go!" Matthew yelled, giving the car a slight push and leaping aboard himself.

Kotler was already struggling with the first stroke by himself when Matthew and Luke joined him at the lever. Fired by adrenalin, the three of them pushed up and down with all their strength. With agonizing slowness, the car began to move and then accelerate.

The bushwhacking riders had now closed to two hundred yards, and the cracks of their smoothbore muskets cut through the air. None of the shots were close, but they did serve to bring the gasping Branson to his feet. His fear-stoked body brushed Matthew aside and took his place pumping the lever.

"Switch...shoot...Rebs," he gasped to the sharpshooter.

Matthew grabbed his rifle from the floor of the platform and fired, but the jolting of the car flung the shot high and wide. Cursing, he ripped his eyes away from the closing horsemen and grabbed another paper cartridge from his cartridge box. Using his teeth to tear open the cartridge, he poured the coarse black powder down the barrel, stuffing the remnants of the paper and Minié ball in after it. In one smooth stroke, he withdrew the ramrod from underneath the barrel and stuffed it all down, replacing the ramrod. Last of all, he pinched another copper percussion cap into place. Looking up, he noticed that the riders had closed to one hundred yards, and he took aim at the one horseman waving a revolver. Matthew fired and began to reach into his cartridge box again without bothering to see whether he had hit the man.

"Use mine," Luke yelled to Matthew. Sweat streamed down his blond brow, and his muscles burned with fatigue.

"Faster!" Matthew urged. "They're gaining!"

Like a spurred horse, Luke redoubled his efforts, pushing and pulling so ferociously that the two railroad men could hardly keep up. Amazed by the young soldier's strength, each of the tired railroad men tried to redouble their own efforts but with less success.

Matthew grabbed Luke's rifle and checked the percussion cap. Whether it had fallen off or had never been put on, he didn't care. Quickly placing another cap on the nub, he raised the rifle, noticing the gap was holding steady now. This time, he changed his aim from the rider to the much larger target of the horse. Using patience that would later surprise him, he waited until he heard the click of a new section of rail, and while on the flat, continuous section, he fired.

Immediately, he set that rifle to the ground and began to reload his. When he looked up again, he noticed one less horseman and an increasing distance.

"Keep going!" he yelled. "We're losing them!"

Taking aim on another horse, and waiting for another smooth section of track, he fired again. One of the riders had his hat whipped off his head by the bullet, although it did not slow him for more than a moment.

Deciding that speed was more important, Matthew put the rifle back down and joined the three men pumping the handcar. Luke was even redder than before, his breaths coming in heaving, panting bursts. Kotler bit his lower lip in exertion, and his nostrils flared like that of a galloping stallion. Bead after bead of sweat dripped off old Branson's nose. His eyes were closed as if that would save some vestige of energy that could be put into the handcar.

Despite their looks of fatigue and exhaustion, Matthew decided that none of the men were letting up in their effort to outdistance the Confederate horseman. They continued exhausting themselves, and the bushwhackers could not gain on them. Gradually over the next few miles, they pulled farther and farther away. Now as much of a test of stamina as strength, they maintained their pace for miles. About five miles short of town, Matthew watched the riders give up the chase. "Praise the Lord," he gasped, "they've given up."

In the distance, Matthew saw one of the Rebel horsemen take off his hat and wave it as if in salute to the Yankee soldiers. Then the bushwhackers pulled their mounts around and were gone.

Matthew and the others continued pumping for another mile, not willing to believe their eyes, but finally it had sunk in that they were safe. Branson dropped to his knees.

"Is that enough excitement for you, Kotler?" Branson said, laying spread-eagle on his back, looking up at the bright blue sky.

Kotler, Luke, and Matthew slowed their pumping to a leisurely level, each man trying to gather himself in his own way. Kotler took his hands off the metal rod and bent over, throwing up over the side of the handcar.

"My sentiments exactly," Branson said, sliding over a canteen that he had tied earlier to a corner bracket.

Luke watched the old man with a sense of curiosity. The stress and subsequent relief had totally changed the old man's attitude. His gruff distemper had changed into a voice of warmth. The dramatic change in demeanor surprised Kotler even more than Luke. Gratefully, he accepted the canteen and swished the cool water around in his mouth before spitting it out.

"Plenty exciting," Kotler said finally after taking a gulp of the water.

"I didn't give you credit, young man," Branson remarked, looking at Luke. "I could see you were a strapping lad, but even so, your strength and stamina amaze me. It was the best I could do just to keep up with you. I feared I wasn't doing anything other than slowing you down."

"Oh, no," Luke blushed. "Your help was greatly needed."

"What happened to not doing physical labor?" Kotler ribbed Branson who surprisingly took it good-naturedly.

"Duty called, Kotler."

"And you," Thomas said, looking at Matthew, "I can see why you are the best shot in all of Kalamazoo County. It's still beyond me how you plucked that rider clean from his horse while on a moving handcar...and from that range!"

Matthew shrugged, not bothering to tell them that he had been aiming for the horse.

"Oh, yes, young man," Branson agreed. "A remarkable shot. Have no fear. Your officers will hear about your bravery, skill, and strength. I assure you of that."

January 23, 1862

"This is ridiculous. They're goin' to kill us like this. I treated my cows better back home," Peter O'Shea complained to James.

He was a man of average height with unusually thick shoulders, strengthened by years of hard work behind the plow. With tightly curled brown hair, thick growth along his cheeks, and a hard stare, he gave many a person the wrong impression. He looked like a man ready to fight at the slightest provocation. Despite appearances though, James had found him to be one of the more practical and reasonable men in Company J.

"Those of us who aren't sick yet," Peter continued, "will be sick before long. An' the ones who are already sick are goin' to die if this cold spell doesn't snap."

James grunted in reply. Cocooned in his battered uniform with a filthy, soiled blanket wrapped around him for additional protection, he tromped slowly over the frozen, snow-covered ground.

He and Peter seemed to be the only ones moving about today. James knew that the temperature had to be below zero, but it was the wind that cut him to the bone like a sharpened bowie knife.

The warm spell of the previous week had left muddy footprints all over Sturgeon, but now in the bitter cold, those muddy footprints had been turned into rock hard, ankle-breaking traps. The wind that blew out from the northwest lashed at James's face, and he knew he better get back inside the livery before frostbite did him in.

Although he wasn't sick yet, nearly one in four of the Western Sharpshooters was feverish.

"What a wasted effort this was," Peter continued as though unaware that the freezing temperatures had muted James's tongue. "How can the regimental surgeon turn away sick men? I know he's filled up in that tiny little house." Peter answered himself, "But leaving sick men in this rotting livery will kill everyone. You all right, James?" Peter stopped, noticing that his companion hadn't made a comment yet.

"Fine, Pete, just cold."

"I know. It's scarcely warmer inside that livery though. The draft that blows through there...sometimes, I think it will blow the fire clean out."

James grunted in reply again. Peter was right, for the effort they went through in getting the army stove, it provided little benefit. The livery was too big and too open to be sufficiently heated by the small army stove designed to heat a Sibley tent.

The two men entered the crowded livery, and James immediately noticed the strong smell of the place. The air was freezing cold outside, but at least it was clean smelling. The livery reeked of sick men, and James forced himself to block out thoughts that he would soon be sick himself if he stayed here in this environment. Making his way over to Patrick's bed of hay on the frozen ground, he went down to one knee.

"How do you feel today?"

Shivering, his normally ruddy face, pale and damp with sweat, Patrick managed a feverish smile. "Better 'n Quinlan," he said, rolling his head to a side and looking at John across the room, mumbling in a delirium.

Unable to hide the concern on his face, James's eyes followed Patrick's across the room.

"He talks more now than he does when he's well," Patrick said in a weak voice, closing his eyes again, as if the effort to speak had exhausted him.

"What did Doc Curtis say?" Luke asked, approaching with his Bible in hand. He had been reading some passages to try to lift the spirits, but if it did, he could not tell. In the back of his mind, Luke's voice kept reminding him that it was only mid-January. He couldn't imagine another two months of this.

"No room," James answered. "Maybe he could take a few of the most serious cases."

"What does that mean? They're all serious," Luke snapped. "Quinlan's dying over there. He hasn't eaten in days, hasn't come out of that delirium for days. He just..."

James pulled Luke aside before he could finish, dragging him from the corner of the stable that was now Patrick's home. "Luke," James said in a hushed voice so that even Patrick could not hear him, "they're all dying slowly, but reminding them of that isn't going to help. Understand?"

January 24, 1862

> *We shiver too much to sleep, and my hand is quickly growing too cold to write much. Tomorrow we march to fix track east of town, at least those of us fit enough to go.*
>
> *—The Diary of James Lockett*

Matthew and Luke stood next to James, equally quiet and preoccupied. The prairie winds whipped at their faces. Any part of exposed skin had long since been flayed red and senseless. A few men had dripping swirls of ice hanging from their beards and mustaches. Yet despite the cold and difficult footing of the frozen ground, James was glad to leave the smell of the stable behind for a while. Though he was still worried about Patrick and the others, the inactivity had been driving the healthy men near insane.

They found the torn-up track six miles east of town. It was a sloppy, hasty demolition. The undamaged rails lay nearby—had it been done right, the rails would have been carted off or placed into fires so that the metal could be twisted into unusable shapes. But given the temperature, James imagined that the bushwhackers were just as anxious to get back to camp as Company J.

The men did not need orders from their officers today. They all knew that the sooner they repaired the track, the sooner they could find a fire. With little direction, the rails were gathered up, spikes broken out, and sledgehammers hoisted.

"Better check up ahead to make sure the track up there is okay," Lieutenant Long said to Lieutenant Simon and Sergeant VanderJagt. "I'll take these ten and check ahead."

"Yes, sir," Simon answered the senior lieutenant.

"C'mon, Lockett," Lieutenant Long said, stalking off, "I don't have time to wait for your lollygagging today."

The directness of Lieutenant Long's address startled James. Other than Walker, rarely did the officer ever address any of the volunteers by name. James handed the sledgehammer to Matthew, who sagged noticeably under the weight.

James smiled slightly and blew on his hands as he looked at Lieutenant Simon who shrugged and waved James on. With a sidewise glance at Matthew, James followed after Lieutenant Long.

They had not gone very far before a sinking feeling penetrated James's cold-numbed brain. Like a dozen little pinpricks, he noticed who Long was leading: Hiram Walker, Isaac Washburn, Bart Randle—basically all of Walker's messmates and James. But he followed on, and began to chastise himself for his paranoia.

While Hiram had not forgotten James's interference back at the farmstead in Centralia, Lieutenant Long had never said a word about it. He had not even looked crossly at James. Long had apparently forgotten all about it.

This was completely the opposite of Hiram. The look of pure hatred was in the large man's eyes every time James made eye contact. Once, James had heard Hiram grumbling to Isaac about getting even. Of course, Hiram had known that James was right there, which caused James to chalk it up as an idle threat meant to bully him and no more.

But as the little group marched out of sight, James found himself less sure of that, and despite his best efforts, he could not dismiss the nagging feeling that pulled on him like a cold hand on the back of his neck. Something was not right, and he knew that it wasn't paranoia.

He glanced at his Dimick and checked that the percussion cap was still on the nub of his loaded rifle. He couldn't defend himself against ten men, but he could take one of them with him! It must be the cold, he thought. The cold must be doing this. There is nothing to fear! The cold, the cold, the cold.

James had become so wrapped up in his own thoughts that he did not notice the small farmhouse ahead with the smoke trickling from its square chimney.

"I think it is time we warmed up a bit," Lieutenant Long said, drawing no disagreement from his chilled men.

Warmth, his mind shouted happily, but James's feet were slow in following. The phantom grip around his neck tightened, and he knew he should not follow Long and the others. He could see it in the bounce of the men's strides—Washburn, Randle, Walker—there was a purposefulness and anticipation to their increasing pace, and it was not just related to the possibility of a warm fire.

But what choice do I have? James thought bitterly. Stand here like a fool in the middle of this frozen field? Wait here like a coward? With a nervous sensation in his stomach, James forced his legs forward. He prayed that his imagination was getting the better of him, that Long and Walker wanted to demonstrate a new quality of conduct.

Was that why Long had intentionally selected me? James wondered, but he could feel in his heart that it was nothing so noble or benign. He had the immutable feeling that something was about to go terribly wrong, so he followed them with his hand close to the trigger of his rifle.

"Cold, Lockett?" Long asked suddenly, turning around with a wolfish smile on his reddened face. "A little something to warm you up?"

The image of Long's leering smile burned into James's brain. Was the man toying with him? Did he sense James's discomfort and want to have a little entertainment at James's expense? He could live with that, he decided, and prayed that there was nothing more to it.

Yet, the half mile to the farmhouse took an eternity as James's mind urgently contemplated a number of other possibilities.

The soft crunch of the frozen ground was all that James heard until they reached the steps of the farmhouse. "What do y'all want?" they heard the foreign voice bark at them. He was a harsh-looking old man, and he glared at them with suspicious eyes.

The stare did not slow Lieutenant Long, nor even draw a comment as the officer climbed the steps. Only when he had reached the top step did Long stop, his eyes thoroughly examining the old man. Despite the cold, the wizened old man had waited coatless for them. Now, his bent frame straightened to its full height and he looked Lieutenant Long in the eye, his thin arms taut against his side.

James clenched his hands, trying to get some feeling in them and shivered.

The old man did not shiver; rather he stared unflinchingly at the men in Union blue.

"We need to check this residence for evidence of aiding and abetting traitors," Lieutenant Long snarled back. "Now step aside."

"This is my house," the old man maintained, "an' I don' want no soldiers in here."

"Soun's like he's hidin' somthin' to me," Washburn hooted from the back.

"Step aside," Long said in a distracted voice, brushing the man away from the door with no more thought than one would wave at a fly.

"Are there no laws left in this country?" the man said angrily, following the men inside.

"Private Washburn," Long said, "please detain this man in here while we search the rest of the residence." Without a look back, Long continued on.

With unnecessary force, Washburn shoved the old man into a small wooden chair in the corner. The old man landed on the chair and then toppled backward over it, knocking his head on the wall as he overturned. Pulling himself upright, he tried to stand only to be backhanded by Washburn.

"Stay seat'd, ol' man, before you get hurt," Washburn said in a pleased voice.

From the front door, James watched with quiet anger. Gripping the rifle as tight as he could, he made no move nor said a word, but the expression on his face communicated all the distress and indecision.

Looking at James, Walker laughed, causing James to look away, boring a hole through the hardwood floor with his gray eyes.

"Put that down!" came a high-pitched shout from another room, followed immediately by a crash and a thud.

Everyone, old man included, rushed to the back room. From the middle of this pack, James arrived just in time to see Lieutenant Long get up, a trickle of blood dripping from a cut in his forehead. Standing in front of him was a young fourteen-year-old girl with the handle of a broken water pitcher still in her hand. Defiantly, the young girl's eyes blazed at the Union officer.

"You thief!" she said, just before a punch from Long knocked her clean across the kitchen.

"Leave her al——," the old man began, but before he could finish the sentence, Washburn wrenched one of the man's arms behind his back with such force that there was an audible pop. The old man howled in pain as Washburn pushed him to the floor.

"Grandfather!" the girl screamed, rising up off the floor with surprising resiliency. Oblivious to her own rapidly closing black eye, she ran towards the old man only to be caught in the grasp of Lieutenant Long.

"Remind you of anything?" Walker said to James with a look of sick pleasure. The ice that had coated his thick beard was melting and dropping to the floor, giving him the look of a rabid beast.

Randle leaned towards James, his fetid breath curled across James's face as he whispered, "How ya gonna help the Secesh this time, Lockett?"

A depraved smirk split Long's face, as he touched his forehead. "I'd say she attacked an officer in the United States Army, boys. According to General Halleck, she ought to be taken back to town." Walker and the others looked back at their officer with knowing grins of their own. "But, I'd say that would be more trouble than its worth. She ought to take her punishment here, the Rebel wench."

"You bastards," James said in a low voice.

The girl's one good eye was wide with terror and confusion. She had gentle blue eyes, but they were now filled with panic as she scanned the room. They were all animals, animals in blue...all but one. She stared at the lanky soldier with gray eyes, and her young, childlike face implored him for help.

James looked at her, trying to disguise the apprehension and fear that he felt. He tried to impassively return her stare. She was so young, he thought to himself, more child than woman. Her long, straight brown hair cascaded down to the middle of her back, and her small, fairylike features were still unblemished by wrinkles or pimples. The gentle features of her pale white face appeared to be crudely damaged by the swelling eye. The look on her young face burned him, scalded him. He could feel the beads of sweat on his chest even though he was ice cold. He knew right there that hers was a face that he would remember for the rest of his life.

"You can't go soft on these traitors," Randle growled at James. "And we're going to teach you the right way to do things whether you like it or not."

Walker leaned closer to James. "Well, Lockett? Cat got your tongue?" He circled James like a predator toying with wounded prey. "Nothing to say? No one here but us...you lily-stomached bastard!" Walker barked suddenly. "You think you know better than our officers! Than General Halleck! Damn muck farmer! What do you know? You think because you is always writin' in that little black book that you's smarter than the officers! Damn muck farmer! Ignorant fool! Think you got a better way to treat this trash?" Walker gestured wildly at the old man still pinned to the floor and the girl caught in Long's arms. "Gonna interfere? Well? Well? No, not this time, I can see it on your face! You frightened sow, you're going to watch the whole thing!"

Lieutenant Long began to slide a hand along the girl's thigh.

James's heart was pounding like he didn't believe possible. It was thunder in his ears. Pounding, vibrating his whole body. Every fiber of his body twitched with fire. Rage!

But there was no noticeable change in his outward appearance.

"Look at him!" Washburn laughed. "I think he's shitted himself!"

Though James's tongue seemed dead and his face passive, he burned to do something. Anything! He saw Randle bent backwards, laughing like a horse, his legs spread far apart to keep his balance.

The girl squirmed futilely to break from Long's grasp, and she gave one last look at James. Her blue eyes were fixated in silent terror.

With a bellicose roar that startled everyone in the room, James viciously kicked upwards between Randle's legs.

The room had become as frozen as the ground outside, and only James could move for the moment. The kick was perfectly placed, and he swung around instantly in the same motion, elbowing Washburn in the jaw. The short, violent blow sounded like a wedge going through a fence rail, and it was impossible to tell which man hit the ground first—Randle or Washburn.

James, acting on instinct, had hardly known what he had done, and certainly had not planned it. Now, his instinct ordered him to raise his rifle up to cock back the hammer, but the spell on the room had finally been broken. He had only raised the Dimick halfway when it was swung high with an upward movement, and James found himself struggling against Walker for control of the weapon.

Walker snarled, one hand on the barrel and the other near the hammer as he tried to wrench the rifle away from his thinner foe.

Swinging around as though they were performing some odd dance, James and Walker struggled for control of the Dimick. The room was ominously quiet, and the glint in Walker's eye told James what they were all thinking, that the larger Walker would surely pull the gun away from him.

Again, instinct answered the call. James snapped his head forward violently, connecting with Walker's nose. Walker still held tight, but he was dazed, and James tried to yank the rifle free.

Crackkkk!

With a resounding echo, the rifle shot reverberated within the walls of the room. Walker's grasp slid from the weapon, and James realized that he himself had pulled the trigger in trying to free it.

"Amelia!" the old man gasped, his eyes widening so that only the whites showed.

Turning a quarter step with the still smoking rifle, James watched Lieutenant Long release the ghastly mess that had been the girl. The color in Long's face rapidly drained to match the bluish mess on his cheek. Flecked with the girl's red blood and bluish brain matter, Lieutenant Long passed out, joining the girl on the floor.

With his mouth hanging open and an inaudible cry on his lips, James gaped at the girl. The Minié ball, fired from the point-blank range, had shattered the entire top of her skull. An enormous puddle of blood spread across the floor in horrible, ever-widening circles around her head.

Feeling himself shaking, James's mind flashed from the original image of the fairylike, brown-haired girl to the gruesome corpse that now lay on the floor. Utterly unable to reconcile the images, they snapped back and forth in his memory like a pulse.

Then, the sharp blow to the back of his head ended the torture, and James hit the ground unconscious.

II

Separate Paths

Word struck town like a tornado. Despite the frigid temperatures, a steady stream of townspeople poured into the old dentist office that now served as Captain Vincent's quarters. They all wanted the same thing—the head of the soldier who had committed this atrocity, Private Lockett!

James contemplated this as he fidgeted in the stiff-backed chair, waiting for the captain. His hands gripped the crude arms of the chair in perfect synchronization with the ticking of the small clock on the wall. But it was not the knowledge of what the townspeople wanted to do with him that caused James to dig his fingernails into the hard wood, it was the constant flashing of the girl's face.

Fairylike and imploring...a dead lump of bluish matter and circles of dark red blood...fairylike and imploring...a dead lump of bluish matter and circles of dark red blood...Over and over again.

He could not stop thinking about it. How could this happen? How God? How could that happen? Why did I have to pull that trigger! James cursed himself, but the empty room made no reply.

He could hardly remember the march back. The blow to the back of his head had been solid, and he had come out of unconsciousness just once, and only long enough to notice two things: that Luke and Gus were carrying him back on a makeshift stretcher and the image of Lieutenant Long. The lieutenant's face was pallid, pasty white, his hair clumped by sticky blood, and one side of his uniform was coated in the girl's blood from fainting into the pool of it.

Had he been told, James would not have been surprised that Walker and the others had invented a tale about how he had murdered a Secesh-loving girl in cold blood.

By the time James was revived, history had been rewritten.

Most of the sharpshooters did not know what to believe, but given no other option, many were forced to believe Walker and the others, even though it made no sense to them.

While James struggled with his own thoughts in Captain Vincent's quarters, Luke shivered back in the livery, but it was not a shiver from cold. He shivered in fear for his friend.

While General Prentiss's orders specifically allowed physical action against suspected sympathizers, Luke doubted that the order would cover the cold-blooded execution of a young girl, as Walker was now portraying it.

Luke had learned long ago that Missouri was a state of divided sympathies. It was truly neighbor against neighbor. There seemed no rhyme or reason in who was a Unionist or who was a Secessionist, but there was one thing that none would stand for, the killing of an innocent girl.

Luke knew that James must be innocent. He was as sure of that as he was that Jesus had died for their sins, but Luke also knew that there was little that Captain Vincent would do for James.

James had been right when he said that Vincent was nothing more than a politician, and as such, the politician in Charles Vincent would do the easy thing. Vincent would not bother to try to ferret out the truth; he would simply hand James over to the local sheriff when they came and asked for him. And they were sure to do that soon. The story had spread like wildfire across the small town.

There was only one thing to do, Luke thought. Find Lieutenant Simon and see what could be done.

But Lieutenant Simon was way ahead of Luke.

Matthew sat quietly in the corner near Patrick, the only ones in the livery not talking.

Man after man gossiped in low voices and speculated on what had transpired. With one side of his uniform covered with blood, Lieutenant Long was a lightning rod for conversation. But most of the debate was about what had driven James to commit murder. Most thought that it had been the intense cold that had driven James insane. He must have been in some type of fury, they mused, to have broken Washburn's jaw and to have bloodied Walker's nose. Some claimed to have seen it coming from the quiet, almost reclusive farmer, although none had ever expected James to have been such a fighter. Most of them steered clear of Washburn, Randle, and Walker. Everyone knew what those men were capable of.

Matthew couldn't believe how quickly many of the men turned on James. Only this morning, James had been the unofficial leader of the group bedded down in the livery, but now, only Pete and Sam were willing to defend him.

"You look like you have a problem," Patrick said in a weak, shaking voice, startling Matthew.

Matthew looked at his once bull-like friend, thinking that Patrick looked even weaker and more vulnerable now than when he had left this morning. His normally thick frame shriveled beneath the two woolen blankets. Even the sun-blotched spots around his eyes were pale, though his heavy red beard hid most of his gauntness. He did not seem to be Patrick McManus looking up at him anymore, Matthew thought, just some pale and weakened stranger.

"There's a problem, Patrick," Matthew said in a soft voice, unsure where to begin.

"I heard. I ain't really asleep. Can't sleep," Patrick said in a cracked voice.

For the first time, Matthew noticed a piece of paper clenched tightly in Patrick's right hand. It was wrinkled and soiled from Patrick's grubby hands, but he still clenched it tightly like some sort of talisman.

Following Matthew's eyes down to the paper, Patrick whispered in a hoarse voice, "The Edgar County boys fixed the bridges south to Columbia. They brought back some of the supplies and mail," Patrick hesitated, and then closed his eyes in exhausted anguish. "Martha's sick," he finished.

"Sick? How sick?"

"Doc Gillam says she has inflammation of the lungs, congestive."

James stood at attention in front of Captain Vincent's desk. The first rays of sunlight were just entering through the frosted pane of the former dentist's office. In fact, most of the dentist's tools still lay on a table along the west wall of the small room. The sun glinted off the long, slender pliers that was used for pulling teeth. That's what I need, James thought to himself, extraction from here.

Captain Vincent still looked well groomed even though his men were now worse off than most horses. The only difference that James could see was that the captain appeared older than before. Crow's-feet had begun to etch themselves into the corner of his eyes, and he had been lacking in his old bravado ever since Hallsville. He looked at James with tired eyes. "Private Lockett," he said in his deep voice that always carried to the back rows of the crowds, "I had heard about your bravery at Hallsville from Lieutenant Simon and Sergeant VanderJagt. I wish more men had seen the courage, then perhaps we wouldn't have been chased off the field like a bunch of panicky women."

Vincent rose to his feet and strutted around the corner of the desk. He peered briefly out the small window, and then began to pace behind the desk with quick, little steps, like a rooster. "As you know, that knock on my head when Victory went down didn't do us much good in Hallsville, but according to Sergeant VanderJagt, you might be the best soldier in this company."

Surprised at what he was hearing, James raised his eyebrows slightly.

"Given that," Vincent continued, turning on his heel to face James, "this pains me so. This company needs all the good soldiers it can get, but I can't have men running off and murdering women and children even if they are traitors."

"But," James began only to stop short, seeing the disapproving look on Vincent's face.

"*Private*," Vincent said, emphasizing the word, "do not interrupt me! Do not lie to me! There is no debate. I have already heard from five witnesses that you murdered that girl, one of them your own officer,

Lieutenant Long. Your guilt is clear. As your commanding officer, I must do *something*." Vincent looked out the small window again. "I have enough trouble with this divided Missouri rabble without one of my men stirring them all up. Lieutenant Simon only yesterday was able to convince some of the townswomen to take in some of the sick. Pitifully few, I'm afraid to say, but some. But now, they are afraid to have 'murdering and thieving' Yankees in their houses." Vincent stopped and gave James a perplexed look. "I am more than halfway tempted to hand you straight over to the sheriff, especially considering that Lieutenant Long tried to prevent you from killing that girl."

The last sentence shook James like a slap in the face. Biting down as hard as he could, he refrained from speaking. Wordlessly, he stood at attention. He clenched his jaw so tightly that it began to bulge.

Seeing the clenched jaw, Vincent changed his tone once again, this time to a more consoling one. "Don't worry, Private. I'm not turning you over. In fact, you are quite lucky. You see, Lieutenant Simon has made the wise suggestion that we try to remove as many of the sick men from here as possible. Those who cannot recuperate in Sturgeon will be sent back to St. Louis by train. Many in our little company have their terms of enlistment ending soon, and it would probably be best for them to recover at home."

More confused than ever, James looked blankly at Vincent.

"I'm going to kill two birds with one stone, Private Lockett. I need someone to go back with the men, someone who is not sick, but I cannot spare a man. That is until now. You will take the men back to St. Louis and then go home from there. When the local sheriff comes asking for you, I will tell him that you have been sent back for a military trial. Is this all clear, Private?" Vincent asked, noticing the odd look on James's face.

More unsure than ever what to make of his captain, James weighed the chances of actually setting the record straight. Regardless of whether Vincent was a moral and just man, James decided that the odds of persuading him were slim. Vincent had already made a decision and a judgement. Telling him that the death was the fault of his nephew and Walker had a terribly low chance of success. No, there would be no setting the record straight. Lieutenant Long had maneuvered him into a corner that he could not escape. James considered himself lucky to escape with his life now, reputation forever soiled or not.

"Yes, sir," James replied. "Perfectly clear, sir."

"Excellent," Vincent said with a satisfied voice. "Lieutenant Simon is in the outer office. He will give you the rest of the details."

"Yes, sir."

"Dismissed, Private."

With that, James left the office, closing the door behind him, wondering how all this had happened, wondering whether he was still asleep and dreaming.

"James," Lieutenant Simon said softly, pulling him outside the building by the elbow, "what did you say in there?"

"Say?"

"Did you argue with him?" Simon asked in a concerned voice.

"Argue?"

"I know about Lieutenant Long and Walker. I know that you stopped them in Centralia."

"What?"

"Luke told me. He didn't know what happened yesterday. My guess is that it was much the same situation, but this time—"

"I was trying to stop them, Lieutenant," James said in a tight voice, the image of the little girl's corpse flashing into his head again. "There was a struggle, and...," James stopped, clenching a fist. "Those bastards," he said in an ominous low voice, glaring at a foe that only he could see.

"That's what I mean, James. Did you try to tell Captain Vincent all that?"

"No," James said stiffly. "I didn't think it would help."

"Good," Simon said with some relief. "When I devised this plan last night that was the only thing I could not prepare for, and it was the only thing that could ruin it. You made the right decision, James. He wouldn't have listened to you. I haven't figured the captain out myself yet, but the one thing I do know is that Lietuenant Long has him completely fooled."

"This was your idea?" James asked.

Simon nodded. "I knew after this it would be best for you to leave. I don't know whether the army and Captain Vincent would protect you from the sheriff, so it's best that you leave. It works well anyway. I've been trying to get Captain Vincent to send the sick back for a while now before they all die of exposure and fever. Lucky for you, the track was repaired yesterday and there will be a train leaving at noon."

"Lieutenant," James said, thinking aloud, "I don't know that I can ever thank you."

"It's okay, James. I'm just trying to do the right and honorable thing."

The right and honorable thing. That is what we are fighting for, James mused. To set things right, to put a country back together. He looked away, his mind elsewhere. *The right and honorable thing.*

James found Luke and Matthew off-loading the supplies from the train that had just arrived. Pausing to stare at the heavy black locomotive with grease clinging to its machinery, James found himself wondering again whether it was all a dream. Was he really leaving the rest of the company behind? Was he really boarding this train never to rejoin the Kalamazoo Sharpshooters?

Dumbly, he walked over to where Luke was pushing a crate off a flatcar. Matthew tugged on one end from the ground level, waiting for Luke to jump off the car and grab the other end.

"You're just in time," Matthew said, spotting James out of the corner of his eye and doing his best to have a normal reaction upon seeing him. "Grab this other end, will ya?"

Obligingly, James headed for the end of the crate still balanced on the railroad car.

"What did the captain say?" Luke asked immediately.

"How's Patrick this morning?" James responded instead.

"Same as before," Luke said from the flatcar, towering above him.

"Johnny Quinlan died in his sleep last night," Matthew added softly. "That makes three. First, Wil Fulgham, then Billy Spencer yesterday."

James took a deep breath and nodded.

"If this weather doesn't let up, there will be a lot more."

"I know," James said softly. "But I think Lieutenant Simon has a solution to that."

"I knew he would come through," Luke said, but James and Matthew did not hear him.

"A solution?" Matthew said quizzically.

"You should know," Luke added, "that Lieutenant Long is telling people that you killed that girl yesterday." His voice was dark and full of compunction. But James showed no surprise at the words, so he added, "But I don't believe it for a second, James. It was the same as before, wasn't it? Hiram Walker again?"

James nodded mutely, unsure what he was feeling anymore. He tried to tell himself that it was not his fault, but the image of the girl kept flashing into his mind. He felt so tired, exhausted really, like rolling over dead.

"Why don't you say anything?" Luke said with a touch of desperation in his voice.

"You can't let this go on," Matthew agreed, remembering the sight of Lieutenant Long stealing the silver. "They're talking about murder, James." The last sentence was said with a hushed voice.

"There's nothing that can be done, Matthew. Not now, not yesterday. It's my word versus Long's, and you know who will win." The voice was cold and certain, and he paused momentarily. With a resigned shrug, he added, "Maybe the girl's grandfather would support me, but I don't know whether he even saw anything, pinned to the floor and all. If he did, I don't know how it appeared to him. Maybe he thinks it was the way Long said it happened."

"But you can't just let them do this to you," Matthew maintained.

"Drop it, Matthew. There wasn't much that could be done yesterday, and there's even less today. The less said, the better." James pulled off his hat and ran his fingers through his oily hair. With frustration turning his face purple, Luke and Matthew didn't know what to say to their old friend. "It doesn't matter anymore," James continued. "Lieutenant Simon...I don't know why really, but he's going to help me...help all the sick ones out too. We're all leaving on this train back as soon as you finish unloading."

"What?" Luke exclaimed.

"I'm accompanying the sick ones back to St. Louis and then Kalamazoo." James paused and gave his two friends a worrisome look. Nervously, he pulled on his cheek with his thumb and forefinger and added, "I guess you two still need to deal with Lieutenant Long, but there's not much that I can do about it at this point."

"What are you talking about? Going back to Kalamazoo?" Luke repeated, stunned by the news.

Carefully, step by step, James took Luke and Matthew through the events of yesterday and this morning. When he was done, James said, "It couldn't get any worse, could it?"

"It could," Matthew said slowly. "Patrick told me that Martha is dying."

Patrick lay on the simple stretcher in the converted passenger car. With fifteen sick men, the car was already beginning to trap some of the revolting smell, but Patrick did not seem to notice. There was a great relief on his feverish face this afternoon. He was on his way back to Martha.

As Luke knelt down to shake hands, he correctly guessed the reason for Patrick's relaxed brow. "You'll see her soon, Patrick. Don't worry, the good Lord will—"

"Pray for her," Patrick croaked. Clearing his throat, he added with a more normal voice, "I know it is in God's hands, Luke, but pray for her."

"Of course," Luke promised. "And I'll pray for you too."

"And James too while you're at it," Patrick said. "He may need it as much as I do." Patrick reached into his pocket and pressed a few coins into Luke's hands.

"What's this for?"

"Lieutenant Simon. Make sure he takes this, Luke."

"Lieutenant Simon? Why?"

"He's paying for this."

"What?"

"The army will get us to St. Louis, but not to Kalamazoo. Lieutenant Simon is paying for the rest of the trip."

"For everyone?"

Patrick nodded. "I saw him give James the money to get everyone home, and I'll be damned if I let anyone give me charity. Make sure he takes it, Luke." Patrick's feverish eyes turned more lucid as he focused inwardly.

"Of course," Luke responded, looking to the other end of the car where James was finishing a conversation with the conductor.

"Take care, Luke," Patrick said in a feverish voice, causing Luke to grin in amusement.

"You take care too, Patrick."

Luke stood and James returned from his talk with the conductor.

"Five minutes," James said to no one in particular and then followed Luke outside for some fresh air. Even the air on the tiny, open-air platform between cars smelled markedly better, and James took a deep breath. "I want to tell you something, Luke," James said, jumping down from the platform without looking.

At the last instant, James saw a figure in a blue uniform walking toward the opening, and he barely avoided landing on the unfortunate soldier.

"Watch where you're going, Private!" Lieutenant Long snapped, stumbling back out of the way.

"Pardon me, Lieutenant," James answered in a stiff voice.

Seeing who it was, Long gave a dastardly grin. The white teeth of his smile glinted in the sunlight. With his wavy, brown hair back in its perfect coif and his red scarf jauntily tied around his neck, Long no longer looked like the dazed wreck he had been immediately after the killing.

"See that you take better care of our men than you do of young girls," Long said in a loud voice, making sure those inside the car could hear him.

Luke was coming down the steps of the platform, and he placed a gentle hand on James's shoulder, but James did not need any restraint. While every urge in James's body was toward fury, he controlled himself and did not give Long the slightest reaction. He wouldn't give him the satisfaction. The ephemeral flicker of hatred that flinted in his gray eyes did not appear until after Long had departed inside the passenger car for one last inspection.

"Ignore him," Luke said quietly, as they stepped out of earshot.

"I'm trying."

Luke looked glum, and James had no words to cheer him. It had only just begun to occur to him that he was returning to Kalamazoo in disgrace.

"Well, James, I guess this is good-bye for now," Luke said finally.

James nodded grimly. While he felt some relief in leaving Missouri behind and getting Patrick home to Martha, he also felt some guilt about leaving Luke and Matthew.

"Don't worry about us," Luke said, as if he could read James's thoughts. "We'll steer clear of Lieutenant Long as best we can."

James nodded, but he knew that was easier said than done. He looked at the black smoke belching from the locomotive's wide stove pipe. "I guess I better get back on board."

"We'll see you after the war is over," Luke said confidently shaking James's hand.

James climbed back on board and found himself face-to-face with Lieutenant Long one last time. There was little room on the steel plate between cars for two men to pass, and James was in no mood to step aside for the man.

When he did not yield, he expected vitriol from Long, but the dapper officer only gave him a smug grin. "You should be thankful, Lockett," he said in a low voice that only James could hear. "I could have had you court-martialed and hung for raising a weapon against an officer."

The train began to move slightly, fighting that uphill battle to gain its momentum. Long began to step around him, when James snapped an arm out, barring his way. "We'll meet again," he vowed in a low voice and then slid around Long and into the passenger car of sick men.

He didn't look back at Long to see his reaction; he didn't care, but he knew he would see the smug face again. One way or the other, James Lockett would see to that.

January 30, 1862

James waited for Patrick's wobbly legs to take him down the steps of the train onto the simple wooden platform. He looked north down Main Street at familiar Kalamazoo. It hadn't changed much since they had left, but it appeared much bigger to him after spending a month in tiny Sturgeon, Missouri. Even the simple dirt road of Main Street impressed James today. Twice as wide as Main Street in Sturgeon, the thoroughfare was lined with wood planking sidewalks, a luxury that James wished the muddy streets of Sturgeon had offered. The four-story buildings that lined Main Street were another sign that the bustling town of Kalamazoo was starting to outgrow its pioneer, agrarian roots.

"When are they going to replace the old depot?" Patrick said, joining him on the uncovered wood planking of the temporary train depot.

"No time soon, I imagine." He remembered the beautiful high-pitched roof of the Gothic structure that had burned in 1853. In his mind's eye, he could still remember looking at the ashes of the building that had once made Kalamazoo so proud. He had never understood the reluctance to rebuild it, especially with all the other growth in the town, but James now had larger concerns. His eyes made it over to the drawn face of his friend. "You sure you're up to the walk back to the farm?"

It was just Patrick and James from here. Five of their original number had died on the trip to St. Louis. Seven more had been deemed too ill to continue on past St. Louis or had insisted on staying in St. Louis so that they could more easily rejoin the sharpshooters upon recovery. One man had stayed in Chicago where he had family, and another had disembarked in Niles, which was closer to his family farm.

James wondered idly what had happened to those who had stayed behind in St. Louis. Had some recovered well enough to continue the journey? He had left them the money from Lieutenant Simon for the train. James guessed that even if a few of them had recovered well enough to continue on, they probably had wasted the money on gambling, drinking, or women. It had been a lonely existence in Missouri, and he supposed he couldn't blame them.

"I told you," Patrick answered with some anger, "I'm feeling better. Just weak, that's all. But I can still walk."

James nodded. Patrick did look a little better. The fever had broken, his forehead was finally free of the small beads of sweat, and finally some of Patrick's natural skin color returned in his face. Though Patrick had never taken on the ashen appearance that the others had assumed before they died, Patrick's pallid skin had at times been too close to it for James's liking.

"Give me that," James said, pulling on Patrick's knapsack.

"I can carry my own."

"Patrick," James said stubbornly, "give me the knapsack. I won't take no arguments here."

With a look of resignation, Patrick shrugged and handed over the knapsack. "When I get my strength back, James Lockett, I'm going to whup you for giving me such a hard time." And they started the walk down Main Street towards their farms almost five miles out of town.

"When you get your strength back, I'll give you the chance. Though I don't want any complaints from you after I have you on the ground."

"Hah!" Patrick said. "Since when did you think you can whup me in a wrasslin' match? I must have been sick longer than I thought for you to get that idea in your head."

James laughed as their boots sounded on the plankings of the sidewalk.

"Where is everyone anyway?" Patrick said, "The town seems half empty."

Pursing his lips, James noticed that Patrick was right. There was little activity on the sidewalks or in the stores, even fewer horses tied up.

"I don't know. The weather's not too bad," he answered, noticing a wagon coming down a side street towards them. Recognizing the figure at the reins, James waved and called out, "Zeke!"

"Boys!" Ezekiel Wilson said in a surprised voice. "What are you two doing back?"

Twenty years their elder, both James and Patrick had known Ezekiel for their entire lives, which wasn't surprising because his farm was just down the road from theirs.

"Term of enlistment is up," Patrick answered.

"Patrick's been sick, and I'm here to make sure that he gets back okay," James added.

"You do look a mite peaked," Zeke commented. "Skinny too. Don't they feed you boys in the army?"

"He's been fighting a fever for weeks," James explained.

"Have you talked to my father or Martha lately?" Patrick interrupted anxiously.

"No, no," Ezekiel said in a reflective voice. "No, I haven't lately, though I did hear a while back that she was sick. Been terribly busy since all you boys left."

"Oh," Patrick said with some disappointment.

"Want a ride back?" Zeke offered. "Just have to do one more errand. Won't take long, and you'll be back on the farm a lot sooner than walking."

"Be real obliged," James replied, fearful that Patrick would stubbornly decline to prove that he could make the walk.

"Well, get in," Zeke said. "I just need to drop off this barrel of dried apples and butter at the Moffat's."

Zeke lightly slapped the reins on the horse, and the wagon crawled along the dirt avenue, taking them into the neighborhood of large houses on the tree-lined streets east of Main Street. Though more impressive in the spring when the large trees were in bloom, the houses that they rode past were still something to see, especially when compared to Missouri. James had never realized before how well off Kalamazoo County was. Besides the influential people who owned the expensive, square brick houses, the farmers in the area were more prosperous than the Missourians. James imagined that it had a lot to do with the rich soil of the Celery Flats and Gun Plain, but some of it had to do with the bustling industry that had blossomed too. Furniture, barrel-making, paper, seemingly anything to do with wood could be made in Kalamazoo.

With the wrought-iron fences, impressive Gothic houses, and fancy dress, families like the Upjohns, Kelloggs, Moffats, and Burdicks had brought much to the county, James realized.

"You seem quiet," Zeke broke the silence, as James observed the scenery.

"Sorry, Zeke," James replied. "Just never noticed the extent of prosperity in our area."

"Not like that out west, eh?"

"Not like this."

"Well, I think everyone will be glad when this is over and everyone comes back, especially people like the Moffats."

"The Moffats? Why's that? He doesn't have any sons."

"No, but he's got plenty of businesses to run, and there's no one around here to work for him now."

James frowned in confusion.

"You see, James, you boys were just the first to leave. Since then, almost every able-bodied male in the county has enlisted somewhere, with somebody."

"Really?"

"So many that Governor Blair is offering volunteers to other states to help fill their quotas for President Lincoln."

"That many?"

"The state is ablaze, James. On fire with patriotic zeal. Well, I guess, I don't need to tell you that. You were one of the first to volunteer. Why, if I was a younger man, I'd be gone myself."

"Lucinda wouldn't like that."

"Probably not, but she wouldn't say nothin'. Warring is part of her blood."

Like a number of others, Zeke had married one of the Potawatomie Indians still living in the area.

"Warring? She's Potawatomie," Patrick laughed. "They've never been known for fighting."

"Not against the white man, but they had plenty of history before we got here," Zeke maintained. "Her brother is even enlisting."

"He is?"

"But he's an Injun."

"Some of 'em are enlisting too."

James raised his eyebrows in surprise. Though there was a significant Indian population in the area, they had lived peacefully for as long as James could remember. Many of them had been Christianized and joined the white man's society, but he didn't know that they had Christianized to this extent.

"I can't believe they would enlist to fight," James said, thinking aloud.

"The county's blood is up," Zeke said. "Reverend Bailey and all the others have stirred everyone up. I s'pose it shouldn't be a surprise, this area has always felt strongly 'bout slavery and the Union."

"I guess there's no better way to end it quick than to have everyone possible take up arms," James reflected more to himself than to the others.

Zeke pulled the wagon through the short, half-moon circle drive and onto the sidelane entrance at the Moffat's. Though seemingly a simple square Gothic design like many of the other houses, the Moffat's house had an air of prosperity that was difficult to match. Whether it was the perfect whitewash coating or the polish of the oil lamps, James didn't know. But there was definitely a feeling that these people had done well.

"Say, James," Zeke said, "I don't s'pose I could convince you to help me carry this barrel of apples in the house?"

"So this is why you offered us a ride home. You need help with your fields probably too," James joked. Just as James hopped out of the wagon, the rear door of the house opened and Mrs. Moffat appeared.

"In the root cellar as usual, ma'am?" Zeke said, doffing his floppy hat.

"Yes, Mr. Wilson," she said as she was joined by a girl about James's age, with rosy cheeks, becoming even redder in the cold.

"Katherine!" her mother scolded. "Get back inside, you'll freeze to death out here."

"It's not bad today," Katherine maintained evenly, her eyes never leaving the blue-uniformed soldier helping Zeke with the apples and butter.

"Don't expect sympathy from me if you get sick, my daughter." Mrs. John Moffat left it at that. Too many times she had tried to teach her eldest daughter the proper and wise way of doing things. But often the girl, who looked like her mother, acted with a stubbornness that was like the father. "John," Louisa Moffat would say to her husband, "that daughter of yours is truly a Moffat. With obstinacy like that, it's amazing I can even talk to her." John Moffatt, of course, always replied that she had married a stubborn man so there must be something Louisa liked about it. To which, Louisa would always turn away with a huff.

Unaware of the audience, James took the first step down the root cellar with the barrel of apples. With his back to the darkness, he slowly felt around with his foot for the step, and then the next.

"Got it?" Zeke asked.

"Got i——!" James replied, just as his foot slipped off the last step. Tripping backwards, he landed straight on his back. The barrel slipped from Zeke's grasp, and it came down full force on James's chest. Instinctively, James grabbed the barrel and held it tight to keep it from crashing and splitting open.

"James? You okay?" Zeke asked.

With the wind knocked out of him, he could not reply that the barrel was still intact and that he was fine.

"James?" Zeke said again.

Still holding the barrel on top of his chest, James craned his head around to the side. The brightness of the day contrasted completely with the pitch-blackness of the root cellar. Then, like an eclipse the light was blocked by two more heads peering down into the root cellar.

"Are you hurt?" James heard a pleasant woman's voice say.

Finally able to reply, James said, "Caught the barrel, Zeke. It's okay."

Chuckling to himself, Zeke hopped down the last step, rolling the barrel off James and righting it. "What a clod. I think I'll do the butter myself."

"Are you all right?" came the heavenly voice again. Looking up in the brightness, James could only make out a shadowy shape. Oddly, with the bright light and clouds in the background, the shape appeared to James almost like that of an angel. Only as he ascended the steps could he tell that it was not a messenger from heaven but an attractive girl about his age.

Her light brown hair was swept up and back, and she looked at him with a gentle, youthful face atop a slender neck. As she stepped back, James thought she moved with an almost regal bearing. Her blue eyes watched him with some concern, but there was also a hint of laughter in the tiny curves of her lips.

Realizing that he was staring at her, James stammered, "Just my...just my pride is hurt, that's all."

"You're one of Captain Vincent's sharpshooters, aren't you?" she said, noticing the red scarf tucked tightly down inside his collar. With only a fraction of it showing, James was surprised she could recognize it.

"Yes, ma'am," he said, self-consciously brushing dirt off his creased and rumpled uniform. Katherine said nothing, but James sensed that she was enjoying his discomfort.

For her part, Katherine also felt peculiar. She couldn't tell whether the goose bumps on her arm were caused by the cold or by the blushing soldier busily trying to straighten months' worth of wrinkles out of his uniform. She looked at his limp brown hair and plain face, knowing there was nothing unusual about them, but it was the clarity in his gray-blue eyes that she noticed from the start. She couldn't remember seeing eyes such as his before. So clear and vibrant, they looked like the eyes that belonged to a man of great knowledge and courage, she thought. Of course, neither of those aspects were readily apparent by the rest of his actions, but that didn't stop her young mind from churning.

"Katherine!" her mother said in a voice she rarely used. "Thank you for your concern for the young man, but I want you inside right now before you catch pneumonia."

Katherine looked at her mother about to argue again, but seeing the rare look of determination on her mother's face, and having heard the serious voice, she relented. "Yes, mother." Turning towards the soldier, she added, "I'm glad you are not hurt. It was nice to meet you, Mr...."

"Lockett. James Lockett," he said hurriedly.

"Inside," her mother ordered again, waving her away. Hearing the door close and with Zeke closing up the root cellar, Mrs. Moffat added, "Thank you for your assistance, Mr. Lockett."

The wagon bounced along the mildly rutted roads, and they made their way back to the farms. Patrick was still looking out ahead when he said to no one in particular, "That was strange."

"What was?" James said, anxious to do anything to pull his mind away from visions of Katherine.

"I think Big John Moffat's daughter was making eyes at you."

Patrick looked at his father standing in the door frame of the house that Patrick had labored over during the previous summer. The elder McManus had opened the door wide at the sound of Zeke's noisy wagon creaking to a stop.

Zeke was already back on the dirt road to his house, but Patrick and James were anchored in their spots. No one said a word.

"Do you want me to go in with you?" James asked hesitantly, his eyes were still on the hardened mask that the elder McManus wore. Balding on top, with his reddish-blond hair mixing with gray, Patrick's father was beginning to develop a stoop that James had never noticed before. Had they been gone that long?

"No," Patrick finally answered in a quiet voice. "I'll come fetch you later." Taking a step forward with a fear greater than any he had known before, Patrick started forward.

"I'm sorry, Patrick. She tried to hang on...," the elder McManus's voice cracked, and James noticed that the hard Irish eyes were filled with tears.

The small gravesite behind the tidy house looks so empty, so out of place underneath the clump of birch trees. I fear two people were buried today. Martha is surely in the cold earth beneath those trees. We knew that the congestive lungs had taken her, but I fear that the Patrick McManus, who I have known since I was a boy, is gone now too.

I know that gasping look of hopelessness. It is the same as the one I wore after father died.

Patrick shed no tears, but I know that look.

He dug the hole where she lays. He insisted it despite his weakened condition. From where the strength came, I do not know. I hope it did more for him than digging father's did for me.

—The Diary of James Lockett

February 6, 1862

"Tell me more about this battle," Daniel Lockett insisted again.

James looked irritably at his brother as they rode along in the wagon. Since he had returned, Daniel's questions inevitably turned back to life in the army, and despite his best efforts, no amount of glossing over the facts was acceptable for his younger brother. With the town of Kalamazoo now within sight, James did not feel like going into life as a sharpshooter, though truth be told, he did find himself missing it. "I don't suppose you'll just pipe down and let us go to Doyle's and then back."

"James!" Daniel said impatiently. "You've hardly told me anything since you've returned. Every time you say, 'Wait until Mother is not around' or 'Wait until Thomas and Jonathan are asleep.' I'm still not sure when you'll go back. I know that you came back to help Patrick, but when will you rejoin the sharpshooters?"

"Don't know, Daniel. I still haven't thought much about when I'll go back to the army."

"But if you don't go back—"

"And no, you can't go either!" Frowning, James looked at the boyish face of his younger brother. "I can see right through you, Daniel. No, you can't sign up. You need to run the farm."

Undeterred that his plot had been so transparent, Daniel quickly responded, "But if you don't go back, you can watch the farm."

"No, Daniel."

"But that's what you want to do. You don't want to fight."

James reined the horse in so suddenly that they jerked forward. "That's where you're wrong, Daniel. You've never been so wrong! I want to fight!" There was a menace in his voice, and an emotive conviction that startled him. He had seen James angry before, but this was different. It took him a moment to realize what it was. It was *passion*.

"I want to fight," James continued, reflecting on how true those words actually were. Though he had never realized it until now, he wanted to be fighting. He couldn't explain it, not to Daniel or even himself, but he knew his place was to be fighting the Rebels, not back on a farm in Kalamazoo. It wasn't a patriotic fervor or boyish romanticism, he realized. It was something else entirely. He had never thought much about his future or destiny; the family had always been too hard-pressed to think about that. But at this moment, sitting in a wagon with his brother, James came to the realization that he had a destiny, and that it was to be a soldier in blue.

Finally looking at his brother again, he added, "But it won't be with the sharpshooters, Daniel." For the next hour, Daniel sat in mesmeric silence as James related every detail of what had transpired in Missouri: from the stolen silver to the cowardice at Hallsville to the murder of little Amelia.

"Ah, James!" Ruth Doyle cried from behind the counter of the general store. "Welcome back." Waddling toward him, Josiah Doyle's wife threw her thick arms around James. "Sorry you had to return home under such circumstances. Such a good friend you are to Patrick." Stepping back, and admiring the blue coat that James still wore. "Still in uniform, I see. When do you return?"

"Not long, ma'am," James said as Daniel busied himself with hunting for their wares. Exactly where or how he would get back, James didn't know, but he *was* going to find a way back into the fight.

"But where is your red scarf?" a soft womanly voice said. Turning in surprise, James found himself face-to-face with Katherine. Her teasing blue eyes made him think that he was the object of some joke, but the friendly smile on her red lips changed his mind. Unperturbed by James's silence and staring, Katherine boldly extended her hand, "So nice to see you again, Mr. Lockett."

"James, please," he said, taking her small hand. Fearing that such a small and smooth hand would be fragile in his grasp, he squeezed only lightly and was surprised by the powerful grip she delivered. She smiled in satisfaction at the look on his face.

With a bemused sigh, Ruth silently withdrew from the conversation. Katherine had a reputation for impetuous behavior that rankled some in Kalamazoo, but Ruth found her spirit quite admirable and well suited to life in western Michigan. Now what Katherine saw in the quiet, ever serious James Lockett, Ruth had no idea, but it would certainly make for good gossip.

"I was very sad to hear about your friend's wife. I had no idea."

Nodding, James said nothing, not at all surprised that word had spread quickly.

"You must be a good friend," she added, "to accompany a sick friend all the way back home."

His gray eyes showed no reaction, but silently he studied her. Was she hinting at something else? She seemed to be insinuating something else. Or was that just her manner? He could not tell. "Anyone would have done the same," he finally answered. Something about those striking blue eyes and that long, slender neck was making him uncomfortable, and he could feel himself sweating beneath all of the layers of winter clothing.

"We heard the Rebels caught you by surprise in Missouri. Was it bad?"

"It was certainly not good," James answered more evasively than he intended. He suddenly remembered the backs of Long and Walker as they ran from the bushwhackers. He had half a mind to mention that their task was made impossible by the incompetence of their officers, but he didn't say anything. It wouldn't help matters now, and Katherine could surely care less. She was just making polite conversation, however pointed her style.

"But it sounds like you made up for it the next day."

James gazed quizzically at her.

"And now that you chased the Rebels from Missouri, the Western Sharpshooters are on their way to a new state."

"What?"

"Oh, yes, I suppose you couldn't know that," she said truthfully. "It was only telegraphed here yesterday."

"What?" He could tell that she took pride in knowing something that he did not.

"I'm sorry. I sometimes forget myself. Lieutenant Long sends my family letters quite regularly, and my father owns the telegraph office—"

"Lieutenant...Long?" James said, feeling the bile rise in his throat.

"Yes."

"Orrin Long? He is your fiancé?"

"Well, not fiancé...yet."

Knowing that an impassive mask had dropped across his face, James felt some relief knowing that Katherine had no idea of the bubbling rage inside of him. Just the thought of Long was enough to roil him like no one ever had. The twinge of jealousy that Long was courting Katherine certainly didn't help, although James reminded himself that he was just a farmer and had no reason to be jealous.

The door to the general store opened with a blast of cold air.

"Ah, there you are, Cousin," a thin young man in an officer's uniform said. Noticing the soldier next to her, he added, "Oh, hello there."

"Ainsley," Katherine broke in immediately, "I want you to meet James Lockett of the Kalamazoo Sharpshooters."

Reaching his hand out only after realizing that the lieutenant had already extended his, James cautiously said, "James, please, sir."

"Ainsley Stuart."

"Lieutenant Ainsley Stuart," Katherine corrected.

"I think I should salute you, sir," James said seriously although their hands were still locked in a handshake.

"That's quite all right, James. I'm actually not official yet. I was only wearing the uniform to show my cousin here."

"You look dashing," she said.

"Dashing?" he laughed. "You are too kind, Katherine. Anyone can see that a gangly, long-nosed fellow like myself is anything but dashing."

"I still say you look dashing."

"So you're one of those who volunteered with Vincent?" Ainsley said to James. "How have you found the enemy so far?"

"Tough, sir," James said honestly.

Surprised by his answer, Katherine interrupted, "Surely you exaggerate. From what Orrin, I mean Lieutenant Long, tells me, it will all be over quickly."

James instantly realized that he had an opportunity to give Katherine a taste of her own medicine, and the bile that rose in him at the mere mention of Long cleared his conscience. With a dose of her arrogance and a touch of his own sarcasm, he replied, "Been fighting a few Rebels up here, ma'am?" He took petty joy in her astonished face. "No, it won't be over soon, Miss Moffat. I think we have only seen the beginning of this."

Before Katherine could argue, as she was prone to do, Ainsley broke in, "I agree completely, James. Few of my Northern friends concur of course, but I do not think the Southerners will lose one battle and simply give up. I had many friends in Washington, most of them now on the other side. They are smart and courageous, and they absolutely believe in what they are doing. I believe you are right, James. We have our work cut out for us to preserve this Union."

"Now Ainsley—"

"And too many of us are unfamiliar with battle," he continued, looking at his cousin. "Men like yourself are at a premium for the Union, James. You've been in battle and know what it is like."

"You are more right than you know," James said softly, remembering Long's turned back.

"What are you doing back here anyway?"

"He came back to help his friend."

"Oh, yes, I remember hearing about you now. I imagine you'll be rejoining your friends again soon."

"Actually, my term of enlistment is up now, and it sounds like they are already on the move elsewhere."

"Really?" Ainsley said. He stopped in thought. With a sly smile, he looked at James. "We could surely use some experienced men. Have you ever considered a transfer?"

"Transfer?"

"Yes, to the 12th Michigan. We could surely use some experienced sergeants. All of the boys are as inexperienced as I am."

"Twelfth Michigan?"

"Yes, Colonel Quinn is raising a new regiment in Niles."

"Never thought much about it," James said slowly, wondering what kind of officer the informal and friendly Ainsley Stuart would make. With a long, thin frame and narrow face, he certainly looked more bookish than rugged, but James knew he shouldn't hold that against a man. Long looked for all the world like a romantic hero, and he clearly was not. The question was, did this friendly, yet aristocratic-looking, Stuart have the courage to face the fire and advance into it?

"You don't need to decide now, but if you want to join, I can arrange it. Come see me tomorrow. I'm staying with Uncle John."

With one last look at Katherine's still glowering face, James heard himself chuckle. "Until tomorrow then, Lieutenant."

Luke's father always says that the Lord works in mysterious ways. The older I become, the more I seem to find proof of that. Today, I found a way back into the fight. I pray that the situation is a better one than the last.

I convinced Patrick to come with me. There is nothing for him here, not right now at least. It does him no good to stare out that window to his wife's grave all day. He takes no visitors other than me, even his father. I pray this new journey we embark on heals him, for surely the last journey nearly destroyed him.

—The Diary of James Lockett

February 7, 1862

Dear Sister,

Thank you for the kind letter. I received it two days ago when we arrived in St. Louis. We left Sturgeon on the 4th via the North Missouri Railroad. None of us will miss the place. Our mood has brightened considerably since we first heard the news that we were to rejoin the war and let the local militias and provost guard worry about the few bushwhackers that remain in Missouri. Finally, we think our sharp-shooting will be put to good use. That is, if there is still a war on!

News of the fall of Fort Henry just reached us. It sounds like the Rebels scattered without even a good fight and retreated to Fort Donelson. While we sit here on the steamer Belle Memphis, *the war may be ending. First, we steamed down the Mississippi from St. Louis arriving in Cairo, Illinois. A more impressive sight, I have never seen as all these giant paddlewheels splash the muddy waters of the great river. With so many ships and men, I wonder why we do not just sail right on down to New Orleans and get it over with. But alas, after reaching Cairo yesterday, we steamed up the Ohio River to Paducah, Kentucky. At this moment, we are on our way up the Tennessee River to Fort Henry. I am told we should be there by morning.*

As you probably know, James and Patrick left with some of the others who were discharged due to illness. The rest of us however have reenlisted for three years like everyone else. Of course, the war will be over long before then and we will be home, but it is good to know that all of the other sharpshooters feel so strongly about seeing this through.

Give my regards to father and all else. I will be home soon.

Your loving brother,

Matthew

February 8, 1862

They waited. And waited. Like the slow downward crawl of the brown mud from the banks of the Tennessee, the men of Birge's Western Sharpshooters made no progress over the hours. While the mud sought to slide into the river, the sharpshooters sought to leave the river for the mud-mired shoreline. They had made the Landing hours ago, yet for some reason, there were no orders for them to disembark. So they waited, and waited.

For days the grand steam transports ploughed through the darkened waters, their giant wheels slapping against its own froth. The two Union gunboats who had joined them on this journey had continued on, leaving the troop-ladened transports behind, but the troops still lingered impatiently on the decks of the transports.

The men milled about where they could on the overcrowded steamers, still conscious of the steamer pilot's warning about keeping an even number of men on either side of the boat. It seemed ridiculous that a boat the size of the *Belle Memphis* could capsize if all of the men rushed to one rail to see something. Impossible, yet something about the coal-eyed look of the pilot had convinced the men, not to test it. Some men who couldn't swim, like Sam Barker, went out of their way to enforce the policy.

While the men grumbled, gambled, and guzzled illicit liquor hidden in their canteens, Luke looked out across the rail to where the *Belle Memphis*'s sister ship was moored. He tipped his hat to another soldier staring back at him. With his wide-brimmed slouch hat, the man was clearly another Western soldier, and Luke tried to pass the time guessing where the man was from. Illinois? Iowa? The man shrugged in reply, as if to say that he too had no idea why they are still on these darn boats.

It was warm, like spring, despite what the calendar said, and the *Belle* reeked of sweaty men packed too close together. Even the sinking of the sun into a brilliant pinkish orange orb did little to reduce the heat. Once it became completely dark, Luke was sure that the chill of night would descend on them just as it had for the past two nights. The men would huddle back to back all across the deck in their filthy blankets so that there was hardly room for one to walk.

A rumor had started hours ago that the delay was caused by the wholesale capitulation of Confederate forces. The pounding of Fort Henry had finally convinced the Rebs of the futility of their task. Of course, a few hours later the officers dispelled that notion. The war wasn't over.

Yet they still waited.

Wordlessly, Lieutenant Simon joined Luke at the rail. For a full five minutes they watched the sun sink lower and lower in companionable silence.

"No coffee tonight," Simon finally commented.

"No warm anything."

The second worst thing about the steamboat was that there was no place to light a fire to cook a meal or to heat some coffee. On the trip up the river, some of the men had figured out that the exhaust pipes that ran through the charthouse could be used to boil a coffee pot, but tonight the *Belle* wasn't going anywhere, and there was no exhaust.

They lapsed into silence for a few moments more before Luke asked, "Officer of the Guard again tonight, Lieutenant?"

"Of course," Simon smiled cheerfully, although to Luke it seemed nothing to smile about. To him, the duty should rotate at least once to Lieutenant Long or maybe even Captain Vincent, yet every night it was always Lieutenant Simon. Still, if the same thought ever crossed Simon's mind, he gave no hint of it.

Luke knew Simon well enough now to know that the lieutenant was no fool, and any fool could tell that Captain Vincent and his nephew took advantage of their positions, or at least were able to bully the junior officer into additional chores. Yet Simon never said an ill word against either. Even when he had helped James find a graceful exit, Simon had said nothing about Long's actions despite knowing the truth.

That was the price of being the junior lieutenant, Luke surmised, and if that was what it meant to be a junior officer, Luke was certain he wanted no part of it. Simon's position entailed all the responsibility and work without any benefits. At least as a private, Luke didn't have to worry about responsibility or dealing with Vincent or Long directly.

A fish jumped out of the water and came down with a loud splash, causing Luke's head to suddenly jerk upwards. With a frown he realized how petty his thoughts had become, and he reminded himself of the bigger picture, the greater cause at hand. Slavery.

"You okay, Luke?" Lieutenant Simon smiled, his scarred cheek wrinkling in a grotesque manner giving the meek officer a ghoulish appearance. Realizing that Luke's eyes were on the still pinkish scar tissue, he stopped smiling. "Pretty horrible, isn't it?"

"Sorry, sir. No, not all. I didn't mean to stare."

"But you were," Simon said accurately. "It's okay. I'd stare at it myself if it wasn't a physical impossibility."

"But it's not what you think, sir. It doesn't look bad."

"Luke," Simon laughed out loud, "you're a terrible liar."

Behind them the grumbling murmur of the sharpshooters changed tone and volume. Men who had been sitting playing cards, writing letters, or reading in the last light of the day suddenly stood up and gathered around the commotion.

"That's the worst part of this," Simon said to Luke as he started to push his way through the crowd. "Too much idle time leads to squabbles."

The wall of human resistance slowly melted away in front of Lieutenant Simon as the soldiers realized that an officer was trying to push his way into the commotion. At the center of it, Walker loomed over another man who was trying to struggle to his feet, nose trickling dark red blood. Yanking the man up by the hair, Walker lowered another meaty fist into the side of the man's head, dropping him to his knees.

Simon noticed playing cards strewn across the planks of the deck and an empty liquor bottle. "Corporal Walker!" he yelled, the words drawing attention only after Walker fired one last punch that put his victim flat on his back. "That's enough!" Simon said, irritated that Walker was not heeding him. "Come to attention, now!"

"Or what?" Walker sneered, turning now to face the much smaller officer.

Even from two arm lengths away, Simon could smell the heavy stench of liquor on the man's breath. Combined with the man's overall dirty and unkempt appearance, greasy tangled beard, and wild eyes, Walker looked more animal than human. He was what most men knew as a bad drunk. But Simon was unaccustomed to dealing with men such as Walker. "Or I'll have you arrested for insubordination," the lieutenant said, his voice sounding meek and chirpish next to Walker's deep, gurgling bass.

"Insubordination?" Walker guffawed. He stopped suddenly. "I'll show you insubordination." With surprising speed and dexterity for his inebriated state, he yanked free his long hunting knife from its sheath and lunged forward, the tip of the knife pointing directly at the middle of Simon's chest.

Stunned beyond belief, the officer froze and watched the silver point of the sharp-edged knife plunge toward his heart. He blinked, and his face twisted into one of confusion when at the last moment, the progress of the knife stopped instantly, as if it had hit an invisible brick wall. Taking his focus off the knife point, Simon's eyes followed up Walker's arm. Like everyone else, he was surprised to see the two strong hands of Luke clenched like a vise around Walker's thick forearm.

Walker frowned, equally surprised at the intrusion and at the powerful grip of the preacher boy. For a moment, neither man made another move. Then Walker's grisly face contorted again, and he took a step to the side to improve his leverage against Luke, but he slipped in the spilt liquor and wet poker cards, and Luke released his grip, letting him fall square on his back. The knife clattered from Walker's hand upon impact, and there was silence on the deck.

Finding his voice again, Lieutenant Simon shouted orders to the men behind Walker. "Grab that man! He's under arrest!" And dutifully the three Wisconsin boys from Company A grabbed the man who had cheated and then pummeled their comrade.

Simon's scarred face gave Luke a look of muted thanks. Luke simply nodded and stepped back, satisfied that the others had control of Walker.

"Clear the way!" Simon shouted forcefully to the crowd, as they marched Walker off to Captain Vincent's quarters on the second deck.

It was early morning with the sky just beginning to lighten when Luke joined Lieutenant Simon at the ship rail. Most of the men were just beginning to stir. Some complaining about sore backs, most just generally grumbling unintelligible words.

"Coffee?" Luke said, offering a tin cup to the lieutenant.

"Thank you, yes. How did you manage that?" Simon queried, hungrily taking the steaming cup. He took a long drink and felt the warmth course down his throat and into his stomach, taking some of the morning chill off his tired body.

"You look tired, Lieutenant."

"I feel tired, Luke." There was an brief pause before Simon added. "I didn't get a chance to—"

"No need, sir. It was just a reaction. If I had thought about it, I probably would have froze up. I just saw what was happening, and something in me reacted."

"Good thing too."

"Definitely a good thing, sir," Luke smiled.

"Luke," Simon hesitated, "I don't know quite how to say this, but you need to keep your eyes open."

"Sir?"

"Last night, Captain Vincent and Lieutenant Long, they—God knows why, but—they decided to give Walker one more chance."

"What!" Luke fairly yelled, drawing startling looks from those still stirring.

"Believe me," Simon said, lowering his voice, "no one is more angry about it than I am, but Orrin convinced the captain not to court-martial Walker. Something Walker said to him before we started spooked Orrin. I don't know what, but whatever it was, it was enough to make him fight to keep Walker out of trouble just this once."

"But he tried to kill you last night!"

"Oh, I know," Simon said. His scarred cheek puckered into a sardonic grin, and there was almost a humorous tone of acceptance in his voice. "But there's little more that I can do about it now."

"This is absurd. This is galling," Luke fumed.

"There is one piece of good news," Simon said gently.

"What's that?" Luke said in a voice that made it obvious he was thinking about something else.

"You're the new corporal."

"Huh?"

"Corporal Bailey."

"Are you crazy,...sir?"

"Not at all," Simon said, ignoring Luke's lack of protocol. "You're the perfect choice. Captain Vincent agrees. Obviously, Walker couldn't go completely unpunished, so Captain Vincent took his stripe away. Rather than open it up to election again and give Walker or his friends the chance to bribe or bully his way in again, the captain has just appointed you the new corporal."

"But I can't do that."

"Of course you can. Of all the men in the company, you're the most natural leader. The men, excepting Walker's cronies, respect you. They've been looking to you for spiritual leadership for quite a while now. They might as well look to you on the battlefield too. Besides, we're talking about corporal, not captain. It's not like it will be up to you to lead us into battle."

"But...," the words lost themselves in Luke's mouth as he suddenly remembered the paralyzing fear of Hallsville.

February 9, 1862

Dear Father,

We never know the path God's divine guidance leads us on.

I know you still harbor second thoughts about my enlistment, and I too have shared those doubts from time to time. But after each prayer to our Heavenly Father, the answer always come back that this is what He wants. I do not understand, but obey.

I have been made a corporal for the company though I never sought it out. I can only attribute this to some greater plan, for I seem ill prepared for any type of responsibility other than shepherding souls.

We are at Fort Henry now, Admiral Andrew Foote having pushed out the Rebels with his gunboats. It seems odd that we are now in barracks that just last week were occupied by the Rebel's 10th Tennessee.

Your Crusading Son,

Luke

The afternoon sun was warm, and Luke was beginning to wonder whether Matthew was right, maybe spring did come early to Tennessee.

Matthew and a number of others had left the earthen fort with a pass to sight their rifles, and Luke knew that he should do the same. Of all the men, he needed the practice the most, but he held back and satisfied himself with cleaning the Dimick. Though the idea of pointing it at another man still seemed unnatural, at least the chore of cleaning and oiling the rifle had become second nature.

A cool shadow across his body blocked the warm sun, and he looked up to see the greasy, brutish features of Hiram Walker and the threatening scowl of Bart Randle.

"I've got a score to settle with you, preacher boy," Walker said belligerently. "Because of you, I lost my stripe and the extra pay that goes with it."

Surprised by the poise he felt, Luke rose to his feet and stood straight and tall, looking down on the thick-chested Walker. In an even voice, he answered, "Because of me, you're still with the company and not locked in chains for murder in front of a hundred witnesses." With a pause, Luke added, "You should thank me."

Luke's words brought on a brief silence, and a look of confusion but only for a brief moment. A second later, the scowl was back. "Don't try foolin' me, preacher boy. You cost me my stripe, and I'm not goin' to forget it. And if you think I'll take an order from you..." He slowly withdrew the large hunting knife from its sheath. Its shining blade had obviously just been sharpened.

"You'll what, *Private*?" a voice barked from behind them, emphasizing the last word. Randle and Walker turned to face Sergeant VanderJagt's equally fierce glare. When nothing was said, the Dutchman prodded further, "You'll what, private? I want to make sure I hear you correctly."

The toughness of Walker's scowl paled in comparison to the furrowed lines in old VanderJagt's thick skin.

"Nothing," Walker finally muttered through clenched teeth, barely at an audible level. Without another word, he and Randle turned and departed. VanderJagt let them go and gave Luke a shrug.

"Fun, ain't it?"

"Fun?"

"Keep your rifle nearby when you sleep and a hand on your hunting knife, son."

"I don't have a hunting knife."

"No knife?" VanderJagt said with a pause, "Then you really do have problems." He laughed in an odd way and left Luke standing there, dumbfounded.

February 10, 1862

There were a few light flurries blowing around Kalamazoo despite the fact that the sun was shining through a break in the clouds. Long, daggerlike icicles dangled off the steep rooftop of the Moffat house, but inside the warm fires and thick rugs made it comfortable.

Katherine looked at the three blue-uniformed men in the parlor. The color of the uniform seemed to be the only thing that they shared in common. Her cousin Ainsley looked so thin and frail in his uniform. In spite of the tailor's efforts, it still hung on his naturally gaunt frame like a half-askew drapery. And even with the golden trim and markings of an officer, he looked so much younger than James Lockett and Patrick McManus. She knew they were the same age, Ainsley had told her such, but it was hard to believe when they were all directly before her.

The two farmboys looked so much stronger and older with the etchings around their eyes and mouth that spoke of the grimness and ardor that they had long since been accustomed to. She focused on James's cautious nervousness. While he could talk light and airy like Ainsley, there was a wariness in his eyes that could not be missed, and

Katherine half wondered whether the tall, wiry farmer was hiding something.

But her suspicions were fleeting. It was much more interesting to concentrate on the awkward discomfort that James displayed from being around her. It had been unmistakable ever since she entered the parlor. She found it somewhat flattering, but mostly just amusing.

James realized that Katherine was looking at his feet, and for an instant, he was certain that he had tramped mud onto the expensive rugs. He had no doubt that the plush red beneath his boot sole cost more than the farm could make in an entire year. With a grimace, he could feel himself blushing, and he looked away, out into the foyer and the broad staircase leading to the second floor. The carved wooden railing of the staircase mesmerized him. James had never seen such detail put into a house, never even considered it. From the diamond pattern engraved in the nine-foot archways above the doors to the curved legs of the furniture, nothing in the house did not speak of regal elegance. To James, it was impossible to believe that the lacquered wood of the Moffat house was the same material as the plain, unadorned wood of his simple farmhouse. This was how royalty lived, he imagined.

Even the brass of the oil lamp appeared unnaturally polished as the sunlight danced off it from the rose-colored parlor window.

Without thinking, he began to twist the toe of his boot into the thick red carpet. In all his life, he had never spent much time thinking about wealth. He was satisfied when his family put food on the table, so the lifestyle of the Moffats was like nothing he had ever imagined. For the first time in his life, James realized that they were *poor*!

He wondered whether Patrick was thinking the same thing, but before he could contemplate it much longer, Katherine's voice interrupted him. "I'm sorry that father and mother could not be here to give you a proper good-bye, Ainsley." Even as she said it, Katherine winced inwardly. There was that word again, *proper*. How she hated that word, yet more and more she found it slipping into her own speech.

"Nonsense," Ainsley said. "This is marvelous. I understand that Uncle John had business to take care of in Detroit, and that Aunt Louisa wanted to see Detroit again. Besides, no one knew that I would be needed at the regiment so soon."

James said nothing. He was glad that neither of Katherine's parents were here. He had a pretty good idea that if Katherine's mother had been here, his soiled boots would never have seen the inside of the Moffat's parlor. And though, being this close to Katherine made him more uncomfortable than any Missouri plains' wind had, he perceived a type of elation just being in the same room with her.

All the while, however, he chided himself for his naive, foolish thoughts. Patrick was right. He was just a farmer, and he could never have a future with someone like Katherine.

"Well, James, do I look the part?" Ainsley said cheerily, his hand resting on the hilt of the family sword that he was so proud of. He had already related the entire history of the sword to James and Patrick, how it had been specially made to fight the British in the Revolution and then used again thirty years later in 1812.

It was an exquisite creation, there was no doubt. Streaming, meandering vines of bronze and silver formed a protective cocoon around the swordsman's hand. James found himself wondering whether it would actually protect one's hand in battle, and who had made the sword—a craftsman or a sculptor?

Ainsley drew the blade from the scabbard, making a sound like a vengeful phantom being awoken. The freshly oiled blade gleamed in the light.

"Looks fit for a prince, sir," Patrick said in an admiring tone. "Needs some sharpening though, I think."

Again, James couldn't help but wonder about his new officer. Was Ainsley Stuart a cowardly son of privilege, like Orrin Long?

"Yes," Ainsley agreed to Patrick's assessment, "but there should be plenty of time to correct that. She is a jewel, is she not? Our family jewel, I suppose."

"Yes, sir, Lieutenant," James answered.

Ainsley frowned at him. "James," he said with some consternation.

"I know, sir," James said stubbornly.

"I understand your point about proper deference when we are in front of the men, but please call me by my Christian name when possible."

"It's not about deference, sir," Patrick spoke up. Though he liked the young lieutenant and appreciated his efforts to curb the arrogance that some officers felt, Patrick knew that Ainsley had little idea of what he was getting himself into. "It's about discipline, sir. Don't worry about whether the men like you or not. It's about whether or not they'll follow you. You're going to ask them to do things that don't make much sense, but they have to do it anyway, without thinking."

Katherine bristled at Patrick's rebuke. Regardless of whether it was well intended or not, it sounded to Katherine like a reprimand, and Ainsley was an officer after all. Worse yet, Patrick had made the comment in front of her. Despite her first instinct, though, she held her tongue and waited for Ainsley to reply, but to her dismay, Ainsley's response left much to be desired.

"Well said, Patrick," Ainsley said, nodding appreciatively. "But I would still prefer to go by my Christian name when possible."

Patrick looked at James with a serious look and then broke out in a short laugh. "Alright, Ainsley. Though it does sound a bit peculiar in my mouth. Maybe Mr. Stuart?"

"Ainsley," the officer replied with an amused grimace. "Nobody calls me Mr. Stuart. That sounds like my father. Though I guess people usually refer to him as 'Senator'."

"Senator?" James said, looking away from Katherine's profile suddenly. "Your father is Senator Stuart?"

"Of course, you didn't know?" Ainsley said with some surprise of his own.

"I...I never made the connection," James stammered, in a state of shock.

"You didn't know that?" Patrick laughed. "What a blockheaded muck-farmer you are!" He laughed deeply, drowning out the laughs of Ainsley and Katherine.

James turned red-faced. There was no greater name in all of western Michigan than Senator Charles Stuart. "So that's why you said you lived in Washington D.C."

Ainsley nodded. "Lived there too long, although I always came back to Kalamazoo to spend the summers with Uncle John and Aunt Louisa. Washington gets unbearably hot in the summer."

February 12, 1862

The morning sun warmed Luke and the rest of the Western Sharpshooters. In rows of four, they tromped towards Fort Donelson as part of Colonel Jacob Lauman's brigade, along with the 2nd, 7th, and 14th Iowa, plus the 25th and 52nd Indiana.

Throughout the easy fifteen-mile march down the Dover Road to Fort Donelson, the excited chatter of messmates could be heard up and down the column. Then, they were stopping again for a rest. It was the second break already, and the rows of men fell out and lounged on a grassy pasture or leaned up against a tree.

"When are these Ai-o-way boys going to find their marching feet, *Corporal*?" Sam said to Luke. Sam and Matthew found particular glee in referring to Luke as corporal now.

"When I heard that it was fifteen miles away, I was a little worried myself," Pete said. "With all the riding we've done on the train and boat, I wasn't sure that my feet were ready for this again, but these green beans are in worse shape than I ever thought I could be."

"Yeah," Sam said, facing in the direction of a couple of Iowans, lounging nearby. "You boys sure march pretty, but you can hardly leave the fort before you need a rest."

One Iowan made a face, but they said nothing in reply to Sam's barb.

Sergeant VanderJagt walked heavily over to them and sat down.

"Tired, George?" Pete asked.

"Don't worry yourself, boy. There's no man in this regiment who cain' outmarch me. I only wish we would stop these infernal rest breaks."

"I agree," Matthew chipped in. "The battle will be over before we get there."

"Ha," VanderJagt snorted. "Wouldn't worry about that, Bauer. They won't start without us. You don't rush a fortified position like Donelson without a second thought or two. No sane man would at least, and I do believe our General Charles F. Smith is a sane man. Old, but sane."

"He is a mite old. I just hope he can lead us in battle. I don't want to stop to let our old general catch up."

"Ha," VanderJagt snorted again. "You obviously don't know much about General Smith. You needn't worry about him. He's an old regular. Seen him in action before. Once those guns start roaring, he becomes the damndest man I ever did see."

"Uh huh," Pete said, lying back and closing his eyes. "Bes' becuz we'll have to take Fort Donelson in a hurry. We took nothing with us but these army blankets, haversacks, and three days' rations."

"Don't forget the forty rounds of cartridges," Sam added.

"That's all a soldier needs," VanderJagt said with tone of finality.

"Well," Luke said in a reflective voice, "it does sound to me that we mean business this time. Three days' rations and no tents? This will be no siege I'd say. This will be real action."

"Hurray for that," Matthew said, leaning back and closing his eyes.

It was a little before dark when Lauman's Brigade arrived within a mile of the fort, joining the rest of General Smith's 2nd Division. Immediately, south of them, W. H. L. Wallace's Division hovered over the eastern approach. To the south of all of them, General John A. McClernand's troops guarded the Confederate positions south of the little town of Dover, which was inside the Rebel fortifications. It was difficult for Luke to imagine that their numbers were so great that they could line up shoulder to shoulder and form a four-mile ring around the enemy, but he had heard that was nearly the case.

As the sky grew even darker, the Union army formed a line of battle and stacked their arms. This only served to push the excitement level even higher for the anxious troops. It was plainly obvious to even the most inexperienced new soldier that the next day would bring a battle, and judging by the fact that they were already sleeping in line-of-battle formation, morning would still be fresh when they attacked the fort.

There were no fires in General Smith's lines, since they were too close to the fort and the batteries of Confederate cannon. Luke wondered whether the Rebels would surrender before the battle truly began, just like at Fort Henry. Somehow, he doubted that would happen again.

The titanic enormity of the task facing the entire nation seemed to fall on Luke's shoulders at that moment. He had seen the remnants of the fortifications at the earthen Fort Henry. It was said that Fort Donelson was a far superior position to hold, and that was why the Rebels had abandoned Fort Henry. If that was the case, Luke feared many a good Midwestern and Southern boy would die tomorrow.

He wondered whether the unseen, uncaring bullet would pick him out of the crowd tomorrow? Or would it find Matthew or Sam? Feeling himself suddenly desperate to read his Bible, he clenched the worn Good Book in his hand, knowing that there was no light from which to read it tonight.

Each man had wrapped himself in his blanket and formed a long, rolled line. Much like when they had been on the *Belle Memphis*, the soldiers were bunched tightly together, some men even shared their backs. Though it was not bitterly cold, it was still cool enough to be uncomfortable.

As he finished his long prayer to the Lord, he found the tightness in his chest had disappeared, and his breathing was slowly becoming more relaxed. Blissfully, Luke drifted off into a dreamless sleep.

February 13, 1862

The Kalamazoo Sharpshooters and the rest of Birge's Western Sharpshooters were roused before first light. Forming their lines at the front of the Lauman's Brigade, they waited. Five minutes dragged into an hour, then two, and impatiently, the men waited in their lines.

"Are we going to stand here all day?" Matthew muttered. "Let's get going."

"I guess General Smith is just making sure that everything is set before we start," Luke said, but his voice was questioning too.

Finally, Colonel Birge returned from his discussions with the general and faced his Western Sharpshooters. With their motley collection of hats and poor attention to detail in dress and posture, they looked like the dregs of the army. The Iowans in Lauman's Brigade marched with practiced precision, and their uniforms were still new and unadorned by individual touches. Rather than the slouch hats preferred by the Western Sharpshooters, the Iowans wore the short-billed caps, or kepis.

But Colonel Birge knew what this motley group was capable of. Though Company J was suspect, he had seen the rest of them overrun the bushwhackers' positions at Mount Zion Church in Missouri. Now, Birge was confident that they would prove their worth again, this time on a much larger scale. He ordered four companies of sharpshooters to the front in skirmish line, and they stepped forward. Lauman's entire brigade would be right behind them.

Luke and the rest of the Kalamazoo Sharpshooters formed their loose, uneven skirmish formation with Companies A, E, and H. In groups of two, they placed themselves in front of Lauman's Brigade, like the tentacles of an elongated blue beast. Their job was to locate the enemy line and drive in the pickets. As skirmishers, they would fight more like individuals than as a whole regiment. They would work in pairs, one covering while the other reloaded. They would advance in short sprints, crouch behind whatever cover was available. Fire at their own rate, fight their own personal battles with the Rebel sentries.

"Redemption, boys," VanderJagt muttered in a determined voice. There was no audible reply made, but Luke saw a number of heads nod. This was the chance for the Kalamazoo Sharpshooters to redeem themselves. They marched toward a small wooded ravine, anxious to butt heads with the Rebel skirmishers and pickets.

With the only sound being their canteens and cartridge boxes jangling against their sides, the skirmishers separated themselves from the main body and began their task of locating the enemy positions.

Luke found his heart pounding with excitement and dread at the same time. They were finally undertaking real action in God's war! But the fear of the unknown, shrouded in the woods ahead, made his feet heavy.

Crack!

The first sound of a shot shattered the morning air. After a momentary pause, there was a series of rifle reports and the sharpshooters to Luke's left began to reply.

Scanning the wood in front of him, Luke could see nothing but the brown and gray of trees and dead leaves. Suddenly two puffs of smoke appeared from the trees, and Luke heard the air above him zing with its first passing shot. Next to him, Matthew raised his rifle and fired at the puffs of smoke.

Luke wondered what he was aiming at, he still couldn't see anything in the woods. Then one of the grayish brown tree forms moved, and Luke realized that he had been looking directly at an enemy soldier. The color of their butternut uniforms blended in almost perfectly with the background!

He raised his rifle and fired at the moving form. Slowly, he lowered the rifle and felt a perverse disappointment when the butternut form did not fall.

The lurching motion of firing and reloading slowed the skirmishers' progress, but the advance was unhalting. They would shoot, kneel to reload, and move forward ten yards before starting the process again. Gradually the distance between the skirmishers and the sentries closed, shrinking from rifle range to musket range. The closer the sharpshooters got, the greater the fire coming out of the tree line. White-gray bursts of smoke sprouted all along the leaveless tree line.

Gus jumped back in startlement as something slapped against the base of his Dimick while he reloaded. Curiously, he studied the solitary ball of buckshot that was buried in the wood.

"Buck and ball," VanderJagt said with a passing glance as he moved forward and fired.

The air was becoming increasingly thick as the Confederate muskets added their buck and ball to the fray. One large musket ball with three small rounds of buckshot, "buck and ball" was notoriously inaccurate at any distance and far inferior to the long-range accuracy of the Dimicks. But as the sharpshooters crept closer and closer, the Rebel buckshot became a greater and greater threat.

Luke saw two more clouds of smoke appear from the woods and heard the air above him slashed with flying lead. All he wanted to do was turn and run! Disappear! This skirmishing was no type of fighting for a coward such as he! There was no sense of security without the massed battle line. Skirmishers fought as every man for himself, or at least every pair. This was the type of fighting for hardened men such as Sergeant VanderJagt or spirited adventurers like Matthew. What was he doing here, Luke's mind cried out.

Still, the three hundred-plus men of the skirmish line pressed forward. And judging by the slackening rate of fire, the enemy pickets were slowly departing from the tree line and falling back to the safety of their own lines.

Luke said a quick prayer for strength, but for once, it did no good. He still wanted to run. Yet, he did not turn and run. Matthew needed a partner, and Luke couldn't abandon him. So dutifully, Luke fired, reloaded, and advanced just like the rest of the skirmishers. Fire, reload, advance.

The sharpshooters lost sight of each other momentarily as they entered the tree line still thick with the smoke from the Confederate musketry. From deeper inside the wooded ravine, the Rebels began firing again, and the two sides traded shots along these rough lines for fifteen minutes, until the Dimicks started to take their toll. The sharpshooters pushed on deeper into the wooded ravine and their already loose formation became even more so.

Yet, as Luke looked down the length of the ravine, he could see the remainder of the Union skirmish line steadily pushing forward. Turning to the front, Luke saw some butternut forms scampering up the other side of the ravine and heard more shots. Slivers of wood scraped his cheek as one of the shots plunked into the tree next to him.

Realizing that he had never reloaded after his last shot, Luke halted and grabbed a paper cartridge from his pouch, tearing it open with his teeth as he had practiced so many times before. He mimicked Matthew's impatient voice of instructions as he poured the powder down the barrel, pressing the Minié ball into the barrel and using the ramrod to stuff it all down. Replacing the ramrod and pinching a percussion cap into place, he started the march down into the ravine and small creek that ran through the middle of it. He could already see some of the more impetuous blue coats down there, taking fire from the thin butternut line at the top of the other side.

"C'mon," Matthew said excitedly. "We got 'em on the run!" He dashed down into the creek, unaware of the two coin-sized splashes that erupted a foot away from him in the ankle deep water.

There was no break for the Rebels. Those who had still not raced back to the refuge of their own lines were taking increasing fire. The forest resounded with the crack of the Dimicks, and the sound of Minié balls splintering tree branches.

Pete and a few others were already climbing up the far side of the ravine. Some of the sharpshooters broke into full runs to chase the last remaining Rebels. It was the best that Luke could do to keep up with Matthew.

Luke reached the top of the ravine and started through the remainder of the woods, but already, he could make out the form of Fort Donelson's defenses through the woods. There were no more pickets to deal with, all of those having now run pell-mell for the safety of their nearby lines.

At this end of the woods, just before the guns of Fort Donelson, Luke could see a number of tree stumps and broken ground leading to a long slope capped by entrenched Confederate rifle pits. Blocking the long slope was an elaborate abatis—sharpened sticks pointing out from all angles, cluttered with thick brush and thorns. There could be no full dash up the slope; maneuvering through all the obstacles would take time, time during which they would be sitting ducks for the Confederate rifle pits. The abatis covered the entire slope up to the rifle pits.

"Gawl!" Sam exclaimed, as he joined Luke at the edge of the woods. "Lookey there!"

"What is all that?" Luke said, equally taken aback.

"We'll never get through there," Sam said. "Even a rabbit couldn't make it through all that."

Suddenly, a small volley of rifle fire sent a shower of branches down onto their heads. A number of Confederate heads immediately disappeared behind the safety of their rifle pits as twenty sharpshooters retaliated.

Behind them, Luke could hear sounds and turned to see additional sharpshooter companies coming up behind them.

"C'mon," VanderJagt ordered, tugging on Luke's sleeve as he ran by. "We're going to try to get around them." With the rest of the

Kalamazoo Sharpshooters in behind them, Luke followed VanderJagt who was chasing Lieutenant Simon who followed the Wisconsinites of Company A.

Ahead, Luke could see the Dover-Fort Henry Road and a number of sharpshooters ducking behind tree stumps and other available cover.

Thwackk!

Just below Luke's kneecap, a Minié ball struck a tree stump, and he became aware that they were taking fire from the rifle pits again.

Suddenly, the earth shook with a thunderous boom-boom-boom. It sounded like the heavens had opened up and unleashed a barrage of thunder and lightning, and it took a moment for Luke to realize that he had heard his first cannon.

Blocking the entrance to Fort Donelson via the Dover-Fort Henry Road was a Confederate battery of twelve cannon.

"Keep those guns quiet!" Lieutenant Simon yelled, motioning the rest of the company to find positions where they could keep up fire on the artillery.

VanderJagt pulled the madly waving Lieutenant Simon lower, behind a tree stump, just as a number of bullets whizzed by overhead, probably saving the young officer's life.

The enemy was two and three hundred yards away, and the sharpshooters' Dimicks began their deadly work, maintaining an incessant fire from behind tree stumps. One by one, the Union left a number of butternut forms sprawled around their guns, until finally the artillery was silent.

A few of the sharpshooters gave a small cheer as the last of the gunners abandoned their cannon. The guns, which were protected by the Confederate rifle pits and in no danger of falling into enemy hands, simply could not be manned in the face of the accurate long-range fire of the sharpshooters.

Slowly, the late morning and early afternoon evolved into a stalemate. The sharpshooters could keep the Rebels away from the cannon, but the abatis and long slope up to the rifle pits deterred any assaults from the main Union body.

Both sides waited for the other to make the next move.

"What do you think is going on down yonder?" Matthew asked Luke later in the day as they crouched behind a fallen tree on the edge of the hollow.

"Well," Luke began only to be interrupted by the crack of a rifle about ten yards away. He looked over and saw VanderJagt begin to reload, seemingly unconcerned as to whether or not he had hit the Confederate head that had foolishly poked itself into view. "Well," Luke began again, "I suppose you're talking about all that cannonading south of here?"

The rolling sound of the cannon battle had continued for so long and with such regularity that Luke no longer heard it. Oddly, it was a not even background noise. Somehow, he had put the sound out of his head and concentrated on keeping his head down and finding targets for his Dimick.

"Of course, I mean the cannons. It has been going on forever. What do you think is happening?"

"How should I know?" Luke shrugged. "This is the first battle I've been in too. Maybe Wallace's Division is making a charge on the center."

"Sounds like a lot of cannon for a charge," Matthew said skeptically.

"Maybe he's softening them up first."

"Wish I knew what was happening."

"Why?" Luke laughed. "You can't do anything about it. Best pay attention to keeping your head on your shoulders."

"I wonder whether we're going to attack today. It's getting late."

"I don't see anything happening, Matthew. Old Smith has made some demonstrations, but I think he's no more ready to try to cross all that than we are."

"We can carry it."

"Don't look easy to me," Sam interjected from nearby, looking out at the abatis again.

"And that's without anyone shooting at you. As soon as we form a line and advance, those rifle pits are going to come alive."

"At least we can keep those big guns quiet."

Luke nodded in agreement. He had never seen canister rip through a solid line of battle, but VanderJagt had told him more than once, and in too much detail, about the devastation wrought by the iron can packed with lead balls. The cannon had to be kept quiet.

Lieutenant Simon came up behind them from the deeper part of the hollow. It had begun to rain minutes ago, fouling weapons and chilling spirits. As the rain came down even harder and the temperature dropped ever closer to freezing, the only solace that the Western Sharpshooters could find was thinking that their counterparts across the abatis were enduring the same miserable weather.

Despite the deteriorating conditions, the only look on Simon's face was that of excited pride. "Hello, Luke!" he said cheerfully, dropping to his knees in the mud.

"Lieutenant," both Luke and Matthew replied.

"Good news, sir?" Luke asked, noticing the excited and pleased look that Simon wore.

"No, nothing new, Luke. It is rather exhilarating though, isn't it? The way we drove them in today."

Surprised that Simon and not Matthew was showing giddiness, Luke blinked. "I think they feel much safer behind those pits, sir," he said.

"True," Simon said, still unabashed. "But it was a good showing for us today. A start towards removing our stain."

"Yes, sir," Matthew said, feeling himself emboldened by the lieutenant's confident words. "When are we going to take a crack at their lines, sir?"

"Not sure, Matthew. Rest assured though that General Smith knows the best time. It won't be today though. We're to pull back after dusk. No picket duty for us tonight, thank God. I hardly slept last night, and I wouldn't want to make it two nights in a row."

"In that case, I want to claim that same piece of rotten wood again tonight," Matthew said. "It made a mighty nice pillow."

"Wish this rain would hold up," Luke said, plucking his soaked uniform off his freezing skin. The rim of his hat dripped with water and any shape the poor excuse had retained was definitely gone now.

The first evidence of the rain turning to snow appeared later that evening. By the time the Kalamazoo Sharpshooters returned through the ravine to where they had started, the snow had become heavy enough to cover the wet ground.

As they exchanged places with Company C, the Illinoisans told them about the failing of W. H. L. Wallace's assault in the middle. The volleys of rifle and cannon fire killed many, but it was word of the fires that were started by the battle which burned the wounded where they lie that shook Luke most of all. Worse yet, any of those who had survived the fire now had to deal with the freezing snow in the middle of this no-man's land. He said a prayer for the men and tried to keep the faith that prayer was enough.

February 14, 1862

The Kalamazoo Sharpshooters stood at attention in the exact same spot as the day before, but today, they needed to stomp their feet to warm up, which turned the two inches of snow into a muddy slush.

It was still dark, just before the first light of the day, and Luke was chilled all the way through like the rest of the sharpshooters. Even tucking his head inside the blanket like an animal inside a cocoon brought no relief from the blasts of cold air that had tormented him all night. When he had awakened from the intermittent sleep in the morning, there had been an inch of wet, icy snow coating his blanket.

The coffee that Matthew had cooked over a small twig fire had brought some relief. At least now he could stand at attention without violently shivering.

"Who do you suppose that is?" Matthew leaned over and asked.

Luke looked in the direction of Matthew's gaze and studied the two generals in the light of the nearby cookfire. One was obviously their own General C. F. Smith with his ramrod posture and flowing white mustache. Luke looked at the other general, much younger than Smith with smooth skin and trim black hair combed over the side. A long goatee covered the length of his neck like a veil, without which, he would have looked quite young.

"General Wallace?" Luke suggested.

"General Grant," VanderJagt interrupted.

"Are you sure?"

Although Luke believed the old sergeant, the question was never actually answered as Captain Vincent and then Colonel Birge addressed them. The soldiers were to go back to the same area as the day before and keep the Rebel gunners away from their cannon. To a man, this sounded like exactly what sharpshooters were supposed to do, and despite the cold, most were glad that they were here instead of chasing bushwhackers in Missouri.

With the generals listening curiously, Colonel Birge dispatched them. "Canteens full?" Birge reminded. "Biscuits for all day?"

Luke consciously patted his haversack, feeling the stiff piece of hardtack.

"All right," Birge finished. "Hunt your holes, boys."

Like a group of Indians, the sharpshooters left camp and found individual positions from which they could harass the Rebels and keep the cannon quiet. Many men found positions behind trees and stumps; some men carried small shovels with them and scraped better positions behind barriers; a few men even climbed trees and waited.

And waited.

It was near three o'clock in the afternoon when the first gunboat engaged the Fort Donelson shore batteries, just under a mile due east of the sharpshooters. The air suddenly became alive with the pounding of large guns as the gunboats traded blows with the Confederates.

From his vantage point high in a tree, Matthew strained to see what was happening beyond him. In spite of the cannon, the sound of musketry had not yet been heard in volley that day. There had been some attempts by the Confederates to use the artillery battery blocking the Dover-Fort Henry Road, especially after sighting the battle flags of various Union regiments demonstrating out of musket range.

And more than once, it looked to Matthew that a full-scale assault of the Rebel positions was due at any moment. It must have appeared the same to some Confederates as they foolishly tried to rush to their cannon, only to fall again under the well-aimed fire of the sharpshooters. Matthew had to admit that he much preferred fighting like this than maneuvering as a whole body. The sharpshooters were truly independent, each man taking care of himself and acting under his own orders. To this point, there had been no shoulder-to-shoulder charges into the enemy fire. He wondered whether that would remain the case or whether they would have to form up and follow Smith's main body into the abatis when the time came.

Wedged in the convenient crook of a tall tree, Matthew found himself almost too comfortable with one limb supporting his back like a chair. Better yet, the main trunk of the tree protected him from any fire that could be directed at him from the rifle pits. The only problem was that reloading was awkward and cumbersome, but given the rest of the benefits, this was the best position on the battlefield, despite Luke's early requests that he come down before he fell out of the tree and killed himself.

Down the road, he could see the new battle flag of one of the Iowa regiments in Lauman's Brigade. Unfurled in anger for the first time, it bore no resemblance to the tattered Rebel flag that waved behind the breastworks, a recipient of numerous Minié balls.

Meanwhile the gun battle raged between the shore batteries and the gunboats. Determined not to be bullied into submission by the gunboats like Fort Henry, the Fort Donelson shore batteries were putting up a determined fight.

Matthew watched the four black ironclads close on the fort. Each one bore on steadily despite the increasing fire from the shore batteries. At eight hundred yards, Matthew thought they would stop, but they did not, trading shot for shot.

Then five hundred yards.

Then a mere four hundred.

The shore batteries made numerous hits, yet none slowed the chugging gunboats.

The Confederate fire was beginning to slacken, and Matthew began to think that the gunboats would blast the Rebels into submission.

Then, like the swinging of a pendulum, the course of the battle changed with one fortuitous shot from the shore batteries. The lead gunboat, about three hundred fifty yards off, took a solid shot through the pilothouse. Seconds later, another ironclad found its tiller ropes severed and began floating helplessly downstream, turning around and around in the eddies like a piece of driftwood.

Seeing their comrades disabled, the other two ironclads closed in and tried to protect them with their hulls. Matthew could hear an excited Rebel cheer mix in between thunderous cannon shots, and the intensity of the shore batteries immediately increased.

The ironclad gunboats began to withdraw but not soon enough. The lead ship took another shot through the flag and chimney, bringing another Rebel cheer.

It had been an hour and half gun battle. The neat forms of the Confederate embrasures had been thoroughly torn by the gunboat assault, but they had held. For the second straight day, the Confederates could claim victory.

Dear James,

I hope this letter finds you well. Sam Barker and the others wanted to pass along their regards. Much has changed since you and Patrick left. As I write this, my hand shakes from the cold, and there is little light to work by so please pardon any errors. We have closed the second day of our siege of Fort Donelson. Though the sharpshooters have performed gallantly and redeemed any mistakes from Missouri, the Secesh still hold onto their fort, and after whipping the gunboats, they are quite full of themselves, shouting down jeers from their breastworks.

The fortifications are impressive sights, and I do not relish the thought of having to take them. Apparently, General Smith is of like mind, because he has only probed their position thus far. There have only been two killed and fourteen wounded out of the entire division.

At this rate, it looks like we are to starve the Secesh, but that seems a poor choice. Many of us shiver in our blankets without tents, and we brought only three days of rations. The sleet is beginning again. I am camped in the mud beneath a wagon to find a dry spot to write you. It is only the terrible cold that keeps me awake long enough to write you this letter.

I do not know what tomorrow will bring, but it cannot bring more of the same. The men can only take so much of this. I have no need to tell you, but disease has already taken more boys than battle, and these kind of conditions are one reason for it. I am sure General Smith is planning out a new strategy. The boys think very highly of him. He spent the day right up in the front of the demonstrations with the rest of boys, trading grim jokes with even the lowliest private. I've no need to tell you how rare that is in an officer.

I'd best be finishing. Either the writing or the cold is making my hand cramp. Keep up in your prayers, my friend.

Your Friend,

Luke

Luke blew out the light of the hooded oil lamp that he had badgered one of the quartermasters into borrowing. Laying his head down, he wrapped his wet blanket around him and tried futilely to sleep.

As he shivered miserably in his shelter, he said a small prayer for those on picket duty tonight. Though it sounded selfish to his ears, he was very glad that he was not a sentry tonight. As humble as the underside of the wagon was, it was a full mile better than nothing at all.

The night wore on, yet Luke found himself no closer to sleep. He rubbed his aching neck and wiped his red nose on his sleeve, but it was not his physical discomfort that robbed him of sleep. Not tonight. It was his mind. No effort seemed capable of shaking the sense of foreboding that he felt.

Though he knew no reason why, he could sense that tomorrow would be more than a day of sniping. It would be a day of something he had never seen before. It would be a full-scale battle, and Lauman's Brigade would have to charge up that long slope of obstacles and climb over the enemy rifle pits. And beyond all that, there was still the fort itself.

He tried to trick himself into thinking that the breastworks were not that tall and imposing, but he couldn't do it. He had seen them up close for the last two days.

Charging those works seemed a possibility beyond all human bravery and gallantry.

February 15, 1862

The Kalamazoo Sharpshooters walked through the gray light of the predawn, descending down into the ravine as they had the previous two days. Nearby, other clumps of sharpshooters walked stiffly with their rifles slung, trying to shake some life into their bones. A few men cursed as they slipped and fell over the slick ground.

"You kept that rifle covered last night, didn't you, Luke?" VanderJagt asked. Each of the first two nights, the old soldier had gone around the company making sure that the men were protecting the firing mechanisms of their rifles from the dampness of the night by wrapping a dry strip of cloth around it. With a zealotry that Luke had seen only with the most devout members of the church, Sergeant VanderJagt harangued each man, lecturing on the importance of keeping the rifle in prime working order.

"Of course I kept her clean," Luke replied with a yawn.

"Her?" Matthew laughed. "You've become so familiar with my father's Dimick that it is now a 'her'? You've only really used it for two days." He shook his head with amusement.

"They've been quite a two days," Gus said, slapping Luke on the back. "We are soldiers now, eh?"

For two days now they had kept those cannon silent. For two days, they had forced the Rebel infantry in the rifle pits to take extra caution in keeping their heads below the lip of the rifle pits.

"Humpphh," VanderJagt grunted. "Fire a couple of random shots, and you boys think you are soldiers? You'll not be soldiers until we mount those parapets before us."

Though they were still deep in the ravine, and the abatis was shrouded in darkness, each man saw the imposing defenses in their mind's eye. The obstacles beckoned them, challenging.

Luke spoke eventually, "I have a feeling that we'll test them today."

The others looked at him with some skepticism. Sniping was more likely than an assault to them, but as if on cue. The sound of sporadic picket fire from the south reached them. No one thought much of it. There had been various shots in the night since they had arrived. But then something else entirely reached their ears in the early morning gloom, the sound of volley fire.

"Hummphh," VanderJagt grunted.

"I didn't realize we had an early morning assault planned," Gus said.

"We don't, or we wouldn't be walking back to our holes like the last couple of days."

"Secesh?" Matthew said.

South of them, the firing increased with intensity, alternating between sporadic bursts and volleys. Cannon suddenly roared, and it was obvious to all of them that this was the beginning of a major battle taking place south of them.

By ten o'clock, the firing south of the sharpshooters was still hammering away at such a pace that they knew the issue must still be in doubt. A Union charge would not take this long for an outcome, some of the men, Lieutenant Simon and Sergeant VanderJagt in particular, speculated. The Confederates must be trying to fight their way out of the trap.

Luke tried not to think about it too much. It frustrated him that there was nothing he could do about it, and that he knew so little of what was happening. He tried to concentrate on finding targets in the Confederate breastworks here on the northern end of the siege line, but the Confederates were far more careful today. He had yet to see one decent target.

"Why don't we do something?" Matthew said abruptly from behind his fallen tree.

"Do what?" Pete said from the hole he had scratched out behind a stump.

"I don't know. Go join the battle down there."

"Humphh," VanderJagt said from twenty yards away. "I think y'all should leave the generaling to the generals."

"I hate it when that Texas accent gets into your voice," Sam complained without malice. "I think I accidentally fell asleep sometimes and ended up inside their lines." He lay with his eyes closed, unseen behind a clump of trees.

"Ha," Pete said, laughing. "We know you're asleep half the time. Some time, we might just leave you behind so that you *do* wake up next to some Johnny Reb."

The sharpshooters sprinkled throughout the area gave a short laugh.

Behind them, the sound of the trampling of brush interrupted them and Lieutenant Long emerged, his face flushed bright red and lungs wheezing.

"Sir," Lieutenant Simon said, saluting, but not rising from behind his hole.

Without missing a beat, Long frowned. His normally clean, shiny face flecked with dirt, his skin chafed from the cold, and his trim brown mustache matted with something other than saliva or sleet, Lieutenant Long certainly did not look himself today. Yet despite appearances, the unmistakable tone of arrogance was still in his voice. "You will rise when you salute me, Lieutenant. Just because you fancy yourself the sharpshooter, that is no reason for lack of protocol."

Without complaining, Lieutenant Simon rose to his feet, exposing himself in front of the Confederate breastworks. "Yes, sir," he said saluting again. Around him, all of the sharpshooters were amazed at the evenness of his voice when a crack sounded out from the breastworks.

The young lieutenant pitched forward, face first into the dirt. He reached up a hand to the side of his head, and dark red blood began to seep between his fingers.

"Lieutenant!" Luke was the first to say, scampering toward him in a low crouch. As he reached the fallen officer, Luke looked up and was angered to see no remorse on Long's face, but he ignored the urge to strike out at the man and concentrated on his fallen friend. "Sir?" Luke said in an anxious voice.

Simon rewarded him with a soft moan, and Luke gently pulled Simon's hand away from his head, fearing the worst.

"Hallelujah," Luke breathed when he saw that the shot had winged Simon. The Minié ball had sliced the top of his ear from his head, but done little more.

Simon began to stir, and Luke pulled a bandage from his haversack.

"I take it, I'm still alive," Lieutenant Simon moaned, letting Luke help him lean against a tree.

"I...," Lieutenant Long began, but clamped his mouth shut, half aware of the ugly looks he was receiving. But the moment of self-doubt dissipated in an instant. "Put your eyes back on the breastworks," he snarled at the sharpshooters. "What I came here to say was that General Smith is going forward finally. He's going to take these works, and we are to keep that battery silent."

"Yes, sir," VanderJagt said, sarcastically emphasizing the last word.

Long immediately turned on his heel and retreated back through the hollow. To where, no one knew or cared at this moment.

"Take the works?" Matthew questioned as more firing erupted again from the south. "But the battle is south of here. Shouldn't we be going down there?"

"Afraid of the defenses? Thought you were all anxious to prove yourself a soldier?" VanderJagt snapped, still angered by Long.

"No," Matthew retorted. "But why go through all that when the battle is down there?" He pointed to the imposing, fencelike obstacles with sharpened sticks pointing in all directions.

"Seizing this position makes perfect sense," Luke said, a peculiar look on his face.

"It does?" Sam frowned. He was inclined to think like Matthew. Why fight through all those defenses when there was a more even fight south of here?

"If the Rebels are making a push south there," Luke explained, "that means they're strong down there. These lines, therefore, must be weaker. They can't be strong everywhere at once."

The sharpshooters all looked at him, at first in surprise and then in admiration. It did make perfect sense. Now might be the best time to take these positions.

It was actually the Confederates who alerted the sharpshooters that General Smith's battle line was nearing. With a flurry of activity, the butternut hastened to their defenses. The gunners frantically tried to load their cannon.

Immediately, the sharpshooters retaliated with a red hot fire. From their hidden positions, they sent a hail of well-aimed Minié balls into the Rebel artillery. Even the shots that missed could prove deadly as they ricocheted off the cannon barrels. With a grim satisfaction, the Kalamazoo Sharpshooters prevented the Rebel gunners from firing a shot.

Finished reloading, Luke raised up the rifle again and slowly picked out another target. Squeezing the trigger, he withdrew the rifle without bothering to watch the outcome and began reloading and following the same process again and again. Soon, he found his hands becoming more than warm from the barrel. The more he shot, the hotter the octagonal metal barrel became, so that as he rammed another Minié ball home, he could feel it burning the skin on his hands.

The blue wave of the Smith's vanguard swept past him a hundred yards to his left. They were the Iowans of Lauman's Brigade, and they marched forward towards the long slope and abatis. What they lacked in marching precision was more than made up for by the steadiness of their agonizingly slow advance. The Iowans were in musket range now, and the Confederate breastworks came alive.

The Southerners unleashed a storm such that Luke had never seen before. Their volleys poured down on the men below like a screeching band of demons. The subsequent long veil of smoke obscured the Rebel faces and weapons, although above one of the black powder clouds, Luke could see a Rebel banner waving defiantly.

From their elevated positions, the Confederates fired shot after shot so that the air was alive with the twittering, zip-zip-zip of flying lead.

Pausing to look to his left as he reloaded, Luke watched the blue line start up the slope. Riding in front of the advance, in perfect alignment with the colors of the 2nd Iowa, General Smith sat fully erect in his saddle, calmly moving forward. He faced directly to the front, occasionally glancing from side to side to check the alignment of the battleline but never flinching. The air around the general was filled with whipping lead as the Confederates concentrated their fire on the horseman. With his battle dress regulation perfect down to the golden braid, his perfect stature and his flowing white mustache, General Smith was the perfect target.

But Luke found to his utter amazement that despite the unending fire from the breastworks, not a shot hit General Smith!

The white smoke from the Rebels' incessant firing had fully obscured the breastworks now, but Luke knew that the smoke was not the reason for their inaccuracy.

As he looked behind the advanced blue wave, Luke saw that it was the trees and brush that suffered from the Rebel fire. Their fire was going too high.

Matthew saw it too. The Rebels were not adjusting their aim for their elevation, and many of the shots zipped narrowly, but harmlessly, over the blue-coated line, into the forest.

Even so, to Luke victory seemed impossible. From the safety of his hidden position, he could see the first Union bodies lying on the field. And though the line moved on, always closing up to fill any gaps created by the unfortunate, the Yankees hadn't even reached the abatis yet!

The continual roar of the Confederate guns was overwhelming.

On sound alone, Luke was terrified, even though he knew the fire was being directed on the advancing infantry and not on the hiding sharpshooters. It was a tremendous, reverberating, deafening crash of hundreds of muskets and rifles, over and over again!

But the sight of the old general with the flowing white mustache, erect in his saddle and unconcerned, inspired Luke like no sermon his father had ever given. The general was as calm and confident as any man Luke had ever seen. The air around the man was clearly boiling with enemy fire, yet he was utterly unconcerned.

He had to follow this man, Luke knew. There was something entrancing. He had to lend his weight to the advance, if only to save their general! They had to go forward!

Leaping to his feet, Luke chased after the advancing blue line as they washed by. Unbeknown to him, a number of sharpshooters followed his lead.

They reached the abatis. The fire reached a new crescendo. More men fell, and the assault wavered. Seeing their hesitation, General Smith turned and put his cap on the point of his sword. "No flinching now, my lads!" he yelled above the fray, holding the cap aloft on the gleaming sword. "Here, this is the way! Come on!" His horse picked its way through the jagged maze of tree branches and obstacles, zigzagging back and forth to find openings, all the while General Smith held the hat aloft on the tip of his sword.

Lauman's Brigade swarmed after him, determined to keep up with their brave, old leader. Formations lost all cohesion as men picked their way through tiny openings; others climbed over the obstacles, and more still tore the barricades apart.

Up the ascent, General Smith rode.

Luke climbed between the protruding, pointed sticks of one of the fencelike obstacles and then through a gap created by the Iowans ahead of him. He ran to his right where there was another opening and followed the others upward. Before his very eyes, those in front of him were whipped with fire, and they twisted and flung themselves in contortions, hitting the ground in all sorts of grotesque angles.

Luke was alone. Another fence of jagged sticks barred his way, and he tugged futilely on it, trying to drag it through the cold mud so that others could follow. A musket ball buried itself in the wood, but he struggled on.

And then Sam and Pete were at his shoulder. Wordlessly, the three of them pulled the obstacle aside, dragging it like a heavy gate through the dirt. Two dozen other men surged through the gap just as they did. The rush knocked down Luke, but he jumped to his feet and followed the surge forward.

The front ranks of this surge fell as Confederates in the rifle pits spouted flame, smoke, and lead. But Luke and the rest of the Union soldiers pressed on, stepping over their fallen comrades.

Their eyes watered from the hazy white smoke, and their tongues could taste the bitter gunpowder, but they stumbled over shredded blue bodies and kept moving forward.

Then suddenly, they were clear of the abatis, and men launched themselves into the Confederate rifle pits. There was no order anymore. Companies were intermingled with other companies; regiments were mixed with other regiments. But it didn't matter, every man from the lowly private to the highest officer knew what to do to capture these rifle pits! Exhilarated beyond belief to be through the abatis and finally upon the enemy, the men from Lauman's Brigade fought like enraged brigands.

Behind the first disorderly mass of men hitting the rifle pits, a company of the 2nd Iowa had somehow maintained their cohesion. Surging past their general finally, they fired for the first time, unleashing a murderous volley point-blank into the breastworks. Without pausing to reload, they leapt into the rifle pits to engage any survivors.

But the only survivors were already retreating, abandoning the rifle pits and praying that there was safety behind the walls of Fort Donelson itself.

All along the entrenchments, Lauman's men were gaining the upper hand. The rifle pits were falling. For another fifteen minutes, they battled the most stubborn of the Rebels, but then they were clear. The rifle pits were theirs! The four regiments—the 25th Indiana, 2nd, 7th, and 14th Iowa—planted their regimental flags in the works as the retreating Confederates raced for the safety of the fort.

But the battle was long from over. Turning to the right, Luke and the others saw a counterattack forming. Five regimental flags and two more Rebel regiments came from Fort Donelson itself.

They had captured the works, but would reserves arrive in time to help them hold it? Desperately, the tired men of Lauman's Brigade looked behind them. Where was the support? They would need the rest of the division to join them in the rifle pits. They would need help, or these hard fought gains would be for naught.

Behind Luke, additional Union units of infantry and artillery appeared to be too far down the abatis.

"Don't just stand there, boy!" VanderJagt yelled in his ear. "We got more fightin' to do!"

Obediently, Luke turned around and fired into the growing mass of butternut, bent on retaking their defenses.

It was total chaos. Some of the Federal soldiers sought cover from which to fire behind, others elected to stand shoulder to shoulder in small groups and fire into the enemy that rushed them from two sides.

The spearhead of the Rebel counterattack fired a ragged volley, and Luke felt a body sag into his legs. Looking down he did not recognize the face, but the ghoulish sound of a Rebel yell snapped his attention back to the front. He and the others in the area fired into the mass without visible effect.

Unwilling to simply wait for the charging Rebels to reach him, VanderJagt charged forward by himself with a primal growl. Watching him for a half-second, the other Union soldiers followed and charged after him.

The Rebel spearhead and the small cadre of Yankees collided with the sound of steel, wood, and bone. Just in front of Luke, VanderJagt drove his bayonet through the stomach of one Rebel. A butternut figure with wild dirty hair clubbed one Yankee and then turned his attention on VanderJagt.

Seeing it a split second before impact, the old sergeant tried to dodge the blow, nearly succeeding. But the glancing blow knocked him down and the dirty Rebel raised his rifle butt to bring it down on VanderJagt's head. Without a bayonet on his Dimick, Luke lunged forward with his rifle. The muzzle only served to knock the man off balance, but Luke's momentum carried him fully into the Rebel, and they went down in a tumble. In a mass of limbs within a world of raging yells and gunfire. Luke's sheer size pinned much of the man down, but he found himself aware of the man struggling to pull out a knife. Acting on survival instinct alone, Luke reached desperately for the man's hand, slicing his forearm as he grabbed the man's wrist in a viselike lock.

He could smell the man's breath near his face and for an instant their eyes locked, each red-rimmed and desperate. They rolled around, clinging to each other, but somehow the man slid from Luke's grasp and struggled to his knees. He was about to plunge the knife into Luke when he suddenly arched upward. Wide-eyed he stared at Luke and then pitched forward.

Looking down at him, Luke saw a bright red bullet wound in the man's back. Luke looked into the background, but it was utter chaos. He had no idea who had just saved his life.

"C'mon, boy!" VanderJagt yelled, grabbing Luke by a sleeve and pulling him back.

Slowly, the blue coats were falling back to the rifle pits again, and for a second, Luke feared all the effort would be lost. But before the Rebels could take advantage of the weakening Yankees, Union reinforcements arrived through the abatis and clambered into the rifle pits that their comrades had fought so hard to take.

Joined by Cook's Brigade and some artillery, Lauman's Brigade fought back. Two Parrott cannons had been physically dragged up the slope by the determined Yankee cannoneers, and they fired with an echoing roar.

Canister!

The tin can packed with lead balls and sawdust burst out of the cannon's mouth, spraying its contents into the gray line advancing.

"Reload, Double Canister!" the order was instantly given, but the shot had already had its intended effect, and Hansom's Kentuckians halted their charge and fell back in disarray.

"Seen Matthew?" Luke yelled to VanderJagt as he reloaded his Dimick with surprising familiarity.

Grinning at the naturalness of Luke's actions, VanderJagt fired his own rifle. "No," he said. "But that don't mean a whole hell of a lot. When we saw you follow the charge, a right bunch of us jumped up behind you. I didn't bother to watch who all came along."

"You were following *me*?" Luke yelled above the din as he fired at a puff of white smoke.

"We didn't know you were such a hellbent leader, preacher boy!" VanderJagt laughed with a kind of perverse pleasure amid all the carnage.

Luke could think of no reply, and he rammed a new ball down his scalding hot barrel.

"Don't worry 'bout Matthew," VanderJagt said seriously. "He may have a mouth like the Miss-a-sip, but he can take care of himself."

Luke nodded, knowing that only a few of the men around them were from their own regiment, much less the Kalamazoo Sharpshooters. In the chaos beyond the abatis, men sought the safety of other blue-coated men, regardless of regiment. Keeping order was an impossibility, so men settled in where they were.

With the air thick with white smoke, the two sides slammed away at each for another hour, but eventually, the Rebels recognized the futility of trying to drive out Smith's men. Grudgingly, the Mississippians, Kentuckians, and Tennesseans withdrew to an inner line, and an uneasy peace came over the battlefield.

As night fell and the bitter cold dropped on them again, Lauman's Brigade bivouacked on the ground they had gained. Ever the leader, General Smith shared the bitter night and difficult conditions with them.

Exhausted, Luke bound up the wound in his forearm and closed his eyes. He fell asleep immediately, even before fatigue parties had been selected to collect the wounded that lay scattered across the abatis and inside the works.

February 16, 1862

Light had not yet broken the cold early morning hours when Luke awoke with a start. He felt a tug on his sleeve and smelled the pungent odor of tobacco. Good tobacco.

"Dreamin' of the Secesh, boy?" VanderJagt asked.

"What? What's happening?" Luke said, somewhat amazed at how instantly awake he had become. His eyes flashed around, expecting a whirl of activity, another Rebel counterattack, but there were few men stirring. Most slept rolled back to back where their exhausted bodies had worn out.

"Time to get back with our own regiment," VanderJagt said, taking another puff on the long drooping pipe that dangled from his mouth.

Taking a sniff, Luke said, "That smells like real tobacco, not the stuff we've been using for the last few months."

"Exactly right, my boy," he smiled, removing the pipe from his mouth momentarily. "Good num'er of these Southern boys had the good stuff. I grabbed it while the fatigue parties helped the wounded."

"You took it off a dead body?"

"Well, now, he wasn't gonna use it anymore, was he?" VanderJagt said with a touch of indignation.

"I suppose not," Luke said, deciding to drop the issue. He arched his stiff back with a soft moan.

"C'mon," VanderJagt said. "Y'all is too young to be creaky already, and we need to join up with the others.

A couple hundred yards away, most of the sharpshooters slept in their own dogpile. Some were beginning to rise, but none as completely awake as VanderJagt. Luke knew that he had fallen asleep before the older man, and that he had only woken because of him. It would not have surprised Luke if someone told him that the old sergeant never slept, because he couldn't ever remember seeing the man do more than doze.

Luke wandered over and sat down next to the square frame of Pete O'Shea, who shoved something in his pocket at the last moment just as he recognized Luke in the dark. Luke didn't see exactly what it was, but he had a pretty good idea that it was more booty from Confederate dead. After a second, Luke could smell exactly what it was, liquor.

"A little early for that, isn't it, Pete?" Luke said, staring out across the darkness at the unseen Fort Donelson.

"Er, probably," Pete said hesitatingly. "It's not what you think though. I was just...testing it, you know...it's real Tennessee whiskey...and I need to shake this chill."

"It is still the Lord's Day," Luke said softly.

"It is?" Pete said with genuine surprise and thought about it for a few seconds. "By gum, you're right. It is Sunday. I had completely forgotten."

"Don't know whether I much like the idea of fighting on the Lord's Day," Luke said. "You think Generals Grant and Smith will make this a day of rest?"

"Well, I'm sure they're both God-fearing men, but I doubt it, Luke," Pete said, glad that the subject had turned away from himself. "Besides, we have the Secesh exactly where we want them."

"How's that?" Luke said.

"Well, we're right on top of Fort Donelson now."

"Is that good?"

"Better than good, Luke. Now that we hold this line, there is no protection for their shore batteries. After we force the shore batteries to leave, Admiral Foote's gunboats can come back, and together we pound the fort with cannon. Pound it into dust. This is all but over."

Luke sat, thinking. After a moment's reflection, he nodded and smiled in the predawn darkness. He had been expecting another day of hard fighting, maybe even assaulting the fort itself. But what Pete said made a lot of sense to him. The Confederates were completely trapped and nearly defenseless now.

More of the sharpshooters and other Union regiments were beginning to roll out of their frozen blankets. Their faces were tired and worn from battle with both the Confederates and the conditions, but steeled by their success, spirits were high.

"Luke?" He heard his name called and turned to see Matthew standing behind him, an anxious look on his face.

"Matthew," he answered cheerfully. "Good to see that you're in one piece. Have you seen Lieutenant Simon? I want to see how he's doing."

Dawn was finally beginning to break. It was another cool, gray day, but there was finally light. Behind Matthew, Luke looked into the abatis that they had plunged through the day before. From the position they now stood, the Rebels had fired down on them. Even from here, he could see the underbrush and saplings shriveled from the hail. Here and there a cartridge box lay on the slope. Across from one cartridge box his eye noticed a canteen with a bullet hole in it. As his eyes scanned the field, he saw anything and everything: a wide-brimmed hat, a blue regulation kepi, a shredded knapsack, its writing papers blown into the abatis' entanglements, hardtack, a broken musket.

Behind him, there was the sound of commotion, and he saw Matthew's eyes widen. "What?" With a look of wonderment, Luke watched a Rebel enter their camp. He carried a dirty white rag on a pole above his head and was accompanied by a lieutenant and corporal from the 14th Iowa.

Matthew stood in open-mouthed amazement.

The Confederates had surrendered. Fort Donelson was now theirs.

III

Shiloh

February 20, 1862

Matthew set his Dimick across his lap and looked at the Stars and Stripes flapping overhead. The bright red was illuminated by the sunlight from behind, and immediately, his mind flashed back to the waving banners as they had taken the outer works at Fort Donelson.

He could still smell and hear it all. The crack of weapons, the shouts of battle, the moans of the wounded, but it was the smell that overpowered all other sensations. The lingering smoke, the acrid gunpowder, the stench of burning flesh, the revulsion of decaying bodies. The battle was finished, and the fatigue parties had collected the wounded and buried the dead, yet the smell remained over Dover, Tennessee.

Overhead, the flag rippled aloud in the breeze, and Matthew looked up at it again.

And then, there had been the sight of the various flags moving in battle. Some were tattered, some were new, but they all marked the various progress of individual groups of men, Kentuckians, Iowans, Mississippians, Hoosiers, Michiganders. All had their own flag.

The sight of their own regimental flag and the Stars and Stripes planted in the enemy ramparts was an exhilaration all its own.

He examined the rifle in his lap again. Satisfied that it had been properly cleaned, Matthew leaned it against his side and worked to free a pouch of tobacco. Luke called it a filthy habit, but Matthew had discovered that a smoke with the clay pipe was relaxing. Yet another bad habit he had picked up, Luke had said with frustration.

The preacher's son didn't approve of the card playing and gambling either, but there was little else to do here in the little town of Dover, Tennessee. After capturing Fort Donelson, the Western Sharpshooters had been assigned to garrison duty in the town of Dover, which had been inside the Confederate lines during the battle.

It was a pleasant enough town, and much like Missouri, they had found a number of Union supporters. Most of those locals who despised the blue-coated soldiers stayed out of sight and out of the way as much as possible.

Puffing on the tobacco, Matthew couldn't help but remember where the tobacco came from. He had never imagined that after a battle so much energy would be spent plucking clean the dead bodies. While he couldn't bring himself to do it, Matthew had seen plenty of other sharpshooters going through the haversacks and pockets of the butternut and even blue-coated bodies. He knew that Walker was funding his current drinking and gambling with money taken from the dead.

But as Matthew puffed on the good Southern tobacco, he knew he was in no place to criticize. While he could not take the tobacco off the dead himself, he had accepted the pouch that Sergeant VanderJagt had tossed him. Matthew could still see the dead Rebel's dirty, bearded face of anguish, eyes shut, and mouth frozen open in rictus. There was no visible wound, but the Rebel had been dead surely enough.

Without regard to the faded picture of the man's wife that came from his pocket as the old sergeant had ripped free the two pouches of good Southern tobacco, tossing one to Matthew. Out of reflex, he had caught it, but now he wished he hadn't.

Perhaps, if the pouch had fallen to the ground...he sighed, maybe then he would not be plagued by the memory of the dead Rebel's face or the picture of his wife blowing across the battlefield into oblivion.

The general inactivity of garrison duty only made it worse. There was little to do except think...and gamble. Neither one seemed very rewarding right now. Rumors flew around the camp: some said Chicago was under siege from Rebels; others said the war was over. The latter seemed to be the more prevalent theory, especially in light of their victory at Fort Donelson.

As Sam said, the Rebels had been given a good whipping and were now streaming out of Tennessee. The war was nearly over, if it wasn't already. Sam was already making his plans for leaving the army now that the war was over, and Matthew knew Sam wasn't the only one.

Home, he thought blankly. He never thought he would want to return to Kalamazoo so quickly.

Dear Father,

By now, you have surely heard of our victory at Fort Donelson. I am still alive and unharmed, and we performed our duty in excellent fashion. After the battle, General Grant commended Colonel Birge on our valor, and we were given the honor of entering the fort second, just behind the Iowa boys who led the charge.

I am told there were over ten thousand prisoners taken, and I believe it. I have never seen so many men corralled together before. I think this little adventure is nearing its end. Many of us around here think this was the victory that was needed to bring the Secesh back to their senses. I will see you soon.

Your son, Matthew

The laughter of men—young and old—drifted across the camp and into nearby Niles, Michigan. As James sat cross-legged in front of the wedge tent he shared with Patrick and two other recruits, he could not help but think how similar the laughter sounded to the throaty boasting of the Kalamazoo Sharpshooters. Much like before, he found himself surrounded by patriotic Michigan men, certain that their weight would force the South into submission and bring about a quick end to this war.

But that was where the similarities stopped. The former horse fields that they marched upon were clustered with an entire regiment of nine companies instead of just one small company. And unlike the sharpshooters, whose amateur officers paid only token attention to the finer points of battalion movement, the 12th Michigan spent an inordinate amount of time marching. Colonel Quinn, Major Powell, and every officer on down took an active part in the training, and it was obvious to James that there was a large difference between a professional soldier and a congressman-soldier.

The supplies were also a dramatic departure from his previous experience. Whereas the sharpshooters had to struggle for tents and uniforms, the 12th Michigan found itself amply supplied. Yet despite their ample supply, James and Patrick stubbornly kept their old uniforms. Faded and wrinkled, they looked much different than the crisp blue coats of the others. They also kept their Dimick rifles rather than taking the government-issued Enfields.

"James, what are you doing?" Ainsley said, approaching from the side.

The senator's son still looked out of place with his ill-fitting uniform draped across his gaunt body, but he had proven to be a diligent officer to this point. James was gratified to see that Ainsley required no special attention or treatment unlike Long and Vincent had.

On a whole, the entire officer's corps of the regiment was a marked improvement. James found himself especially liking the well-spoken Major Powell. Square-jawed and statuesque, the old army man had an air about him that caused men to instantly respect him.

"I'm just thinking, Lieutenant," James finally answered Ainsley.

"Don't think too long, James, or you'll miss seeing my cousin."

James tried to show no reaction, but he must have failed.

"Hah," Ainsley laughed. "I knew you were thinking of her."

James tried to protest, but he knew it was a lost cause to convince Ainsley of anything else. Ever since they had left Kalamazoo, Ainsley had taken singular pleasure in teasing James about his cousin, Katherine.

"Don't know what you're inferrin', sir."

"You can keep up your act all you want, James," Ainsley chuckled, "but you're not fooling me."

"I don't follow, sir."

"Stop with the 'sir,' James. There's no one around."

"Sorry."

"Anyway, Katherine is accompanying her parents to Chicago. The train stops here in Niles this evening, and they wanted to meet me for supper. I thought you might want to accompany me."

"Ainsley, I'm not sure that's such a good idea," James said hesitantly.

"Nonsense. I'll be back at five," Ainsley said with a smile and departed, just as Patrick and James's new messmates returned.

Joe Tucker was laughing loudly with that rumbling, raucous tone that seemed so out of place with his tiny frame. Tucker was a small, rail thin man with a quick smile and even quicker poker hands, James had observed. His short, tightly curled hair was laced with sweat, but his excited eyes and wide smile told the story.

"What happened?" James asked.

"Old Paddy here thought he could chop more wood than me," Tucker smiled triumphantly. Patrick shook his head wordlessly. "Now he cooks in my spot the next three times."

"Are you sure that's a reward?" James smiled back. "Might be a punishment for all of us if you ask me."

Ezra Lampkin laughed. He was a younger man than Tucker, with a bigger, softer body. He had a slow moving gait and gentle brown eyes. He too was quick to laugh, but while Tucker's laugh was one of knowing he had gotten the better of you, Lampkin's laugh was a mild, almost dull-witted laugh of good-naturedness.

"Never thought that little runt had a chance," Patrick said, rubbing his sore shoulder. "But he never slowed down, not for a second."

"You should know better," James said. "You've seen Joe rube others already."

"I know. But this time I thought his mouth got ahead of himself. We were chopping wood! I'm twice his size, I thought—"

"Never underestimate Joe Tucker!" Tucker interrupted with relish.

There wasn't much to Niles, Michigan. In fact, as James followed Ainsley into the hotel next to the depot, he wondered whether there would be anything in Niles at all were it not that the train to Chicago passed through town.

Though his face betrayed no emotion, James followed Ainsley up the steps with trepidation. Logically, he knew he should not have come and would be best served to stay away from Katherine and forget all about her, but in the end, he knew he could not resist seeing her.

He steeled himself for the encounter by telling himself that this time, there would be no avoiding the fact that he was deluding himself. He thought the dose of cold reality would snap him out of it, and for that reason alone, he told himself that this trip was worth it. Ainsley, of course, had no idea that this was his friend's motivation.

It was James who saw Big John Moffat first. His name implied that he was a large, physically imposing man, but he was not. In size, he was of average height and girth. Still, there was a reason that everyone called him Big John, and that was the force of his presence and determination. As James looked at the man with his tall stovepipe hat and finely tailored suit, which was so new that the material still gleamed, there was no mistaking Big John Moffat as someone of importance. Even his proud, erect walk revealed that he was from a class above James. No one ever would have guessed that a young John Moffat had once been as poor as James.

"Ah, punctual as usual, nephew," Moffat's loud voice could be heard by passers-by across the street. "You caught us just on our way to investigate the fare of this little berg." Moffat grasped Ainsley's hand in a vigorous handshake, and Louisa Moffat stood by her husband's side, warily eyeing James.

"Ma'am," James said, tipping his cap, feeling very uncomfortable with her scrutiny.

Realizing for the first time that Ainsley had a companion, John smiled. "Sergeant, is it?" he acknowledged but did not bother to shake hands. "There is a saloon across the way for you while we feed our skinny lieutenant."

"Yes, sir," James answered dutifully.

"But—," Ainsley began.

"I'm afraid the offerings in Niles will not be as elegant as the last time we dined, nephew, but that was our nation's capital."

"But—"

"Ah, yes," Moffat interrupted again, "Your cousin is not feeling well and has retired for the night. It will just be the three of us this evening."

"But—"

"I'll be over there, if you should need me, sir," James said, pointing to the saloon. There was no disappointment in his voice. If anything, he felt relief.

Giving James one last look, Ainsley shrugged and followed his uncle into the restaurant.

James sat at the far table. The saloon was mostly empty, just two other souls sitting at the bar. Stagecoach men who made the run to Grand Rapids by the look of it, James guessed from their dusty appearance.

He sat quietly, wondering how long the Moffats would eat dinner. James was unaccustomed to saloons and really had no purpose for one. With a sigh, he realized that he had received the dose of cold reality that he had been seeking. The Moffats outclassed him that they did not, and could not, notice him. Though he knew it was for the better, it did nothing to lift his spirits.

"May I join you?" he heard a familiar feminine voice ask him, and he looked up in astonishment at the smiling face of Katherine. She looked at him with a catlike grin of teasing amusement. The elegant lines of her face and neck looked terribly out of place in the rough hewn bar. Just as before, James could not help but think she looked like an angel.

"Katherine," he said, scrambling to his feet, "I mean Miss Moffat." She sat down, leaving him standing, and after a confused moment, he took a seat also. "I thought you were not feeling well."

"I just told mother that because I knew she would be difficult about having you eat with us."

James blinked in confusion, unsure what to say.

"And I so wanted to see you again."

"Me?" James managed in surprise.

"Of course," she said, enjoying the effect she was having on him. She paused, watching the confusion and discomfort pass over him. It was so genuine that she could not help but be warmed by it. It was a type of flattery that was so different from the casual superiority that Orrin displayed. She hated being taken for granted and that was exactly the way Orrin treated her sometimes, she thought.

"But why see me?" James said, both praying for and against a positive answer, sure that he must be misunderstanding something.

She shrugged and carried on with something else, but noticing that James was paying her no attention and still trying to find an answer to his own question, she returned to the topic, "So straightforward, Mr. Lockett. That is one reason that I like to talk to you. I know that I need not worry about what game you are playing, or what gossip you are spinning. Why, it wouldn't surprise me if you had never told a lie in your life."

"Huh?" he uttered, giving her a bewildered look, wondering whether he had come into the conversation halfway through it.

"Besides, I thought I would pass onto you how your old friends are doing." There was a gleam in her eye that set James's suspicions aflight. Something in her voice betrayed her when she said "old friends."

"What do you mean?" he said slowly.

"The Kalamazoo Sharpshooters played a significant role in capturing Fort Donelson."

He searched her face for a clue as to what she was hiding. "I read that in the papers, Miss Moffat."

"But did you know that they were given the second place of honor upon entering the fort?"

"I did, and I also saw that none of my friends ended up on the casualty list."

"They say that the war might be over after this victory."

"Who says that?" James said with a snort.

Insulted by his reaction, her stare turned colder. "The same person who said that you killed a Rebel sympathizer in Missouri."

James's hand instantly clenched his knee. Orrin Long.

Somehow he was able to remain seated, despite the charge of hate-induced fire that surged through his body. His face flushed with color, but the eyes remained steady, locked onto Katherine's baiting blue eyes. "A letter from Orrin Long?" he queried in an impressively mild voice, wondering what game she was playing.

"Yes," she said with a note of triumph. "And he mentioned in passing that one of the sharpshooters had been sent home after murdering a Rebel sympathizer."

"Did he now?"

"Yes."

"And you believe that?" James said very slowly.

"Believe it? Of course, why wouldn't I?"

"And he said it was me?"

"No," she admitted. "But I am right, aren't I? You seemed too healthy to be traveling back on discharge." James gave no reply, and a smile of triumph crossed Katherine's face. She knew that she had deduced correctly. "Rather smart, aren't I?"

"Smart?" James said starting to lose the tight rein he had held on his tongue. "If you are right, you're sitting across from a murderer, Miss Moffat!"

She pondered his retort for a second. "I suppose you're right about that. I hadn't thought of it that way."

James shook his head with a sad face. The surge of hate was evaporating, leaving his veins with the bitter residue that was disappointment. He had hoped the dishonor was left behind in Missouri, that he could pick up again without any trouble. What foolish thoughts those were, he frowned. The tales that Walker and Long were weaving were no doubt being told and retold, probably becoming more sinister each time. How foolish it was to think that he could outrun the stain on his reputation!

"You shouldn't believe everything you hear, Miss Moffat," James grumbled. He picked up his cap, thinking that he would leave.

"But don't leave, James. I don't care. It was a Rebel sympathizer. We are fighting a war."

"Don't care?" he demanded, staring at her in shock. "We are talking about taking a human life."

"But—"

"You damn fool!" he growled with a trembling anger that stunned him. "You have no idea!" The grotesque images of little Amelia flooded his brain. Pixielike and imploring...then a shattered corpse, spilling more blood than seemed possible for her little body to contain. So much red blood!

"But this is a war, people die in war. That's why we're fighting one."

"I'm fighting to keep people alive, not to kill innocent people! I'm fighting to end this war before my fool brother enlists and gets himself killed!"

"But that's why it's okay."

"God in heaven, Katherine! You don't understand! That girl in Missouri was no sympathizer! Even if she was, it wouldn't matter. I was trying to *save* her, not kill her!" He paused. Telling her about Long's treachery would do him no good. She would never believe him...It would do him no good to try to tell people the truth.

Angrily, he slammed his cap onto his head and stalked out of the saloon. The sooner they left Niles for the battlefields, the happier he would be!

February 24, 1862

Dear Father,

These are the most curious times. Garrison duty gives the men too much time for temptation. Such dens of iniquity thrive here where there are gambling and liquor and idleness.

I thought perhaps we would be leaving that behind today. We marched eighteen miles to Metal Landing on the Tennessee River, and the rumor was that the war was over, and we were heading home. It set off such a search for souvenirs that you would not believe. Broken sabers, Confederate buckles. Why, Sam Barker put a twelve-pound cannonball in his haversack! It felt like a hundred pounds by the time we reached the Landing. You should have seen the look on his face when the orders were countermanded upon reaching the Landing. We had to march all the way back!

Only Pete O'Shea didn't mind the return march, because he has his heart set on the shopkeeper's daughter here in Dover.

Will write more soon,

Luke

March 15, 1862

On March 15, they finally departed Dover once and for all. Again, the speculation had been that they were going home, but instead they marched and were carried by steamship further south.

But their disappointment passed quickly. Most men where still convinced that the conflict was near its end, and besides, every man had to admit that they were now part of an impressive expeditionary force. If the Secessionists had not caved in already, this force was surely the instrument to do it. Fifty-eight steamers took twenty-seven thousand men south, accompanied by two gunboats, the *Lexington* and the *Tyler*.

But it had not taken long for a new topic of conversation to quickly rise to the front of everyone's mind. It had been a week since the news first broke. Their general had been demoted! Their leader, the man who had orchestrated the falls of Forts Henry and Donelson, General Grant, had been replaced!

"But why?" Matthew had asked his messmates. No one answered. He bent over the small cookfire and put a biscuit next to the bacon in the skillet awash with grease.

"Don't make no sense to me ne'ther," Sam agreed eventually, kneeling over the fire and warming his large hands. "Relieve General Grant after he won us the greatest victory of the war? Makes no sense."

"I heard he was slipping back into his old habits," Pete commented.

"Who cares?" Sam snorted. "Don't matter to me that he partakes a little. In fact, I think I can only trust a man who does...not including current company, Luke," he hastened.

"Sounds more like jealousy between the generals than alcohol if you ask me," Luke observed.

"General Smith? Jealous of Grant?" Sam asked.

After all, their former division commander was now the commander of the Army of Tennessee since General Grant had been recalled.

"No, not General Smith," Luke said. "He wouldn't do that. Besides, he was Grant's subordinate. He didn't have the power to get him removed. It must be General Halleck back behind his desk in St. Louis."

"Desk general," Pete grumbled. "What does he know about generaling in the field?"

March 16, 1862

Dear Sister,

We have reached our new destination. There isn't much to see here in Savannah, Tennessee. There is really only one small street lined with dilapidated wooden buildings that have seen the worst of a few storms. But the folks are friendly. Once you get used to the we'uns and the yes'ms, they can be quite hospitable people. Most of Savannah is Unionist, believe it or not. I'm told we are only twenty miles from Mississippi too. One man told me that Savannah voted two to one against Secession. It is saddening to think that even so, they have been forced to turn on their country because of the rest of the state. I am humbled to admit that this is what I have learned from being in the sharpshooters. For all of the fiery rhetoric heard in Kalamazoo County, many of these folks are honest, loyal Americans.

From Savannah, we have had a number of raids into the countryside, but mostly we have been opposed only by the weather. Where the Rebel army has gone, no one has any idea.

Your faithful brother, Matthew

March 17, 1862

Luke walked alongside VanderJagt on the narrow dirt road. They had departed the tiny town of Savannah this morning and were setting up camp.

"I'm not so sure that I'm glad we left," Luke said to VanderJagt, as the younger man bent down to retrieve some clear water from the small pond just beyond a peach orchard.

They were eight miles south of Savannah, on the opposite bank of the Tennessee River at a place called Pittsburg Landing, a flat, rolling plateau equally intermixed with field and forest. It had first been the camp of General William T. Sherman's troops after one of his weather-aborted raids south, and now the entire Army of the Tennessee had moved to join the high-strung, red-haired general.

VanderJagt laughed. "When are you going to learn, boy, that it doesn't matter what you think? It only matters what the generals think."

"I know that! I was just—"

"Besides, we should just be grateful that we have old Sam Grant back in command again."

It was true, Luke thought. They should be grateful to have their general back. The newspapers had taken to calling him U. S. Grant, for Unconditional Surrender, after he refused to give the Rebels any terms at Fort Donelson. Only immediate and unconditional surrender would be accepted, Grant had declared. In a war where the North had yet to find a true champion, this bright spot of a victory had been the only story that mattered for the nation's newspapers.

It seemed odd to think the newspapers could wield such influence, but it was their weight that had overwhelmed General Halleck's jealous vendetta against General Grant. Grant had his army back, but one couldn't help but wonder when General Halleck would try to take it away from him again.

Luke finished retrieving the water from the pond, and they walked back up the River Road. The sharpshooters were camped in an open field with the rest of Lauman's Brigade. No doubt the Cloud family wasn't happy that a thousand men were camped on the bare patch of earth that they had scraped out.

There wasn't much to Pittsburg Landing, Luke thought, just a few poor farms carved out of the tangled thickets on this plateau above the Tennessee River. Luke thought he should be thankful for the elevation at least. Just north of them, the creeks and watersheds had flooded the low-lying area due to the torrents of rain earlier in the week. At least, camp was on dry ground.

"Took you long enough," Matthew said, taking the water from Luke, as he began to make some coffee, resting the blackened tin pot on a bed of burning twigs.

"Luke! Luke!" Sam said anxiously, pulling himself away from a conversation with Pete. "Pete O here says that Miss-sippi is just beyond those trees." Sam looked at Luke with excited eyes. Often, the other men enjoyed teasing and generally making a fool of Sam because he was a little slower than the others, but Sam knew that he could trust Luke. The preacher's son never participated in the others' little games, causing some to say Luke was a spoilsport. "So, is that really Miss-sippi down there?" Sam asked again.

With a tired look at Pete, Luke said, "Not quite that close, Sam. Another twenty miles is what I heard. That's where all of General Albert Sidney Johnston's Rebel army is waiting for us."

"Not waiting, *cowering* in Corinth is what I heard from some of Sherman's men," Matthew corrected. "General Johnston is just waiting for us to go down there and chase him out of there too, just like we've chased the rest of his forces out of Tennessee."

"Y'all won't chase him out like that," VanderJagt said, trying to guard against being too harsh. "I know Sidney Johnston. He'll not run so easily."

"Hah," Matthew said. "Those were his men at Fort Donelson. He trained those men."

"But he wasn't there to lead them, Bauer. You'll see a different Rebel soldier when Johnston is on the field."

"You sound like you know him," Luke chuckled.

"I do know him," VanderJagt said. "We fought together in the war for Texas independence."

"Texie! That was a long time ago," Pete whistled.

"You don't have to tell me," VanderJagt said, tugging on his thick beard. "I didn't even need to shave back then, that's how young I was, but y'all don't forget a man like Sidney Johnston. He's a big, barrel-chested man, easily over six feet tall."

"Six feet!" Matthew exclaimed in a disbelieving tone.

"Was he your general then, George?" Pete asked.

VanderJagt laughed. "Yes and no. When I first met him, he was a private. A few months later, he was a brigadier general."

The others gaped and were silent. It was Sam who eventually spoke up, "They can do that?"

"Don't get your hopes up, Sam," Pete chided, drawing laughs from everyone. "You'll be lucky to ever make corporal."

"Besides, son," VanderJagt said with a rare grin, "you didn't go to West Point like Johnston did."

"Oh."

The others burst out laughing again.

"Well, this General Johnston may be some kind of Mex-ie-can fighter, but we ain't Mex-ie-cans. We'll still whip him sure enough. That is if we ever see any Rebels again," Matthew boasted confidently.

Nodding agreement, the men turned back to their individual chores and activities. Luke looked around, remembering how confident and carefree the entire Union encampment was across the plateau. Safe in the thought that the Rebels were far away and in disarray, there had been no mention of building earthworks, and the pickets were thinly extended from the main encampments.

Luke turned around and looked through the trees at the far edge of the Tennessee River.

"See something?" George VanderJagt asked him.

"No," Luke said slowly. "Just thinking."

"Didn't I warn you about that already?"

"George," Luke said even more slowly, "we are on the same side of the river now as General Johnston's army down in Corinth, and the river is at our backs. I think I would feel better if it was *between* us."

March 20, 1862

The three steamers that carried the 12th Michigan plodded down the wide Mississippi waterway, and excitement ran high as many of the Michiganders saw the famed river for the first time. They did not know exactly where they were heading, but everyone guessed it was someplace in Tennessee.

As usual, James and Patrick kept primarily to themselves, but they still heard the rumors just like everyone else. There was no mention to anyone else, but first and foremost in the former sharpshooters' minds was whether they were headed to join General Grant or General Don Carlos Buell. They knew Luke and the others were with Grant, readying themselves for the invasion of Mississippi, but that was not the only large Union army in Tennessee. General Buell's Army of the Ohio was in Nashville. Was that where the 12th Michigan was headed?

The newspapers in St. Louis had been full of stories about making one final push in Mississippi, that such victory would surely bring about peace, despite the Confederate success in Virginia.

James was not so sure, but he did know that this time he was leaving with a better-equipped, better-led group of Michigan men.

March 25, 1862

It was Grant's army they were to join.

"Peabody's Brigade," James mumbled to himself as the 12th Michigan stepped off Pittsburg Landing and began the short march to where they would camp. Oddly, he and Patrick were to be in one of General

Prentiss's brigades again. The leather-faced general, who had cleaned out Missouri with his iron-fisted ways, was to be James's commander again.

The 12th Michigan was to join Peabody's Brigade, one of three brigades reporting to General Benjamin M. Prentiss.

The knowledge that they were to serve General Prentiss again immediately made James remember Missouri. It had been this general's heavy-handed directives in regard to the treatment of civilians that had opened the door for Long's behavior and led to James's downfall. James couldn't help but rationalize that in some distant way General Prentiss was partly responsible for what had happened to little Amelia.

It could only be a bad omen that he found himself in Prentiss's Division again, James thought gloomily. As telltale as the appearance of a raven.

They had spent three hours lingering on the sandy embankment of Pittsburg Landing while Colonel Quinn and Major Powell tried to find the regiment's orders. While they waited, Patrick discovered that the Western Sharpshooters were here also and still assigned to Lauman's Brigade. The Fort Donelson veterans were camped at the Cloud family farm near the peach orchard next to the Hamburg-Savannah Road.

As the 12th Michigan marched by the edge of Cloud's field, following the Corinth-Pittsburg Road to their encampments, Patrick could see a great number of white tents stretching across the field. The faces of the sharpshooters were too far away, but he made a mental note of the location.

"They'll be surprised to see us," Patrick commented with a smile.

James nodded but made no other reply. His mind was too fogged with thoughts of little Amelia now.

The 12th Michigan marched down the dirt road with many of the men whistling, excited to be in the camp of what was called the Army of Tennessee.

"Where you boys from?" one soldier asked as they passed by. He looked up from adjusting a battered tin pot that was boiling. Another soldier poked his head around the tent side and watched the newcomers march by. "Whar'?" he repeated with an odd Southern Illinois drawl.

"12th Michigan," Ezra replied proudly.

"Never heard of ya," the Illinoisan laughed.

"Well, you will. Just you wait," Ezra promised. "Soon as we find them Rebs, you'll have heard of us."

"Only cuz y'all were saved by the 57th Illinois," the first Illinoisan jeered.

The road left the field and cut through a surprisingly green jumble of trees and dense thicket. The only clear space in the dense, mazelike thicket was a shallow ditch made by a rutted wagon trail that cut perpendicular across it.

"This ain't exactly Sain' Louie, is it?" Joe commented to James as they marched another mile before pitching their tents with the rest of Peabody's Brigade, just beyond Barnes Field.

March 26, 1862

Luke and Matthew anxiously walked to the encampments of the 12th Michigan and looked at the fresh white tents of the new regiment. Unlike the sharpshooters' A-shaped wedge tents, the 12th had been supplied with teepeelike round tents.

"I guess new regiments get new tents," Matthew remarked to Luke.

The two Kalamazoo Sharpshooters could not have been more surprised the previous day when Patrick had strolled into their camp just beyond the peach orchard. At first, the men of Company J stared at the red-head like he was a ghost. It had actually been Walker who said the first words with a throaty, "What in the tarnation are *you* doing here?"

After that, the men gathered around Patrick with hardy backslaps. It had taken an hour for much of the novelty to wear off.

Little Lewis Searcy, who had begun to pass the time by creating little songs to be sung with his fiddle, was already trying to work the appearance of their old comrade into a new song.

James had not accompanied Patrick on his visit. Although Patrick had not brought it up until the crowd had cleared some and tried to explain that James did not want to cause a stir, Matthew was still bothered by the slight. Luke accepted it as a wise decision, but Matthew could see no logic behind it. Missouri was a long ways away now, and he knew James had nothing to fear from anyone...except maybe Walker, and that was certainly no more than Luke had to fear from the man.

But today was a new day, and Matthew grinned upon seeing James. He looked relaxed and happy, not like James at all, Matthew thought jokingly.

"*Sergeant* Lockett?" Luke said with a wan smile. "When Patrick told us that, I laughed. I was certain that he was pulling our leg, but there are the stripes."

"I was thinking the same about you," James chuckled. "Corporal? Who would have guessed? Why, I can still remember Matthew trying to teach you how to shoot."

"I think his title as best shot in the county is still safe," Luke grinned in reply.

"But he earned that stripe at Fort Donelson," Matthew piped up, proceeding to relate the tale of Luke's charge into the abatis.

James listened and immediately remembered past picket duties with Luke—remembering when the preacher's son had confessed his consuming fear. It didn't seem possible, but he had no doubt that Matthew was not exaggerating. Luke wouldn't have stood for that.

April 4, 1862

James walked amiably with Ainsley to the southwestern edge of the Union camp, where General Sherman's troops were encamped. He didn't know why, but he was in a particularly good mood today. There was no reason for it, but he was bright and cheerful despite the looming gray clouds and rain. Ainsley, on the other hand, who always seemed to be ever so chipper, was consumed by his own thoughts today.

They were headed to the camp of the 72nd Ohio to meet with one of Ainsley's friends from Washington, D.C., another congressman's son. James was just glad to get out of the camp, even if it meant putting himself at risk of another torrential downpour like the one they had seen this morning. The mood of the men was becoming increasingly antsy. Drilling and waiting was growing tiresome.

Although on a rainy day like today, everyone was glad that they were not marching anywhere, and they were equally thankful that they were camped on the high plateaus, rather than in the swampy lowlands north of the landing. The torrents of rain had turned their camp slick with mud, but at least it wasn't flooding.

"This will be the first time I've seen any of Sherman's men," James noted, trying to start up a conversation with the strangely muted Ainsley. The officer gave no reaction, so James continued, "The newspapers in St. Louis called him insane."

Ainsley nodded, and James shrugged. At least, he was listening.

"The newspapers also talk about how the war is almost won in Tennessee," Ainsley finally replied. "And I know you don't believe that either."

"True," James pondered. "I suppose I shouldn't spread rumors about Sherman since I don't know the man."

In the distance, there was the sound of musketry, and the two Michigan men looked at each other. The sound of gunfire was nothing new in camp. Besides men getting passes to adjust their sights, there had been a number of reports of Confederate activity; however, they had all been disregarded as overblown encounters with bushwhackers and nothing to be concerned about.

The musketry sounded again for another twenty seconds, and this time, more sharply than before. It was definitely not training.

A minute later, two companies of Ohioans cut across the road ahead of them to investigate.

"Those bushwhackers have bitten off more than they can chew this time," Ainsley said, watching the two companies disappear into the thick woods. James made no reply and they began to walk again when Ainsley surprised James by turning suddenly and saying, "I'm glad you decided to accompany me to see William."

"Why?" James grinned. "Thought the Secesh would come through our pickets and take you back to Richmond?"

"No, actually, I need to ask you something. You see, I'm confused about something."

"What's that?"

"It's about Katherine," he said, and the good humor that James had been feeling dropped away instantly. "I just got a letter from her, and she told me to tell you that she was *sorry*? She said she was wrong about what she said in Niles? Did you...did you see her that night in Niles?"

James knew that Ainsley did not mean to make him uncomfortable, but he had. Since that night in Niles, Ainsley had stopped teasing his sergeant about his young, blue-eyed cousin. In fact, he had not mentioned Katherine at all until now.

"Yes, I saw Katherine that night while you were eating dinner," James said slowly. "She was waiting for me in the saloon. It was all part of her plan. She," he hesitated, but then plunged ahead, "she knew that your uncle and aunt would not allow me to eat dinner with them, so she pretended to be ill and then surprised me in the saloon." James grimaced, "surprised" was the right word. He had never expected her to unravel his Missouri misfortune, or to present it to him in so blunt a fashion.

"That does sound like Katherine," Ainsley said with a face. "She is a bit headstrong." He turned back to James and said, "But why didn't you tell me any of this?"

"I'm sorry, I just—"

"It wouldn't have angered me, James. While you may be right, and my uncle and aunt may think less of you because you are a farmer and not a founder, I don't. I have a sense about you, James, that's why I wanted you to be sergeant. There's something about the way that you carry yourself. Why it wouldn't surprise me if you were an officer before this war ends."

"An officer?" James laughed heartily. "That's absurd, Ainsley. They don't make men like me officers. I have no money, no connections."

"But those officers aren't necessarily the ones who will win this war."

"That may be, Ainsley, but that's the way it is, and personally, I don't mind. I saw the attraction that officers draw in Missouri." Even the ones who are running away, he thought bitterly. "Officers are magnets for the bullets. Lieutenant Simon of my old sharpshooting company has been wounded two times already, and they've only been in two battles." James noticed that Ainsley was silent. "Sorry, sir. I didn't mean to spook you. I'm sure you're the one officer who will come through unscathed."

Ainsley laughed. "Probably because they'll look at this scarecrow in officer's clothing and decide it is better if they let me continue to lead."

"You're a fine officer, Ainsley," James said seriously. "The best lieutenant that I have served with."

"Better than Orrin Long?" Ainsley said with some surprise. "He certainly looks the part, and according to my cousin, he has acquitted himself quite well."

Orrin Long.

James's face turned dark and his eyes blazed. "You are his superior in every way." He looked at Ainsley with a burning intensity that the young officer had never seen before in his stolid sergeant. "Orrin Long acquitted himself well?" James finally added scathingly. "A man so full of himself could say anything, but the truth remains the truth."

Still, taken aback by James's reaction, Ainsley said nothing for a moment before commenting, "That's the strongest reaction I've ever seen you have, James. I think if I lit your blanket on fire in the middle of the night, you would have a milder reaction."

"I have my reasons."

"I take it you don't like Orrin," Ainsley chuckled, trying to lighten the mood. He was unsuccessful.

"No, sir, I hate the man," James declared unequivocally.

Ainsley looked at the ground for a moment. He had seen how James looked at his cousin. "Does this have something to do with Katherine?"

"No, Ainsley," James answered in a suddenly tired voice. "Roots of my hate go back well before I ever laid eyes on your cousin. Although, she has done her fair share to stoke those feelings."

"And this is why she is sorry?"

James nodded in reply.

"What *did* she say to you in Niles?"

"Ainsley, if I told you, you wouldn't believe me, and that would harm our friendship, and though I want to tell you, I've come to treasure our friendship more than a poor farmer's son should."

"Tell me," Ainsley ordered in a serious voice.

James looked carefully at his friend. The son of privilege was perhaps naive and gullible, but Ainsley was honest and tried to do right, he thought to himself. With a deep breath he began to relate the entire tale, from Long's stolen silver to Long's cowardice at Hallsville to the killing of young Amelia.

James half-expected an astonished face or disbelieving look from Ainsley, but there was none, only the words, "James, I believe you, my friend."

Rain pelted the already soaked sides of the tent near the small wooden structure of Shiloh Church. The constant pattering played on without let up. "I don't envy Colonel Buckland and those men chasing the bushwhackers," Lieutenant William Peterson said to Ainsley.

Ainsley's Ohioan friend was a determined-looking young man, whose receding hairline made him appear older than he was. Only Peterson's voice was a give away that he was much younger man.

"At this rate," Ainsley replied, "the Rebels don't need guns. They just need to get enough of us out running around in the rain. Pretty soon, everyone will be sick."

Peterson laughed.

"It has been a few hours, and this rain isn't letting up," Ainsley continued. "We should probably head back to camp. A pity to stay dry this whole time only to soak ourselves on the way back."

The sound of sodden troops reached their ears, and just as Peterson was about to comment, the flap of the tent whipped up to reveal a drenched and muddied young lieutenant. The man stood in the opening with sheets of rain whipping against his unwrinkled face.

"William!" the breathless lieutenant rushed, then he noticed there were others in the tent.

"It's okay, Stephen," Peterson said, rising to his feet. "This is my friend Lieutenant Ainsley Stuart of the 12th Michigan and his sergeant, James Lockett."

As if an afterthought, Stephen nodded and then addressed Lieutenant Peterson in an excited voice, "I think you need to get your company ready, Will."

"Why?"

"I just came back with Colonel Buckland from that patrol to investigate the shots."

"Yes?"

"It wasn't bushwhackers. When we reached the picket posts, all seven pickets were missing, not a sign of them! That seemed like too much for a few bushwhackers, so we chased after whoever it was when we ran into some Rebel cavalry. Good thing it was raining so hard, because neither side could see each other real well, and they certainly had us at a disadvantage being only two companies of us."

"But why do I need to get my company together? I wouldn't think that Rebel cavalry is cause for concern, Stephen."

"Wait, William, I'm not finished. The 5th Ohio Cavalry fortunately came to our rescue and scattered the Rebs, chasing them back. I thought it was all over when a few minutes later our cavalry came racing back to us."

"What? Why did they do that?"

"Said they saw a long line of Confederate infantry and artillery. Colonel Buckland is informing General Sherman right now. The Rebels are here!"

Ainsley looked at James. "I guess we better get back to our posts, rain or no rain now."

Saying good-byes and pulling on their hats, James and Ainsley began their walk back through the downpour. Their path took them right past the tent of General Sherman. Even in the pounding rain, they could hear the voice of the general chiding Colonel Buckland and his "green Buckeyes" for exaggerating nothing more than enemy reconnaissance.

As they passed the open tent flap, James looked over his shoulder at the disheveled general with red hair sticking out in almost every direction.

"What are you looking at, sergeant?" a goateed major at the tent's entrance snarled, hurrying them on their way.

The entire way back, James could hear General Sherman's mocking tone echoing in his head, "Rebel infantry? Hah! That's the problem with you volunteers! You green Buckeyes! One little bushwhacking party becomes an entire column of Johnston's infantry! There's nothing out there, Colonel! Nothing!"

April 5, 1862

The large man listened politely.

His jacket was partially unbuttoned, as if his thickly muscled chest prevented it from being any other way. The steady firmness of his brow never wavered, and the full mustache never curled in either disagreement or agreement as he listened to his subordinate outline his fears.

Then the large man, General Albert Sidney Johnston, commander of the Confederate army, stood up. He towered over his bureaucratically chosen second-in-command, General P. G. T. Beauregard.

While Johnston looked the very picture of a rugged leader and man of action, Beauregard was a swarthy-skinned Louisianan who looked like the clever, cunning fox—a man certain that his raw intellect was far superior to any man's, including General Johnston's.

Beauregard had just spent the last twenty minutes trying to convince Johnston of the obvious, but a flicker of doubt never clouded the larger man's face. So Beauregard tried one last time, in as blunt and simple of terms as possible, "We no longer have the element of surprise, sir."

Beauregard forced himself to say the last word, but even giving proper respect did not seem to impress Johnston. He still stood there, as confident as ever that they were about to destroy Grant's army of Yankees.

Johnston gave a small smile of confidence. "No, my friend," he started, even though Beauregard was far from a friend, "we will attack, and we will surprise them, and we will trap Grant's army against the banks of the river."

"But the attack was to have been launched at dawn yesterday!" Beauregard was right, the muddy roads and raw recruits of the Confederate army had made for an agonizingly slow pace upon leaving Corinth. They would not be ready for the attack until dawn the next day.

"Grant is still unaware," Johnston said with such a calm confidence that Beauregard half-believed him even though he knew the man could not be right. Surely by now, the Yankees realized their presence.

"But if Buell's army has already arrived—"

"They have not arrived, General Beauregard. Don Carlos would not push his men so hard. They still march. And this is why we must attack, before he can join Grant."

Beauregard knew Johnston had a point. It was better to fight when the odds were even, rather than when outnumbered two to one. But the element of surprise surely must be gone, and an attack would be foolhardy now.

"We will attack at dawn tomorrow, and we will surprise them," Johnston said with finality.

Beauregard frowned at the lost debate. He knew an order when he heard one.

"Trouble, sir?" Ainsley asked Major James E. Powell of the 12th Michigan.

The dark eyes of the major were focused on something far, far away, and it took him a moment to realize that he had been spoken to. Looking at the skin-and-bones lieutenant, Powell relaxed slightly. Despite the young man's unsoldierly appearance, Major Powell liked Stuart.

"No, Lieutenant Stuart, all is well."

"That's good, sir. I thought for a moment more of the pickets had disappeared," Ainsley chuckled ever so slightly.

"Lieutenant?" Major Powell said with a puzzled look.

"Like the 72nd Ohio and their pickets, sir."

"What are you talking about, Lieutenant?" Powell questioned, and Ainsley related what he had seen yesterday in Sherman's camp.

"By damn!" Powell cursed when Ainsley was finished. "What's wrong with the man?"

"Sir?"

"Sherman just ridiculed Colonel Appler too. Just took the man down to his bootstraps in front of the entire 53rd Ohio."

"What for?"

"For sounding the long roll after hearing some shots. General Sherman told him to take his Buckeyes back to Ohio—that the enemy is no closer than Corinth."

Powell turned and looked over his shoulder in the direction of their brigade commander's tent, Colonel Everett Peabody. The mountainous colonel was a well-liked, garrulous man, but he was a cautious man and no fool either. Colonel Peabody would not take the news lying down—rumor or not.

He gazed around their encampment. There were no earthworks, and the river was at their backs. The days had been spent drilling the men. So much of the army was raw, he knew, and the drilling was needed, but now it seemed incredibly foolish to have neglected the defense.

Ainsley looked at the Major Powell's pensive face, knowing what he was thinking. But even if the Rebels were here, would they dare attack? "With General Wallace's men nearby now, we number forty-five thousand," Ainsley thought aloud.

"Surprise would make up for the numbers, Lieutenant. Besides, we've known that Polk and Hardee have been marching. All reports say that the enemy is concentrating in Corinth."

"But if they are concentrating here instead?"

"That is exactly what I fear, Lieutenant Stuart."

"But why would General Sherman be so adamant?"

Powell paused before answering. "The papers in St. Louis said he had lost his nerve, had overestimated the size of the Rebels in the past. Maybe now he is overcompensating."

"Pardon me for saying so, sir, but perhaps the general is not like you and just does not trust us volunteers."

"Perhaps, Lieutenant. God knows there are enough of those who think that the old army has been corrupted by you volunteers." Powell smiled slightly to take the edge off his words. They were quiet for a second when Powell turned serious again and looked Ainsley straight in the eye. "Say nothing of what was said here, Lieutenant. Do you understand?"

"Yes, sir."

"I need to go talk with Colonel Peabody."

With a sense of urgency, Major Powell had related his fears to Colonel Peabody who shared similar ones. Feeling that the safety of the army may be at stake and that there would be no harm in investigating, Colonel Peabody went to their divisional commander, the leather-faced General Prentiss.

Predictably, the general was his normal contentious and abrasive self. Had he spoken to Peabody in such a manner outside of the army, the massive colonel would have taken issue, but being in the army, Peabody answered a stiff "Yes, sir," to each rebuke.

But Colonel Peabody had made up his mind. He would disobey orders and send Major Powell and five companies on a march down the Seay Road and determine whether there was an enemy out there in the darkness. He would be damned before he just sat there and did nothing.

Just *one* mile away from Peabody's camp, forty-seven thousand Confederates shivered in their soaked and muddied clothes. Exhausted and chilled from the long march in the rain, they still lit no fires for fear of discovery. As they huddled in the darkness, they could faintly hear the Yankee soldiers—unaware and singing "Home, Sweet Home."

April 6, 1862

"I was standing right there when Colonel Peabody gave Major Powell the orders," Ainsley said to James as they began to march off in the darkness. It was scarcely four o'clock in the morning, and James was tired, cold, and a little worried about marching off in the darkness of the hour. "I believe the colonel's exact words were to 'Find the enemy. Drive in the guard and open up on the reserve, develop the force, hold the ground as long as possible, then fall back.'"

"So let me get this straight, sir," Patrick said in a hushed voice. "We're marching off here in the darkness because we think the whole Rebel army is out there—not just some bushwhackers—and our job is to pick a fight with them, with just five measly companies."

Ainsley paused before answering in a reflective voice, "I suppose that is accurate. I hadn't thought about it that way."

"It's better than sleeping comfortably in our tents and waiting for them to come at us," James said, remembering the 72nd Ohio's missing pickets.

"There's probably not much out there," Seth Dreyer chipped in from behind them. "Just a few bushwhackers in for a big surprise."

Before James could answer, Major Powell appeared besides them in the darkness. "Quiet!" he demanded in a low, angry voice. "What do you think this is, an excursion for night air? No talking! Understand?"

"Yes, sir," they all answered in muted voices.

"Chrissakes, Lieutenant, you're an officer," Powell muttered before heading back towards the front of the patrol.

They were five companies strong, two hundred seventy men. The two largest companies being the ones from the 12th Michigan.

Quietly, they marched southwest of their camps towards the Corinth Road. In the pitch-dark, only the sound of rustling uniforms and the occasional jangle of a cartridge box and canteen broke the stillness of the night. Unconsciously, James stroked the smooth octagonal barrel of his Dimick. Patrick fussed with the cartridge box, and Ezra sniffled and wiped his running nose on his sleeve.

They were only three-quarters of a mile from their camps when each man snapped erect and alert at the crack of two muskets, and then a few more. In the dim light, James could barely make out the shadowy form of two mounted sentinels.

"Skirmish line! Skirmish line!" Major Powell ordered frantically, and the men reacted as best they could in a state of confusion in the darkness, stumbling and tripping but forming a thin staggered line.

The fire of the vedettes was soon joined with that of a couple Confederate pickets in the trees. The hastily formed skirmish line turned slightly and advanced into Fraley Field.

"My word, they were close to camp," Ainsley said behind James.

"Sir!" James growled, knowing that an officer had more important things to do than give commentary. "Sir," he repeated less harshly.

"They are close," Joe observed.

"I cain' hardly see a thing," Ezra complained.

Patrick raised his rifle and took aim at where he had just seen a flash.

"Not yet," James whispered to his friend and reluctantly Patrick returned the rifle to a ready position across his body. In the dim light of the early morning, James thought he spotted dark forms moving in front of the trees on the other end of the field.

"When do we get to fire on these bushwhackers?" Seth said impatiently from down the loose line.

"When the major gives the word," James said, his voice sounding gruff and threatening without even trying, "and not before!"

Behind them, Ainsley peered into the middle of the patrol's small skirmish line, searching for Major Powell's silhouette. Taking his family sword out of its scabbard and pulling out the pistol with his other hand, Ainsley looked odd, even with the darkness hiding his gaunt and awkward frame.

But also hidden was the determined look on his face. To himself, Ainsley quietly recited Colonel Peabody's orders, "Drive in the guard and open up on the reserve." They were in the process of doing just that.

Suddenly, the stationary figures—one hundred eighty yards ahead—changed the peaceful dawn with an eruption of noise and flash. Ainsley wasn't the only one startled by the small volley. Seth halted in his boots only to be unceremoniously shoved forward by James.

"Come—," James began, only to be interrupted by Major Powell's order to return fire. On this far end of the line, James and the others never actually heard the command, but it was clear enough that the order had been given, a ragged volley ran down their line.

"Independent fire! Independent fire!" James heard the echoed order after they had all emptied their weapons.

He was already reloading his Dimick when he noticed some of the other men slow to do so. "Just like we drilled before," he said in a calm voice that was still loud enough to be heard by those around him. With individual cracks and flashes, the Confederates fired.

Slowly, James's ears became deadened to the crack of rifles and the occasional zing of a bullet, but it was the thump of a ball meeting flesh that caught his attention.

With a puzzled expression, he looked to his left where the peculiar sound came from and saw a pair of boots lying in the grass. His eyes followed the boots up to the trousers and uniform. Although it was still too dark to see a face, he knew exactly who it was from the full stomach that strained the uniform.

"Ezra," Patrick said matter-of-factly as he rammed another Minié ball into his Dimick.

"Keep up the fire, boys," Ainsley interrupted from behind them. Aware that a few men were gawking at the company's first casualty, he shouted encouragement to them with a voice that none of them had heard before from his skinny body. A resonant tenor shouted at them with a calm presence. "Hot and steady, boys! Hot and steady!"

The fire picked up pace again, and despite the seriousness of their actions, James knew he was smiling a little. Ainsley was going to make a good officer after all.

James aimed at what he guessed was a Rebel, although it might have been a tree. As if in answer to his question, a flash appeared from the spot, and James instantly answered it. Although he was sure the shot had been true, and with his Dimick it was well within his range, he could not tell whether the silhouette was still there or not. As he took another paper cartridge from his box and tore the end off with his teeth, he wondered how the Wisconsin boys at the other end of the line were faring. He knew that they had been equipped with heavy Belgian muskets, and it would take an excellent shot and a little luck to hit anything with a musket from this distance.

The black of night slowly turned to a dark blue and in the growing strands of light, James lost count of how many times he had fired.

The change in daylight and the rate of fire from the Confederates was almost imperceptible, but slowly, the patrol was getting the upper hand and though there were a number of blue-coated men down, they were maintaining a higher rate of fire than the Rebels.

Major Powell noticed it also and gave the order to advance. Obediently, the patrol edged closer.

Even the cry of pain from his left did not shake James's attention as he focused on the Confederate pickets.

"Forward, company! Forward!" Ainsley urged above the intermittent firing.

A few more bullets whizzed by overhead, and the patrol stopped in its tracks but not because of the bullets. It was the sight of an entire Confederate line of battle emerging from the trees—*thousands* of men all shoulder to shoulder in two rows, stepping off in near unison.

"Oh, my God!" Tucker gasped.

James's eyes flashed from one end of the line to the other. The butternut line stretched as far as could be seen. James didn't even want to know what was hidden beyond sight in the trees to the right. It was obvious to every man that this was more than anyone anticipated.

This was Johnston's army! Stunned, James realized that they had bumped headlong into a massive Confederate assault. No army could organize so many so quickly. The only way that so many men could be in a line of battle already was that they had *already* been marching. The Confederates had planned a surprise attack!

Were it not for their patrol, the entire Army of the Tennessee would have been caught in their tents!

"Steady!" James said more out of instinct than anything else. But holding his ground was the last thing on his mind. He could feel some of the men creeping backwards. He had not wanted to retreat at Hallsville, but this was different! This time, he wanted to run—run far and fast. Against this battle line, there was no hope for victory. No bravery could save the day.

"It's the entire Rebel army!" one soldier uttered slowly in a low voice.

"Aye," Patrick said.

"Orderly withdrawal!" Ainsley echoed the order as the entire patrol began to retreat.

"Orderly!" James snapped, watching one man take off in a dead run. "I'll shoot the next man who runs!" he added, and the fierce look on his normally impassive face declared that he was not bluffing.

They retreated back down the Corinth Road, past the fork in the road. Most of the men in the company had only one thought, to pull back as fast as possible, but James bit his lower lip, knowing that they were not far from their camps. Had the sounds of fighting been enough to rouse Prentiss and the other generals from their stupor? Where were the others? Had they given the army enough time to form a defense behind them?

They were met just beyond the crossroads by Moore's Brigade.

"Where are the rest?" Patrick said solemnly to James. "One brigade will do nothing."

James nodded. Patrick was right. Although this tripled the size of their little patrol, every man who had seen the Confederate battle line knew that they needed much, much more. Still, they dutifully formed a new defense line and waited for the Confederate wave to appear again.

Just behind James, Major Powell was in animated conversation with Colonel Moore.

"Ainsley," Major Powell called, motioning him over. "Get back to camp and tell Colonel Peabody that we are being driven back. Even with Moore's men, we won't be able to hold this lot. We are facing an entire division or more."

"Yes, sir!" Ainsley said, and he took off in a gangly ramble down the road back to their camp barely a half-mile away. Awkwardly, he held his scabbard to the side of his leg while he ran.

With sweat streaming down his bony face, Ainsley dashed breathlessly into camp, immediately spotting the massive two hundred forty-pound frame of Colonel Peabody.

"Sir, sir!" Ainsley cried, dramatically bounding in front of the colonel and saluting. "Major Powell reports that the patrol is being driven back. It's a division attack, sir."

"Division," Peabody scoffed, looking sidewise, and Ainsley noticed the Philadelphia journalist who had been in camp the past few days. The man looked oddly out of place in his brown suit and bowler.

"Sir, I've seen them," Ainsley began again only to be interrupted by a tremendous volley of musketry that sounded like a thunder crack from heaven or hell.

The sound of such violent musketry quickly changed Colonel Peabody's tune. No longer skeptical, he ordered the long roll sounded, and like ants from their mounds, men piled out of their tents and left their morning cookfires burning.

How any of them could have been sleeping through all this, Ainsley would never understand.

But with a speed born of desperation and shock from being roused by an imminent threat, Peabody's Brigade began to form up.

As Ainsley stood dumbfounded in the middle of the camp, he heard the sound of galloping hooves. The draconian glare of General Benjamin M. Prentiss looked down at Ainsley, still damp with sweat in his lieutenant's uniform, and then the general's eyes found the much larger frame of Colonel Peabody about to mount his horse.

With a slew of curses, General Prentiss addressed Peabody, but it was the only final words that Ainsley would remember.

"...a direct flouting of my authority, Peabody! You are held personally responsible for bringing on this engagement!"

"General," Peabody interrupted and saluted from his steed, "if I brought on this fight, I am to lead the van!" He yanked on the horse's reins and chased after his men forming up to block the road just beyond their own tents.

The thunderous volley that Ainsley heard in camp was the work of Woods's Mississippians. The musket and Minié balls slammed into Moore's Brigade and Powell's patrol with devastating effect. James looked around at the cries of agony on either side of him. Some men were returning fire; others were dazed into stony inaction; others were dead already.

It was a slaughter with one possible outcome. There was no chance for victory, but James and a few others knew they had to stand and fight. They had to give Grant and Sherman time. They had to slow the enemy!

Grudingly, they gave ground, firing as they slowly shuffled back. James raised his rifle and fired into the approaching mass of butternut still shrouded in the white smoke of their volley. Missing seemed impossible against the advancing wall. Slowing the wall seemed equally unlikely.

"Close the gaps," Captain Baker ordered, bleeding heavily from a shoulder wound. Obediently, the defenders crowded together to erase the gaps caused by fallen men. Then new gaps would appear as the musketry whistled through the branches, snapping bone and wood alike.

Captain Baker began to wave his sword with his good arm and was about to give another order when he was struck down by a musket ball. Seemingly oblivious to the loss, the men continued to fire as fast as they could load.

Taking another paper cartridge from a cartridge box that he had taken off a dead comrade, James began to reload as he inched back with the rest of the men. He bit into the end of the cartridge and tore off the end. This time, he did not bother to spit the few grains of black powder out of his mouth. At this point, the powder was all he could taste, and spitting it out was an exercise in futility.

With Patrick on one side and Tucker on his other, he fired and fired again. So many times that he lost count, but always, they were forced to give ground. He knew they were giving as good as they could, but their line continued to shrivel while the long lines of Confederates never seemed to shrink. Ponderously, the Confederates would move forward, always threatening to overlap the outgunned defenders on both flanks.

It was shortly after seven now, and James was vaguely aware that the sounds of battle were spreading. As he reloaded yet again, he thought he heard fire from their distant right where Sherman's men were camped. For a moment, he wondered how Ainsley's friend Lieutenant Peterson was faring.

He finished reloading and aimed his Dimick into the advancing wall, but his shot harmlessly flew into the upper branches of the trees as he was jostled by the soldier behind him, crowding forward for his own shot. Without a word or face of disgust, James ignored him and dropped the butt of the gun to the ground and began the process all over again. The burning hot barrel stung his hands, but he hardly noticed. Finished, he pinched on another percussion cap and raised the Dimick, firing into the distant, but ever oncoming, line of Rebels.

Ainsley watched Peabody's Brigade form up. Miller's Brigade guarded their left flank. Two brigades and a battery of artillery weren't enough men, he knew. And what of Major Powell's patrol? Anxiously, Ainsley chewed on his lower lip. Those were his men up there, ahead somewhere—bearing the brunt of the fulminating attack.

As if in a daze, Ainsley started to walk through Peabody's line into the forest up ahead. He could see no men, but the sounds of battle were coming through loud and clear—echoing, threatening.

"Sir!" an anxious voice cried out to Ainsley as it was obvious to all that the rail thin officer was about to disappear in the cacophony of fire raging in the trees ahead. Ainsley turned to see another lieutenant chasing after him.

"Where are you going?" the fresh-faced young man said to him.

"To rejoin my men," Ainsley said dumbly.

"Sir, I wouldn't do that. You're as likely to run into the Secesh as you are to meet up with your men now."

"But those are my men," Ainsley said, anxiously wondering whether James and the others could possibly survive the increasing pace of fire in front of them.

"Sir," the young man said, "I would consider it an honor if you would fight with us, sir. There is nothing else you can do for your men up there."

Ainsley hesitated, pondering the truth in the man's words. With a sorrowful face, he nodded and walked back to Peabody's line with the man. It was only then that Ainsley recognized the young lieutenant as a fellow officer of the 12th Michigan.

With a nervous silence, Peabody's line waited for the appearance of the Confederates. Suddenly, the firing in front of them stopped and a few minutes later, a few blue forms raced out of the woods, like animals escaping a forest blaze.

"Hold you-r fi-re!" The order quickly rang down the line as the remnants of Moore's Brigade raced through the line. Some of the men stopped to join up with the Peabody's line, but many continued to flee from the onslaught without breaking stride.

"Johnny Reb send you running?" jeered one of the Wisconsin men in Peabody's line.

Quickly, James grabbed Tucker by the back of the collar, knowing that as tired as they were, Tucker was still liable to go after the man.

"Save it, Joe. This day has only begun, and you're going to need all the energy you can muster."

With a sense of the inevitable, they waited to confront the Rebels for what seemed like the hundredth time already, and it was only 7:30 in the morning. One of Peabody's men next to him gasped, and James looked up into the now familiar sight of mismatched butternut that stretched the edges of his vision.

"Steady, stea-dy," the order rang up and down the line. Slowly and steadily, the line advanced towards them. To their left, a shrill and ghoulish yell rose up from the Rebel ranks, reverberating...a sepulchral call.

Six months of memory passed through James's mind as the massive Confederate volley tore into the blue line of defenders. Minié balls whipsawed through the air, snapping branches off, slamming into trees with audible thuds, shrieking as they raced overhead, and some knifing deep into men's bodies. Yet, James somehow heard none of it while his mind raced from Kalamazoo to Missouri to Kalamazoo to here.

He snapped awake as he went to his knees. The man behind him had fallen into his legs. James had not felt the breeze of a bullet pass by his head, smashing a gruesome hole into the face of the soldier behind him. James remained on his knees for a moment, not sure whether he had been shot or not, not sure at all what had happened.

"James!" he heard a concerned cry from next to him.

Blinking, James pulled his legs free from the man's lifeless body, and rose to his feet. "I'm okay, Patrick."

The Peabody line survived that first devastating volley. With a mixture of pride and surprise, James saw that the line had held intact. There were so many holes in the line, but they were still fighting. Fighting for their very lives, but they had not run!

The men kept up their fire, and the two sides traded blow for blow. The Yankees were holding the Rebels for now, but James could see through the trees that some Rebels were moving to the right, heading for the unprotected flank.

Behind his men, Colonel Peabody rode, rallying them with his presence and voice.

For a half-hour, Minié balls and musket balls filled the air with a familiar zip and zing. Each man fighting an individual war against a faceless butternut-clad enemy, firing as fast as he could reload. James looked behind him as Peabody rode by again, and he found himself stirred by the presence of the large man. Though suffering from four wounds, Peabody seemed to be unaffected and determined to win.

A musket ball whizzed by close overhead, and James wondered how many more could possibly be deflected by this invisible shield that seemed to protect him. For a moment, he wondered again whether God intended for him to die here, in this wooded thicket in Tennessee—so far from home, so far from preventing his brother from joining the army and finding the same fate. Yet, so close to friends like Patrick, Ainsley, Luke, and Matthew.

Even as his mind wandered, he mechanically continued firing and reloading. But the wanderings of his mind were halted by a cry of despair behind him. With a quick glance over his shoulder, he saw Colonel Peabody lying on the ground, shot in the head. The line began to break as a few men decided they could take no more and began to run back through the trees. Seconds later, a cry came up from the far right as the Confederates overlapped the line and began to turn the flank. There was momentary panic as it seemed that some of the Rebels had gotten in behind them!

Suddenly, the entire line gave way, and panicked men began to stream backwards towards their own tents. It was pandemonium and every man ran for himself!

Bending down to grab another two cartridge boxes from the dead around him, one of whom had been the shaken boy, James raced after Patrick and Joe. They sprinted through their camp in Barnes Field. There seemed to be Rebels everywhere. Firing! Taking prisoners!

The men rounded one neat row of tents and were surprised by two filthy, patchily dressed Confederates emerging from one of the tents, each with a loaf of bread in his hand. Patrick knocked one into the other, as they streaked past. James dodged the falling Rebels and hurdled the still burning cookfire in one clean jump. He did not look back at the equally stunned Rebels who now sat in the mud, but with their prized bread safely held high.

Those who could, dashed to the far end of camp, beyond where there seemed to be any Rebels. James paused momentarily behind one of the quartermaster's wagons to catch his breath and fire at the pursuing Rebels.

The Confederates were charging en masse now, swooping in on the disorganized and shattered Yankees, taking dozens of prisoners.

But other Yankees were escaping. Some made the mad dash across their old camp, but many suffered the greatest indignity of all, shot in the back as they ran. It was chaos all across the encampment.

Some of the remnants of Peabody's and Miller's Brigades paused to fire at their pursuers as James had done before continuing the retreat through the field. From behind wagons, tents, piles of hay, and trees, they sporadically spat back at the enemy, but it was like throwing peas at the side of a barn. Their efforts had no visible impact on slowing down the Rebels.

James and the others ran until they reached the low, wooded ridge just beyond their camp. Pausing there to reload, James looked with astonishment at the number of bodies strewn across their old camp. But it was not the sight of the dead and dying that shocked him. It was the sight of the Confederate's advance grinding to a halt! The Rebels were plundering the camp! More intent on booty than on pursuing the shattered Yankees, the Confederate advance had stopped!

"I don't believe it," Joe mumbled.

James noticed more than ever that the butternut wave was not homogeneous. In fact, the enemy appeared almost like a ragtag mob. Some had full uniforms of butternut, some wore only coats with civilian trousers, and some had no uniform at all. Nearly all of them, however, paused their attack to scrounge around the captured Yankee camp. Coffee that had been left on cookfires was now devoured. The fresh bread that had been the luxury of the camp was now being devoured by men from Mississippi, Alabama, and Tennessee. Soldiers ducked into tents and came out with watches, tin plates, anything that could be stuffed into a haversack.

"Think they'll take your writin' book?" Patrick asked, reading James's mind.

James shrugged. “S’pose so. Looks like they intend on taking everything else.”

A few Confederate officers struggled to regain discipline. Some were able to convince their men to collect prisoners instead of booty, but most were unsuccessful.

Even so, James could see that the Confederates had another problem now. The Rebels were ill prepared to deal with that many prisoners. Like the temptation to loot, the number of prisoners accomplished what Peabody’s Brigade had not been able to do, slow the Confederate assault.

For a shockingly long hour, the Rebels were held at bay with nothing more than an occasional pot shot to disrupt them.

By 8:30, Birge's Western Sharpshooters had begun to march down the River Road towards the peach orchard with the rest of Lauman's Brigade. Up in front of them was Colonel Williams. Behind them was the young, fresh-faced General McArthur and his brigade from W. H. L. Wallace's Division.

Marching in the rear of Lauman's column, Matthew looked over his shoulder at the 50th Illinois in McArthur's Brigade. "Look at those funny hats," he said.

"They're called berets," Luke replied.

"Plenty of Scotsmen once wore those," Pete added.

"I like the little ball on top," Sam laughed.

The conversation continued down such an idle path as a guard against their nervousness. The sounds of intense fighting had been heard all morning, and now they were marching closer to the ever booming and cracking sounds. The steady stream of refugees from Prentiss's Division did little to cheer them. While some were genuinely wounded, many were just badly scared. So scared, that the normal jeers had no effect on them. The shirkers continued to run for the landing.

Up ahead of the column, an officer of the 3rd Iowa announced that any man seen deserting his post would be shot. His regiment gave a resounding cheer.

"Think James and Patrick are okay?" Matthew said. He had been searching the faces of the shirkers as they passed by, each and every face. He didn't expect to find James or Patrick, but he thought he might recognize someone from their camp. It was a fruitless vigil.

"You'll not see Jimmy or Paddy with this riff-raff," VanderJagt answered.

They passed the pond and the blossoming peach orchard. Williams's Brigade had taken up a position on the opposite end of the old cotton field. The sharpshooters and the rest of Lauman's Brigade filed in beside them, forming a right angle on Williams's left.

It was nine o'clock, and they waited as the sounds of battle neared. Surely, the Rebels couldn't have pushed this far already, Matthew thought to himself.

James, Patrick, and Joe fell back out of the wooded ridge having given token resistance. Despite their sniping, the Confederates had gathered some semblance of organization again and were pushing forward.

Scarcely better than individuals, the Union remnants retreated again, diagonaling away from the Eastern Corinth Road, heading north. It was as if they were retracing their steps back to the Landing.

"I'm getting damn tired of retreating," Joe grumbled. There was blood on his leg (someone else's), on his shoulder (his), and two scratches on his forehead from flying pieces of tree. The musket ball had passed clean through the muscle beneath his shoulder, and the arm hung limply in place. James had noticed what a struggle it was for Joe to reload his weapon, much less raise it and aim. But Joe was not about to skedaddle with the rest of the wounded.

"At least you can say we were the last to retreat," Patrick said as a couple of Confederate shots zinged by overhead.

"I'd say those who got captured get that honor," Joe grimaced through clenched teeth, "but point taken."

They passed through the edges of Davis Field and saw another line of Union blue forming up, waiting for the Confederates to appear. As they crossed through the far right of this line, Patrick recognized the battle flag of the 33rd Indiana in Lauman's Brigade.

James shouted to one of the Hoosier officers who watched them intently. "The Rebs 're right behind us, sir."

The officer nodded and pointed behind the line. "The rest of your brigade is reforming behind us."

"Yes, sir," James answered automatically.

"How 'bout that, we get a rest," Joe mocked.

"That was Lauman's Brigade," Patrick interjected, looking at James. "I recognized their colors."

"Wonder where the sharpshooters are?" James said, spinning around and scanning the line while he walked backwards, but he could not tell where their friends were.

As they reached the thin wagon cut in the dense thicket, they heard a familiar voice cheer them.

"Sergeant Lockett!" Ainsley yelled, bounding up to greet them.

"Ainsley!" James said in a grateful, but tired voice.

The sounds of battle sprang up again behind them as the Confederates engaged Lauman's and Williams's Brigades.

"I should have known you three would be on the horse's tail," Ainsley said in jest with a grin.

"Where've you been, Lieutenant?" Tucker said, thirstily emptying the officer's canteen.

"Don't tell me you missed all the fun," Patrick cracked.

"Never fear, Private McManus. I've had plenty of fun." Ainsley lifted the rifle that he had been leaning on so nonchalantly. "Plenty of fun."

"There will be more where that came from," James said. "How about some ammunition?" Three empty cartridge boxes dangled around James's neck.

"Back here," Ainsley said, pointing and walking back with them. "I ended up helping Hickenlooper's Battery get away. How about you?"

"Hickenlooper?" James said with some surprise. "They made it away?"

Ainsley nodded. "They've formed up over there with the rest of us from Prentiss's Division."

"And how many is that?"

"About five hundred."

Patrick and Joe stopped what they were doing and looked aghast at Ainsley.

"Five hundred? Out of the whole division?" Joe said in disbelief.

"What about the 12th?" Patrick asked.

"Some of it is here. It's hard to say, Patrick. We're all so scattered. There could be more of them scattered anywhere from here to the river to the landing. So scattered...why, it must be some sort of miracle that brought the four of us back together."

"Yeah, a real work of divine intervention," Patrick grumbled, but he too was pleased to be reunited with their affable lieutenant.

They refilled their empty cartridge boxes amidst the crash of weaponry. The Rebels had now run into Lauman's line from the sound of it.

"Glad to see at least you put away that silly sword and picked up a rifle, sir," James said, tapping the battered rifle that Ainsley held.

"The sword wasn't much use," Ainsley admitted. "But it's not silly. It's a sign of honor."

"So we're to stop the Rebels here, sir?" Patrick interrupted. "Along this wagon cut?"

"Yes, we will stop them here on this sunken road."

James looked skeptically at the wagon trail that had been worn down over the years, like a shallow trench. "I suppose it is as good a place as any we've had to this point."

Luke watched the 13th Ohio battery unlimber their six guns, as the sharpshooters waited. They had seen the last remnants of Prentiss's Division come through the field and forest, and everyone along the line knew what would be just behind the retreating soldiers.

The men of Lauman's Brigade had seen battle before at Fort Donelson. The boom of cannon, the crack of musketry, and the zing of Minié balls were nothing new to Lauman's Brigade, but Luke found himself wondering how the untested Ohioans, manning the cannon, felt.

Rebels began to appear at the edge of the wood across the field, just behind the Hamburg-Purdy Road. There was surprisingly tentative musketry exchanged. Being at the right angle joint between Lauman's and Williams's Brigades, the sharpshooters were well placed to retaliate with their long-range Dimick rifles.

Matthew took aim at a Confederate holding their flag aloft and fired. With a flash of satisfaction, he saw the flag fall from the man's hands as he fell. The moment was fleeting, however, as another Rebel instantly rushed to pick it up.

Matthew hurried to reload and then took his time finding a target again. He had come to the conclusion that shooting an ordinary soldier was a poor use of his skills. Instead, he patiently scanned the field for an officer or flag bearer. Spotting a soldier waving a sword, he fired and was disappointed as the man retreated unharmed back into the trees.

Southwest of them, Confederate cannon opened up, and Matthew suddenly felt very vulnerable. While the Union cannon roared in reply, Matthew could not tell where the Union cannon were aiming, if indeed they were aiming at all. In contrast, the Confederates were clearly attempting to silence the Union batteries. Chunks of earth were torn up as the shells exploded near the Ohioans.

Then instantly, Matthew was blinded by an enormous flash. The very air exploded, and a blast, like a tornado, knocked him to the ground where the earth still shook from the tremendous explosion. Minutes seemed to pass before the soft ground of the cotton field quelled its reverberations, longer still before the gritty dirt and debris ceased raining from above.

A lucky Confederate shell had found a Union caisson, and the subsequent explosion, fueled by the ammunition, obliterated any trace of the caisson, the six pull horses, or the eight artillerymen. The cannon, twenty yards in front of the caisson, had been flipped upside down.

But worst of all, the explosion unhinged the 13th Ohio. Immediately, they abandoned all of their cannon and fled the field in a panic.

Matthew felt a firm hand pull him up from the ground. The same hand stopped Matthew's gaping with a not-so-gentle slap to the back of his head. "Eyes front!" VanderJagt barked. Or at least, that was what his lips seemed to say. Matthew couldn't hear a thing, not a ringing, just nothing, like a bottomless tomb. Just vast, vast cavernous silence.

Despite the lack of artillery support, Lauman's Brigade and the rest of General Stephen A. Hurlbut's troops held their position. The sharpshooters sniped from long distance at the Confederate infantry in the woods, but mostly, they flattened themselves as best possible from the continued barrage of artillery.

To Matthew, it was unbearable. But as Colonel Lauman and Colonel Birge conversed behind the burrowing sharpshooters, the two officers appeared as calm and unconcerned as if they were chatting aimlessly on an ordinary spring day. But finally, fearing a Confederate infantry assault, Hurlbut pulled his two brigades back. Matthew and the rest of the sharpshooters agreeably fell back across the cotton field and ended up lining the fence around the peach orchard.

"That's a fair amount of open ground for them to cover now," Lieutenant Simon yelled in Luke's ear.

Luke looked around him and noticed immediately that he did not see Captain Vincent and that the company looked smaller. He had heard a few of the telltale thumps of lead meeting flesh and had seen one shell shred two unfortunate men, but the company looked too small.

"Where is everyone?" Luke asked. "Did we get separated on the withdrawal?"

"We are a little out of place," Simon said, noting that they were tucked between companies of Colonel Pugh's regiment of Illinoisans. "But I think you are referring to our few shirkers."

"Shirkers?"

"By now, at the pace they were running, Walker and his friends are probably back at the landing."

Luke bit his tongue to hold back a flow of unChristian curses. "What about Lieutenant Long?"

"He's still here, I think."

The battle had tapered off, and yelling was no longer necessary.

"They're gathering themselves for a charge," Lieutenant Simon deduced.

"I know. Where's Captain Vincent?" Luke asked, still not seeing him.

"Down on the right. He was hit in the hand but is still on the field. Don't worry, Luke, for all our problems with the captain, he won't leave us."

James felt a peculiar rumbling in his stomach and looked up to the sun high above, marking it as not even noon. But any ideas of food were erased by the crashing sound of cannon. As he looked down the line, he could see three batteries of cannon and knew there was more Union artillery north of their position.

Men flattened themselves to the sunken road, but the shallow trail provided little protection and Confederate shells slammed in front of them and behind. The earth beneath him trembled and shook each minute, like an angry beast awakening slowly from a slumber.

Federal cannon returned fire, and James put his arms over his head and closed his eyes. The shriek of each shell seemed to be crying something, and James prayed that none of them would screech his name.

A shell crashed into the trees directly behind them with a splintering crash. A second later, he heard a large branch crash to the ground, but James and the others still did not stir from their position.

"I think I'd rather face muskets with my sword than this," Ainsley yelled in his ear. "I hate the idea of being blown to bits by some unseen cannon shell."

A shell shrieked overhead and shook the earth, showering them with dirt.

"Don't be jinxing us now, Lieutenant," James hollered back over the din.

Another shell landed among a clump of men forty yards to their north, leaving lifeless blue clumps. James shut his eyes tightly, wishing he had not seen that.

"I'm sure I'll get my wish though," Ainsley yelled back. "There will be a charge behind this bombardment for certain."

Patrick wriggled closer to them, raising his voice, "What's the debate here? Anything is better than lying here throughout all this."

Suddenly, the shrieking shells stopped and the only sound was the Union batteries, and soon they stopped too, realizing that the Rebels had quieted. James and Patrick looked at each other.

"Ready?" James said to Ainsley, tapping the percussion cap on Ainsley's rifle.

They peered into the thicket ahead of them. James guessed that he could only see forty or fifty yards into it, so thick it was with brush, tangles, vines and trees. And even then, he doubted he could get a clean shot through the mess greater than twenty or thirty yards.

From the thicket came the ghoulish yell of defiance that had become all too familiar. All along the sunken road, men from Iowa, Wisconsin, Illinois, and Michigan packed in, shoulder to shoulder, along the fence rail and waited.

"Here they come!" came up a cry, and James could see movement of some sort all along the front. With an agonizing slowness, the movement came closer and closer. Finally, James could make out the actual forms of Rebels struggling through the tough thicket. They were fifty yards away now, and he could clearly see that they were having trouble maintaining their formation in the brush. But with an arrogance, they paused from time to time to reform, either oblivious or unconcerned about the Union defenses ahead.

"Wait, steady!" the unknown major from Iowa said from behind James as he paced up and down the line.

The Confederates closed to almost one hundred paces, and James fought to concentrate on his aim and ignore the fact of how close and how many there were. They held their fire, waiting.

"Fire!" came the order.

What seemed like a mile-long blaze of flame erupted from the Union lines. With a chorus of snapping wood and cries of pain, the Confederate line shuddered and buckled.

James went about the familiar process of reloading. He had scarcely fished out the paper cartridge when the Union batteries added to the mayhem. With thunderous booms, they fired loads of canister into the Rebel line. Like a giant shotgun, the lead balls shredded tree and man alike.

A few Confederates returned fire, plucking some Iowans off the fence rail, but most of the Rebels began to retreat back into the thicket. Their painstaking efforts to maintain some sort of formation were no longer adhered to, and they fell back, each man at his own speed. Their lines had been torn with gaping holes.

"They'll think twice about doing that again," Joe said, as he finished reloading. He rested his rifle on the top fence rail, making it easier for him to shoot with one arm.

As the first wave fell back, James felt some relief as he looked down their long line. For the first time today, he thought they might have a defense organized well enough so that the Confederates couldn't simply overlap them and force them back. With most of W. H. L. Wallace's Brigade on the right and Hurlbut on the left, they might have enough to stop the Rebels. Finally, the Rebels were facing more than piecemeal opponents!

"Here they come again!" the cry went up a few minutes later, and James again saw movement in the thicket.

This time there was no waiting for a massive volley. Musketry and cannon immediately reacted to the movement, and the attack was again beaten off, this time before the Rebels had even come close.

From behind the fence railing in the peach orchard, Luke and the rest of the sharpshooters watched the stunning sight of three Confederate brigades in line of battle emerge from the woods. With the green wall as a backdrop, their flags waved brilliantly in the breeze of the sunny day.

Luke scanned the long line of unfamiliar uniforms. Some wore the usual butternut like those at Fort Donelson had. Others were wearing no uniform at all, and a few wore bright uniforms that were more appropriate for a great costume ball with their bright red and blue knee-high leggings and fezlike caps.

Though their uniforms were different, the Confederates all moved with the singleness of one great, giant machine. Lurching forward, the Rebels began to move towards the sharpshooters and the rest of General Hurlbut's men. With each step, the line seemed to become more and more in tune with each other's stride.

Plumes of white appeared from the Confederate artillery supporting the attack. For some reason, Luke had long ago stopped noticing the booming echo of cannon as they traded shot for shot.

But now, the fire intensified, and it was impossible to ignore. Shells shrieked overhead and burst with thunderous bangs behind him. One shell tore open a gash in the earth, another ripped a peach tree from its roots, another obliterated a rider on his horse. One moment, the man was riding madly to the front, a messenger no doubt, and the next moment, rider and horse disappeared in the heavy smoke. Only when the smoke began to lift some, did Luke see the horse twitching on its back. The rider was nowhere to be seen.

Luke stared around them in a sense of wonder. The peaceful, new blossoms on the peach trees fell like fresh snow amid the hail of lead, coating everything around it with a surreal white blanket. The barrage continued for fifteen minutes. By the end of it, Luke's smoke-irritated eyes would have sworn that it had snowed in the little peach orchard. Everything was covered with white, and a number of blossoms floated in the air like gentle snow flurries.

Looking to the front, Luke noticed that the slow-moving Rebel assault was within range. Some of the sharpshooters had already begun to fire. Union artillery shells fell among the Rebels, throwing up mounds of earth, and small gaps were already beginning to appear, but more Rebels filled in.

The Federal soldiers packed behind the fence railing put up a heavy fire. Luke couldn't imagine advancing into such a continuous wall of flame. Even if the shots were utterly inaccurate, the mere vision of such firepower had to be a deterrent.

Yet, the Rebels traded shot for shot. Shoulder to shoulder in the open field, the Rebel brigades returned the fire coming from the peach orchard.

Matthew scanned the area. He could see the Secesh officers urging their men forward. He sighted a rotund gray-coated officer grabbing the regimental banner from the hands of the color sergeant, waving it dramatically as he stomped forward, daring his men to follow their flag. With a squeeze of the trigger, Matthew spun the officer around in a circle. The brief advance halted in confusion and disarray.

All along the peach orchard fence rail, men reloaded and fired as fast as they could. It was the rare sharpshooter like Matthew who actually paused to pick a target.

The Confederate resolve began to waver in the face of the murderous fire. As if to spur them to a decision, the Federal artillery belched rounds of double canister, and the hundreds of lead balls mercilessly cut men down where they stood. Their spirit faltering, the Rebels began to inch back, firing as they went. A few could not take it any more and broke for the safety of the woods. But most slowly, and stubbornly, walked backwards in the face of the fire, as if to say that the blue coats may have won this round, but they were not broken and would try again.

Gradually, as the Rebels removed themselves, the cotton field revealed the crumpled forms of so many men...hundreds and hundreds.

Without a sigh of relief or remorse, Matthew lowered his rifle until the butt rested on the ground and closed his eyes.

James and the rest of the patchwork Prentiss's men watched another Confederate wave move through the thick underbrush, their lines again completely tangled and in disarray as each man tried to maneuver through the thicket. Next to him, Joe rested his rifle on the fence rail for support, Patrick similarly took aim, and even Ainsley appeared to know how to handle his rifle, although his reloading time was much greater than the others.

James picked out whom he guessed was an officer and waited for the man to get closer.

"Patience, patience," he mumbled to himself, as he fought the urge to pull the trigger. From this angle and position, James guessed he had a better view of the Confederate officer than did the man's own men, and James was thankful that he wasn't the one making the charge through the dense thicket.

Holding their fire until about twenty-five yards this time, the Union line erupted again in a wall of flame, decimating the Rebels who were stumbling through the woods. Cannon roared from near point-blank range, ripping giant holes in what remained of the disarrayed Rebel lines.

Smoke shrouded their position and blurred vision, but it was ignored as each man now hurriedly reloaded and fired again into the smoke-filled forests. Confederate retaliation was mild as their line broke again and retreated in the face of such horrific fire.

The forest was quiet for a moment, when James saw two lone figures rise to their feet. Each was wounded and dragging a leg, but one was by far worse. Using his comrade as a crutch, the mangled Confederate tried to limp out of the thicket, dragging his leg and shattered arm behind him. Without thinking, James raised his rifle and took aim. Then he felt a hand on his barrel, pushing his aim down.

"Leave them be, James," Ainsley said in a calm, but forceful voice. "We won't be troubled by them again today."

"Yes," James gulped, realizing that he had been about to kill a man—a man with a family and life probably not unlike his own. Suddenly, James felt a terrible distaste for this war, for what it was doing to them all. They had become animals and butchers.

Surely, the fields were littered with enough dead, dying, and maimed to fill the whole country. But with a dark realization, James knew that no amount of distaste could end the war now. Like it or not, the war was real now and would continue. There would be more death, more killing. Closing his eyes and clasping his hands, James gave a quick prayer for them all on both sides. The sooner this war ended the better, but he knew they were all powerless to stop it now.

Through the thicket, the Southerners came on again, having regrouped and again they were cut down by murderous, unforgiving fire. Again, and then again over the next hour and a half, the same group of battered Rebels tried to reach the Union position, and each time they were driven off with heavy losses.

Though each Rebel charge knocked more blue-coated men off the fence rail, James couldn't imagine that the Southerners had enough men to continue at this rate. But each time, they came back again.

With an unspoken sense of dread, Luke watched the Confederate battle line emerge from the woods again. This time, he counted four brigade flags, and it looked like a fifth one down to the east.

"They're attacking the length of the flank this time," Lieutenant Simon remarked, ducking instinctively as cannon bursts landed in front and behind them again.

"Doesn't look any different to me than the other two times," Matthew said, uncorking a shot from long range. His face had been blackened from the day's fighting, and his hair was matted to his forehead with sweat. He did not look young anymore.

The Rebel ranks moved closer and closer, and the two sides traded shots. With thick white smoke beginning to shroud the Union line again, Matthew searched for another officer and spotted a man on horseback actively rallying his troops, making himself as conspicuous as possible. Matthew fired and began to reload. As he replaced the ramrod, he looked up, surprised to see the rider still there. Again, he fired at the man.

And again, he looked up to see the rider still there. This time, the Confederate was getting close enough so that Matthew could see that the rider was waving a tin cup in the air to urge his men forward.

Nearby, Pete recoiled and stumbled backward. With a stunned look on his face, he stared at the spreading crimson on his chest. He dropped to his knees, unseen by anyone else, and died with none of his friends aware of what had happened.

Seconds later, a Rebel shell found the zigzagging split rail fence and tore out an entire length of railing, spraying men down around it.

The fighting was as hot and furious as Matthew or Luke had ever seen. Lead flew thick through the air, and the ground shook with the stomping of thousands of men and the impact of cannon shells. Smoke blocked vision and a million things seemed to be happening at once, all accompanied by the deafening sounds of gunfire and wounded men, but Matthew was only partially aware of it. Again he fired at the rider, knowing that his aim was good enough to hit the man, even from this distance.

"By God!" VanderJagt said from two spots down, "there's General Johnston himself!" He pointed at the large man on horseback waving the tin cup.

Finally, the Federal line began to buckle under the onslaught. The Confederates did not slow this time, and the Federals could sense that there was no stopping them. All around Matthew, there were blue-coated casualties. Sensing that the Yankees were close to breaking, the Rebel officers redoubled their efforts, convinced that this charge would succeed where all others failed.

With a startling realization that the left had given way, Matthew, Luke, and the rest of Hurlbut's line were ordered back. Nothing could stop the Confederates now. They owned the entire left flank. W. H. L. Wallace's and Prentiss's remnants were on their own.

As they retreated, Luke remembered the pond behind the peach orchard and licked his blackened, parched lips, but the sight of the pond sickened him to the point of vomiting instead.

Facedown at the edge of the pond, some even floating in the middle of it, were a number of dead bodies, and even dead horses, their blood turning the pond red in color. Wounded men, desperate for one last drink, had expired on the very edge of the water hole.

Grabbing him by the arm, even as the preacher's son was throwing up, VanderJagt pulled Luke along to the new line of defense that they were setting up to block the River Road just beyond the bloody pond.

"C'mon, son," VanderJagt yelled amid the roar of cannon and continual musketry, "I've already lost Gussie, I'll not lose you, too."

Ainsley returned with more ammunition for their little cadre in the middle of the Federal line.

"This can't still be the same day," Joe sighed, leaning forward with his eyes closed and head resting on the lowest rail of the fence.

"Aye," Patrick said. "It's the same day, and darkness is nowhere near yet."

"How can these Johnnies keep coming?" lamented one of the Iowans.

"They can keep coming," James said, "because they know it's only another mile until they drive us back into the river, and then all of Grant's army will have to surrender."

"I'm not spending any time in a Secesh prison," Joe snapped angrily.

"Then we better hold them here as long as we can," Ainsley said, "because Buell's Army of the Ohio must be nearly here. If we can hold on for reinforcement."

With the sounds of battle still crashing to their left, they had no idea that their protection over there had been driven back through the peach orchard.

It was just after 2:30 when James and the others stirred again and watched another Confederate line bash its way through the thicket. Just as before, the air was full of lead and smoke. The zing and zip of Minié balls cut through the air with such regularity and frequency that it seemed that they were in the middle of a hornet's nest with millions of maddened insects diving through the air.

Zip, zip, zip. James heard the shots whiz by, just overhead. With a start, he jumped back as one shot smacked into the wood railing and deflected just past his ear with a zing.

The smoke was beginning to build again. But no longer was it merely fueled by rifle and cannon. Now, the thicket itself was on fire, and through the smoke, the Confederates marched. With the gray pall behind them, they seemed like a force of demons cast out of hell and bent on destruction. And despite the frenzied Yankee fire and terrible losses they were suffering, the Southerners continued towards the sunken road, firing as they went.

From his position on one knee behind the fence railing, James worked the ramrod down his fouled Dimick. The spent black powder from so much use clogged the barrel and made it difficult to ram the Minié ball all the way down. During the periodic lulls between Rebel charges, the men lining the sunken road would try to clean their weapons. Without any hot water nearby to remove the clinging clumps of powder, the soldiers used the next best thing, urine.

Despite his efforts to clean it during periodic lulls, no gun could handle such a rate of fire without fouling, and James angrily set it aside for now and picked up the rifle of an Iowan who had fallen. Anxiously, James pulled the trigger and fired into the Rebels, who were now only thirty paces from the sunken road.

Ainsley worked free his pistol and emptied it into those struggling through the thick brush.

Though they were close to the sunken road, it was too much for the Confederates, too many of them had fallen, too few were left to capture the Yankee's position. The few Confederates left standing, made their way back through the thicket as fast as they could, no longer caring about their appearance, only their lives.

Gasping for air as if he had just run a long race, James collapsed alongside his weary comrades. The Confederates had gotten close that time, too close. He wondered how much more they could possibly take.

To their front, a wounded Confederate gave a horrifying scream as the fire in the thicket engulfed him. After his yelling resounded along the front for what seemed an eternity, it stopped abruptly.

Another wave of Confederates struggled through the brush, as determined as ever to break the Union center.

"How many charges is this?" an Iowan asked with some weariness, as the firing resumed.

"I stopped counting after five," Patrick said. "Maybe eight or nine now."

The firing intensified, and the defenders clung stubbornly to their line. Their numbers were dwindling now, and they were rapidly running low on ammunition, yet they hung fast.

Hickenlooper's Battery, now out of canister, had begun firing the less effective solid shell into the advancing Confederates. Yet, the Rebels continued forward. Remorselessly, they stepped on and over the bodies of dead comrades, firing as they went.

James's face was so blackened from powder now that he looked like a miner. His lips were caked black, and his hands were callused and burned from so much firing that he could scarcely feel anything any more. With red eyes no longer capable of watering, he squinted through the smoke and fired into the fog that had developed from the fighting again.

"James, I'm out of...," Joe began and then spun around, collapsing to the ground.

"Joe!" James cried, crawling over on his knees to the small man.

"I'm all right," Joe said through grinding teeth, holding a shattered right arm with his weakened left arm. Through the gushing red blood, James could see a speck of white bone poking out.

"You got to get back now, Joe. No more arguments. You can't fight like that."

"By damn I can, Lockett!" Tucker snapped back with his eyes shut and a pained grimace.

"You can't raise a rifle with that arm—"

"Give me Lieutenant Stuart's revolver. I'll shoot with my other arm."

"Joe," James implored, knowing that the man was dying before his eyes, "you'll bleed to death."

"Joe Tucker never loses," he said, rising to his feet between James and the fence railing.

The thump of a Minié ball finding flesh sounded all too close to James's ears, and he looked at the blank expression on Joe's face. Ever so slowly, the small, wiry man pitched forward into James's arms.

"Tuck," James said softly in a choked voice.

Joe coughed twice and opened his eyes one last time. Without a word, he stared up at James. Coughing once more, his head dropped, and he was gone.

Holding the light body in his arms, James knew that another brave man had been cut down in the prime of his life. Rapidly, the blood from Joe's wounds coated James's pant legs.

"Get back in line, sergeant!" the patrolling major said from behind.

James snapped his head around with a burning glare at the officer but saw that the major too was bleeding from an arm wound. With a deep breath, James answered, "Yes, sir." Gently, he laid Tucker's head down and picked up his borrowed rifle and rejoined the line.

And again, they drove off the attackers.

Luke and the other sharpshooters stood shoulder to shoulder in Wicker Field, firing at the Confederate battle line as they approached. Luke fought with VanderJagt on one side and Matthew on the other. With a painful inevitability, they gradually gave ground, hustling back to form another defensive position with a reserve regiment. They held momentarily before being forced to do it all over again.

Wallace's and Prentiss's last reserves appeared from the woods on the right, but even the cross fire wasn't enough to stop the Confederate wave. Despite their losses, the Rebels could sense victory was at hand. They had finally broken the stubborn Yankee defense line that had held all afternoon. Now, victory was at hand. The Yankees could be swept up piece by piece.

The sharpshooters fell back through their camps in Cloud Field.

Suddenly, Luke felt a powerful burning sensation on the side of his head. His vision of the approaching Rebel flags blurred, then blackened. Oddly, he was still aware of falling to his knees and then hitting the ground. He could hear his own voice talking to him in calm tones but knew that he was not trying to speak. The voice softened, and there was a comforting sense of knowing that the Lord was with him. Then all was black.

The barrage of cannon was like nothing anyone had ever experienced. Despite the continual bombardment of some sort throughout the day, this new hammering was like nothing else. Instead of a few batteries trading fire with Hickenlooper and the other Union cannon, this felt like all of the Rebel cannon west of Virginia had gathered together for one massive bombardment.

In fact, this was virtually true. After repeated attempts to crack the Union center, Confederate General Daniel Ruggles had gathered every piece of artillery on the field for a massive bombardment of the area the Confederates were calling the "Hornet's Nest."

It would have come as no surprise to James and the others to learn that Ruggles had gathered more cannon for this bombardment than had ever been gathered before in the history of North America. It had taken an ungodly amount of time and human cost, but the Rebels had finally realized that the Union position was too strong for the brave, but foolhardy charges. Now, the Rebel cannon were going to pound the position at the sunken road into submission.

The earth-shaking thunder roared continuously without break or reprieve. As soon as one cannon fired, another was lit off, and again, and then again. As James, Patrick, and the other survivors braced themselves and scratched deeper into their meager cover, an infinite number of cannon pounded away at them. Spouts of flame and dirt sprung up around them like wellsprings.

The soldiers lost track of time as the cannon fired repeatedly, driving off the few Union cannon that were still functional.

"I don't think we'll be able to stop them this time," Patrick yelled into James's ear. He wore a pained expression as another shell slammed in behind them.

"We don't have enough ammunition as it is now," James shouted back in agreement. "Unless Ainsley gets back here with more, we'll have to give ground."

"I doubt he'll try to come back through all this," Patrick said skeptically as the earth spouted again.

"He'll try," James said worriedly. "I just hope he makes it through." He looked over to where Tucker's body still lay. The men had no time to do anything for him. The best they could do was cover his face with Ainsley's handkerchief.

James watched behind them as shells rained in. Finally, through the spikes of flame and dirt, he saw the familiar outline of Ainsley running towards them. With his hand again clamped to the bouncing scabbard at his side, he ran half bent over, his head tucked into his bony shoulders like a turtle trying to protect itself. Other than the rifle the young officer carried in his left hand, he appeared empty-handed.

Another shell screamed by overhead, and James buried his head in the ground, knowing this one was close. When he looked up through the smoke and falling dirt, he did not see Ainsley.

"Ainsley!" he yelled, jumping to his feet. He spotted a body on the ground near where the shell had landed. Oblivious to the other shells crashing down, James sprinted to his friend's side, sliding to a stop and covering Ainsley's body with his own as another shell sent deadly shrapnel flying in all directions.

"Ainsley," James croaked, looking at Ainsley's contorted face.

With a sickening feeling, James saw no foot where Ainsley's boot had once been. The top of his boot deteriorated into a blackened stump where dark, red blood began to flow.

Patrick skidded up next to them. He whipped off his belt and immediately pulled it as tight as physically possible across Ainsley's stick-like thigh. Knowing that bleeding to death was Ainsley's worst enemy now, James whipped off his uniform jacket and tied it around the stump in what he feared was a futile effort to staunch the bleeding.

"No ammunition," Ainsley choked out the words.

"We have to get him out of here, back to a surgeon!" James shouted above the crashing shells. Though he could not hear him as another shell exploded, Patrick nodded in agreement.

"McClernand and Sherman gave away," Ainsley struggled. His face contorted in pain.

"Hang on, Ainsley. We're getting you out of here."

They began to lift him when Ainsley spastically spat out the words, "The sword, James!"

Seeing the scabbard that had been cut from his body nearby, James ran over and grabbed it. "I have it, Ainsley! I won't lose it, I promise!"

With a cry of agony from him, they lifted Ainsley. Patrick had his Dimick slung over his shoulder. With one hand on Ainsley's belt and another under his shoulder. On the other side of the fallen officer, James's one hand held the sword, the other grabbed Ainsley's light body by the belt, his bleeding leg propped high on James's shoulder between his arm and neck. Together, James and Patrick hoisted Ainsley and moved through the carnage.

The news of McClernand's and Sherman's retreat caused them to fear the sight of Rebels appearing from the west, but what they saw first were Rebels from the east.

"Hurlbut's given way too!" Patrick huffed.

Behind them, they heard the Union line open fire as it had so many times that day. The Rebels were making another charge at the sunken road, but that was the least of their worries now.

James's eyes flashed from the Rebels on the right to movement on the left, spotting more Confederates emerging there too. Rebels on both sides! Ahead of them was an ever closing gap that led to safety. *The Hornet's Nest that they had manned so long was surrounded.*

A few bullets whizzed in, smacking into trees and earth, as Confederates ran forward, firing on the run to stop anyone from escaping their trap.

"Leave me," Ainsley moaned, stirring from his near unconscious state.

Without wasting their breath on a reply, James and Patrick ran faster, but the gap to safety seemed a hundred miles away.

"Faster," James gasped. The opening was closing, and more and more Confederates were nipping at their heels, angling to block their escape. It was like a nightmare. From all sides, the forest seemed to crawl with Rebels and that terrible Rebel yell. The cries chased the three boys from Kalamazoo.

James could see light at the edge the forest, and he prayed that the meadow that lay beyond them was still Union held, or at least, a no-man's land.

More shots zinged through the air, one of them tugging at Patrick's jacket. Ahead of them, one speedy Confederate had managed to make it to the opening before them. He leveled his rifle, expecting the Yankees to surrender, but with lungs bursting and legs and shoulders burning, James and Patrick continued directly at him.

As they closed to twenty-five yards away, James began a desperate, throbbing yell. It was not unlike the Rebel yell they had heard all day, but James's scream spoke more of bloodthirst and complete desperation. All he could see was the opening and the sight of the lone man blocking their path. Knowing that nothing was going to stop them, he continued to yell as they hurtled toward the Rebel.

With a stunned look on his face, the Confederate looked down at his rifle after it had misfired, the hammer falling on a dud percussion cap. He began to turn the rifle around like a club, but it was too late. Without breaking stride, Patrick lowered a shoulder and ran clean over the man.

They burst out into the meadow like drowning men surfacing for air. Running for all they were worth with their load, James and Patrick churned across the meadow, ever fearful of being shot in the back. Ainsley's blood had drenched James's undershirt, turning the entire right side a dark red. It was sickly smelling and warm, and Ainsley continued to moan with each step.

But at least, he was still alive, James thought.

Ahead, they could see Union blue hidden behind the tree line. They had run the gauntlet and survived, he thought wildly!

Completely winded, James and Patrick collapsed to their knees just in front of a fresh-faced, clean-shaven captain beneath the banner of the 15th Michigan.

Spotting the officer's sword in James's hand, he mistook James for an officer. "Sir? Are you all right, sir?"

"The Lieut'ant...needs to see...the surgeon...right away...," James gasped, pointing to Ainsley.

"Of course, sir," the captain said, and three men came forward, sliding a blanket under Ainsley to use as a stretcher.

"And you better...get ready...to hold...this position," James continued between panting breaths, not realizing that the captain had James confused for an officer. "The Rebels are...right behind us."

"Yes, sir," the captain responded, worriedly looking into the meadow. "The colonel should be back soon. He's still trying to find us some ammunition."

Patrick looked around and noticed that their arrival had caused half of the regiment to gather around curiously and gawk at the three wildmen who had burst from the wooded hollow.

"Get ammunition?" James questioned sharply.

"Yes, sir," the man answered, now wondering what rank this imperious, coatless officer held, thinking James must surely be more than a captain to take such an aggressive tone with him.

"Yes, sir," one of the lieutenants added for James's benefit. "We just arrived."

"Hell," one unseen man in the crowd crowed, "we only mustered in last week. This was our first night sleeping on the ground."

My God! James thought, realizing how close they must be to the landing. The Confederate army is about to burst from the hollow, and we have to stop them with completely green soldiers who have no ammunition!

"Captain," James growled angrily, his frustration from a day's fighting flowing over, giving his voice strength and venom that he did not think that he had. "The Rebels are about to come through that meadow, and we have to stop them! Here!"

"But we have no ammunition," the captain said meekly.

"You have bayonets, don't you?" James snarled before he knew what he was saying. "We haven't bled this much today to surrender now!"

"Bayonets!" James heard someone order, and it was echoed down the line.

"Here they come!" cried another voice, spotting the loose butternut skirmish line emerge from the hollow.

The gaggle of soldiers from the 15th Michigan was already dispersing into a ragged line. James clenched the Stuart family sword tightly and glared at the Rebel menace now coming through the meadow. His face was black with powder burns and powder residue. His shirt was drenched in blood. His hair was heavy with sweat and matted to his head. Before James knew what he was doing, he took two steps to his front and bellowed in voice that was not his own, "Mich-i-gan! Show 'em your steeeeeel!"

A booming, tremendous "Hurrah!" rose up from the hollow and echoed across the meadow, and then the Michigan men broke double time from the woods. With bayonets flashing in the sinking sunlight, the 15th Michigan charged across the field.

Stunned, the Confederates in the meadow stopped their progress and began to fire into the haphazardly organized charge.

The fire slowed the Michigan men at first, but not James. With Ainsley's sword held high over his head and his shirt drenched in blood, he was a fierce sight as he charged to the front. With his legs burning and his mind trapped in blood lust, he did not bother to look behind him to see whether the 15th Michigan was following him. He would attack by himself if he had to now.

Seeing his disregard for the fire, the Michigan men gathered momentum and fell upon the Confederates with a clashing of steel and the cracking of rifle butts.

Many of the Confederates retreated against this unexpected counterattack, but some remained in the field and battled hand-to-hand with the Michigan men.

James slashed wildly at a butternut-coated man, cutting across the man's arm as he attempted to swing his rifle.

All around James, there was a blurring frenzy of swinging rifles and lunging bayonets. So much happened, so fast, it was hard to distinguish color—friend or foe in the melee.

With a cry, James launched himself at a Rebel who was focused on charging another man in blue. With slash across the back, the man fell, and James ducked instinctively as another Rebel swung his rifle at James, grazing the top of his head. Though his mind was foggy, James's instinct knew enough to lash out with the sword as he fell, and he felt it penetrate the soft flesh of the man's belly.

James wobbled to his knees, ready to fight on when his foot hit a blood-slickened patch of grass. With a flash of astonishment, he felt himself crashing onto his back, noticing just before impact that there was a Rebel officer looming above him, sword raised, ready to drop it on him. James started to futilely roll to his side to avoid the blow when the Rebel's face shriveled in pain and confusion.

Removing his bayonet from the Confederate officer's side, Patrick gathered James by the arm.

The Rebels were falling back into the forest, awestruck by the ferocity of the Yankee counterattack. Wisely, the 15th Michigan did not pursue. Without a foe to fight in the meadow, the 15th gradually made its way back to the tree line, having stunned the Confederates and given them second thoughts about advancing.

Wearily, James returned to the tree line. With a mixture of satisfaction and concern, he noticed that Ainsley had been taken away. The captain from the 15th motioned towards James, and an extremely irate colonel approached.

"How dare you lead my men on a suicidal charge!" the colonel raised his voice, waving a finger at James. "Who are you? I'll have you written up for this, sir! I don't give a damn what rank you are! You killed some of my boys!"

Before James could answer, another colonel on horseback with a neatly groomed uniform and mustache that wrapped around behind his ears approached. This second colonel reined in his snorting black steed. "Well done, sir!" the second colonel said, bending down and reaching out for James's hand. "It would be an honor to shake the hand of the man who led such a brave charge. That was exactly the kind of tactic we needed to give us time to form a new defense line."

"And who are you?" the 15th's colonel snapped, not recognizing from the uniform that the man was not a field officer.

"Colonel Webster, General Grant's chief of staff," came the answer in a foreboding voice.

"I see," the 15th's colonel replied in a soft voice.

"Now, as I'm sure you were just saying, Colonel," Webster continued, "you were about to tell Mr...."

"Lockett," James filled in.

"Thank you. Mr. Lockett, here, about how critical and wise that charge was in stopping the Rebel advance."

"Yes, sir. Exactly, sir," the 15th's colonel said, swallowing his pride.

"Well done, Mr. Lockett," Webster said, righting himself in the saddle and pointing to Ainsley's blood all along James's shirt. "I believe you should have that wound looked at immediately."

"Yes, sir."

"Afterwards, I'd be obliged if you come see me, Mr. Lockett."

"Yes, sir. Thank you, sir."

Colonel Webster rode off. The 15th's colonel watched him go and then turned wordlessly on his heel.

For a moment, James stood alone and puzzled.

"They thought you were an officer," Patrick chuckled softly, tapping the Stuart's family sword and noting that without a coat, James wore no insignia of rank.

His mind whirling from the charge and what had just happened, James violently shook his head.

"What?" Patrick said. "That Reb musket butt scramble your brains?"

James looked at the darkening sky and listened to the ebbing sound of battle. The day was finally dying.

"No," James said slowly, "I'm all right...I suppose...let's go find where they took Ainsley."

James and Patrick leaned back wearily against a tree. The sun had gone down, but the place still rang with the boom of cannon as the two Federal gunboats on the Tennessee River pounded where they guessed the Confederate positions to be.

But it wasn't the sound of the cannon that kept their exhausted bodies awake as they leaned back against the tree. They still hadn't found Ainsley. The sheer number of wounded was shocking. They had walked through endless areas of wounded men. Lying in haphazard clusters near confiscated cabins or large white tents, the moans of the dying were still upon their ears.

Some of the wounded at least had blankets beneath them, but most were simply laid on the ground. James did not know how many they had seen, or even how many clusters they had seen, but he knew that Ainsley was in one of them somewhere.

The smell of death and dying was still strong in his nostrils, mixing with the heavy smell of gun smoke that James guessed he would never lose now. His mind was also infected by the images of the gutshot, the amputee, and the dead.

There were more wounded to search, but neither James nor Patrick felt up to the task at this moment. They had learned that Ainsley might not even be at Pittsburg Landing anymore. From asking around, they had already learned that many of the wounded had been taken by steamer back to Savannah.

They had also learned about more than just the wounded. They had seen with their own eyes the number of frightened shirkers milling about the landing. It wasn't hard for them to believe that throughout the day the number of terrified men swelled into the hundreds, maybe even thousands some had said.

They had heard about entire regiments breaking and running away, like the 53rd Ohio, and of other regiments making courageous and desperate stands against overwhelming odds all across the battlefield. But every time, these piecemeal defenses of individual regiments and brigades had collapsed under the weight of the Confederate juggernaut.

Patrick had heard about how they had fought the entire day without General Lewis Wallace's Division. They got "lost" on their six-mile march from their camp at Crump's Landing, arriving from that northern point only after darkness had fallen.

They had heard about how General Grant had been in Savannah when the first Confederate hammer blow had fallen.

Most frightening of all, they had seen how close their last line of defense was to the river. *There was no more ground to give.*

Both James and Patrick knew this army had been beaten today and that they would be driven back into the river the next morning except for one thing. They had seen deliverance firsthand. It was the arrival of reinforcements. General Buell's Army of the Ohio was arriving, stepping off steamer after steamer. Each trip brought more fresh troops to the battered Union lines.

"I s'pose I should go see Colonel Webster now," James said in a tired voice with his arms crossed as he shivered without a coat.

"I'll wait here," Patrick replied. "Then we'll go look for Ainsley again."

James waited inside Colonel Webster's tent.

"I'll be with you in a moment, Mr. Lockett," Colonel Webster said without looking up from the papers that covered a second line of desks in his tent.

The first set of tables stood between James and the colonel, and James couldn't help but notice the large map of the area. In dark writing, James read the words "Last Line" next to the jagged dashes that were perilously close to the river.

Colonel Webster scratched out his scrawl on his writing desk as James's eyes scanned the tent. It was different from the glimpses he had seen of Captain Vincent's tent so long ago. Webster's tent was practical and obviously a place of work. Lit by two lanterns, James could clearly see that the mustached colonel had been busy organizing a defense.

Finally turning around and looking up with a calm face, Webster said, "Good to see your wounds were not too serious, Mr. Lockett. I'm surprised to see you so soon. That is quite a bit of blood on your shirt."

"Not my blood, sir. Actually, sir, I'm not wounded at all." Pointing to the dried blood on his shirt, James added, "This is my lieutenant's blood, sir."

"And the pants?"

James looked at the blood on his pant legs and took a moment to remember Tucker. "No, sir. That's someone else's."

Webster nodded sympathetically. "You've seen a great deal today, I am sure, Mr. Lockett. What regiment are you with?"

"Twelfth Michigan, sir. Peabody's Brigade."

Webster's face betrayed no emotion but his voice did. "You *have* seen a lot today, Mr. Lockett. But you are not wounded?"

"No, sir," James answered again. "I didn't mean to disobey your orders, sir, but I was searching for my lieutenant to give him his sword back. I promised to return it to him safely."

"I see," Webster replied, eyeing the sword still at James's side. "I take it that you have not found him yet."

James shook his head. "No, sir."

"I didn't think you were an officer," Webster continued, looking down at James's pants and simple leather boots.

"Sir, I never told anyone that I was an officer..."

"You just let the 15th Michigan assume you were."

"Yes, sir," James answered slowly. "I'm just a sergeant."

"And you did nothing to dissuade the 15th of their assumptions either? You just let them follow you?"

"Correct, sir," James answered with less hesitation this time.

Surprisingly, Colonel Webster cracked a small smile. "Good thing the 15th didn't recognize your trousers as an enlisted man's like I did."

James blinked in surprise.

"That charge was exactly what was needed at the time, Sergeant Lockett. It broke the Rebels' momentum, gave them a reason to think a little bit about doing it again, which was exactly what we needed. Time. It makes no difference to me, Sergeant Lockett, who led the damn charge, only that it was made. It was the right decision at the right time."

"Yes, sir," James answered with some confusion.

"We have too many officers who got their positions because of who they know, not what they know. Too many officers who are not leaders of men. *You* are obviously a leader of men, Lockett." Webster stopped and looked James over from head to toe. The young sergeant had a muted confidence with a quiet steely-eyed look, Webster thought to himself. Even so the young sergeant appeared to be a generally unassuming man, not unlike General Grant himself. "This army needs men like you, Lockett. In five minutes, you convinced a group of strangers to follow you in a bayonet charge without ammunition. You led without looking back to see whether they were there. That's the kind of leader General Grant wants."

James blinked again, unaccustomed to such praise and unsure what it all meant. "Sir, I don't mean to contradict you, but I'm just a farmer."

"So was General Grant," Webster shot back, "and not a very good one at that. Why, before the rebellion started, he was an ordinary shopkeeper in Galena, Illinois."

James looked at him in complete surprise.

"You're his type of man, Lockett," Webster paused with a peculiar smile on his face. "How would you like to be Lieutenant Lockett instead of Sergeant Lockett? Sam Grant doesn't care where you came from if you can lead and fight like that."

James's eyes widened. "Lieutenant? You can do that?" he managed.

"Hell, I can do damn well anything I please, as long as General Grant agrees, and I'm sure he'll agree to this."

A lieutenant? James thought to himself.

"This battle is not over yet, Lockett. With Buell's men and that laggard Wallace finally here, we can turn the tables on the Rebels tomorrow. What I need you for is some of these bits and pieces. We have a number of broken units that could be put together as reserves, and I could use a few officers to lead them. What do you say, Lockett, like to help lead one of these fragments? Are you up to the challenge?"

"Yes, sir," James said confidently with a salute.

"Excellent," Webster smiled, scratching out some orders. "Give this to the quartermaster for a new first lieutenant's uniform and report back here before dawn to Lieutenant Colonel Calliford."

"Yes, sir," James saluted enthusiastically. He was about to leave when the tent flap opened and a bearded man with observant eyes and a rumpled general's uniform entered.

"General Grant," Webster said, rising to his feet and saluting.

"Colonel," Grant returned, curiously casting his eyes at James and the dried blood that covered his clothes.

"This is the Lieutenant Lockett who led that charge I mentioned earlier. He was just on his way out."

"Well done, *Lieutenant*," General Grant said with a knowing smile.

"Thank you, sir," James said, saluting and leaving Webster's tent.

James wore the new lieutenant's uniform with a new scabbard belt for the Stuart family sword and carried two rubber gum blankets under his arm that he had coerced the quartermaster into giving him. Colonel Webster's signature went a long way he had discovered.

Still stunned by the dramatic turn of events, James slowly walked from the quartermaster's tent. He was exhausted, yet elated. He was an officer!

In the dark, with his mind completely somewhere else, he did not see the man crossing his path, and they bumped into each other, although neither man fell. The other man snapped around and glared at James. "How dare you...," he began before his angry face melted into one of disbelief and then anger again. "You! What are you doing here, Lockett?"

James immediately recognized the voice and felt himself straighten up, a scowl furrowing his brow. With a clenched jaw, James looked squarely into the eyes of Lieutenant Long.

"I asked you a question, Lockett," Long sputtered.

James did not answer and instead studied his old nemesis's uniform. Was he another cowardly shirker milling about the landing?

"Where are the sharpshooters?" James asked in a calm voice instead of answering Long's question.

"We were separated. I don't know," Long said, bending closer in the dark to examine James's new uniform. "An officer?" Long said aghast. "Impersonating an officer! You can be shot for that! Why, you should be hung just for returning to the Army at all!"

Something inside of James snapped at that moment, and he reached out with both hands and grabbed Long by the neck. His hands dug into the soft flesh around the man's windpipe. Long's arrogant eyes bulged as he gasped for air.

"You coward!" James snarled menacingly. "You abandoned your men again, just like at Hallsville! And you threaten me, you child murderer?" James squeezed even tighter. He could see the whites of the coward's eyes bulge further. "I should kill you now!" James said through a clenched jaw.

Long struggled futilely for breath, his hands clawing weakly at James's wrists.

"You make me sick!" With a final squeeze, he released his grip and threw Long to the ground. Without another word, James gathered the gum blankets off the ground and turned on his heel, heading off into the black night. Long sat on the ground gasping, wordlessly rubbing his bruised neck.

James had barely composed himself by the time he found Patrick sitting under the same tree.

"So they made you an officer?" Patrick said immediately with one look at the new uniform.

James stood in front of his old friend, suddenly at a loss for words.

"Daniel is ne'er going to believe this," Patrick remarked, clapping him on the shoulder. "C'mon, I found another batch o' wounded back near this cabin. Maybe Ainsley is there."

They made their way through the rows of wounded lying in a field beyond a weather-worn cabin and billowing white surgical tent. Illuminated from the inside by lanterns, James could see the silhouettes of a surgeon sawing something. The delirious cries of pain echoed in the night air, and James quickly lowered his eyes.

Slowly, he and Patrick walked through the chaotic clusters of men lying on the bare ground. It was difficult to make out faces in the dark, and walking was treacherous with randomly laid men sprawled around. More than once, James had lightly stepped on an errant limb, although depressingly, cries of pain came from the man's lips only half of the time.

James stared into the contorted, dirty, sweat-caked faces of the dying and the dead. He had already seen the cart piled high with limbs behind the cabin, and now as he looked at many of these men, he could not help but remember it.

He saw men without arms and legs, men with head wounds, and others with chest wounds. Wounds of every sort imaginable were around him on this field. The smell of blood, infection, and death hung heavy on the air. It was impossible for James to believe that they were in an open air pasture and not trapped inside with the odors. The stench made him remember his father's last days, and he visibly shook himself to forget the memory.

After what seemed an eternity, Patrick came and grabbed James, pulling him to where he had found Ainsley.

Ainsley was lucky, he still lay on the same blanket that the men from the 15th had transported him on. Blood from his wound covered the bottom quarter of the blanket. He was just barely alive. Unconscious and unresponsive, James's only clue that Ainsley had been attended to was that a bandage had replaced his coat around Ainsley's stump. Between a slit in the bandages, he could make out the medicinal plaster that coated the end of the limb.

Ainsley's pale face and shallow breathing gave them little reason for optimism as they stared down at their fallen friend.

"He's still out," a weak, hoarse voice told them.

Looking over, James saw a one-armed lieutenant watching them. Paler and even more weak looking than Ainsley, the man twisted slightly on the blanket next to Ainsley.

"The Reb shell did the doc's work," the man croaked hoarsely. "There wasn't much more for him that they could do."

"Thank you," James said, not knowing what else to say.

"He hasn't been awake since I came to, Lieutenant..."

"Lockett," James answered. "How about you, sir? Anything I can do for you?"

"Nothing that can be done," the man laughed bitterly. "John Wesley Powell, at your...," he coughed roughly, "...service." Lieutenant Powell rubbed his jaw with his remaining hand and added, "On second thought, a sip of water would be greatly appreciated."

Patrick was already uncorking his canteen before the man had even finished the sentence and helped hold the container while the man drained the remaining half of the canteen, spilling a good section of it across his chin. When he finished, he looked up with a tired smile and said, "Didn't realize how thirsty I was." James nodded and focused his attention back on Ainsley.

"I'll keep an eye on your lieutenant as best I can," Powell added.

"I would appreciate that," James answered. "I'll be here through the night, but come tomorrow, I s'pose I'll have some more Rebels to attend to."

Patrick held out his hand and felt the first droplets of rain. "God, save all," he said dejectedly. "On top of all else."

James spread out one of the rubber gum blankets across Ainsley. "How about some protection from the rain?" James asked, already spreading the second gum blanket across Powell.

"Thank you mightily, sir," Powell said in a weak voice as the clouds opened up and torrents of rain descended on Pittsburg Landing.

James looked across the pasture at the wounded helplessly soaking in the rainstorm.

Powell spoke up one last time for the night. In a weak voice, he said, "I'm from Illinois, Lieutenant Lockett. Where do boys who stick together like you three come from?"

James pulled his cap lower over his eyes. "We're Michigan boys."

Matthew and the rest of the sharpshooters wandered in the trees just east of Chambers Field, far north of where their camp had been the night before. Despite their sacrifices, they had failed to hold the Confederates and had been pushed north with the rest of Hurlbut's and McArthur's men throughout the day.

While their losses were not as heavy as some, like the piece-by-piece destruction of Prentiss's Division, the sharpshooters were at half of the strength they had left Kalamazoo with. Disease, losses at Hallsville, and today's battles had taken a heavy toll on the company.

Pete and Gus were now gone, and they had carried Luke back to the surgeon, his head creased by a Rebel Minié ball. A dozen or so Kalamazoo Sharpshooters were missing, due mainly to desertion, Orrin Long among them. The captain's nephew had disappeared after the peach orchard, and no one had seen him since.

Lieutenant Simon had been wounded yet again but remained on the field. For whatever reason, the man seemed to have a guardian angel, because again, his wound was minor.

As Matthew shivered in the pouring rain, he listened to the gunboats keep up their continual fire. He found it utterly impossible to sleep despite the exhaustion that racked his body. He had trouble focussing his fatigued mind, but eventually, his thoughts came back to wondering about James and Patrick. Had they escaped? He heard that a few of Prentiss's men had shot their way out of the trap. Were James and Patrick among them, or were they like the Dobbins twins, prisoners? Or were they lying like so many others across the fields?

The rain kept on, and he knew he should get some sleep because there would be more tomorrow. Lew Wallace's men had finally arrived and filled in on the right. The fresh troops probably meant a counterattack in the morning.

But sleep would not come. So like many others on both sides, Matthew spent a sleepless night wandering among the trees and heavy raindrops.

April 7, 1862

Again, the crack-crack of skirmishers' rifles sounded, but this time it was different for Matthew and the rest of the sharpshooters who made up the skirmishing line in front of Lauman's Brigade. Today was a new day, and with the remaining units of Sherman's and McClernand's Divisions on either side, Matthew found himself in the vanguard of the first organized Union counterattack of the battle.

Beyond Sherman, Lew Wallace's fresh division anchored the right flank and also marched on the small creek of Tilghman's Branch.

To the east, Buell's Army of the Ohio began to march through the ground that the Confederates had abandoned during the night.

Startled Confederate pickets fired solitary shots before fleeing in the face of the crushing force before them. The battle that they thought they had won had suddenly turned against them. Even in the dim light, the Rebels could tell the size of the behemoth bearing down upon them.

North of Matthew, the sound of Union musketry drew closer at first, and then farther away, as Wallace's fresh men drove the Confederates from Jones Field and outdistanced the tired survivors of April 6.

Behind the sharpshooters, the battle line of blue tried to ignore the stiffness in their bones and the heavy wetness of their drenched uniforms. The sun was just over the horizon. A new day, a new battle, a new outcome.

But they were tired and the advance was slow and ponderous. Still, the sheer size of their firepower began to overwhelm the outnumbered Rebels, and slowly, ever so slowly, Lauman's Brigade neared the creek.

Then with a blink of amazement and dejection, Matthew saw a Rebel line of battle counterattack to their right, ready to recross the Tilghman Branch and drive Lew Wallace's and Sherman's men back.

VanderJagt stood next to Matthew and watched in surprise also but without the dejection. Rather, a serious look of approval appeared on his face. "We have the brave fools this time," the old soldier said, pulling on his dirty beard.

"What?" Matthew asked.

"Today, we're all better organized. They cain't collapse a line with that charge. We'll enfilade them."

"What?"

"We'll turn right and catch 'em in a cross fire, boy."

A minute later, Lauman's Brigade received the order just as VanderJagt predicted. Before he knew it, Matthew was looking down the length of the Confederate line. He took aim at the Confederate flank with the rest of the Yankee soldiers. Just as they had received at Hallsville, now they were getting the opportunity to enfilade the enemy flank. The edges of the enemy line crumbled. More and more Rebels looked to their right in surprise to see fallen comrades and advancing Yankees.

Bravely, the Confederate attack continued. Whether through courage or ignorance, the Confederates disregarded the mounting losses on their right side and continued to plow directly into Wallace's and Sherman's line where they were already receiving brutal fire.

Matthew was beginning to wonder what it would take to stop these Rebels. Perhaps, James had been right after all, these Rebels would fight with an unstoppable vengeance to protect their homes. But finally, the Rebel line began to shudder to a disjointed stop. Human endurance could no longer face such fire, and with a stubborn reluctance, the Southerners began to fall back, firing as they went. Pride refused to allow most to hurry back, and many paid a price for that pride.

The advance continued, and Matthew resumed the heavy-footed march through the trees. Holding a position in the line was difficult because one had to step around trees and other obstacles, but the line always moved forward. It was surprisingly difficult to keep up.

Again, they stepped over and on the bodies of fallen Rebels. Before yesterday, Matthew had tried to avoid stepping on the bodies, both

Yankee and Rebel alike, but now it was too common. If a body happened to be lying in his stride, he would step on it, just as he would a fallen tree.

Sometimes the body would stir ever so slightly. This time, however, the body did more than stir. With only a quick glance down Matthew had noticed the shabbily dressed Rebel in simple trousers held up by worn suspenders, but as he stepped on the body the man yelped and leapt up to his feet, starting to run, but not sure which direction to head.

Matthew fell, and though he got up immediately, he had already lost his place next to VanderJagt and Barker as the line continued to move forward at its own pace.

The Rebel who had been playing possum seemed to dance in place, unsure which direction to run in. Cut off from his comrades, the Rebel stood there in momentary confusion. Matthew stared blankly at the man while the sporadic sounds of battle echoed ahead of them as the battle lines clashed again.

The Rebel held his dirty hands in front of him as Matthew pointed the rifle at him. "Awl-right, Yank," his frightened voice said, and Matthew noticed beneath the dirt and grime that the Rebel was a boy even younger than himself.

"Matthew!" Lieutenant Simon called, trotting back. "What are you doing back here?"

"I have a Rebel prisoner," Matthew said in a slightly stunned voice.

"I see that," Lieutenant Simon said. "Well, take him back. There's a detachment of Sherman's Buckeyes taking back some prisoners. Why don't you catch up to them and then hurry back."

"Yes, sir," Matthew said, motioning the Rebel back through the woods.

It was cumbersome keeping a pointed rifle at the man, but with each step, Matthew found himself growing more relaxed and more cocky.

"We're going to push you and Johnston all the way back to Corinth today," Matthew boasted.

"Johnston?" the Rebel said with a cackling laugh. "He was kilt yes'day. Some Yank sharpshooter got lucky! Beauregard leads the army now, and for that, y'all should be thankful. If Johnston was still here, you'd be *my* prisoner."

Matthew quieted and remembered his errant attempts in the peach orchard at the tin-cup waving general. Maybe my aim wasn't off after all, he thought to himself.

Lieutenant Lockett marched forward with his small company under the command of a Captain McGee, a Chicagoan whose previous company had been mostly captured north of the sunken road. With four other motley companies, they made up part of the reserve for Buell's advancing division.

They were Hawkeyes, Hoosiers, Buckeyes, Minnesotans, Wisconsin and Michigan boys. For once, James did not observe any boastful rhetoric among the men. This group was too tired from the long night and too dejected from the previous day. Despite their varied backgrounds, they did have one thing in common, they all had tasted defeat one way or the other yesterday. Some like Sergeant Milton Bosworth of the 53rd Ohio had tasted it in particularly bitter fashion.

"We had them in that field," Bosworth had related to James earlier in the morning. "More'n half of them was already down on that field when our colonel cried out, 'Retreat! Retreat, save yourselves!' We had them, Lieutenant Lockett! There was no need to retreat."

When Bosworth had said that to him, James sensed that he himself was now under the sergeant's scrutiny. Left unsaid was Bosworth's true question, was James like the colonel of the 53rd?

They marched four abreast past the Dill Branch and lingered within sight of Lauman's old camp in Cloud Field. Patrick looked at James but said nothing. They knew exactly what the other was thinking. How had the sharpshooters fared yesterday? Luke? Matthew? VanderJagt and the rest?

There was firing up ahead where Hazen's Brigade led the march through ground that the Confederates had withdrawn from during the night. The firing continued for another hour, but the motley reserves held their place. Some rested their weary bodies, lying down in the mud, or sitting on fallen trees. And they waited...waited for Lieutenant Colonel Calliford to give them the order to advance in support of Hazen's Brigade, Buell's Division.

Patrick sat silently, listening to the echoing fire, staring off in the general direction of the dense thicket around the sunken road.

James conferred with Lieutenant Colonel Calliford, and as Patrick watched the exchange, he was surprised at how normal it seemed to have James as an officer. They had been taking orders from James ever since Hallsville. Now, he just had the position to go with the authority that he appeared to naturally command.

"If they're just gonna hold us in reserve all day—," Milton Bosworth groused.

"You'll what?" Patrick said with a smirk. The sergeant from Ohio was a nonstop talker.

"I don't know...but I'll be mad as a hornet."

"We'll be in reserve all day," Alexander Harper, another 53rd Ohioan, chipped in. "They think we're a bunch of yella-tailed cowards after yesterday."

"That's why we need another chance!" Bosworth replied stubbornly.

"We're not all 53rd Ohio here," one of the men said. "And they don't raise no cowards in Wisconsin."

Bosworth jumped to his feet, only to be grabbed around the collar by James, which was probably fortunate for Bosworth since the Wisconsin man was bigger and ready for him.

"No one calls me a coward," Bosworth said, still straining but not very hard. He was not a small man. With his squat neck, broad back, and hunched shoulders, he could have easily pulled free.

"I left half my friends on the field yesterday! You think I'm worried about you, Buckeye!" the Wisconsin man snapped.

"Shut your trap, both of you," James said evenly. The only two names he knew were Patrick's and Milton's, and at this point, he had no intent of learning any more. Looking at Bosworth, James added, "You're a sergeant, so act like it, Milton. Get the men together. We're moving out."

On the double quick, they marched through Cloud Field and then Wicker Field, where the smell of gunpowder still hung over the new corpses from this morning's skirmishes.

The sense of déjà vu chilled James. They were headed back through the woods to the sunken road. As they hastened to join up with Hazen's and Smith's Brigades, the sound of Confederate cannon filled the air. Nearby, Bruce's Brigade attacked south across the cotton field beyond the peach orchard.

Though the roles were reversed, the outcome was still the same as Confederate muskets and cannon shattered the charge and sent the Yankees back.

But unaware that Bruce's charge had been foiled, Hazen's and Smith's Brigades moved forward in two lines, coincidentally sweeping into the area where the Confederates were moving in counterattack, protected by a company of Louisiana artillery.

James and the rest of Calliford's reserves rushed to catch up to the main body. In the tangle of the thick woods they accidentally veered south and suddenly found themselves as the vanguard, instead of the reserves. With a moment of confusion, they broke from the woods and found themselves face to face with the Confederate artillery.

The Rebels were faced to the northeast, ready to defend against an attack from the main body. They had no idea that they were now squarely in the sights of Calliford's reserves.

Lieutenant Colonel Calliford trotted up to the lead company, curious what the delay was.

"We seem to be the van, sir," James said drily.

"So we are, Lockett," Calliford replied. "We best get out of column and into line of battle."

Astonished that the Confederates had yet to realize their presence, the four companies of reserves spread out in a miniature line of battle. With a simple nod from Calliford, they surged forward into Davis's wheat, toward the unsuspecting cannon. James quickly wished that he still had his rifle and not just a borrowed army revolver from Powell and Ainsley's sword. But it was too late now.

Startled at the sudden appearance, the Louisiana battery began to wheel their weapons around to meet the new threat. "Fire!" the order came, and the Yankees emptied their weapons as they advanced. The hail of Minié balls cut down a number of Louisianans around their cannon.

"Reload and advance! Independent fire! Independent fire!"

Some of men stopped to reload, but most hurried forward, not bothering to load again. They had decided that it was better to be in amongst the cannon rather than in front of them.

Even so, the Louisianans were still able to wheel some cannon around, and one spouted a deadly hail of canister, disintegrated the entire left side of the Union charge, killing Captain McGee.

"Capture the guns!" James cried. He could hardly believe his luck. Other than capturing a regiment's colors, the capture of cannon was the biggest prize of all. And there they were for the taking in front of them! These men who had tasted nothing but defeat the day before launched themselves forward like starving animals.

Another blast of canister shredded three Minnesotans as it fired just yards away from them, but it was too little, too late as the Union troops swarmed over the battery.

In the blur of motion, smoke, and sound, James was vaguely aware of the man next to him dropping to his knees. Looking up to see a cannoneer with a smoking pistol, James raised his revolver and fired one for the first time in his life. The recoil snapped his wrist upward and the shot flew wide and high.

The cannoneer hurriedly bent his revolver in half and tried to quickly reload.

James did not hesitate. He ran forward in a full sprint, worthlessly firing the revolver as he went. None of the shots hit the Rebel, and with the Stuart's family sword in his left hand, he dove madly on top of the man just before he could finish reloading.

All around him, the field had turned into another wild melee of hand-to-hand fighting. Shots went off at point-blank range and rifle butts clashed with two foot long bowie knives. But James did not hear or notice any of it at that moment as he struggled with the cannoneer in the mud. Feeling the Rebel go limp after he had smashed the butt of the pistol into the man's temple, James struggled to his knees and looked up.

Bosworth was about to drop the butt of his rifle down onto a man's head, and Patrick too was fighting like a wild man. Holding his Dimick extended like a club, he looked for another target. At his feet were already two fancifully dressed Louisianans.

James raised his pistol again and realized it was empty. He had lost track of time when he heard a new cry and from the corner of his eye, he saw two Rebel infantry regiments rushing forward to assist the overwhelmed cannoneers. Shots began to whip in among them, thudding against flesh, zinging away from cannon barrels. Worse yet, James knew they were exposed. There was no reserve coming to help them hold this position. They were the reserve after all! And they were lost!

Even if they could finish capturing the guns, they would never be able to hold them. With no choice, Calliford gave the order to fall back.

Milton fired once more and then looked at James. The words of his flapping mouth were drowned out in the sounds of battle, but James knew well enough what was said. They were retreating again.

On the right flank, Grant's army had progressed. By mid-afternoon, they were again in control of McClernand's old camp and nearly in possession of Sherman's.

It took Matthew most of the day to catch up to the sharpshooters, but it was not the distance that slowed Matthew's rendezvous, it was the wounded. As he made his way across the fields of battle, fallen Rebels and Federals alike littered the ground. Some were dead, but many were wounded and primarily unattended. Matthew had stopped to try to help the first two, eventually leaving his canteen with the second, but the sheer number was overwhelming. He saw men on the ground, collapsed behind fence rows, behind trees, anywhere that an eye could see.

Matthew found himself ashamed by the naivete of his early boastful words. They had left Kalamazoo so certain of their ability to end the war, never realizing how insignificant they were. On this one pasture alone, there were more dead than there had been Kalamazoo Sharpshooters three times over.

James had been right. This was no great adventure full of glory and victory. It was a test of stamina. Who could take more bitterness? Who could ignore the destruction around them and continue on with a blind eye?

How many men had the sharpshooters lost? Was Luke among them now? Had VanderJagt, Barker, or any of the other sharpshooters, whom he had grown so close to, been killed today? And what of James and Patrick?

With tear-filled eyes, Matthew fled...but in the direction of the battle. There was strength in comradery. The sooner that he found his comrades, the better for his aching heart. Matthew ran.

James and the rest of the company waited leisurely. They were "his" company now. Captain McGee was dead, but James spent no time reflecting on that. Instead, his eyes were glued to the sunken road that lay ahead of them. They were at a different section of it than he had defended the day before, but he knew exactly where he was.

The bodies of a few dead Federals still lay where they had fallen. Whether they had been cut down the day before or today, James did not know or think about. His eyes skirted down the narrow trail—curving around the bend—to where he guessed that he, Patrick, Ainsley, and Joe had so steadfastly fought the day before. He contemplated wandering down there, to see whether Tucker's body was still where they had left it, but James shook the thought from his head.

They were in reserve of Crittenden's Division now with a number of other piecemeal units. And this was *his* company now, his responsibility. He needed to focus on his duty and not sentimentality.

He looked over at Patrick and was not surprised to see his old friend similarly subdued, listening to Bosworth chatter on. The Buckeye did not seem the least bit fazed that Patrick was only paying him scant attention.

Ahead of them, they could still hear the sound of skirmishing as Crittenden's men assessed how stiff the Rebel resistance was across the Purdy Road. Not far beyond that road was the field where they had camped with Peabody's Brigade. It seemed so long ago now to James. Even retreating across that road and through the field seemed so long ago to him now.

I am oh, so tired, he thought wearily.

It was near two o'clock when Lieutenant Colonel Calliford received word to move his ragtag group forward to reinforce Crittenden.

"We'll be making an assault for certain," one of the Iowans commented to no one in particular as they moved through the thicket. They aimed for the Corinth Road, which would take them south to Crittenden's line, but the shortcut did not materialize as they struggled through the tough thicket that was littered with dead Rebels.

James was shocked at the carnage his defense of the sunken road had wrought. He knew they had withstood at least ten separate charges, and he had seen the dead Federals near the sunken road, but he was still not prepared for the wretched sight of hundreds upon hundreds of dead Confederates, lying at every conceivable angle in the thicket.

All ordinary conversation stopped as they marched through.

Ahead, James struggled not to step on one of the dead as they passed through a line of fallen Southerners who must have been cut down in one devastating volley, like grain being scythed. They lay neatly in line next to each other, a grotesque patchwork carpet.

"Good God," Bosworth mumbled.

James had known that they were exacting a terrible toll on the charging Confederates, but what courage drove such men to continue over and over again, over the very top of so many of their comrades?

Patrick cleared his throat and tried not to look down. They had another battle coming up, and he knew it would do them no good to ponder this for too long. But looking away was impossible. He *had* to look at them, otherwise he would trip.

So many men...twisted, contorted, trapped, as if the thicket itself had reached out and snared these unfortunate souls.

Finally, they reached the Purdy Road and fell in line with the rest of Crittenden's men.

The Rebels had formed at the edge of the woods that blocked Peabody's old camp from view. If the Yankees wanted it back, they would have to cross the open space of Barnes Field.

Confederate artillery began to shell the tree line where Crittenden's men were forming. To many who looked across that open expanse, it looked like ten miles.

How many times could he face death like this and still be breathing in the next hour, James wondered more out of curiosity than anxiety. He felt strangely alone, like he wasn't even here, even as a shower of twigs fell down on him from a shrieking shell blasting through the treetops. It was like he was watching himself from somewhere above.

"By God, we have something to prove," he voiced aloud without thinking. He paused and turned to his small, mismatched company. "We've been pushed and pushed for two days. Not one of us here knows what it is like to capture ground." Though uncomfortable at the reminder, he had the men's attention. "God as my witness, we'll not withdraw this time!"

His little company gave a resounding, "Hur-raaah!" Then, from somewhere down the line, another deep, guttural "Hur-rah!" sounded, and then another, and another, far beyond where James's voice could possibly have carried. For a moment, the hurrahs sounded even louder than the cannon fire being traded back and forth. His insignificant little company was not the only one ready to advance!

Minutes later, the order came, and the entire line started forward, disjointed at first, and then with each man shoulder to shoulder with the next.

Bosworth gave a loud whoop and raised his rifle in the air with a clenched fist.

In front and behind them, shells burst, sending dirt into the air, but James did not notice. His eyes were anchored across the field, as if that could calm the nauseating fear that tried to grow inside of him.

"One final push will break them!" a galloping colonel yelled as he rode behind the advancing line.

The shriek of another shell, close over head, made many men duck on instinct, but James continued forward, as if unimpressed by the near miss. His men struggled but succeeded in keeping up with him.

Confederate musket shots cracked through the air. Some zinged by overhead, some ploughed into the muddy ground in front of them, some thudded sickeningly into the blue line.

One company of Federals stopped to return fire and reload, but James and his men continued forward, holding their fire until they were closer, oblivious to the growing carnage around them—the eye-watering smoke, the sickening smell of powder and flesh, the deafening and unceasing roar of the guns. These men were all-too-familiar with it now.

They were halfway across the field, and James watched impotently as a Rebel cannoneer adjusted his aim, pointing it directly at James.

The Rebel finished ramming home a load of canister shot, just as a Union shell exploded behind the cannon, showering it with dirt and smoke and causing the gunner to drop to his knees, but it was not enough. A different Rebel ran forward and pulled the chord attached to the lanyard, igniting the touchhole of the gun.

Like a giant shotgun, the cannon sprayed death around James. Some lead balls flew overhead, many hit the soft ground in front of the advancing line. Some of those buried themselves in the soft mud, but many bounced up, still capable of shattering a man's leg or tearing into his lower torso.

But most of the canister ripped directly into the line. The Iowan slightly ahead of James dropped to his knees immediately, howling and holding his face with both hands before falling silent.

Instinctively, James grabbed the man's rifle as he marched by. He felt naked with only Ainsley's sword in hand.

The Federal rifle fire began to intensify as fewer and fewer men held back. The thickly packed Union troops began to have an effect, and James started to notice small gaps appearing in the thin Rebel line. No longer were the Secesh one long line of men, shoulder to shoulder.

In the middle of the defense, the Rebel cannoneer began to reload as James and the others drew even closer. They were less than fifty yards away, and the Union artillery had stopped for fear of hitting their own.

Musket balls zipped around James and the others.

The Rebel cannoneer withdrew his ramrod from the giant muzzle, and James could see they were seconds away from firing another devastating blast of canister. A few shots winged off the thick cannon barrel, and James sheathed the sword and readied the Iowan's rifle on his shoulder.

Peering down the long four-foot barrel of the Enfield rifle, he could see the large black hole of the cannon muzzle aimed directly at him and for a moment there was nothing in the world besides him and the cannon. There was no sound as he watched the cannoneer placing the lanyard in the Napoleon's touchhole. The gunner stepped back, ready to touch off the shot.

James pulled the trigger, his Minié ball spinning through the air, racing against the cannoneer's arm as he stretched the triggering chord taunt. Time stood still as James looked down the length of the rifle and watched certain death await him.

But the instant before the man could pull the lanyard free and fire the Napoleon, James's shot hit square in the man's chest. Like a mule kick, the man collapsed inward, arms flapping and the chord slipping from his hand.

The Federal line rushed forward on the Southerners.

Rebel reinforcements emerged from the woods behind to their cannon, but not to fire. They came to pull their cannon away from the advancing Yankees, to remove them to safer ground. They stiffened their defense and met the Yankee charge, trying to give the gunners enough time to get away with their Napoleons and Howitzers.

The Confederate infantry succeeded in giving them time to hastily withdraw their cannon, but the battle had been won. Grudgingly, the Rebel infantry began to backpedal and the retreat was on.

Angered that the cannon were escaping, James sprinted toward them, sword waving, only to be blocked by the sight of six infantrymen cutting him off before he could reach the woods or the cannon. Dropping the spent rifle, he whipped out the revolver and fired once into them.

The long, menacing bayonets gleamed, and the Rebel infantrymen moved towards him, having already fired their muskets. James was about to fire the puny revolver again when a wave of blue coats surged past him and engaged the courageous, but now overpowered Rebels, wounding three of them and sending the other three running.

The battle swirled for a few minutes more, but the outcome was never in doubt. Barnes Field was theirs.

Three hours later, James and Patrick walked into their old camp with the rest of Crittenden's men.

All across Pittsburg Landing, the Confederate line had given way—on the right, in the middle, and on the left. The Confederates were now in full retreat back to Corinth. The sound of rear-guard action could still be heard, but for James and most of the Yankees and Rebels, the battle of Shiloh was over.

As they made their way back to what had been Peabody's camp, and then a Confederate camp for Breckinridge's men the next night, James searched for his old tent.

Milton and Patrick watched curiously as he stepped around the facedown body of a Rebel and peered into the tent. It was still standing despite being ripped and torn with bullets.

From his knee, James could see his journal and pencil exactly where he had left it, as if he had just returned from his patrol with Major Powell. Gathering it up, he said nothing as he rubbed the leather-bound book, his mind flashing from one event to another.

They had survived. Somehow, God in heaven, they had survived. With a silent whisper, James thanked God for his protection, and in his next breath asked that the war end, but in his heart, he knew the end was not near.

Peering in from the opening of the tent with his finger poking one of the bullet holes, Milton cleared his throat, "Ah, Lieutenant, sir? Are you all right?"

“Fine, Milton,” James answered. “I just wanted to see whether my journal was still here.”

“Going to do some writin’ about all this here?” When James said nothing, Milton added, “It’ll make a fine story, sir.”

“Milton,” James said with a pause, looking up at Patrick standing behind the Ohioan, “I fear, this story is only beginning.”

Historical Background

Part I—The Boys from Kalamazoo

Chapters 1–6

While the Kalamazoo Sharpshooters are fictional (based loosely on units with fanciful names like the Coldwater Cadets, Jackson Grays, and Michigan Hussars), Birge's Western Sharpshooters did exist and experience much of what the Kalamazoo Sharpshooters experienced. Truly a combination of farmboys from various states (primarily Illinois, Wisconsin, and Michigan), Colonel Henry W. Birge's men fought bushwhackers in Missouri, silenced the cannon at Fort Donelson, and found themselves on the bloody fields of Shiloh. Though their name changed later in the war to the 14th Missouri and then the 66th Illinois, most still referred to them by their original name, the Western Sharpshooters.

The state of Michigan was aflame with the early fervor surrounding the Civil War. When President Lincoln asked for volunteers, Michigan was among the first to answer the call. By the opening battle of the war, the first battle of Bull Run, only one Western state managed to send a regiment to Washington, D.C., in time. Michigan's quick answer to the call led President Abraham Lincoln to proclaim his famous, "Thank God for Michigan!"

Fueled by antislavery hotbeds and Underground Railroad stops like Kalamazoo, Michigan soon found itself with more volunteers than needed for President Lincoln's quota. Many Michigan men found themselves helping other states fill their quotas and serving in their regiments.

Chapters 7–11

Missouri had been engulfed with internecine warfare long before the arrival of the Western Sharpshooters. The political and vigilante maneuverings of the "Wide Awakes" in St. Louis were of particular importance as their possession of the Federal armory was a serious blow to Confederate fortunes in Missouri and the West in general.

One company of Western Sharpshooters did suffer a stinging defeat at Hallsville, but Colonel Birge's men redeemed themselves with a resounding victory the following day at Mount Zion. This devastated bushwhacker activities in that part of Missouri.

While Matthew's and Luke's encounter with bushwhackers and the escape via railroad handcar sounds fictional, it is actually based on the sketchy accounts of one of the Michigan boys of Company D in the Western Sharpshooters.

Part II—Separate Paths

Chapters 12–20

While the Moffats were one of the founders of Kalamazoo, and Senator Charles Stuart was one of the most popular and well-known individuals in the state, there was no Ainsley Stuart or Katherine Moffat. Nor are they based on anyone. They are simply fictional characters.

In contrast, the actions of the Western Sharpshooters at Fort Donelson are factual. Amazingly, the charge of General Charles F. Smith is also true to life. Time and time again in researching the capture of Fort Donelson, I found several accounts describing their astonishment and exhilaration in seeing General Smith proud and erect in his saddle, leading the charge through the abatis as if protected by God himself. For whatever divine reason, despite drawing much of the Rebel fire, General Smith was never hit during his audacious assault.

Part III—Shiloh

Chapters 21–33

The battle of Shiloh was the bloodiest event in American history up to that point in time. By the end of April 7, 1862, more American soldiers had died in that one battle than in all of the preceding American wars combined.

Historians can only speculate why Generals Sherman and Grant were so oblivious to the looming Confederate threat. Were it not for Colonel Peabody's disregard for orders in sending out Major Powell's patrol, the outcome of the battle and war may be have been quite different. The warning that the patrol gave the Union army, while partially ignored, did save them from waking to find forty-seven thousand Confederates in their camp.

Even with the warning, it was only the stubborn resistance put up on the Sunken Road for six hours that saved Grant's army from complete destruction.

As with many stories, it is the "what if" that makes it interesting. At the Confederate's high point of the battle, General Albert S. Johnston personally led a charge on the peach orchard. Unbeknown to even himself, the commander of Southern forces was shot just behind the knee. The blood from the wound drained into his high riding boot, and even after Johnston slumped from blood loss, his aides could not find the wound. Tearing open his shirt, his aides watched the general die in dismay. A simple tourniquet to staunch the bleeding may have saved the general's life. Would Johnston have pressed the attack that night rather than waiting for morning like Beauregard? It is impossible to say. It would have been asking a lot of his exhausted troops, but maybe.

It is here that I must confess taking a bit of literary license. While the 15th Michigan, its troops mustered in only two weeks prior to the battle, did make a courageous bayonet charge because they had yet to receive ammunition for their weapons, it was slightly earlier in the battle and obviously not led by James Lockett. But, of course, James had to lead someone.

And yes, Lew Wallace, future author of *Ben Hur,* was there, and the famous one-armed explorer and discoverer of Lake Powell, John Wesley Powell, did lose his arm at Shiloh.

But it is only 1862. The war is not yet halfway over, and it is after Shiloh that the Union finally comes to the grim realization that this war will not be won so easily.

There will be many more battles before James Lockett and company can return to Kalamazoo.